Will
Do
Magic
For
Small
Change

ALSO BY

ANDREA HAIRSTON

Master of Poisons

Redwood and Wildfire

Mindscape

Will Do Magic For Small Change

A NOVEL OF WHAT MIGHT HAVE BEEN

Andrea Hairston

A Tom Doherty Associates Book
New York

WILL DO MAGIC FOR SMALL CHANGE

Copyright © 2016 by Andrea Hairston

A Tordotcom Book
Published by Tom Doherty Associates
120 Broadway
New York, NY 10271

www.tor.com

Tor® is a registered trademark of Macmillan Publishing Group, LLC.

Library of Congress Cataloging-in-Publication Data

Names: Hairston, Andrea, author.
Title: Will do magic for small change : a novel of what might have been /
Andrea Hairston.
Description: First Tordotcom Edition. | New York : Tordotcom, Tom Doherty
Associates, 2022.
Identifiers: LCCN 2022021129 (print) | LCCN 2022021130 (ebook) |
ISBN 9781250808738 (hardcover) | ISBN 9781250808752 (ebook)
Classification: LCC PS3608.A54534 W55 2022 (print) | LCC PS3608.A54534
(ebook) | DDC 813—dc23
LC record available at https://lccn.loc.gov/2022021129
LC ebook record available at https://lccn.loc.gov/2022021130

Our books may be purchased in bulk for promotional, educational, or business use.
Please contact your local bookseller or the Macmillan Corporate and Premium Sales
Department at 1-800-221-7945, extension 5442, or by email at
MacmillanSpecialMarkets@macmillan.com.

First Edition: 2016
First Tordotcom Edition: 2022

Printed in the United States of America

0 9 8 7 6 5 4 3 2 1

Book I

What is life? It is the flash of a firefly in the night. It is the breath of a buffalo in the wintertime. It is the little shadow which runs across the grass and loses itself in the sunset.

—Blackfoot proverb

Public Display

"Books let dead people talk to us from the grave."

Cinnamon Jones spoke through gritted teeth, holding back tears. She gripped the leather-bound, special edition of *The Chronicles* her half brother Sekou had given her before he died. It smelled of pepper and cilantro. Sekou could never get enough pepper.

With gray walls, slate green curtains, olive tight-napped carpets, and a faint tang of formaldehyde clinging to everything, Johnson's Funeral Home might as well have been a tomb. Mourners in black and navy blue stuffed their mouths with fried chicken or guzzled coffee laced with booze. Uncle Dicky had a flask and claimed he was lifting everybody's spirits. Nobody looked droopy—mostly good Christians arguing whether Sekou, after such a bad-boy life, would hit heaven or hell or decay in the casket.

"Why did Sekou give that to you?" Opal Jones, Cinnamon's mom, tugged at *The Chronicles*. "You're too young for—"

"How do you know? You haven't read it. Nobody's read it, except Sekou." Cinnamon wouldn't let go. She was a big girl, taller than her five-foot-four mother and thirty-five pounds heavier. Opal hadn't won a tug-of-war with her since she was eight. "I'm not a baby," Cinnamon muttered. "I'll be thirteen next August."

"What're you mumbling?" Opal was shivering.

"Books let dead people talk to us from the grave!" Cinnamon shouted.

Gasping, Opal let go, and Cinnamon tumbled into Mr. Johnson, the funeral director. The whole room was listening now. Opal grimaced. She hated *public display*. Mr. Johnson nodded. He was solemn and upright and smelled like air freshener. Opal had his deepest sympathy and a bill she couldn't pay. Dying was expensive.

"Why'd you bring that stupid book?" Opal whispered to Cinnamon, poker face in place.

"Sekou said I shouldn't let it out of my sight." Cinnamon pressed her cheek against the cover, catching a whiff of Sekou's after-gym sweat. "What if there was a fire at home?"

Opal snorted. "We could collect insurance."

"*The Chronicles* is, well, it's magic and, and really, *truly* powerful."

"Sekou picked that old thing up dumpster-diving in Shadyside." Opal shook her head. "Dragging trash around with you everywhere won't turn it into magic."

Cinnamon was losing the battle with tears. "Why not?"

Opal's voice snagged on words that wouldn't come. She made an *I-can't-take-any-more* gesture and wavered against the flower fortress around Sekou's open casket. Her dark skin had a chalky overlay. The one black dress to her name had turned ash gray in the wash but hadn't shrunk to fit her wasted form. She was as flimsy as a ghost and as bitter as an overdose. Sekou looked more alive than Opal, a half smile stuck on the face nestled in blue satin. Cinnamon inched away from them both.

Funerals were stupid. This ghoul statue wasn't really Sekou, just dead dust in a rented pinstripe suit made up to look like him. Sekou was long gone. Somewhere Cinnamon couldn't go—not yet. How would she make it without him? *Pittsburgh's a dump, Sis. First chance I get, I'm outta here.* Sekou said that every other day. How could he abandon her? Cinnamon brushed away an acid tear and bumped into mourners.

"God's always busy punishing the wicked," Cousin Carol declared. She was a holy roller. "The Lord don't take a holiday."

Uncle Dicky, a Jehovah's Witness, agreed with her for once. "Indeed He don't."

"So hell must have your name and number, Richard, over and over again," Aunt Becca, Opal's youngest sister, said. "This chicken is dry." A hollow tube in a sleek black sheath, she munched it anyway, with a blob of potato salad. Aunt Becca got away with everything. Naturally straight tresses, Ethiopian sculptured features, and dark skin immune to the ravages of time, she *never* took Jesus as her personal savior and nobody made a big stink. Not like when Opal left Sekou's dad for Raven Cooper, a pagan hoodoo man seventeen years her senior. The good Christians never forgave Opal, not even after Cinnamon's dad was shot in the head helping out a couple getting mugged. Raven Cooper was in a coma now and might as well be dead. That was supposedly God punishing the wicked too. Cousin Carol had to be lying. What god would curse a *hero* who'd risked his life for strangers with a living death? Cinnamon squeezed Sekou's book tighter against her chest. God didn't take a holiday from good sense, did he?

None of Opal's family loved Sekou the way Cinnamon did. Nobody liked Opal much either, except Aunt Becca. The other uncles, aunts, and cousins came to the memorial to let Opal know what a crappy mom she was and to impress Uncle Clarence, Opal's rich lawyer brother. An atheist passing for Methodist, Clarence was above everything except the law. Sekou's druggy crew wasn't welcome since they were *faggots and losers*. Opal didn't have any friends; Cinnamon neither. Boring family was it.

"I hate these dreary wake things." Funerals put even Aunt Becca in a bad mood. She and her boyfriend steered clear of Sekou's remains.

"The ham's good," the boyfriend said. He was a fancy man, styling a black velvet cowboy shirt and black boots with two-inch heels. Silver lightning bolts shot up the shaft of one boot and down one side of the velvet shirt. His big roughrider's hat with its feathers and bolts edged the other head gear off the wardrobe rack. "Why not have supper at home, 'stead of here with the body?" He helped himself to a mountain of mashed sweet potatoes.

"Beats me." Aunt Becca sighed.

Opal couldn't stand having anybody over to their place. It was a dump. What if there was weeping and wailing and *public display*? Aunt Becca glanced at Cinnamon, who kept her mouth shut. She didn't have to tell everything she knew.

"Some memorial service. Nobody saying anything." Becca

surveyed the silent folks clumped around the food. "Mayonnaise is going bad," she shouted at Opal over the empty chairs lined up in front of the casket. "Sitting out too long."

"Then don't eat it, Rebecca." Opal sounded like a scratchy ole LP. "Hell, I didn't make it." She needed a cigarette.

"Sorry." Becca pressed bright red fingernails against plum-colored lips. "You know my mouth runs like a leaky faucet."

Uncle Clarence fumed by the punch bowl. His pencil mustache and dimpled chin looked too much like Sekou's. "Opal couldn't see the boy through to his eighteenth year. I—"

Clarence's third wife read Cinnamon's poem out loud and drowned him out:

Sekou Wannamaker
Nineteen sixty-six to nineteen eighty-four
What's the word, Thunderbird, come a streaking in that door
A beautiful light, going out of sight
Thunderbird, chasing the end of night

Cinnamon joined for the final line:

What's the word, Thunderbird, gone a shadow out that door

"Hush." Opal turned her back on everyone. Maybe it was a stupid poem. "Sekou talked a lot of trash. You hear me?" She touched the stand-in's marble skin and stroked soft dreadlocks. "When he was high, he didn't know what he was saying—making shit up. Don't go quoting him."

Cinnamon chomped her bruised lower lip. "*The Chronicles* is a special book, *magic,* a book to see a person through tough times." She threw open the cover. Every time before, fuzzy letters danced across the page and illustrations blurred in and out of focus. If you couldn't stop crying, reading was too hard. The pages were clear now. The letters even seemed to glow. She dove right in.

Dedication to *The Chronicles*

The abyss beckons.

You who read are Guardians. For your generosity, for the risks you take to hold me to life, I offer thanks and blessings. Words are powerful medicine—a shield against further disaster. I should have written sooner. Writing might help me become whole again. I can't recall most of the twentieth century. As for the nineteenth, I don't know what really happened or what I wished happened or what I remember again and again as if it had happened. I write first of origins, for as the people say:

Cut your chains and you become free; cut your roots and you die.

Chronicles 1: Dahomey, West Africa, 1892—Stillpoint

Kehinde was fearless, an *ahosi*,[1] king's wife, warrior woman, running for her life, daring to love and honor another man above Béhanzin, the king of Dahomey. She saw me come together in scummy water tumbling over smooth boulders, my eyes drawn from rainbows, feet on fire, crystals melting into skin. Momentum carried her through the cave mouth toward me as bright green algae twisted into hair, and I sucked in foam and slime to form lungs. Even if she had wanted to run from an alien creature materializing from mist, dust, and light, there was nowhere to go. Enemy soldiers rushed past our hiding place, bellowing bloodlust. Seeing me emerge into human form, Kehinde did not scream or slow her pace, but accepted the event, an impossible vision, a dream/nightmare unfolding before her as truth. Her disciplined calm eased my transition. Yet, nothing prepares you for the first breath, for the peculiar array of new senses or the weightiness of gravity. I was stunned by the magnetic field and the urgency of desire—for food, for touch, for expression and connection. The first experiences are paradise.

As I selfishly reveled in the miracles of this universe, in the delight of a new body, danger threatened at Kehinde's back: bayonets, bullets, and a hundred furious feet. She gulped the humid air and glared back and forth between me and the watery entrance. Her deep brown flesh was torn and bleeding as her heart flooded bulging muscles with iron-rich, oxygen-dense blood. An unconscious man was balanced on the fulcrum of her shoulder. He bled from too many wounds, onto the knives, guns, water gourds, ammunition, bedroll, food, wooden stool, palm leaf umbrella, human skulls, and medicine

---

1 The appendix to *The Chronicles* offers a compendium of words and information from the Wanderer's world for handy reference.

bags that hung from a belt at her waist. She settled the man against the damp earth. She kissed his eyes, stroked his hair, and murmured to him. Foreign projectiles were lodged in his organs. He'd soon bleed himself away. Abandoning him would have improved her chances of survival, yet she had no intention of doing this. Kehinde's spirit appealed to me at once. My body settled on a form close to hers.

She aimed a rifle at me. Later I would learn she was a sharpshooter, *gbeto*, an elephant huntress, a merciless killer of her enemies. In these first moments I understood the murderous device yet felt certain she would not set its lethal projectiles in motion. Too noisy, why give herself away to harm me, a naked being just coming to my senses? She could not fathom the risk I posed. Trusting me for the moment was reasonable.

I pushed her weapon aside with my still spongy cheek and bent to the suffering man. Kehinde shifted the rifle toward the cave opening and held a knife at my writhing algae hair while I ministered to him. If I knew then what I know now, I might have been able to save him. Perhaps it was better for me that I was so ignorant of human bodies. He might not have embraced a newly formed Wanderer, and Kehinde might not have become my guide. Lonely Wanderers fade back into the spaces between things or fracture incessantly until they are next to nothing.

"Kehinde," the man groaned and reached for her. "Somso . . ." I covered his mouth quickly. Kehinde dripped fragrant, salty fluid onto my face, silently urging me to act, to aid the broken man. With minor core manipulations, I eased pain, calmed turmoil, and gave them a few moments to share. The man came swiftly to his senses and gripped her calf. She thrust the rifle into my hand. I grasped it clumsily and monitored the cave mouth. I doubted my resolve and my accuracy—my bones were still gooey, my muscles rock hard. She crouched down, and they passed soft sounds between them, inhaling each other's breath. She never betrayed his last words to me, yet I'm sure he exhorted her to leave, to let him die with the hope that at least she had a chance to live. Kehinde shook her head, resisting his demand.

The people who carried her death in their minds raced again through the water outside our cave. The man heard them and clutched a blade at her belt. "Somso!" Insistent, he ground his teeth and spit this word at her, a name I would later learn. The sound made my throat ache. Someone splashed close to the entrance. Kehinde's heart raced. The dying man nodded at her and closed his eyes.

Kehinde sucked a ragged breath. "Somso," she said. Her hand shook as she forced her cutlass through his heart.

He did not cry out. My own heart rattled in my chest. Kehinde pressed her lips on his as blood burbled to an end. She wiped the blade on the damp ground and threw a wad of cloth toward me. Words rained down, a frothy hiss, barely audible, like steam bubbling through a hole. I understood nothing and waved the cloth at her stupidly. My new body was starving for language. I gorged on her sounds, gestures, smells; I lapped up the twists and turns of her nose and lips, swallowed the flashes of light and dark from her blinking eyes. Her expressions were tantalizing and rich, but sense would only come after more experiences. Abandoning me would have greatly improved her chances of survival. She had no intention of doing this either. I resolved to know her completely. Kehinde would be the *stillpoint* of my wandering on this planet.

A rash decision, but Kehinde was taking a similar foolhardy course. A storm of feet headed our way. She gripped my wrist and dragged me through the cave. We crawled on our bellies, twisting and turning through a labyrinth of darkness. Kehinde hesitated at an intersection of four tunnels. She lit a lantern, whispered *Somso,* and chose the narrowest opening. A distant spit of light might have been illusion. Just when I thought the walls would crush us, we tumbled out into a forest.

Kehinde lurched about dropping gear: umbrella, water gourd, bedroll, and several human skulls. How she chose what to abandon and what to keep was a mystery. She explained nothing. What would I have understood? She snatched the cloth I clutched stupidly, threw it over my nakedness, and cinched it with a belt. She reconsidered abandoning two skulls and wrapped them and bags of ammunition and food on the belt around my waist. Angry voices and clanking weapons echoed in the cave. Kehinde pointed to the bright orange star sliding behind trees. I mimicked her gesture. She ran. I followed, matching her cadence, stealing some balance. Luckily a new form yields quickly to the demands of the moment, to the first experiences.

Racing through dense forest over rock-hard roots, we kept a punishing pace until the star's bright light faded from the dome of sky. My lungs expanded, increasing their volume with each tortured breath. Indeed, my whole body strained to match the warrior woman's. I admired the powerful limbs, muscular buttocks, and indefatigable heart that she'd had years to develop. I had a few hours of struggle and pain to match her physique. Exhaustion accumulated in my cells; torn muscles generated more strands; my feet bled new blood. The trees sang comfort to me. Birds let loose battle cries, goading me on. So many strong chemicals assaulted us. My skin, tongue, and nose burned. Dizzy, I faltered, but the rhythm of Kehinde's breath and heart guided me through the maze of sensations. Our human pursuers could not fly across the ground as we did. Soon our sole companions were unseen animals and the wind.

We camped in cold moonlight on burnt ground. Kehinde had tools to make a fire, but resisted offering a sign of our location to her enemies, my enemies now. Nursing bloody feet, ripped muscles, and an empty stomach, I intertwined limbs under a scratchy blanket to sort and assimilate the first experiences. When Kehinde thought I was asleep, she hugged a dead tree stump and swallowed sobs. Distant creaks and rasps from the bushes made her flinch. She scanned the darkness for spies on her grief, for enemies about to attack. Pushing away from the stump, she spit and hissed, stomped intricate patterns in the dust, then obliterated them with furious swipes of a horsetail whip. She fell to her knees, threw back her head, and shuddered wordless anguish. As she forced herself back up, my eyes watered.

Spying on Kehinde felt wrong; yet, as I rehearsed her dance in the theatre of my mind, her love and anguish claimed me. I resolved to be a good witness.

My memories waver. Coming from another dimension and manifesting in this flesh form, who would not be uncertain? This drawing is what I make of that funeral night. It was a fevered moment. Such is life on Earth.

Guardians and Wanderers

"It wasn't a lie," Cinnamon whispered to the Sekou-stand-in half-smiling at her from his flower and satin fortress. "The Wanderer's like Daddy, an artist who sorta lost his mind."

Cinnamon stroked images of Kehinde dancing in the moonlight. The warrior woman was muscular and fierce, scary and beautiful. She was sad too, like Cinnamon, over losing someone she loved. Trees and bushes retreated from her, pulling in stalks and limbs, turning aside leaves. Animal eyes peeked from caves, nests, and prickly branches. Stars glittered above her, or perhaps a swarm of flying insects flashed fluorescent butts. Kehinde threw ample hips and brawny arms around like lethal weapons. Wide eyes were pulled into a slant by tight cornrows that covered her head in delicate swirls. Full breasts stood up on a muscular chest. Thunder thighs and big feet made a storm of dust in a rocky clearing. The drawing captured the Wanderer's fevered vision with photographic detail but was also dreamy like those painters Sekou loved, Marc Chagall or Lois Mailou Jones. The Wanderer was a good artist, showing how that night in old Africa had felt.

Despite the beautiful painting, it was hard to *believe* in an alien Wanderer *writing for his life*—to Sekou and now Cinnamon. Space aliens usually zoomed into big cities like New York, London, or Tokyo, and they came right now or on a distant tomorrow to conquer the world (mostly). Whoever heard of aliens going to Dahomey in 1890-something? Cinnamon looked up from the book. Opal was so embarrassed by a drug-addict son who'd maybe OD'ed on purpose that she almost didn't have a memorial service. Cinnamon resisted doubt. Sekou always dug up cool things nobody else knew.

"Good Lord, what size are you already?" Aunt Becca waved a

chicken wing at Cinnamon. "You better learn to push yourself away from the table."

"I didn't eat much." Cinnamon hadn't eaten *anything*. Tears pounded her eyes.

Opal pulled Cinnamon aside. "Nobody wants to see that." She scoured away tear dribble. "You promised not to be a crybaby today. Sekou wouldn't want you crying."

"I knew him better than you did." Sekou wouldn't want Cinnamon to be sad forever, still he'd appreciate a few tears. "There's plenty he never told you."

"Your brother was no good. That's why he's dead this day." Opal poked the book. "I gotta dump that junk of his. Can't have it around the house doing us no good."

"*The Chronicles* is all true. Can't throw truth away." Cinnamon hugged it close. "The more I read, the truer it'll get. Sekou got it from a weird and wonderful Wanderer."

Opal wheezed. "Some homeless, trash-talking cokehead told Sekou that Wanderer lie 'cause—"

"No. Sekou said the Wanderer trusted him to keep several illustrated adventure, uhm, adventure journals of top, top secrets safe."

"Don't get wound up—"

"Can't have it drop on somebody who doesn't *believe*." Words flooded Cinnamon's mind from everywhere and nowhere at the speed of light, a story storm. "It's a, a treasure, priceless. We're talking about a Wanderer from the stars, I think, or no, wait, hold up." The floor tilted under her feet. Her tongue tingled. "A Wanderer from another dimension, from *the spaces between things*, come to chronicle life here on Earth. Without me reading, the Wanderer is dust! I'm a, a lifesaver."

"Lifesaver?" Opal snorted. "You wish!"

"I don't know if the extra dimensions have stars. Anyhow we're the Wanderer's *Mission: Impossible*. Only the Wanderer is like Buckaroo Banzai crossing the eighth dimension, and wait, I remember exactly: *A Wanderer from different stars traveling the spaces between things*. That's it. New pages can appear anytime. Sekou made me

Guardian of the Wanderer's *Earth Chronicles*—if anything should happen to him."

Opal stamped the tight-napped carpet. "Stop this motormouth nonsense."

Cinnamon couldn't stop. Consonants smashed into each other around whizzing vowels. "The Guardian should memorize *The Chronicles* in case the book is ever destroyed. Sekou worried about letting the ancient, marvelous Wanderer down. But he had me as backup, with my steel-trap memory. Hear it once, remember forever."

Opal gripped Cinnamon's face, digging jagged nails into her cheeks. "What did I tell you 'bout lying and making up crap? You're too old for that."

Cinnamon slipped from Opal's grasp. "Pages I don't read will disappear. Sekou said we're about to forget everything, but memory is the master of death!" Last week, standing in line for a sneak preview of a John Sayles movie, *The Brother from Another Planet,* Sekou had handed Cinnamon *The Chronicles.* He didn't say much beyond the life-and-death-Guardian bit. Cinnamon had to fill in the blanks. "*The abyss beckons.* Sekou said I should read to fortify my soul against Armageddon."

"You don't even know what Armageddon is." Opal pressed chapped lips to Cinnamon's ear. "Sekou was depressed and high all the time, and his baby sister was the only person dumb enough to listen to his crap."

"I don't see anyone from the other side of your family." Uncle Clarence crept up on them, sniffing flowers and eyeing sympathy cards. "Sekou was no relation of theirs—"

"Sekou's pronounced SAY-coo. And Granddaddy Aidan, Miz Redwood, and Great Aunt Iris are going to be here shortly unless they hit further delays." Riding story-storm energy, Cinnamon lied easily. "They were supposed to come yesterday. A freak blizzard ambushed them in Massachusetts."

Opal adopted a poker face; yet trial lawyer Clarence shook his head and wrinkled his nose, like lies were funky and he smelled a big one. His two grown-up sons sniggered in the corner. Their younger sister did too, and she wasn't usually mean. Sekou claimed people got mean in a crowd, even nice people. They couldn't help it—human beings tended to sync up with the prevailing mood. Sekou refused to hang with more than four people at a time. He hated handing his mood over to strangers. He and Cinnamon practiced throwing up shields against mob madness and other bad energy for when they might be surrounded by hostiles. Cinnamon tried to raise emergency fortifications, but sagged. Getting her shields up without Sekou was too hard. He'd left her alone, defenseless against *infectious insanity*.

"Miz Redwood is a hoodoo conjure woman, and she married herself an Indian medicine man," Aunt Becca explained to her boyfriend, who was a recent conquest and not up on the family lore.

"They never got married, not in any church," Clarence said. "Aidan is a plain ole Georgia cracker, no Indian anything—"

"Hoodoo?" the boyfriend said over him. "What? Like *Voodoo?*"

"Nah! Old-timey *real* black magic." Becca rubbed Cinnamon's hunched shoulders till they relaxed. "You know?"

He didn't.

"Not Hollywood horror, not zombie black folk going buck wild." Becca pursed her lips at Clarence and his grown kids. "They say old Miz Redwood can still *lay tricks* on folks who cross her."

"Rebecca, don't nobody believe that old-timey mess," Opal said. "Lies and backcountry superstition."

Cinnamon winced. Opal was syncing up with the enemy.

"When you get along to my age . . ." Becca's boyfriend didn't look old: handsome as sin, a little gray in a droopy mustache and powerful muscles pressing against the velvet shirt. "Going on strong is what you want to hear about."

That was two on Cinnamon's side.

"Devil worship and paganism." Uncle Dicky took a swig from his flask. His hand was shaking. Jitters broke out everywhere in this god-fearing crowd.

Clarence wanted to hit somebody. Becca shoved a plate of chicken and gravy-soaked biscuits at him. "Eat," she said. "Don't nobody want to be carrying this food home."

Opal pulled Cinnamon away. "Read your book." She sat her in a chair by a window overlooking a vacant lot and hissed, "Quit telling tales."

"Words are my shield too!" Cinnamon watched the sun head for the hills and cold fog rise off the river. A homeless man struggled with his shopping cart through dead weeds. "I know they're trying hard to get here. Nobody better tell me they're not."

"Your grandparents can't be running down to Pittsburgh for every little thing," Opal whispered. "They're old as the hills. You shouldn't be calling them up and bothering them."

"I didn't. They just *know*. They're coming to keep us company, 'cause we're sad."

"You're making up what you want to happen."

"They love us more than anybody, except Aunt Becca." Opal didn't deny that. "I'm their favorite grandchild."

"Only grandchild." Opal groaned. "How did I get stuck with a stupid optimist?" She sighed. "I'm hurting inside and out. You're not the only Guardian swallowing a flood of tears. Sekou put a knife in my heart every day, but I miss him too."

Cinnamon licked a bruised lip. "Sorry."

Opal scrutinized her. "You been fighting at school again?"

"No." Not *at* school. Cherrie Carswell and Patty Banks jumped her two blocks from school by the library, calling her the dyke from the black lagoon. Cinnamon thought they wanted to be friends. They had more bruises than she did. Nobody ever wanted to be her friend.

"I better not hear about you fighting. I couldn't take it." Opal staggered away. "Read *The Chronicles of the Great Wanderer* and let me have some peace."

"OK," Cinnamon said.

"What is he doing out there?" The funeral director cracked a window on December chill. "Move on, man," he shouted at the homeless man limping with his rickety cart through the vacant lot next door. "They got a shelter in East Liberty."

"East Liberty is a long walk, Mr. Johnson," Cinnamon said. "'Specially pushing your whole life on rusty wheels. He could hobble all the way there, and the shelter might be full."

Mr. Johnson turned from the window and scowled. Cinnamon clamped her mouth. She shouldn't fuss at someone her mom owed piles of money to.

Mr. Johnson marched toward the casket. "The family thanks you for coming." His voice was a soothing rumble. "Visiting hours are up in twenty-five minutes."

"Only twenty-five? We just got here." Clarence rolled his eyes. Opal couldn't afford to pay for more memorial time to impress him. Nobody wanted to be here a second longer anyhow. "A budget funeral," Clarence muttered.

"Driving a bus doesn't pay like telling lies in court for guilty people with money to burn." Cinnamon blurted this out fast.

"Where'd she get that from?" Clarence sneered.

"Cinnamon's a bright child, making up her own mind," Opal replied.

Becca's boyfriend gave Opal a cup of tea. Becca stuck out her jaw, put her hands on her hips, and kept Holy Rollers *and* atheists at bay. Cinnamon opened the book. A breeze from the window flipped pages to just past the first drawing.

Chronicles 2: Dahomey, West Africa, 1892—Spirit Guides

I wandered into a new body, into a new life at the end of a war.

The kingdom of Dahomey fell to the republic of France in 1892 when French Legionnaires defeated King Béhanzin's army just outside of Abomey, Dahomey's capital city. The French were led by Colonel Alfred-Amédée Dodds, a Senegalese fighting man whose mercenary army included African enemies of Dahomey. The fighting was brutal, and losses were great on both sides. King Béhanzin's *ahosi*, his warrior women wives, displayed exceptional valor, frequently leading the charge. All combatants acquitted themselves well, but the French possessed the deciding technology: Lebel rifles with high-velocity projectiles, quick-firing machine guns, and twenty-inch fixed bayonets. Dahomean valor was no match for these advantages.

Kehinde and I lived running and hiding for months, in search of Somso—a person of great importance. *Somso* was the last word spoken by the man Kehinde mourned. I understood so little at first, but whenever Kehinde was agitated or uncertain, whenever her heart raced at the gurgle of a stream or the cackle of insects, as if these were enemies about to attack, I made her tell stories. Slowly human words and gestures made sense. And I must confess, this intoxicating world possessed me. Much is missing from what I wrote earlier: the whir of ten thousand red bats swarming overhead at twilight; the taste of burnt earth, burnt flesh on the air; the musty tang of our exhaustion. Monkeys teased us from fat iroko trees, spitting and defecating. Fragrant lilies filled our mouths with oily pollen. Stinging insects drank our blood and left fever and diarrhea behind. Flying tapestries of butterflies would cloak my still body until the clattering of Kehinde's rations, weapons, and keepsakes set them to flight.

Near the coast, Dahomey's climate was drier than in the rainy jungles inland. Farmers were blessed (cursed?) with cool sea breezes, rich soil, and great flat expanses. There were no hills or natural defenses. Much of the population lived and died as slaves or soldiers, laboring for local lords and distant captains of industry. (Kehinde had been stolen from her people in Yorubaland to fight for Dahomey.) Royal plantations had replaced crops of maize, millet, bananas, sugarcane, potatoes, and melons with palm oil to sell. Many people went hungry as the war raged. Plantation slaves revolted. Villages were burned and looted; smallpox devastated young and old. The turmoil challenged me. I had to become supple, always ready to improvise.

King Béhanzin staged his last stand against the French in the sacred city of Kana. From distant treetops, Kehinde and I watched as *ahosi* warriors were sliced to shreds or riddled with bullets. Spirit houses and sacred shrines to the orisha—ancestors, forces of nature, cosmic deities—were demolished. Béhanzin escaped with *ahosi* warriors to Atcheribé, thirty miles north of Abomey. French Legionnaires scoured the countryside, eliminating Béhanzin's allies. The king eluded capture while seeking *ahosi* survivors and new recruits. He hoped to rebuild his army and fight the French again. Kehinde stayed one step ahead of the French and Béhanzin's forces. The *ahosi* considered her a traitor—because of the man whose misery she cut short in the watery cave. Mourning him fueled her search for Somso. I longed to understand her grief. Kehinde had stories for everyone and everything except the dead man.

One hot afternoon, right after the fall of Kana, we sat in the high, cool branches of an iroko tree and watched as, half a mile away, French Legionnaires plunged twenty-inch bayonets into the dummy bedrolls we'd left behind to trick them. They set fire to brush, hoping to smoke us out. Instead, the wind carried the flames back to them. Many soldiers sizzled and screamed in death.

"Let them all kill each other," she hissed. "Let them kill those they love most."

That night we ran from a barrage of bullets flashing in the dark and doubled back behind our path. Silent as a shadow, Kehinde ambushed a rebel slave who'd harassed us for days. To him, Kehinde was still Béhanzin's woman, enemy of the slaves. The acid of revenge fueled his bloodlust. He was young, not yet grown to the fullness of his bones: hair just sprouting at his genitals, testosterone reeking in his sweat. As she strangled him, I ached for the lovers who would never know his touch, for the mysteries he would never glimpse, for his song unsung. How could Kehinde not feel this agony? Dying, the man fired off several rapid rounds. His body toppled over, and Kehinde caught the long, heavy Lebel rifle he'd gotten from the French.

"They recruit rebel slaves with promises of freedom and sacks of bullets." She tossed his rifle to me. "I prefer Winchester, yet, see the damage this Lebel does?" She stuck her fist in a palm tree's mortal wound. "The French massacre so many at once, zack, zack, yet say we *ahosi* warriors are savage killers." She listened to the darkness. "Hurry, *civilization* comes this way to *tame* us."

We dashed through a grumbling stream to throw pursuers off our trail. Dense foliage along the water blanketed the stars. Creatures roared and squealed. Some monster thing jumped into the water and displaced the flow with a guttural bark. Kehinde growled and churned the stream like a massive beast. We passed without attack. A water warrior, beloved by the river goddess, Oshun, and the ocean deity, Yemoja, Kehinde rode the rough torrent easily. I was just her acolyte. The unruly current stole my hard-earned balance. I stumbled countless times, and she held me up. When both feet got jammed between rocks, I went under. A hot-blooded, clear-eyed predator leapt from the bushes onto Kehinde's rapidly drawn cutlass. The mortally wounded creature clawed her belly before relinquishing its last breath. Kehinde ripped the blade through its mouth and rested her trembling arm on my back. We gulped air. The smell of gunpowder, urine, and rum rode the fog toward us. After long days on the run, exhaustion claimed even her muscles.

"Enemies snap at our heels," she said. "We need rest." Abandoning me would have improved her chances of survival. Instead, she carried me to a cave obscured by vines and a sister stream pouring down a scruffy hill. We dropped underwater and crawled up slippery rocks into the dark. Hidden behind a veil of mist and roots, we watched Béhanzin's scouts. They searched the banks with lanterns, hunting for signs of clumsy feet stomping onto land. I smelled blood on their cutlasses and frustration on their skin. As an orange moon peeked between black trees, they faded into darkness. These scouts feared the French as much as they lusted after our blood.

"In the north few would hunt us, but before leaving this coast-land, I must find Somso and her son perhaps, a baby," Kehinde said. "Do you understand?"

I nodded, eager to please. Kehinde spoke her mother tongue, Yoruba, a language mostly lost to me now: *Ajeje owo kan o gbe'ru d'ori, ohun a ba jo wo gigun ni gun.* Or: It is impossible to place a heavy load on your head with one hand; whatever we consider together is bound to be successful. Optimists. Beware their simple-minded truth.

Kehinde lit a fire. Deep in the cave, a river snake coiled around the statue of a big-bellied, big-breasted water deity, Oshun or Yemoja, and slept. Instead of cutting off the snake's head, Kehinde danced, chanted, and made offerings of cinnamon, rum, and fish to the mother of waters. She turned our hideaway into a spirit house. For Ogun, father of iron and war, she cut patterns in the muddy ground; for Eshu Elegba of the crossroads, she molded a clay figure with cowry-shell eyes. She thrust a red feather in its crown, laid a knife at its feet, and whispered praise songs.

"When my brother and I were young, we ran away and spent the night in a cave like this." She sank down beside me (at the edge of tears?). "This time with you is a triumph. Lost memories return, of before I was *ahosi* warrior, before the Fon of Dahomey stole me and made me kill for them." She touched my head. "Shall I tell you?"

I craved stories more than food. She had never offered a tale from her former life. Thrilled, I nodded.

"I'm Yoruba from near Abeokuta, a city in a distant land. The Fon and Yoruba are ancient enemies, yet we share *Ifa* wisdom and orisha deities. My village was small, beautiful, and full of aggravating elders who kept secrets. My brother and I wanted to know everything, like you." She smiled at the memory. "It was the day when a masquerade—do you know this, a dancing full body mask—would sweep through the village, chasing children, threatening to poison and eat us. It was an *aje* masquerade, a dangerous, powerful grandmother with large wooden breasts, a wise green face, and two blue-and-yellow snakes for hair. The English say *aje* is witch; they don't understand powerful women. The *aje* uses her powers for the good of the community if we don't displease her. My brother and I went to spy on dance preparations. As they muttered secret words to call down the *aje,* my brother was too excited. He stumbled through a bush and fell in the dancer's path. The *aje* tripped over him and screamed curses. The helmet mask tumbled and cracked. Dance masters, market women, and elders cursed too—blights, infertility, pox!

"We ran away as fast as we could, ashamed for endangering the community. We ran until it was dark and cold and we were lost. Hungry creatures howled, and terror choked me. *I'm not afraid,* my brother said, *so you're not afraid either.* My fear faded with his words. Oshun guided me. I found a cave hidden by water and started a fire. We slept in each other's arms. In the morning, a snake curled at our warm feet. I said to my brother, *I'm not afraid to return to our village, so you aren't either. They won't be angry, only happy to see us.* His fear melted. In daylight, the way home was clear. Father was too happy to scold. Mother couldn't remember to be angry. She cooked fish and yams for her youngest blessings." Kehinde swallowed a sweet taste of *before.* "My brother and I share a spirit, in life and death. We make a path for each other." She grew silent, pulled away from her smile, away from me and back into mourning. I curled around her like a snake, and she managed a fitful sleep.

Chicken Fun for All

Clanging metal startled Cinnamon. Outside, the homeless man danced with his shopping cart. One leg was shorter than the other. His gait was off, as he stumbled, leapt, and shook his behind. Cinnamon grimaced and turned away. She traced the Wanderer's drawing. Her fingertips grazed charcoal? pastel? paint? caught in the rough surface of the parchment. It was like touching old Africa. For the first time since she found Sekou sprawled on the basement stairs last Sunday, she smiled.

Words like *indefatigable, array, momentum,* and *cadence* made her feel good. She'd look these up and also *Armageddon*—to be sure. Sekou was a dictionary hound, stealing tomes from bookstores and libraries. Nobody believed he'd do that, even when they saw him lugging a fifty-pound *Oxford English Dictionary* out a side door. Looking up words with Sekou was an adventure. Opal better not toss his dictionary collection.

An alien writing his Earth escapades in Africa to Sekou was amazing! Maybe the Wanderer was a she, if its form was like the warrior woman's. Either way, he/she wouldn't have trusted a *faggot loser* with *Mission: Impossible* secrets. Cinnamon jumped up. She could prove how incredible Sekou was.

"Africans sold my ancestors to get rich." Clarence roared like a lion.

Opal leaned against the coffin, clutching Aunt Becca, crying inside, 'cause *nobody wants to see that.*

"They still got slavery over there." Clarence was on a roll. "Why call yourself Jigga Juba or Sekou? I am not African."

"Shush. Nobody's saying you are." His third wife shoved cole-slaw at him.

Becca ushered Opal out for a cigarette.

"It's good to know we got some history," Becca's boyfriend said.

"Nothing wrong with *made in America*," Clarence replied. "Africans still got their history, and they're a hot mess, going downhill fast."

"Time is up!" Mr. Johnson said, an edge to his hospitality smile.

Cinnamon looked at her watch. "We still have five minutes!"

A loud creak followed by screeches worthy of horror movie hinges made folks jump. Mr. Johnson freaked as the heavy emergency doors nobody ever used swung wide. Instead of Count Blacula or a no-name zombie extra, a tall old woman wearing red silk pants under a quilted jacket stepped through ground fog. Elegant and regal, like an African queen, she strode into the parlor. Multicolored emergency lights pulsed in the street behind her. She paused to adjust an orange satin turban on a majestic crown of white hair. Mr. Johnson raced over and fussed with latches and bolts. The woman stroked an eagle feather dangling from her waist between two white seashells. Her breath whistled through clenched teeth. The whole funeral parlor stopped gossip, complaints, and chat to stare.

A sturdy old fellow who could pass for white loped up the stairs and stood breath-close to the woman. He had a straight back, strong features, and must have been a handsome young blade back in the day. His bright patchwork coat came to just below the knees, surely a coat for celebrations, costume dramas, or Halloween, not a memorial service. He had smoky green eyes. Her eyes were bright and clear. She blinked sorrow at the coffin. Her man sighed sorrow and pulled a mane of thick white hair back into a long ponytail. Every gesture was dancer-elegant, accentuated by the gentle music of silver bangles, velvet pouches, and glass-bead necklaces.

Another old lady, who could have passed for the first woman's twin, appeared behind them. She sported a beaded Native American blouse and full green pants under a maroon brocade coat. She leaned against her companions. These old folks were magnificent and strange and more colorful than the flower fortress around the casket. Cinnamon wondered if they'd come in the wrong door and death had caught them off guard.

"This is always locked." Mr. Johnson couldn't get the door shut. "How'd you get in?"

Mourners at the food table cut their eyes at the late arrivals as Clarence shouted, "Show people, making an entrance, when it's almost over." He glowered at Cinnamon.

It had been over two years since she'd seen them, long enough for her to forget how anybody looked, but not—"Miz Redwood! Granddaddy Aidan! Great Aunt Iris! You came! Before they kicked us out too." A story-storm lie come true.

"Of course we come for the service." Miz Redwood opened long arms.

Crying but also smiling, Cinnamon ran into her grandmother who didn't fall or lose her turban when she banged into her. Miz Redwood squeezed Cinnamon to a sweet-smelling bosom then passed her on to Granddaddy Aidan.

"We was sitting up in ice and snow, missing you, letting life slip by." He hugged her tight, scratching her face with his rough cheek. Finally he let Aunt Iris get ahold of her.

"They can talk me into anything." Iris kissed Cinnamon. She was soft and spicy. Papery skin was covered with light brown splotches where darker color had faded.

Redwood laughed. "Baby sister, you the one had us out there wrassling with sleet and hitchhiking like old hippies and hobos to get here fast."

"Train engine broke down. What're you going to do?" Iris pushed Cinnamon an arm's length from them. She stroked Cinnamon's strong jaw, squinted at long legs and thunder thighs, and brushed down frizzy braids.

"Growing faster than a weed tree." Redwood nodded approval.

"She's making a run for you." Aidan winked and squeezed Cinnamon's nose. She took comfort in their backcountry Georgia drawls. "How you doing, honeybunch?" Aidan leaned close. Cinnamon shook her head and sputtered awhile. The elders nodded, as if she were telling a good long story.

"How's your mama?" Redwood scanned the room.

"Opal blame herself, but," Iris sighed, "Sekou took every mean thing happening in this world to his heart." Sekou had written to Iris all the time, and she had written back. He could write her anything—even about boyfriends dumping him.

"Is it God punishing us for being bad people?" Cinnamon asked.

"No," Iris declared without even thinking.

"That isn't why bad things be happening, like to Daddy and Sekou too?"

Aidan took Cinnamon's hand and squeezed. Redwood stroked her head. "Who told you that *plague on bad people* nonsense?" she asked.

Cousin Carol spoke up. "You know Cinnamon has a lively imagination—twisting innocent words into a fabulous tale."

"What innocent words?" Redwood glared, storm mad.

Electricity snapped up people's backs and flashed in their eyes. Icy fog surged through the window. Cold damp snaked around folks' shins, assaulting ankles. They squirmed and broke out in funky sweat. A good person shouldn't take pleasure in misery, but . . .

"Hold your horses." Uncle Dicky staggered forward. "We're all civilized here and this is . . . this is . . . a . . . a . . . whatcha . . . a . . . Christian funeral." Actually, his slurred words sounded more like *chicken fun for all*. He extended a cup of coffee and booze to Aidan, whose lips curled at the first whiff. Aidan batted the offering away. Dicky kept repeating *chicken fun for all*. He was too drunk to see how much trouble he was in.

"You're making a fool of yourself, Richard. Sit down and shut up." Clarence shoved him into a chair. "Look . . ." He gawked at the elders. Even facing a hostile judge and jury, Clarence always had something to say. His third wife clutched his arm.

"We were talking against drugs, against abomination, the *sins*, not the *sinner*." Cousin Carol managed to speak while edging away from the emergency exit.

"*Unnatural sinners bring God's wrath down on themselves,*" Cinnamon quoted Carol. "*Running 'round with faggots and losers put your*

*daddy in a coma and Sekou in a casket. God is punishing the wicked.
No wonder he OD'ed."*

Redwood and Aidan took a deep breath. Iris muttered in some
other language.

"You ought to be ashamed, talking 'bout *anybody's* god like
that." Redwood's voice could fill a big auditorium.

"Did you come spoiling for a fight?" Clarence asked. "We're
grieving a young man snatched from us before his time, like your
son. We don't have good young men to spare."

"That's true, Clarence," Aidan said. "But did you speak up
and defend Sekou or Raven Cooper or Cinnamon against foul-
mouthed ignorance?"

Clarence was speechless a second time.

Iris ushered Cinnamon to the casket. "Hard things happen to
a person." She touched Sekou's cheek and spoke softly. "You lose
loved ones or every good thing you worked for. But it isn't the fates
weaving your misery or God mad at you."

Redwood stepped behind Cinnamon. "Raven Cooper"—she
stumbled on her son's name—"got shot in the head 'cause some fool
with a gun was 'bout to cut down innocent folks who loved each
other, 'bout to shoot 'em in cold blood, 'cause he couldn't stand to
see their love." Tears ran down her face. "Raven stepped in the line
of fire. His spirit called him to sacrifice. Those two women were his
friends."

Cinnamon gasped. "They said Daddy saved strangers, not
friends. He wouldn't have been anywhere near that faggot bar if
he hadn't been hunting bad-boy Sekou."

"Raven was a man doing what he believed." Aidan took hold of
Redwood. Grief washed through them, but did not linger. "Love
is what you got to do to be free."

"We all have a generous spirit in us," Redwood said. "Got to
hunt it down, get it working."

Aidan put a blue velvet pouch around Cinnamon's neck, filled
with herbs, rocks, and secret things. *Mojo*, a prayer in a bag. He'd
given her one before, but she'd lost it. He touched her cheek, drawing

a hoodoo sign on her face. "There's a mystery moving the universe." He sang as he spoke. "We are part of it, part of what moves the stars, what sends birds flying thousands of miles and keeps rivers winding to the sea, what makes flowers wilt even if we don't cut them. We are stardust, sharing the mystery of the Milky Way, of birds and storm clouds riding the wind, and to live is a blessing, our precious miracle. Sekou knew the wonder and the terror. We are blessed to have known him, to have loved him, and to still be part of his story."

"Let the church say amen!" Aunt Becca stood in the front doorway with Opal, whose mouth hung open. "That's what we need for a memorial service."

Redwood, Aidan, and Iris squeezed Opal's hands, stroked her back, and cried tears she couldn't, saying, "We know how you feel, losing a son."

Iris wrapped nine strands of some hairy root around a cloth book. She waved it at the head, heart, and feet of Sekou's dead dust stand-in and then laid the book among red flowers—more hoodoo spells. "I brought Sekou's letters to keep you company while he walks the star road home."

Someone in the back snickered over *noble savages and hoodoo Negroes.* Clarence?

"You shoulda been a preacher, Aidan." Uncle Dicky extended his flask.

Aidan pushed it aside gently and clapped Dicky's back. "I gave up drinking before you were born. I was a mean drunk, fighting everybody and trying to kill my ownself."

Dicky sputtered, gobs of spit flying from his lips. He bumped a fist against Aidan's chest. "You're all right, man." He staggered away. "He's all right, ain't he?"

Somebody whispered, "Redneck cracker."

"I don't have no truck with backcountry hoodoo." Cousin Carol spoke the mob meanness loud, but Cinnamon had her shields up.

"The family is grateful to everybody who has come to pay their respects." Mr. Johnson closed the casket. "But you're running over time." He ushered folks out.

"Did Cinnamon call you? Rebecca wouldn't dare." Opal glared at Redwood, Aidan, and Iris. She worried the buttons on her one black dress. "How could you show up like this, no warning?"

"*You* should have called us," Redwood said.

Becca dragged Cinnamon away, before Opal launched into something nasty.

Generous Spirits

The funeral crowd jostled out the narrow front door to the parking lot. Mr. Johnson stood guard at the wider (and still open) emergency doors. The sun sat low in a saddle between western hills, casting spooky shadows. The homeless man pushed his cart toward departing mourners. Icy fog was waist high and even stinging a few cheeks. Rot and poop in the vacant lot assailed irritated sinuses. Becca plowed through nosy questions and rude glares. Cinnamon hugged her orca knapsack. Inside, *The Chronicles* throbbed, a steady beating heart next to hers.

"Opal is on a hard road," Becca said. "Let's cut her some slack." She deposited Cinnamon by her car and headed back inside.

In a stand of weed trees, Lexy Wood, Sekou's nineteen-year-old boyfriend, yelled at a woman in a coat with a furry hood. Seeing Cinnamon, Lexy raced off, as if cops were after him for dealing love to minors. She never told anybody about him and Sekou doing it in the laundry room behind the clanking dryer when Sekou was supposed to be babysitting. Lexy was grinning and gasping underneath Sekou like they were on the Big Dipper roller coaster at Kennywood park, coming 'round the bend and plunging into a ravine. Opal would be ripped if she knew what Cinnamon had seen, but it wasn't *sin*. It was as good as Sekou's glistening eyes and Lexy shouting, "Wheee Lord!"

Lexy probably knew all about that night in the bar, about the two ladies loving one another—Daddy's friends, friends he took a bullet for. A wild man had come gunning for love. How weird was that? Had there been a trial, or did the gunman get away? Nobody told Cinnamon anything but lies. Almost thirteen, yet everybody treated her like *the baby*. Her knapsack tumbled into the dust. The homeless man grazed her thigh with his cart. She gripped the handlebar and broke a nasty fall.

"Twilight upsetting your heart spirit?" The man smelled like dog breath and old running shoes, his last shower an ancient memory. He wore a slimy coat made of this and that held together by safety pins and electrical tape. Scars crisscrossed his face; shifty eyes wouldn't settle. Cinnamon hunted down her generous spirit and nodded thanks at him. He offered a broken-tooth grin and pointed at a speck under a distant streetlight—Lexy. "That boy was fond of your brother."

"Sekou called him Dr. Bug-Man. They had a big blowout two weeks ago. Lexy wanted to take Sekou to see Daddy at the nursing home." Cinnamon halted. "I'm talking too much."

"I got Lexy to listen at the emergency door. A fine service today for Mr. Sekou Wannamaker." The homeless man had a strange accent, foreign *and* down home. "Love *is* what you got to do all right." He took a carved stool from his cart and set a velvet donut on the hard wood. "I been waiting for love to come on back in style." He sat down, setting out a sign: *Veteran, jacked up in the war. You got peace. Can you please help me?* He was maybe twenty-five, no hint of beard, no Viet Nam edge to his eyes.

Mr. Johnson stomped up. "What I tell you about harassing mourners?"

"He ain't hurting nobody," Cinnamon said.

"I *will* call the police. Don't push me." Mr. Johnson talked over her. "Move on!"

"I'm not trespassing." The man shook his cup at mourners dashing for their cars.

Mr. Johnson kicked the stool. Wooden animals snarled and clawed. He yelped and clutched a ripped cuff. "What the?" He retreated inside. "Jail will be your own fault."

Cinnamon bent down to inspect the stool. The wild beasts were still, but warm to the touch and fragrant, a hothouse jungle scent.

The homeless man winked crusty eyes. "By the time the cops

get around to answering Mr. Johnson's call, even a broken old soul like me, with a bad butt and crooked feet, could be long gone."

"Can we give him some money?" Cinnamon said to her approaching family.

"No. Don't encourage him." Opal grabbed Cinnamon and thrust the killer whale knapsack at her. "You'd lose your face if it wasn't plastered to your skull."

"I knew where it was every second!" Cinnamon snatched the orca.

Aidan offered two twenty-dollar bills. The homeless man folded each into a tight square and stowed them in the mouth of a leopard in the stool bottom.

"That belongs in a museum." Opal wrinkled her nose and pulled Cinnamon away into prickly weeds. "He probably scams more money in a day than Clarence."

"I doubt that," Iris said. "Clarence hits up desperate rich people."

"I appreciate your sacrifice." The homeless man stashed the stool. "Spirits we recognize always come to our aid. Blessings on you as you fit grief in your good hearts." He pushed the cart away. His right leg didn't want to go the same direction as his left.

"Becca and her boyfriend drove different cars here," Opal said to the elders. "He'll drive you all wherever you want to go." Becca's boyfriend waved from his car.

"They're staying with us," Cinnamon said. "Right?"

"We ain't driving back to Massachusetts." Redwood crossed her arms over her chest. "You got to put up with us for one night."

"Opal!" Clarence spun his BMW's wheels through a sharp turn and threw gravel at their shins. "Call me if you need anything." Opal looked at her feet. "Don't make us the ogres." Clarence flailed and banged the horn. He sucked blood spurting from a knuckle and sighed. "What I mean is . . . Let me help you, Sis."

"You're doing plenty." Opal waved him on without mentioning the funeral bill. "I'll call you if I can think of something."

Reluctantly he drove on. Opal wasn't going to call him, and he knew it.

"Clarence remind me of Brother George," Redwood said. "A fire-breathing dragon, making folk tremble, but burning up his insides too."

Cinnamon never considered how a dragon felt inside, or Clarence either. "I want to ride with Miz Redwood, Granddaddy, and Aunt Iris," she yelled. "Please!"

"Your brother's up in there, dead. Hush that noise. Have some respect." Opal pulled out a cigarette and struck a match. It sputtered.

"Please," Cinnamon whispered and bent her head.

"Fine," Opal said. "Watch out," she told Becca's boyfriend. The old folks stood serenely by his car, ancient angels, fog curling over their heads. "You think butter wouldn't melt in their mouths, but they're the wild bunch and"—she wagged a finger at Cinnamon— "space is the place for this one."

The woman in the hooded coat, who'd been fussing with Lexy, tapped Opal's shoulder. "Do you have a minute?"

Opal turned and froze. "What?" She lit the cigarette.

The woman pulled her hood down. It was Star Deer, one of Daddy's best friends from *before*. Energetic and lean, she had a warrior's ferocity and a dancer's grace, even standing still. Star was Cherokee, one of the *noble savages* who worked Clarence's nerves. "I didn't come to fight."

"What you come at all for?" Smoked curled from Opal's lips.

"Sekou and I were friends." Star was godmother to Cinnamon *and* Sekou.

"The funeral's over. You paid your respects. Bye." Opal pushed past Star and escaped into Becca's car.

Cinnamon glared at Opal. "Sorry about Mom wigging out."

Star's face softened, and she hugged Cinnamon. "Grieving, nobody has to be nice. I'll call her later." Star murmured a greeting to the elders, pulled her hood up, and strode into the fog.

Becca's boyfriend drove a big Toyota wagon with plenty of leg and butt room. He opened the doors. "Are you as old as they say? Sorry, if that's not a polite question."

"I was born when dirt was invented," Iris said. "Sis and Crazy Coop are older still."

"I'll Crazy Coop you!" Aidan squeezed Iris's nose.

"They're stage people," Cinnamon said as they settled in: Iris up front with Kevin—she asked his name right off—and Cinnamon between her grandparents. "They've traveled everywhere, doing plays, writing books, making movies. I'm going to be an actress too. The theatre keeps you young."

"More power to you." Kevin tipped his roughrider hat. "Becca says you're an Indian medicine man, I mean, uhm, Native American."

"Medicine man? I don't know 'bout that." Aidan smiled at this black cowboy man. "My father was Seminole; my mother come over from Ireland." Not *a plain ole Georgia cracker* like Clarence always said. Aidan worked his jaws and lips without speaking. He looked tired and feeble—lost in another time.

Reaching over Cinnamon, Redwood squeezed his arm and said, "Miss O'Casey was running and Big Thunder was mourning loved ones dead too soon. They found each other on an island in the grassy water of the Okefenokee, where swamp currents rock the land and carry some of your sorrows away. Grieving—"

"I hate funerals," Cinnamon declared. "I'm not going to another one."

"I guess we'll have to hang on a while longer, see you through," Redwood said.

Iris nodded. "We've been saving ourselves, hoarding strength for you."

"Nobody better die anytime soon," Cinnamon said to Aidan, so it was clear.

He perked up. "We can wrassle that boneyard baron a little longer then."

Kevin honked at mourners blocking the exit. "Seat belts fastened?" He headed out.

Cinnamon wrestled *The Chronicles* from her knapsack, then lost her nerve.

"What you holding to your heart there?" Redwood said.

The Earth Chronicles of an Alien Wanderer." Cinnamon held it up. "Sekou gave it to me before he . . . died." She opened to the second chapter. The pages glowed. "See?"

Aidan squinted. "Print's too tiny for my old eyes." He ran his fingers across bright images. "That's a handsome drawing though."

"Can I read it to you?" They'd understand—the hard words for sure. Iris had given Sekou his first three dictionaries, *Random House, Merriam-Webster,* and *Cambridge.* Being hoodoo conjurers, they might even understand underneath the words. "It's a good story."

Redwood pulled the book to her nose. "Dahomey, 1892? Historical fiction?"

"Science fiction too," Cinnamon said.

"We got time," Iris said. "Traffic's backed up across the bridge to the Parkway."

"Really?" Kevin stuck his head out the window. Red lights glowed to infinity.

"Iris put her mind to it, she can see things the rest of us don't," Aidan said.

"Uh-huh." Kevin drew his head back in, spooked.

Redwood laughed. "Isn't this road always jammed up?"

"Well, yeah," Kevin said. "It's the only way, unless—"

"You want to take the bridge to nowhere," his four passengers said in unison.

Kevin grinned. "The wild crew, huh?"

"Read, honeybunch," Aidan said. "It'll do my heart good to hear a story."

"It will?" Cinnamon said.

"Stories are medicine too," the elders said in three-part harmony.

Kevin studied each one of them in turn. "Ain't that the truth."

Thankful for the traffic jam, Cinnamon started back at the beginning of *The Chronicles* and read right on to new pages.

Chronicles 3: Word Dance

The morning after taking refuge in a spirit cave, Kehinde woke uncertain. Her heart played a troubled beat; her breath caught on jagged emotions. She walked in circles, avoiding me. The past haunted her steps; the future was mist. What is a warrior without war? A woman without a family? Bandit, traitor, slave? Being a *stillpoint* for my journey meant nothing to her yet. I wanted to tell her: Wanderers value experience above all; without it we are a map of static. To know a world is to drop into its soil, water, and atmosphere, and risk everything to become a citizen of history.

Ignorant, untested, reckless, I ran ahead into the bright horizon. Kehinde followed me as I stalked hyenas, spied on villagers and soldiers, dug up anthills, and awakened sleeping pythons. She stood guard as I teased angry rebels, ruthless French liberators, and danced in a thunderstorm, daring the lightning to twist my spirit into a better form. One evening, she talked elephants out of ripping up the tree I climbed. A grandmother stroked her cheek before lumbering off.

"Why? Why harass an elephant?" Kehinde fumed at me. "We are lucky. These aren't elephants I shot at!"

In awe of her elephant talk, I shook my head.

"My brother found a baby elephant once, lost and tangled in thick roots. She was bigger than he was and yowling. A grandmother elephant trumpeted a distant reply. Lions had caught the scent and sound of despair. My brother was just one spear. He called for me to join the rescue. I resisted. Why risk our lives to save an elephant? Lions need to eat. *Let them eat someone else,* he said. *This one is my friend.* So I stood guard, shouting, waving his spear at hungry lionesses while he cut roots to free fat, clumsy legs. I thought we were about to die on lion teeth. But grandmother elephants thundered in, routed the lionesses, then charged us. The ground shook. They halted, toe to toe with my brother and me, waving their trunks. The baby wrapped her trunk around his waist. He cut the last root. The baby touched my cheek then ran under her mother." Kehinde stroked her face. "The elephants escorted us past hungry lions. I still hear their voices in my bones." Kehinde circled me, poking muscles, noting reflexes. "So like intrepid Taiwo come back to me."

"Taiwo?" I struggled to mimic her sounds.

"Taiwo." She pointed to my face. "A true name calls you to yourself."

"Taiwo." The first word my mouth mastered I took as a name.

After the elephants, more words came, but days disappeared. Or perhaps I lost them. Arrogance and joy are potent drugs. Seeking Somso and eluding Béhanzin and rebel slaves, Kehinde appeased my hunger for experience. In the chaos of war, many fields lay fallow. Once beautiful villages were deserted. We avoided cities, hunted in forests and rivers, and took what we needed from farmers. They were confused by an *ahosi* strutting into their compounds as if Dahomey's glory times had returned. They averted their eyes as we helped ourselves to mangos, peanuts, and yams. We were never greedy. Kehinde left metal or seashells as payment. No one had news of Somso. This displeased and relieved Kehinde. She wanted to find Somso but feared finding her too.

Disguised as refugees, weapons hidden, we slipped into the coastal city of Ouidah. Kehinde winced at the falling-down forts and dilapidated houses. Cracked porticos, overgrown verandas, and rotted auction blocks leaned toward the sea. The once mighty Portuguese fortress had become a Catholic mission. A brown rash covered pockmarked white walls. Wrought-iron gates and ban-isters were twisted and rusty. We sidestepped mounds of refuse and rivulets of offal. Mats of tiny creatures ate human and animal waste, discharging pungent gasses. Deformed beggars waved broken fingers at us; Kehinde smacked them away. I tossed shells and metal at them, and she did not protest.

"A tavern once." She pointed to a mound of rubble. "Good rum and dancing." She sighed. "When money flowed from selling captives, the villas had fine gardens, sweet fish swam the lagoon, no grass grew in the streets." She swatted a horsetail whip at biting flies. "Nothing but bloodsuckers and thieves living here now."

She asked everyone for news of Somso. They laughed, growled, or shrugged off her queries. The streets were crowded with stories I wanted to experience, history I wanted to join. I longed to explain this desire to Kehinde, but human language required endless rehearsal to orchestrate glands, bowels, skin, and tongue.

"Today, I creep through this wasteland, a shadow." Kehinde's sweat tasted wrong. Her magnetic fields were erratic. "Once I commanded many warriors. They sang praise songs to my valor. I didn't run when a bull elephant charged. I shot him in the eye at close range. The Fon of Dahomey stole me, made me fight and kill, but I was never a slave. Never *nzumbe*—living dead."

My body ached with her contradiction and pain over the lost grandeur of Ouidah, over her own stolen life. In this world, what one body felt was echoed in another's—a world of magic indeed. I was restless and impatient to master this magic.

"Soon." She felt me as I felt her. "We're nearly there."

An ancient iroko tree loomed over the ruins of a modest dwelling. I stopped in its shade, bowed my head, and stretched my arms around the girth of its trunk. The braid of black wood was cool and smooth. The high crown of dense green nodded and whispered to me. Roots arched across sandy ground and disappeared under low buildings to share an aquifer with a battered well. The iroko sucked water through its veins to feed new leaf buds as hot starlight powered its growth.

"You feel the iroko's power? It speaks to you?" Kehinde asked. I nodded. "Good. My destiny is not ruin. You are a sign of that." She paced behind me. "This is Kpassezoume, the sacred forest, where all the *vodun* powers reside. Centuries ago by French reckoning, King Kpasse, the founder of Ouidah, disappeared from his palace, fleeing enemies who would destroy him. At death's gate, his spirit took refuge in this iroko tree, a tiny shoot then, but grown mighty now.

King Kpasse lives on in the iroko and hears our hearts." She placed an offering in a clay pot nestled at the base of the tree. She pressed her lips against smooth bark and talked of Somso with the old tree, too softly for me to hear details. In its long life, Kpasse's sacred iroko had heard sorrowful epics, sweet lies, and hard truths. Like a good Yoruba priest, the iroko listened without judgment or reproach and offered those worshipping at its altar the wisdom of their own minds. Refreshed, Kehinde turned to me. "We go north. Perhaps Somso and her child escaped in Béhanzin's wake. We need bullets."

In the center of Ouidah, we found two mercenaries from Senegal to sell us ammunition. Their twisty magnetic fields were confusing. Kehinde smelled treachery. She opened the bundles they were selling and exposed a false bottom of pebbles.

"You dare cheat me?" She threw off her disguise. The gun across her back, the cutlass at her waist made them pause.

"We spit on Fon warriors! We defeated you. You're nothing." One thief waved a knife at me. The other reached for a pistol. Kehinde wielded her cutlass, and in a breath, their hands were ribbons of blood. I stuffed rags in their mouths, grabbed bundles of ammunition, and ran. Shaking with fear and rage, Kehinde stood above them, about to cut off their heads. I sang the hyena hymn that woke us in the night and made her spitting mad. She sheathed her cutlass and hurried after me. We ran several hours. The thieves would bleed out or be too weak to chase us.

"Quick death is mercy," Kehinde said when we slowed to a trot. "Who wants to linger in pain and humiliation? Why not go on quickly to dance with the ancestors?"

Killing the thieves was a waste, but my tongue tangled the words.

"These rogues didn't care that I am *ahosi*. They wanted to cheat and rape us then slit our throats. Don't waste good feelings on them."

"Death. No more changes," I sputtered. "Dreams dissolved, story over. A shame."

"You talk nonsense." Kehinde flicked long fingers in my face.

"You mourn only one dead one. Why not others?"

She grunted and marched ahead. I could barely keep up.

Heavy with bullets and supplies, we pushed north around swamps, slipped by French scouts, and ran until the war was far behind us. We came to barren lands with few human inhabitants. Scrub brush clung to rocky soil. Thousands of flying foxes hung like dark hairy mangos in the sparse trees that dotted the savannah.

"They migrate, seeking a new destiny," Kehinde remarked.

The rains came. We searched for Somso in pounding wet and endless mud. Kehinde stayed in an ill temper. Who could fault her? We vomited much of our food away. Fever and chills robbed the night of sleep. I studied our anatomy and the tiny creatures who would make us—our flesh, our cells—their slaves. When we finally negotiated a blood peace, we had narrowly avoided death.

Far north of Abomey, to celebrate the end of the rainy season, Kehinde schooled me in the ways of *ahosi* soldiers. I was reluctant to learn Fon warrior ways, but practicing war dances with bare hands, feet, and weapons made the challenge of speaking easier. Running over rocks and ruins, dodging spear thrusts, knife swipes, and machine gun fire, I held the cutlass with both hands and sawed the air, twisting my wrist to signal the enemy's head had fallen. The tongue is a subtler dancer than feet or hands, but a dancer nonetheless. With new patience I worked through the words and music of human language. Kehinde treated me sometimes like a baby, patiently repeating phrases and actions, tolerantly correcting foolish errors and demonstrating nuance. Other times she offered complex insights that even initiated priests of *Ifa*, the Yoruba's highest wisdom, would have barely grasped. My tongue ached day and night. Eventually responding to magnetic, chemical, and tonal fluctuations became automatic. My tongue rejoiced.

We came upon crumbling interconnected buildings that resembled giant clay pots with straw hats. Doors opened to the west and were flanked by dilapidated altars to *vodun* deities, close kin to the Yoruba orisha that Kehinde worshipped. Kehinde paused at a female *vodun* of the waters. I was drawn to Legba or Eshu, master of the crossroads, trickster at the gate of life and death.

"Hungry orisha desert lazy supplicants," Kehinde muttered as we tended neglected altars. "When angry, Eshu beats a stone until it bleeds."

Who knows what pain we spared or what blessings we shared? "What is this place?" We walked through bright, hot starlight toward a river.

"An old fortress of the Somba kings," Kehinde said. "The name has crumbled like the buildings, like the high clay wall. We are nowhere and need no name."

"A person doesn't get out of the way for someone who rode a horse yesterday."

"Yoruba wise words." She laughed at my perfect syntax. "Well spoken."

"Somso . . ." I'd rehearsed what to ask about the man Kehinde mourned, yet faltered. How could I bring up grief when she was laughing?

"You're right. Somso wouldn't come this far. I run from her." Kehinde staggered down the bank into the river. "*Omi gbogbo l'osun*—all waters represent Oshun." Before the undertow claimed her, I clasped her waist. Tasting her grief made me weep. "Warrior *ahosi* never cry." She touched my tears. "We can't have love or a family as other women. Warrior *ahosi* must be loyal to the king. Nothing but valor in battle and honor in death matters. We're men not women. *Ahosi* who return from a campaign without defeating the enemy and taking many captives must die. No retreat, ever. We conquer a village or bury ourselves in its ruins. King Béhanzin has given birth to us again. We are no longer Yoruba, Igbo, or Ewe. We are his wives, daughters, soldiers. War is our pastime; it clothes and feeds us."

She sat down in the water, tears held tight in her throat. I sat beside her. The river banged our hips and splashed our faces. Kehinde hung her head and whispered, "I've betrayed everyone who believed in me." She dropped her Winchester rifle in the mud and blocked my attempt to retrieve it. "My twin brother was shot down by me, who saw only an enemy of Béhanzin and aimed to fill his rebel slave belly with bullets."

The intrepid brother she loved? The one who chased masquerades and made friends with elephants? I could not blink or swallow.

"You saw him die."

I had seen many die by her hand, yet I hadn't seen her *shoot* anyone.

"What do you say to that?"

No words danced on my tongue.

"The Fon of Dahomey killed my family. They stole me, remade me. What am I now?" She curled her lips and grasped my throat in rough, callused hands. "Who are you to take pity on me? A masquerade, a spy? Why do you trust me?"

Her grip was too tight for breath, for sense. Did she mean to kill me?

Remembering

In the twilight, fog turned to sleet. Cinnamon squinted at the next chapter of *The Chronicles*. Letters blurred into squiggles. Achy eyes slid shut, and she almost fell asleep. Kevin's Toyota bumped through a pothole and jarred her awake. A drawing sparkled in somebody's high beams. Kehinde danced in mist. Silver water pounded at her back, spraying light in every direction. A blue snake circled the neck of the Oshun-Yemoja altar in the spirit cave and spit its forked tongue at Kehinde's cutlass. Several snakes wound around the *vodun* or orisha's body and through a snarl of black hair.

"Where is Dahomey?" Cinnamon rasped.

Aidan scratched his neck. "It was a country in old West Africa."

"It's Benin now," Redwood said. "Maybe a small part of Togo."

"They met folks from there, when Sister dragged Aidan to the 1893 Chicago World's Fair," Iris said. "Dahomey had a village at the Fair with a show of fighting women." This must have been one of Aidan and Redwood's hoodoo adventures—magic spells twisting time. "Some folk say that Dahomey was evil, brutal slavers, murdering savages, cannibals." Iris paused dramatically. "Others say it was a mighty kingdom, wondrous, well-organized and efficient, a paradise for their fighting women, Amazons to the Europeans, *ahosi*, wives of the king, *mino* in their own language—our mothers."

Cinnamon sat up. "The king of Dahomey really had warrior women wives?"

"We don't know much about those women, but that doesn't make them untrue."

The road did a hairpin switchback in the dark. Kevin veered away from a dented guardrail and rickety houses clinging to the hillside. "Pittsburgh always looks ready to fall into a ravine or a river. I'm from Philly by way of Detroit. I can't get used to being a cliff dweller." The close call had everybody's heart pounding. "What's your address?"

They were a few blocks from Opal's house, but Kevin careened down the wrong street. Cinnamon didn't tell him. Getting home wasn't high on her list. She thrust *The Chronicles* toward Kevin. "This drawing is like from a museum."

Aidan pulled her hand back. "Kevin has to keep his eye on this wandering road." He stroked Kehinde and Taiwo on an elephant. "The Wanderer has a fine hand, like—Raven." Aidan and Redwood spoke their son's name together.

"Nobody throws paint like Daddy." Cinnamon refused evidence to the contrary. Opal sold, hid, or burnt Raven's paintings, but Cinnamon remembered his style and the excitement she'd felt staring at his dreamy images for hours.

"Get a light, motherfucker!" Kevin swerved around a cyclist in dark gear. "I don't want your sorry-ass soul on my ledger!"

Iris pressed her foot against phantom brakes as they came upon the flashy red wingtips and chrome butt of a vintage Cadillac Eldorado, the sort of pimpmobile Clarence sneered at and Sekou and Lexy drooled over. Cinnamon cringed. Would everything remind her of Sekou or Daddy? Kevin pumped the brakes. The cyclist zipped past them through a red light.

"Suicidal motherfuc . . . Excuse my French." Kevin hunched his shoulders. "Sekou give you that book? Spooky."

Cinnamon swallowed tears; she was tired of crying. "Yeah."

"Where'd he get it from?" Kevin asked.

"Opal says Sekou was too nice, you know, *doing any stupid thing for no-account trash who always be taking advantage of fools,* but uh, if he saw something good that needed doing, Sekou never let you down. So . . ." Cinnamon's tongue tingled. "So when the Wanderer said it was life and death and asked him to be Guardian, Sekou said yes! Being an ancient alien makes it hard for people to *believe* in you, even if you're talking truth. Sekou understood, 'cause he was like a brother from another planet too. I'm the only one who really knew Sekou, besides Lexy, the Bug-Man, his uhm, best rapper friend. Sekou made me backup Guardian."

"That's a heavy load to drop on his little sister," Kevin said.

"No, it's not! What you remember makes you whole." Cinnamon smacked his seat back. Redwood grabbed her hands.

Kevin sputtered. "I don't mean to upset anybody."

"Of course you don't." Iris patted his shoulder.

"Sekou let me read any book of his. *The Chronicles* is tame compared to—" Aidan and Redwood shook their heads. Cinnamon didn't need to tell all. She stuffed *The Chronicles* through the toothy grin of her orca knapsack. A fabric fang on each side stretched over the spine, so the swollen volume just fit. Relieved that the backpack and *The Chronicles* had worked out their *issues,* she murmured, "Sorry. What I mean is, uh—"

"Remembering does make you whole," Kevin stammered.

"You're tired, honey. Put your head in my lap." Aidan eased Cinnamon against his patchwork coat. The scent of licorice and fresh cut wood calmed her.

"Sekou left you a story that won't wear out or break down." Redwood stroked her back, pulling out knots that Cinnamon hadn't realized were hiding there. "A good story can last you a lifetime."

"I'm too old to *believe* stuff like that." Cinnamon fought sleep.

"Well, Miz Lady, watch out for the tales you be telling." Redwood stroked the mad out of her too. "Lies have a way of taking over from truth, wiping it out the picture. I say, don't cast a spell you can't live with, you hear me?"

Cinnamon sniffled. What did lies have to do with stories or spells? "Do you think the man Kehinde carried into the cave at the beginning was her brother?"

"What do you think?" Iris was professor emeritus from Oberlin College. She always made you look up things and figure stuff out for yourself.

"But, what do *you* think?" Cinnamon pleaded.

"I think I made a wrong turn." Kevin wiped the inside of his streaky windshield. "Down here, right?" He turned onto her street.

Cinnamon whispered to Iris so Kevin wouldn't hear. "Do you think Wanderer-Taiwo is a boy or a girl or both? I think both."

"In *vodun*, realizing full male and full female spiritual evolution simultaneously is the highest state of the physical body," Iris replied—not so much an answer as a puzzle.

"You'll have to keep reading to find out." Redwood patted the knapsack.

"What's the number?" Kevin asked again.

"Tell the man how to get you home, honeybunch," Aidan said.

"7654," Cinnamon muttered.

"I knew we were close," Kevin said. "They should fix those busted streetlights."

"Nobody want to find this street." Cinnamon quoted Opal as the car pulled up to the house. She had to make a face to hold her eyes open.

Aidan hobbled out of the car first, his bones cracking and popping. Kevin scooped drowsy Cinnamon up, like she didn't weigh a thing. The Doberman next door threw herself at the fence, snarling, despite a choke chain.

"Some welcome committee." Kevin carried Cinnamon up the steep stairway as if she were a little child. The Doberman trailed them, growling and clanking the chain.

"Hush, Rain, it's me," Cinnamon muttered at the dog. "They're on our side."

It was twenty-three steps to the front door. Rain was silent for the last five.

"What took you so long?" Opal said through a curl of cigarette smoke.

"The train quit on us before Hartford," Aidan said.

"We were stranded on the rails." Iris shook her head.

"A whiteout. Snow thick as a bale of cotton." Redwood jabbed the air.

Opal took a drag on her cigarette. Kevin's legs trembled. Cinnamon was getting heavier by the second. "You letting us in, Opal?" he said.

Opal stood aside. Kevin carried Cinnamon through the door. She closed her eyes on how mad her mom was. The elders' voices were a cornbread molasses tumble, slow and sweet, thick and chewy.

"I didn't think we'd make it on time."

"Miz Redwood worked a spell."

"I waved down a car."

"Heading for Route Ninety-one South."

"Snow was gone outside of New York City."

"The wind . . ."

"Singing a storm song the whole way."

"This nice young person drove us right to the funeral parlor . . . Aria?"

"Such a flimsy car. I thought we were goin' fly off that bridge."

"No, Ariel, the spirit who would be free."

"An actress . . . How you holding up, Opal?"

Aidan whispered in Cinnamon's ear. "I'll take you to see your daddy, if you like."

Cinnamon was thrilled. "Soon? There's no time to lose."

Aidan nodded as they tucked her under the comforter and turned out the light.

"Old as the hills," Kevin whispered. "A miracle they're still walking."

Cinnamon must have fallen asleep, because grizzly old hills stood up, shook cold snow into the Ohio River, then walked off toward West Virginia. The phone rang and woke Cinnamon up to shouting. Her door was cracked.

"She'll call you back, Star," Aidan said.

"I will not. Half this mess is her fault!" Opal yelled. Star heard that across town.

"Star think you need to go see Raven at the nursing home," Redwood declared.

"I don't see you going." Opal never went to see Daddy. "Star is worse than you backward hoodoo fools—"

Cinnamon slammed her door. She'd call Star tomorrow, when

Opal wasn't around. The orca knapsack slid off the bed, spilling *The Chronicles* onto the floor. Opal would hate her reading such a nasty grown-up story. Too bad! Cinnamon jammed headphones from Sekou's new Walkman on her ears and climbed under the comforter with the book. Tina Turner wailed, *What's love got to do with it?* as Cinnamon read new pages.

Notes (#1) to the Current Edition of the Earth Chronicles, Dec. 1984

In this twentieth century, I've been tracking lost memory, desperately trying to conjure *scattered* history. After seeing Kehinde's Yoruba homeland in Nigeria, I traveled to Benin. I visited the coastal city of Ouidah and braved the three-mile slave walk to the sea. It was a good-natured day, breezy and sunny. The sand was golden, the sea black jewels. A parade of tourists and pilgrims was led by Daagbo Hounon, the highest priest of *vodun,* the ancient Fon religion gone worldwide on slave ships. We supposedly traced the footsteps of African ancestors, paying tribute to souls lost in bondage, celebrating spirits who survived slavery.

I offered sacrifice at a shrine to the water mother, *Mère d'eau,* called Mami Wata nowadays. Our guide claimed this *vodun* had protected captives (who jumped, fell, or got thrown overboard) from treacherous reefs and sharks roaming coastal waters.

"I tell true story," the guide insisted. "Not Hollywood *Voodoo.*"

Near the end of the memorial path, we came to the Tree of Forgetfulness. Wretched captives who had been gagged, branded, and held in close quarters before Middle Passage were marched counterclockwise around the tree, seven times if female, nine times if male. With the past thus wiped from their minds, they were prodded through the Gate of No Return to slave ships and the horrors and triumphs of the New World. I stumbled eight times clockwise around the tree and fell to the ground with other tourists. We wept in black crystal waves.

During several hundred years of slave trade with insatiable Europeans, Dahomey grew wealthy (and avoided a slave destiny) by forcing millions of captives down many routes to the sea; this one slave walk is a grand fiction. Yet, tourists and pilgrims take this staging of a legendary past as the past itself, as stolen memory restored, as healing for the aching ancestors in our hearts. I found not a building or a rock or a tree that looked familiar, not an echo of Kehinde or our past anywhere. It was as if we had never happened.

Beware, dear Guardians.

Perhaps the stories I write are the convenient lies I tell on myself until they seem true. Or perhaps I've fashioned a performance around stolen memories to reclaim my spirit. Or maybe my life since that time with Kehinde in Dahomey has made me a simple-minded cynic who doubts truth.

Chronicles 4: Dahomey, West Africa, 1892—Books

I don't know how long we sat in the river, Kehinde squeezing my throat. Starlight burned our scalps as the water stole our warmth. She had many jagged scars, deep purple signs of her fearlessness in battle. I struggled for a breath and touched a scar on her collarbone that I hadn't noticed before.

"How can you trust me?" Kehinde relaxed her grip. "Why are you with me?"

"I was a heavy burden slowing you down." My voice hurt, yet I shouted over the rushing river. "You didn't abandon me when death chased at your heels."

"I'm good at running. Flight can masquerade as freedom."

"I'm a witness, a chronicler of life. Wanderers lose their minds to fill them with Earth stories, your stories."

She frowned at me. "Wanderers forget who they were before?"

I nodded. "Who knows why we are born to a life? We make it up as we go."

"I too wish for memories to die . . ." She shook herself. "But you talk nonsense."

"Teach me." I bowed my head. "I wish to be brave, swift, and wise, as you are."

"I'm a coward, not brave. The Fon bent me to their will."

"You are no coward."

"I ran when they first tried to make me a warrior *ahosi*." She touched the collarbone scar. "They dragged me back and beat me, but wouldn't kill me."

"Who?"

"The Fon of Dahomey aren't my people. The English call my people Yoruba as if we're just the language we spoke. I poured libation to ancestors in Abeokuta. Fon warriors led by a fierce young captain, Yao the incorruptible, raided our village. Yao was all muscle with deep-set eyes, scars over his heart, and a handsome lion face. He came for captives to ship to Cuba or to work royal plantations near Ouidah. Yao took my father's head and raped my sisters." She blinked slowly. "My brother and I hid in *aje* masquerades. Yao mistook me for a boy, strong enough for labor, too young for a threat. He sent my brother to a royal plantation and me to the ships. I leapt into the ocean near Ouidah. Bloody fangs and battered fins swam toward me—sharks. Men were devoured in three bites of their dagger teeth. Blood spurted in my eyes. Heavy chains and flailing bodies dragged me down. Holding my breath, I wondered if the ancestors would greet me. I'd neglected them. Satiated sharks swam by me. The chain digging into my neck was no longer attached to anyone. I struggled up for air.

"Near me, men flailed to reach the very slave boats they'd leapt from. Fon soldiers laughed as sharks ate their legs. The hope of escape died in the eyes of captives on deck. Yao had tricked us into escaping to scare others. Fon warriors whispered greetings to their ancestors before hungry sharks swallowed a captive. In death we should still be slaves of Dahomey. I refused messages to their ancient fathers and great uncles. I spit their words back at them and banged a curious fish in the nose.

"*She fights off sharks!* Yao pointed at me thrashing in bloody sea water. *We must have her fight on our side.* Yao fished me from cruel waters. I didn't struggle against his rescue. I was a coward, choosing life, not honor." She leaned her head back and shuddered.

I stroked her cheek with my cheek, my eyelashes brushing her forehead. I slipped my arms around her belly. She was startled into speaking again.

"Yao took me back to Ouidah. I was far from the altars to my ancestors. My brother had been sold, my family slaughtered. The life I could have was as a slave. I thought of killing myself in this very river. The water wouldn't take me." She grasped a ripple in the fast-moving current. "Women scouts of King Glele, Béhanzin's

father, claimed me. Abla, the strong one, child of fire and captain
of new recruits, made an offer. She would train me to be a warrior-
wife. If I craved death, I could find it on the battlefield where there
is honor in death. If I fought well, I should have power, slaves of
my own, and live as a man with no one but Glele and his lords over
me. A warrior makes her own destiny. Indeed, slave women have
risen to *kpojito*, reign-mate of the king."

Kehinde stood up, green froth clinging to her skin. "I accepted
Abla's challenge. I would learn the warrior way and speak Fon oaths,
but remain true to myself. I would offer sacrifices at the Fon's *vodun*
shrines, but also pour libations to the orisha who watched over me—
Oshun, mother of waters. I'd show Abla and Dahomey the mask of
loyalty and wait for the day that revenge was possible." She laughed
like a hyena.

"But in time I forgot myself and enjoyed what this warrior life
offered. To bow to no one—how many women can boast of this? I
can shoot and kill, and I don't fear death. I've taken many heads."

I gasped.

Her lip curled. "I can't recall my first, second, or even tenth head.
The first battle, I was full of rum, fear, and pain where Abla had
beaten me. They woke new recruits to train at night. The smell of
death, shrieks . . . like a nightmare. Abla claimed I ripped a man's
throat with my teeth when I ran out of bullets. Ten heads that
night—Abla said I'd be rich and rise high. She lied." Regret shivered through her. "The powerful have subtle ways to seduce and
conquer. I've done terrible things." She gripped my arm. Her fingernails broke the flesh. "Yet, I came home to myself." Her face twisted
into a predator's grin. "Béhanzin's scouts sought an oath-breaker, a
traitor."

"I know."

"You don't know." She cupped my face in rough hands. "For
ahosi there is no greater crime, no enemy so base as one who breaks
a promise to other *ahosi* or to our husband and king. Only Eshu
knows why I go on living."

"To find Somso, of course, and to share your world with me."

Kehinde looked at me, baffled. "You do not give up hope?"

I plunged her fingers into the water and onto a fish that would be our supper. She laughed in surprise at the quickness of my move and the slick skin of the fish. I guided her up the riverbank and made a fire. We feasted. The fish was succulent and sweet. I roasted yams to accompany it—her favorite meal. I sang birdcalls she loved, shook a rattle for her to dance, and mimicked graceful moves so poorly she laughed again. Knowing what she would like, planning small joys for her was delight. Despite my efforts, Kehinde crumpled in the mud as the moon rose. I folded her into the sphere of my arms for the first time. Uninitiated in romance, I nuzzled her neck and belly and filled the air with pungent scents. Her sleep was beautiful, and I managed to cloak consciousness a few moments myself.

The next morning, Kehinde awoke renewed, hopeful. We headed south, determined to find Somso. Although war had transformed Dahomey into a dispirited, alien landscape, Kehinde resisted despair. As we slipped through broken countryside, teaching me gave her pleasure. Reanimating the ruins with stories allowed her to mold my thoughts and name the future. We kept a relentless pace, resting only a few hours now and then. Kehinde feared never finding Somso.

One afternoon, the home star was too hot. Our lungs were full of dust and our feet were bloody. "We should take refuge in this deserted spirit house," I demanded.

She relented. We slept by an altar to a green-eyed deity with stringy hair. After several unconscious hours, Kehinde shook me awake. I was covered in sweat. My throat ached.

"You were choking." She leaned against the one sturdy wall. "Breathe when you sleep, or you won't return from dreams."

I shook off lingering drowsiness. "Sleep is too much like death." She winced at my words. "What are you doing?" She clasped a dusty leather treasure against her belly. It was filled with thin, crisp sheets of cloth. It absorbed her attention like quicksand.

"I couldn't sleep anymore. I read my books for . . . inspiration."

"Books?" I grunted at these inexplicable weighty things. "Why carry these—"

"You disapprove? Fula women always warned me, capturing a *gawlo*, a griot storyteller like this, locking him away in a book, is very bad for the memory and everything else. How can we trust distant words from nobody? How do we recognize truth without hearing a voice, seeing the eyes, or smelling sweat?"

I shrugged. We had met few Fula people—a griot playing his *hoddu* lute and a woman with tattoos singing under the stars. They were no wiser than anyone else.

"I say, who remembers every story? Who can call up ancestors so clearly they sing in your mind? A person can lie out loud to my face or on paper behind my back." She handed me books purchased in Ouidah: a slim weather-beaten thing (Sufi poetry?), Jules Verne's *Vingt Mille Lieues sous les Mers (Twenty Thousand Leagues Under the Sea)*, and Charles Dickens's *A Tale of Two Cities*. "I read and write Arabic, French, and English. I learned to be a proper British lady in a school where they hoped I would love Jesus." She indicated a broken glass painting above her head. "Jesus was a powerful orisha who walked on water and called the dead back to life."

I handed the books back to her, indifferent to their magic. My stomach grumbled. "Do we have food?"

"My parents wanted me to understand European cunning and Arab secrets."

"You're tired. Sleep, and I'll watch over you." I gobbled the last of our fruit.

"Eshu Elegba doubts everyone and everything. But—"

"The powerful have subtle ways to seduce and conquer."

She jumped up, sneering. "You will school me?"

I didn't answer. Why give inexplicable anger more fuel?

She shouted. "My father was a *Babalawo*, an *Ifa* diviner, a master of mysteries, a guide to our highest destiny; and my mother an *Iyalawo*, also a priestess of *Ifa*, a mother of secrets. She saw me writing in a vision. My father said words were my destiny and sent me to school when who would think of such a thing for a poor girl."

I stood up too, close enough to drink her breath. "Your destiny has never been defined by what others think," I said softly.

"The Fon stole me before I was truly initiated into the secrets of the Yoruba, French, or English wise people. I've been lost a long time—"

I kissed her sweet lips to end our foolish disagreement.

We tasted tongues, brief intimacy that she ended too quickly. She shoved the two cities' saga in my face. "You will learn."

Chronicles 5: Dahomey, West Africa, 1892—Blood Oath

As we wandered through sparse savannahs and approached Abomey, I came to know many languages, spoken, written, and danced. I learned the difference between the Yoruba of Abeokuta and the Fon who stole Kehinde to wage war for Dahomey, who made her steal other people from themselves. I memorized what she knew of *Ifa*—the history, wisdom, and spirit guide of the Yoruba rendered in stories and praise songs to the orisha. I read every night. Arabic poetry and European novels made little sense. Stories without bodies didn't interest me. I grew bored learning nonsense.

Kehinde chastised my laziness in the ruins of a compound we had visited before. Blood still stained the ground. "We shall not always wander a conquered land hunting my brother's wife and son."

"Somso was his wife? Your brother had a child? Why not tell me sooner?"

Kehinde hadn't meant to tell me. Her tongue slipped. She flicked fingers at my anger and continued. "There are cities across the waters where we might become someone else."

"We are who—"

"—they make of us." She sneered. "I'm a daughter of a distant land. Dahomey isn't my home or yours. I'm a traitor to everywhere I've been. Eshu knows where we shall make a place for ourselves and be reborn. We do not."

We found no sign of Somso. Still, Kehinde rejoiced at the sight of fields being plowed and soldiers keeping the peace. Finally, home territory.

"The French have spies everywhere. One may have heard of Somso," she said. "We'll make ourselves useful to French lords. Our skills are valuable."

"Well . . ." I had only seen the French recruit male warriors. I clamped my tongue. We tell the stories we want to believe. Sometimes they come true.

"I am *gbeto*, a sharpshooter, and who needs good aim with such a weapon?" She pulled the Lebel rifle from my back. "Don't worry. You will be as *ahosi*."

"Yes, I have completed the training."

"Completed?" She laughed. "Run through there." She pointed at a bush with thorns longer than my hand and sharper than the cutlass at her waist.

"No."

"Go on!" She threatened to whip me with strands of goat knotted with chips of bone and metal—a weapon I surmised and not a musical instrument or, maybe, both.

"Why beat me for protecting delicate skin?" I was swift now. She couldn't catch me.

"You should obey."

"Even what does not make sense?"

"Do you know all the sense there is?"

"Explain why I should do this? Or why I should let you beat me if I don't?"

"How will you ever get tough if you can't bear a little pain, a little blood?" She dropped her gear and raced through the bush that slashed her cruelly. She didn't cry out or falter, but stood waiting for me on the other side, bleeding and breathing hard. "You never know where your enemies hide. Perhaps they live within you. Pain can't be your master. We must be loyal to one another, through blood and pain, in the face of death, then we will always triumph."

"You believe this still?"

"Not everything Abla taught me was a lie."

"Which is lies and which is truth?"

She staggered as if I'd thrust a bayonet in her stomach. "Whoever knows that?"

"We must ask."

"My brother was always pondering lies and truth. He said we

are ignorant children drinking at a river that runs with poison, believing in those who scoop tainted water into our mouths." She trembled. "Which is worse, dying of thirst or poison?"

"Your brother asked this?" I prodded, hoping she would speak more.

"My twin. He was with me when we first met." Her cheeks were stone, her breath fire. "You look like him."

"So do you," I realized. "In the cave, your twin brother, not your lover—he died on your cutlass?"

She bared her teeth in that predator grin. "I spared him the slow death of Winchester bullets in his belly. Honored in life, Taiwo dances with our ancestors."

Taiwo. I shared a name with her brother, a brother she had killed for mercy's sake.

"I live on for us both." She waved at me. "Come through danger and pain, and I will tell you about him."

I ran into the mighty bush with no armor but my pathetic skin. Pain assaulted me. I feared thorns would come from nowhere and take my eyes in a surprise attack. Well-armed plants defending their fruit against tougher skin than mine demanded respect. The tangle of stinging hooks captured me. Thrashing made me more of a prisoner.

"Come!" Kehinde shouted.

I ripped myself apart to reach her.

"Tell me of your brother." I fell at her feet, clutching a burbling wound in my side. "Why have you never told me before?"

"Only a fool trusts a stranger."

"Am I a fool for trusting you?"

She shrugged, then dripped blood from her wounds into a skull. "Will you swear never to betray me?"

"I will swear."

The skull grinned at her as she spurted blood from my wound into it. "This man was a French spy. He raped a palace guard while a cousin from my village pinned me down and made me watch. My cousin called me traitor and planned to rape me too. The pal-

ace guard was a Fon woman who had shown me kindness. We'd
sworn to die for one another. I had no weapon. She flung a hidden
knife in my cousin's eye, saving me instead of herself. The Frenchman crushed her neck before I took his head. No good solution.
Hers was the best plan to save one of us."

"No good solution," I murmured. This grim logic made me dizzy.

Kehinde added gunpowder, palm wine, and fragrant leaves to
the blood. "After you swear, I'll tell you Taiwo's story." She poured
a few drops in the dust and called on the master of the crossroads
as witness:

Eshu Elegba!
Who used his penis for a bridge
Penis broke in two, and travelers toppled into cold water
Eshu the road maker!
Who changes trees into warriors and makes paths into dead ends
Eshu Elegba!
Who threw a stone yesterday and killed a bird today
Witness our sacrifice
Hold us to our oath
We are one spirit now

"I will never betray you." She drank the bloody mixture then
thrust the skull at me. "Speak the oath in your own tongue."

"You ask me to face death." To speak my language was to become no one in particular and broadcast my experiences between
the wavelengths of this place. I might lose my Taiwo-self for
hours, days, possibly forever. "Doing such an oath could scatter a
Wanderer into many beings. I might get lost in the spaces between
things."

She nodded. "Everyone dies. I've sworn to let go of one self to
become another. Only Eshu knows our destiny." She trembled in
front of me. "Life or death, I face tomorrow with you, unafraid."

I gripped her waist. "You must watch over me until I return to
this self."

"Explain." She squinted, as if less light would clarify my meaning. "Stay with this body, no matter what it says or does."

"I have sworn. Do you doubt my oath?" She pushed the skull to my lips.

I drank the bloody brew in one gulp, took a last swallow of air, and promised never to betray her to Wanderers near and far. The ground lurched under my feet. Trees and vines danced across a silvery sky. In my dissolving eyes, ten thousand iterations of her calm face blotted out exploding stars. I collapsed.

Several weeks passed before I was this Taiwo-self again. Meanwhile French soldiers discovered our hiding place as Béhanzin's scouts came seeking a traitor *ahosi*. They fought each other. Although Kehinde worried I had gone on to dance with my ancestors, she threw my body over her shoulder and ran into the forest.

In the deep repose of formless Wanderers, tethered to a fragile human form, I wondered if I could keep my oath to her. Never is a very long time.

Mojo Working

Cinnamon spit the taste of fire out of her mouth and tried to wake up. She was held captive in a bad dream where the house was on fire. Opal jumped around, squealing about the insurance money they'd collect and the bills she could pay. Cinnamon clutched *The Chronicles*, dictionaries, and scrapbooks she'd rescued from Sekou's side of their room, just her room now. A fist of flame snatched the heavy volumes from her hand without burning her; a cloud of smoke sucked thoughts out of her mind. She reached for her treasures and screamed at Opal. "The fire's stealing memories of Sekou and Daddy too."

Raven Cooper, tall and spooky, with smoky eyes and silky dreads twisting 'round a crooked grin, waved his arms in front of a gunman, as two warrior women tasted tongues below a stained-glass Jesus. An image on paper, it melted in blue flame.

"Cinnamon doesn't need to read more faggot fantasies." Opal talked to the fire, egging it to burn higher, hotter, as if she didn't notice Daddy burning up, as if Cinnamon wasn't even there. "She's lying all the time, living in a fantasy world."

Cinnamon bolted up, awake.

Opal was ranting at somebody right now. "I threw out that other *mojo* mess you gave her."

"I didn't lose it." Cinnamon hissed and balled her fists.

"Why take her to church?" Redwood's voice boomed. "For Jesus walking on water and coming back from the dead like a zombie? Huh?"

"Stupid optimist."

"She's twelve," a soft, low voice insisted. Great Aunt Iris?

Cinnamon sniffled. Real smoke made her sneeze. Gray dawn light snuck under the shades and softened the darkness. The bookshelves were dancing shadows. Her *Brother from Another Planet* poster hung crooked against *Starman,* and *The Adventures of Buckaroo Banzai Across the 8th Dimension* was missing a tack at the bottom. Something wasn't right. She'd fallen asleep in street clothes, reading, with the lamp on, no flashlight under the comforter. *The Chronicles* had been clutched to her heart. The dead man was Kehinde's brother, her twin even. On the back of a picture of Taiwo tossed over Kehinde's shoulder, the Wanderer had painted Raven Cooper leaping in the air to catch a bullet with his teeth. The bar, street, and crowd were a blur except for two hands entwined and Sekou's dark brown eyes. Or was that only a picture in a stupid-optimist dream?

Cinnamon groped the floor. Dust devils danced up her fingers. *The Chronicles* was gone. She sneezed into the sleeve of the pink princess PJs she hated and clutched her throat. The blue *mojo* bag Aidan had given her was also gone. Panic closed her throat and nose. A third sneeze exploded inside her head. The Walkman, headphones, and an almost empty knapsack sat neatly on Sekou's cluttered desk. Opal must have come in the night and taken *The Chronicles* and her *mojo* bag when she was dead to the world.

Cinnamon put her fist to her mouth and clamped down on a scream. She peered under the bed. Sekou's stash of secret things hunkered with the dust bunnies behind her sneakers. Counting twelve dictionaries still sitting proud on the bookshelf, she peeked into the *Oxford English Dictionary* resting on its stand/altar under a warped mirror. Sekou had stashed photos of Raven in with his favorite words. Determining that they were safe, she ran to the window and wrestled it all the way open.

"It's our job to spoil her," Aidan said.

"You will not take her to see her father." Opal spit in the fire.

The window looked out on a rocky patch of dirt (that the realtor pretended was a yard) that separated the house from a steep drop to the alleyway behind them. Opal, dressed in a ratty yellow bathrobe, marched around a garbage barrel, emptying a cardboard box into orange flames. Redwood, in billowy pants and robes, moved opposite her as if they were dancing an angry tango duet.

The blue scarf at Redwood's waist could have been the Ohio River raging after a storm. Aidan tugged at Redwood's arm, his long white hair trailing in the wind. He looked like an old Indian medicine man for sure, trying to get his hoodoo witch woman into a dark wool coat. Iris was halfway 'round the corner on the staircase up to the street, her head down, her chest heaving. She had on sensible shoes and an iridescent raincoat, and she carried the bag with their overnight things. They were leaving. Iris also clutched a book or something under her arm.

Opal shouted. "Raven was crazy wild like you all and—"

"You loved him for it," Redwood said.

A few tears slipped past Opal's defenses. "I'm not losing anybody else."

"Raven ain't all the way gone yet," Aidan said.

"Might as well be dead!" Opal snarled.

Redwood hugged Opal and her raggedy tears.

"Aidan's already got one foot in the grave." Opal squirmed free. "When you're gone, I'll be left with the mess." She tossed an envelope in the barrel. The cardboard box was empty. She tossed that too. The fire flared up, spitting ash and sparks into the patchy pink dawn. Redwood eyed the high-reaching fingers of heat that poked in the open window.

"What's to stop Cinnamon from—" Opal sounded wrong.

"Everybody's doing the best they can," Redwood said. "Sekou blamed hisself for Raven getting shot, like he pulled the trigger that sent Raven to a coma."

"It tore the boy up inside," Aidan said.

Cinnamon skipped a breath. Sekou never told her that. Didn't he trust her? How could Sekou believe a lie like that? Daddy in a coma was no way his fault.

"If you're going, go on before she wakes up and begs me to let you stay till Christmas." Opal sounded hollowed out.

Redwood let Aidan put the coat on her shoulders and tug her away. Opal lit a cigarette in the tower of flames and glared at the ground. Marching around the house, the elders glanced up at Cinnamon's window and even managed to smile. A car pulled away in the front, probably Aunt Becca's Kevin taking them to the train station. Aidan wouldn't fly. He had *one foot in the grave.* One wrong step and *Falling out the sky ain't how I plan to go.* Cinnamon couldn't stop an image of Aidan from plummeting into dark earth. Dirt filled his ears, eyes, and mouth. She was choking too, trying to stop a flood of tears. What if she never saw any of them again? *Never*—like Sekou! No. She'd hitchhike up to New England if she had to—

"Shit," someone screeched. "Watch it!"

Opal sprayed a hose of freezing water on the burning trash. A cyclist, no helmet, no lights in patchy dawn, pushed a ten-speed up the hill and cursed the rain of slush. She had a death wish, biking Pittsburgh hills in winter.

"What's wrong with you?" The cyclist brushed wet ash off her boyish figure.

"Me? What the hell's wrong with you?" Opal replied.

"I'm an actor. My bike ride is emotional research."

"Well, I ain't studying you." Opal slumped into the house.

Cinnamon closed the window, raced to lock the bedroom door, then climbed back under the comforter. Crying made it hard to breathe. Opal had sent the elders packing. She was burning *The Chronicles,* a special book, *magic,* a book to see a person through tough times, a book with a picture of Daddy in it! Cinnamon hadn't gotten to memorize or even read much of it. You weren't supposed to throw the truth away. That gave evil a chance to ruin your life. Cinnamon remembered what Armageddon was: a battle of good and evil at the end of time. Sekou said Armageddon was coming, and she'd let him down, let the Wanderer down too. She punched the pillow. Something hard inside bruised her knuckle. She swallowed a whimper.

"I know you're not asleep," Opal tried to open the door. "I hear you crying. Stop that and let me in."

"How could you?" Cinnamon muttered. As she wiped away tears, blood from her knuckles dripped onto the pillow.

Opal rattled the knob.

"It wasn't your book. Sekou entrusted it to me. I'm the Guardian." She poked the pillow. Something was hidden under it. "You burned Daddy's paintings too and now—"

"What are you talking about?"

"Burn your own life, not mine," Cinnamon yelled.

Opal pounded. "We can't be living in the past."

"Sekou said the past doesn't go anywhere. We always got a foot in yesterday."

"He did not say that nonsense. You're making that up."

"It's sorta what he said." Cinnamon sniffled. "Just leave me alone!"

After a few heartbeats, Opal walked back down the hall.

Inside the pillow, Cinnamon found a carved wooden box wrapped in Redwood's river silk. The liquid blue fabric flowed like cool water over Cinnamon's wounded hand and pulled the pain away. The box was shaped like a comet with a tail of silver threads and violet feathers from a Georgia swamp bird. Aidan's handiwork, it smelled of lily of the valley, black licorice, and rosemary oil. Aidan sucked licorice to soothe a cranky stomach. Cinnamon slid the top open. Inside was a yellow mosaic bead on a slim chain, her blue *mojo* bag from Aidan, a fat letter from Iris rolled like a scroll, and the shells and eagle feather that Redwood always wore. *Always.* Cinnamon's hands trembled.

That was something. That was more than something.

She'd have to figure out a hiding place that Opal couldn't find.

Letter from Iris Phipps,
December 1984

Dear Heart,

Don't be angry with your mom.

Opal thinks walking 'round the Tree of Forgetfulness will save you from being haunted by a past you can't do anything about.

Maybe she's right.

Opal loves you and wants the best for you. She loves Sekou too—no hiding that.

Raven Cooper was her whirlwind, kindred spirit. They met in the desert—in a flash flood cloudburst—and promised to hold on to one another.

Opal's heart is breaking.

Didn't Sekou say we had to look out for her? I know you promised him, so hunt down your generous spirit and forgive her in the hard days to come.

We offer you these keepsakes to remember us by:

Aidan's folks found one shell on Enotah, a sacred mountain in Cherokeeland (Georgia); another shell is from the Sea Islands and your great-grandmother, Garnett Phipps. The feather is from a Lakota war bonnet. Aidan and Redwood found it at the 1893 Chicago World's Fair along with the yellow bead from Dahomey. I hope you don't mind us hiding powerful hoodoo magic under your pillow. Guard these treasures well.

Aidan says he's going to set your praise song for Sekou to music as soon as we get home. He also wrote you a song. He says, please excuse the rhyme. Don't mind him. That's an old music-man's modesty. Get him to play both songs on the banjo for you next time we come down:

Nobody can burn
What you're holding in your heart
Nobody can turn
The truth riding on your breath
To ash and smoke, to pain and regret
How much you want to bet
Nobody can set
The spirit on fire, except with love
Nobody can set
The spirit on fire, except with love

Redwood sends you a hoodoo spell to make you a theatre person, like her and Aidan:

1: *Walk down by the river. Watch it flow, until you feel it flowing in you.*
2: *Flow with the river whenever you want or need its power.*
3: *Read a book every day, and you'll find secret lines, written just for you.*
4: *Copy your secrets in a special journal.*
5: *Improvise your own magic words to conjure the world you want.*
6: *Find a friend or two, and share secrets and magic out loud.*
7: *When you want to scream at Opal, tell her how much you love her and why.*
8: *Go on and say why you're mad too.*
9: *Go where you've never been before—an aisle in the library, a corner of Kennywood Park, a museum or picture house, a bridge over troubled water or calm, a building downtown, a block in a strange neighborhood, a secret forest—and watch it flow, until you feel it flowing in you.*

You are the light of our lives shining on.

Write and say how you're doing. We can't wait to see you grown into yourself.

Love,

Aunt Iris, Granddaddy Aidan, and Miz Redwood

P.S. *Aidan slipped* The Chronicles *out of your room while Opal got you into those sweet PJs. Redwood put him up to it, saying, "Take the book for safekeeping. Opal be in a fire-breathing, dragon temper. When her spirit cools, we don't want nasty regret laying her low."*

I've read a bit further. A drawing from the end of Chronicles *5 and these new chapters came loose. I took it as a sign and passed them on to you.*

Magic indeed.

Notes (#2) to the Current Edition of the Earth Chronicles, Dec. 1984

Trusting in words, in the stories of others can be dangerous. Dahomey is beyond the words I have written. Kehinde slips from my grasp, even as I try to write her down.

Eshu laughs at me.

I scoffed at books and writing, but it was learn to read and write or lose my head. Still I swore that I'd never waste precious time writing what could be spoken, danced, sung.

Dear Guardians, beware of promises you can't keep.

After Kehinde's death I write words to generous strangers I may never know, who trust me at least while they read. I seek the pattern, the story we made—a sacred task done in honor of Kehinde. What you remember makes you whole.

I am writing for my life, while I wait for love to come back in style.

Eshu laughs at us all.

Chronicles 6: Dahomey, West Africa, 1893—Return

Having sworn to Wanderers far and near never to betray Kehinde, I came back to the Taiwo-self in a smelly room a few miles south of Ouidah, close enough to the sea to spit in the waves. It was a hot night. Kehinde dripped sweat in my eyes. The usually tight plaits across her head had unraveled, loosening tufts of hair streaked with dust and grit. Her rich, dark skin had gone ashy. Her breasts and long legs were covered by rough brown cloth, the same rough cloth that irritated my skin from ankle to neck. I squirmed against a rash on my hips. Deep-throated creatures howled an alarm outside. I shuddered at the noise and stink of a hungry predator.

Kehinde searched my face, uncertain. "Taiwo?"

We were crammed with too many people in a dilapidated hut where the Fon had once held captives before shipping them to the Americas. The rank air offended my tongue. I didn't mind the unwashed bodies, but the rampant despair nauseated me. I turned from Kehinde to vomit in a corner. A few foul drops came up. A woman with a big belly scooted away from me. She pulled a veil tight against her face.

"Can you walk?" Kehinde asked. I traced a finger across her cracked lips. She was desolate, a dry riverbed. "Let's walk." Kehinde yanked me over sleeping bodies out into a salty sea breeze.

We stood under a field of dim stars. I sucked fresh air greedily. We walked twenty minutes at a fast pace and halted on an empty beach. The dull roar of waves pounded my skull. Sand and grit scrubbed my ankles. I was light-limbed and heavy-headed.

Kehinde pulled me on toward the sea. "Are you really my Taiwo?"

I tried to say, "Who else?" but garbled the words. My tongue tasted of bile and blood. A stab of pain in my side made me stumble. The wound from the armored bush was still tender. I should have healed myself before talking into the spaces between things. "You think I'm a masquerade and not myself?"

"You *appear* to have returned." Anxiety wafted from her pores.

I tripped and almost fell. Kehinde steadied me and retrieved a gourd of warm liquid from behind a dazzling white rock. I guzzled the contents. My raw esophagus burned. The undulating horizon settled and vision cleared. I spied books, medicine bags, and a comb in the sand, but no skulls, weapons, or ammunition. We were naked indeed, at the mercy of any who held our deaths in their minds. I scanned the beach, fearful of ambush. Lapping waves became warrior feet. Wind in the palm leaves was a soldier's labored exhalation. Before panic claimed me, Kehinde touched my cheeks, shoulder, and belly with calloused fingers, tentative at first, ending with a pinch. I groaned. She poured libation from a small gourd into the waves and spoke:

> *Eshu!*
> *Rule breaker*
> *First and last born*
> *Guardian at the gate*
> *Who speaks every tongue*
> *Master of life and death*
> *Whose breasts never run dry*
> *Eshu!*
> *Who knows our thoughts, our hearts*
> *Wise orisha*
> *Who rhymes our reason*
> *Eshu!*
> *I am grateful that you have returned Taiwo to me.*

She flicked a horsetail whip and narrowed her eyes. "I never broke our oath."

I gripped her wrist. "Go on."

"My brother, he was *Omotaiyelolu*, the first to taste the world, the twin who excels. The balance was thrown off when Taiwo died, by my hand. You came and returned the world to balance, didn't you?" She blew sour breath in my face. "Didn't you?"

"I am not your brother."

"I know." She hurled my hand against my belly. I lost several breaths. "You're nothing like him." She lied. To wound me? The sack of brown cloth hung stupidly on her muscled physique. More hair twisted free of deteriorating braids. Black storm clouds covered stars and a sliver moon. A light on a distant boat bobbed in the waves. Dizzy, I wanted to throw up, but I was as empty as the space between galaxies.

"What brings us to the cove"—I blinked away nausea—"where sharks fed on Yoruba flesh and Oshun spared you?"

"You were right about that deadly bush. After being wounded gravely, speaking the tongue of your ancestors took your strength. You collapsed into my arms. Mercenaries were about to attack us. I had to carry you. You were heavy as death. I couldn't get far with such a burden. Stumbling up to a termite tower, hope deserted me. You were barely breathing, an errant heartbeat. Our story almost ended there."

I paced around her brooding silence. What was worse than the tales of betrayal, rape, and murder she'd already told me? "You see me, hear me. I am with you again."

"Yes." She rested her full weight against me, trusting my control of gravity. I staggered, but didn't fall. As I held her in the sphere of my being, her breath turned sweet. The wet heat from her skin soothed me. The rhythm of her blood was delicious. With a swipe of my tongue, I tasted joy in a rogue tear trickling down her cheek. I laughed softly.

She pulled away. "What's funny?"

"Joy." I pulled her close again.

She resisted. "There were others. They laughed at me too."

"Others?"

"In you." She tapped the space between my breasts. "Alien

strangers rode your spirit, and I was afraid you'd never come back to me." She dug in the sand with her foot. The blade of her cutlass gleamed in a shaft of moonlight.

I uncovered the hilt with my toe. "To speak our oath, I risked all." She shivered as my warm breath evaporated sweat on her neck. "Wanderers are restless, always seeking new adventures, new experiences. Why come back to what you've already tasted once?" Wanderers rarely lasted long enough in one place to have a full life. "You and I swore to be one spirit. You can tell me anything."

She slipped away from me, back into her story. "At that termite tower, your other spirits awoke and warred with one another—cursing, shouting, and drooling blood. They clouded your eyes and stole your tongue. They spoke nonsense in languages I had never heard. They moved your limbs, enjoyed your heartbeat, stole your breath."

I shuddered. "What else?"

"They held the Lebel rifle to my head. No matter how hard they rode you, no matter what curse, threat, or horror they spit from your lips—I refused to abandon you."

"Did they harm you?" I swallowed slowly. "Did I?"

She shook her head and hunched her shoulders—yes and no.

"Tell me." I brushed grit from her hair and plucked the comb from the sand.

She touched wayward locks. "I haven't had a moment—"

"I will make you beautiful again." I forced a smile. "Tell me what happened."

"I didn't feed these lost spirits or welcome them in your body. I told them to go away and send you back to me. I called on Oshun, Shango, and Eshu Elegba. I danced a war dance, smashing through madness, taking your invaders' heads with my cutlass. Eshu accepted this sacrifice. Your face became a mask of calm. The Lebel rifle was on your back again. Your fingers caressed my palm with a crossroads sign. Like a person lost in dreams, you wandered elsewhere, but Eshu rode your body, protecting you against the others, keeping the way open for your return."

I murmured a praise poem:

Eshu!
Full breasts
Rule breaker
Penis road maker
Many-headed change

I dug the wooden comb through tight curls, massaging her scalp with the rounded tips. She sighed and sat in the sand. I slipped behind her onto the cool surface of the white rock. Squeezing her shoulders between my thighs, I gathered wayward hair and braided it against her head. "Did the French capture us?" I asked. She shook her head. "Béhanzin's spies?"

"Would we be chatting on this beach if *ahosi* warriors had caught us?"

I stared at the blinking light of the distant boat. "Is that our ship?" She nodded. "Are we slaves now? You traded our freedom for our lives?" She tried to pull away, but I clenched her shoulders and braided a second row.

If this journey is not about patience, I don't know why else I wandered here.

Chronicles 7: Dahomey, West Africa, 1893—Pretty Knots

I plaited her entire head in a swirling galaxy pattern before she spoke more.

"French mercenaries followed my clumsy tracks to the termite tower. I heard their loud approach. I shook you, hard enough to snap your head from your neck and shouted, *Run! I cannot carry you any farther, and if we stand still, we die. Don't let enemies from within defeat us. Fly!* Your eyes were dark clouds. The invaders tried to cackle through your lips, but, Eshu be praised, your body obeyed me. You raced away at the speed of dreams. I followed. My heart wanted to burst. There was blood on my breath, a ringing in my bones. Your swiftness saved us. Lazy French soldiers turned from our path and chased Béhanzin's spies. We watched from a hillside as they charged into an ambush. *Don't rejoice a swift battle,* I said. *The victors will come for us.* We ran on. You flung the Lebel rifle into a lagoon. I threw away most of our things too, for speed. Going at a dream pace, our muscles lasted until Ouidah.

"Filthy and exhausted, we wandered the streets of the city. The invading spirits sang in foreign tongues and argued with shadows. I waited every day for you to return. One afternoon in the market as you entertained an eager crowd, I spied a muscular man with scars above his heart—Yao, the warrior captain who raided my village as a young man. He had pulled me from an ocean death and given me to Abla for warrior training. Yao mistook you for my brother, a rebel slave come back from the dead. It's not true, you are who you are, but Yao recognized me for true, a traitor, an oath-breaker. Yao's head still belonged to Béhanzin. He would have died to bring us down. Without my rifle, I was no match for him. Spectators surged around us, squealing at your madness, cheering. Yao couldn't reach us with his knife. The French must have confiscated his rifle. He screamed, *I will kill you both.* People in the crowd, thinking Yao a thief, wrestled him down. The market women don't abide thieves. I rejoiced. Avoiding their justice would take time. I got you to flee, softly, a shadow feeding the dark, and we escaped."

A distant splash startled me. Reaching for the cutlass, I wrenched my torso and winced.

"Vigilance is a good habit, but fear can't be our lives. We were lucky that day. Yao was alone, without a rifle. It was easy to lose him. Your *aje*—power spirit—put us in constant danger. Despite this, Eshu wouldn't let us leave Ouidah and meet destiny elsewhere." Kehinde gestured at my wound. "That was an angry mound growing worse. You were covered in bitter sweat. Your body obeyed simple commands, but I couldn't heal you. That evening after Yao's ambush, your breath was shallow; your joints failed every second step. We were close to starving. I had nothing left to barter with." She clutched my calf with sandy hands. "Hunger tore you apart. Even with Eshu riding you, the *aje* flapped your limbs in the wrong direction."

My achy muscles remembered this.

"With the last of our gold, I sought a *Babalawo,* a Yoruba man living free from his wisdom. I'd met this father of mysteries when I was first a captive in Ouidah. An honorable man, even if he drove a hard bargain, he'd never betray us to Yao. I'd forgotten the way to his compound. When I spoke this plan, you rallied and in a few hours wandered to his door. Who denies a miracle? The *Babalawo* saw Eshu in you and agreed to perform *Ifa* divination. He tossed the palm nuts, marked lines in the dust. You knocked over the divining tray as he was about to offer *Ifa* verses. *Eshu,* I declared, embarrassed. He nodded and spoke *Iwori Meji.*"

"I don't know those verses." In the north Kehinde schooled me in the *Ifa* wisdom of the Yoruba. Perhaps she'd taught me *Iwori Meji.* My memories were so muddled.

Kehinde recited:

Ifa *says this is a person who wants to go out of town or on a journey.*
The person should sacrifice so her eyes do not see evil where she is going.
Ifa *says this is a person whose relatives cause her trouble.*
They won't let her find peace anywhere, but if she sacrifices—
She will find peace of heart and will overcome all her enemies.

"I sacrificed and asked about a French healer. The *Babalawo* warned me, *The Frenchman knows how to lance a wound, yet can't see for looking. Too greedy. Take his medicine. Ignore the rest.*" She touched the scar at her throat from the Fon slave collar. "We went to the Frenchman, Dr. Pierre, and his price was high."

"Very high?"

She shrugged. "Dr. Pierre declared that as sure as water falls down a cliff, you'd die from the infection if it were left untended."

"You gave the *Babalawo* the last of our gold. How could you pay—"

"I paid his fee. There was no alternative. Dr. Pierre said, *On est dans le coma.* He cooled you in a bath, cleaned the wound, made you drink bitter tea. He said no ghosts haunted you. Is that true? Did the bush send tiny creatures to scatter your spirit?"

"There are in me always others waiting for an opening. As you once said, anyone can become someone else. Only Eshu knows tomorrow."

"You wind your words into a pretty knot." She scratched her neck. "Don't lie."

"I've never lied to you. Wanderers don't know all the lost selves who roam the crossroads, waiting for a chance to take over."

Her hand hovered over my wound. "Can we choose who to be?"

"Perhaps." I slipped down beside her and clutched the cold metal of the cutlass. The blade cut my palm and I dripped blood in the sand. "I sacrifice to our truth."

Kehinde clasped my bloody hand. "I understand why you don't trust sleep."

"Really?"

"Don't underestimate me."

"Forgive me. I'm an ignorant Wanderer."

"In sleep, you're vulnerable to the others who would steal your tongue, feet, and heart. You have many spirits, many bodies—like Eshu." She smiled. "Much ashe—power to make things be."

"I fought the others."

"Instead of fighting, you could sacrifice and go elsewhere for another life?"

"Yes. I might never be Taiwo again."

"Eshu guides every transition." She brushed her cheek against my knuckles. "When Yao and his squad raided our village, my brother and I were dreaming. We slept in an iroko tree—his idea. I dreamt of being a warrior woman. Warrior feet woke my brother. He sounded the alarm. I threw a masquerade over his head and mine. They caught us and dragged us through the village." She paused. "We didn't see what had happened, only bodies burning. My father's head dripped blood on Yao's spike; my sisters screamed; my mother's waist beads were scattered."

"What did your brother dream?" My wound throbbed. I winced.

"Taiwo became the *Babalawo* of his dreams, and I became the warrior woman." She sighed. "After Dr. Pierre wrestled you from *le coma,* I swore we'd make a long journey; we'd find new stories, peaceful sleep. I didn't know how, but *Ifa* isn't cruel. Eshu laughs at our sorrow, for sorrow fades when we turn the corner into a new life."

"The orisha show us a path. We must take it."

"Exactly, you couldn't come back to yourself until we were on our way. So after I dispatched the Frenchman—"

"You killed Dr. Pierre?"

"He violated me many times. He lusted after you as well."

"When I was sick and helpless?" My stomach rolled. "Why?"

"It gave him pleasure." She balled her fists. "Dr. Pierre's medicines dried up bitter sweat and made the angry swelling subside. Yet invaders still whispered with your tongue. *What cure is this?* I asked. He sneered at me, *Je ne suis pas le sorcier de tribu. I'm no witch doctor. Taiwo is in God's hands.* I realized, searching for Somso in this war, I might lose you to Yao's blade. Fon spies could mistake you for me or my brother. Who knows if Somso still lives? Abandoning a dead woman to the ancestors would not dishonor my brother. I decided to journey far and leave enemies behind as *Ifa* said. The night before our departure, Dr. Pierre came to my bed, demanding more than our bargain, saying he deserved me once more and you as a bonus. He'd charged other women a similar price for saving their children's lives. Many returned for regular *treatments*." Kehinde sighed. "I sent him away. I'm not other women."

"You are their champion."

"While you healed, I was Dr. Pierre's assistant." Kehinde fought tears. "He turned no sick person away: Yoruba, Fon, English, Brazilian, Fula, Portuguese, Igbo, French, Ewe, rebel, slave, soldier, or royal prince. He shared French doctor secrets with any who listened. He taught everyone who asked to read. Books and knowledge were his greatest treasures, and he gave them away. I traveled the world in his library, and we talked of noble lands, ancient and in the future. He had me teach him *Ifa* wisdom. We wrote down many verses. At his funeral, only a few women spat on the grave. Most sang his praises. The mothers of the market suspect a jealous husband or an angry lover, but I'm their enemy."

"How could someone so good turn around on himself?"

"That question torments me," Kehinde said and recited:

Eshu slept in a house—But the house was too small for him
Eshu slept in the open—But the open was too small for him
Eshu slept in a nut—At last he could stretch himself!

"Now *you* wind words into a pretty knot," I said.

"You would have spared Dr. Pierre, even though, changing your bandages that last night, he fondled your breasts, spread your legs, and started to mount you. I'd warned him. You weren't part of our bargain." Her heart was a hammer. "He spoke sweetly, *Don't be jealous, chérie, I have more than enough love for you both.* He thrust himself into your helpless form. Love? A person without honor is a dead person. How can he know love?" She spoke softly. "Still, killing him wasn't as easy as taking other heads."

"*Ifa* chose *Iwori Meji* for us both."

"Who argues with a cure? You've come back to yourself."

"Have I?" Wanderer memories were blurry fragments.

"I'm your *stillpoint.* I will know you from beginning to end. That is Wanderer wisdom you spoke to me. *Believe* in who you say you are."

Exhausted from her long vigil watching over me, she curled within my arms and fell deep asleep.

Chronicles 8: Dahomey, West Africa, 1893—New Life

A high-pitched bell sounded on the European boat. Birds passed over the ragged coast, cawing and slapping the air as if their roost had been threatened by predators. Kehinde shivered awake in the first strong breeze of the night. We mingled hot breath. My tongue lapped her salty skin. Desire burned through me, a surprise attack. Despite the past selves I'd forgotten, I still recalled that passion posed grave dangers. Too late. Love ambushes even the vigilant. Our limbs twisted and tangled until we made a braid of our bodies. Heart, breath, and bowels matched rhythms. Nerves fired a storm of static across our skin. Kehinde's sweat soured suddenly and thigh muscles tensed. Rough tones filled her throat and light dimmed in her eyes. Uninitiated in romance, I faltered. What was I to her?

"We shall wander." She spoke softly. "The French do not want women warriors."

"I know."

"I don't have to be who I have been. The new king, Agoli Agbo, is a puppet, not a real ruler. He has only a few wives, and they are plump and beautiful, for his bed, not hard, bony warriors. His French masters don't trust the *ahosi* warriors. We could be Béhanzin's spies, hunters in their compounds, laying charms, destroying the power of French deities. Agoli Agbo has promised to marry the warrior women off." She grunted. "Who thinks I'd willingly go to a common man and be his slave, someone to order about and beat when it pleases him? I won't let anyone steal me from myself again. In America, they say, we can live as who we are, as who we want to be. They have freedom for all."

"How can you believe such outrageous lies?"

"Many people coming to Dr. Pierre told unbelievable tales with no incentives to lie—poets, soldiers, adventurers from many lands. They left stories behind." She waved a book in my face. I couldn't read the title in the dark. "Tomorrow we'll take a boat across the waters to America and see for ourselves if the stories of freedom are true."

"But a slave ship?"

"They're done with slavery across the sea. How could you think that?"

"Dressed as captives in old slave quarters, a European boat clanging in the night, declaring its power over land and sea." I smacked the book. "And you trusting what could be a collection of lies. What should I think?"

"An Italian impresario came looking for *ahosi* warriors or women who could act like *ahosi* warriors. Our clothes were rags. He gave us these for travel. He'll pay us well to show Chicago, America, our ways. We'll perform our dances and do a war-masquerade."

"I'm no performer of masquerades."

"The impresario was impressed with the show your *aje* put on."

"What if this impresario has no honor, like Dr. Pierre? Will you kill him too?" I picked up the cutlass and sliced the air. "How many stories will you abort?"

Kehinde's lips flushed with hot blood, and I regretted my cruel words.

"No good solution. Somso and her child are lost. I've accepted this, and Yao hunts us. I'm a traitor. No village, clan, family. We must go where people write a new story."

A bullet sliced the muggy air above my head and burrowed into wet sand. Kehinde and I rolled opposite directions. Someone emptied a Winchester at us. Clouds cloaked the moon and black water hid us. I peered through sparks and smoke into the palm trees where a rifle spit death. Darkness protected us but also hid our attackers. Four feet ran to the beach as the Winchester was reloaded. Gripping the cutlass, I let dark waves lap over my head.

"Kehinde!" Our attacker knew who we were! "May thunder and lightning kill us if we break our oaths." Bullets sprayed too close.

A sickle moon cut through clouds and spilled silver light on the beach. An *ahosi* warrior woman charged across the sands. She was older than Kehinde. Gray sprouted at her temples. Wide eyes glistened. Scars decorated tough skin. Crystal, ivory, and coral necklaces bounced against her chest and waist. Cuffs of silver and copper covered her forearms. A cutlass rode her hip. She reloaded the Winchester.

"You've lost your rifle. Perhaps your courage too." She fired at the sea. "Yao said you stumbled through the Ouidah market ragged and filthy in the company of a fool. How far you've fallen! Come, face death with your last scrap of honor."

Behind the warrior, a second woman ran slowly, without gun or blade. She clutched a veil around her face and wore the same rough brown cloth that chafed my body. Her belly was big. I recognized her. She'd sat near us in the smelly hut.

"Don't waste bullets on sand." Kehinde appeared a few feet behind our attacker and knocked her in the back. "Abla, the strong one, child of fire and maker of warriors, you were never a sharpshooter."

Abla almost lost grip of her rifle. She turned toward Kehinde as her companion sank in the sand with a shriek. "Don't worry, Somso," Abla said. "At this range, who needs good aim?"

"Somso?" Kehinde relaxed her martial stance. "Taiwo's Somso?"

Many women could have this name . . .

Abla pointed the Winchester at Kehinde's head. "You don't deserve another breath. You betrayed King Béhanzin, your co-wives, and yourself."

Kehinde dropped to her knees. "I'm ready to greet my ancestors."

"Somso tells me her husband, the great rebel leader, was a *Babalawo*." Abla stepped between Somso and Kehinde. "He cast *Ifa* and boasted: although his twin was an *ahosi* warrior, her head wouldn't always belong to Béhanzin."

"Why so much talk?" Kehinde gestured at Somso, her brother's wife, big with child, Somso whose name had been a prayer guiding us. "The Wanderer will take care of the future." Kehinde intended to sacrifice herself for a woman who'd probably betrayed her. "From beginning to end, we share the road." Kehinde closed her eyes.

"I knew you'd try to flee. My spies watched every departure." Abla reloaded an empty weapon.

"Open your eyes!" I sprang from the water with the cutlass. "Abla's talk is a trick."

Startled, Abla turned from Kehinde to search dark waves for ambush. What happened next is unclear. Potent stimulants saturated my muscles. I sucked in enough oxygen for a conflagration. My eyes went dark. Human thoughts dissolved. Kehinde claimed I was no longer in human form. An *aje*—power spirit from the spaces between things—had strayed into this dimension with my Taiwo-self. There are in me always others lurking at the crossroads, ready to seize the moment. Kehinde described tentacle hair, sharks' teeth, deadly tusks, and a fat, poisoned-tipped tail. Bullets bounced off skin tougher than elephant hide. The ground under my feet tasted different; the air sounded wrong, the sky didn't smell as sweet as before. An alien world.

The cutlass sliced mist, muscles, bone, and Abla's head toppled from her body. Her face was a map of disbelief. She had little time to think a last thought. Blood drenched the cutlass, the sand, and my taloned feet. Abla's dead fingers clenched the Winchester's trigger. It spat bullets at the sky. I trampled the rifle, grabbed her body and severed head, and plunged into the waves. I rode the pounding surf, skirting lethal rocks to reach the open sea where I flung Abla into inky foam. The ship's bell clanged an alarm. Pinpoints of light raced across the decks. Later I learned that some poor sailor had been spooked by a giant sea monster and collapsed on the bridge, never to rise again. Two lives wasted that night.

Back on land, fire bubbled up from my gut and burned my tongue. The ugliest feelings I have ever known overwhelmed me.

It was as if I'd lost my soul. Hungry for murder, I waved the cutlass at Somso (Abla's accomplice?), who cowered at the shore. Her eyes danced between me and the waves smashing the rocks, considering which death would be worse.

Kehinde ran between us and clasped my claws. "Spare her," she pleaded. "This is Somayina. Somso."

"Somso." My mouth ached with the last word Kehinde's brother had uttered.

"Brother-Taiwo loved her more than life itself. She is his wife."

"You know me?" Somso clutched her belly. A child stirred in her. Its salty ocean world ruptured and trickled down her leg. The child would follow soon. Curiosity doused *aje* rage. What led the wife of a rebel slave leader to join forces with an *ahosi* warrior? Somso's death no longer tasted sweet in my mouth. I drew away from the *aje* and back to my Taiwo-self, back to new life crowning between quivering thighs, back to

Pizza and Spells

Cinnamon gasped. *The Chronicles* excerpt ended midsentence. A drawing on the back showed a shark-lizard creature with a human face and seaweed hair rising out of a tidal wave. Blue snakes circled scaly arms. Lightning crackled from clawlike hands. Taiwo resembled the Oshun/Yemoja figure in the spirit cave. The image stuttered on the page like a broken video. Cinnamon stopped breathing altogether.

A wet, sparkling baby pushed out of its mother into the world and took a breath in Kehinde's trembling arms. Her brown dress was slick with afterbirth. On a frothy black sea, a tiny ship flashed points of yellow light. Salt tingled in Cinnamon's nose. Somso cried as the baby suckled heavy breasts.

"I didn't burn all Raven's paintings." Opal rattled the door.

Cinnamon fell out of bed.

"You can't shut yourself in there all day." Opal practically read her mind.

"Why not?" Cinnamon prayed the lock was strong. "I don't have school."

"You have to eat. You have to act normal."

Cinnamon blinked sand from her eyes. The magic moving-picture thing rewound and settled into a still: *Aje*-Taiwo waved a bloody cutlass and spewed poison from a fat tail. Fearless Kehinde stood between this monster *aje* and pregnant Somso sinking into sand. About to give birth, Somso clutched Kehinde's ankles. Her eyes were comets, trailing tears.

"Open up."

Cinnamon carefully rolled the pages up; no creases would disturb words or pictures. She'd have to read this chapter again, when she wasn't so whatever she was. Thoughts flooded her, a story storm.

The Wanderer had lost its mind—*The Chronicles* was a hoodoo cure, Redwood's spells #4, #5, and #6—writing secrets, inventing magic, and sharing with a friend. Right now in 1984, the Wanderer was out there somewhere, waiting for love to come back in style. Yesterday at the funeral, somebody else said the same thing. The Wanderer was sending her signs.

Yeah. Coincidences are probability magic, Sekou whispered.

"Huh?" Cinnamon scanned the room. "Is that you?"

Probability magic, Sekou repeated, a ghost talking as quietly as a breeze rustling dust, maybe so Cinnamon wouldn't freak. *Can you hear me?*

"Yeah," she whispered. "But how?"

Your ashe—the power to make things be.

Cinnamon nodded. "Much ashe."

I don't scare you?

"No. You can talk to me anytime." She was excited at the prospect. "Why didn't you tell me about you and Daddy at the bar?"

Opal's on our team, he said, a little louder. *Love makes her crazy.*

"Kehinde didn't ditch the Wanderer. I'm not giving up on Daddy."

"Are you talking to yourself in there?" Opal asked.

Mom's a drama queen. You better say something.

Cinnamon tried Redwood's spells #7 and #8. "I love that pizza you do from scratch, even if I'm mad at you for sending Miz Redwood, Granddaddy, and Aunt Iris away. How could—"

"Nothing except frozen peas, ancient cereal, and black cherry ice cream in the kitchen." Opal sounded wrong again. "Bread's got mold and the milk is lumpy too. We can go to the store, stock up. You can help with the tomato sauce. Open the door."

Cinnamon shoved Iris's letter and *The Chronicles* pages back into Aidan's comet box. Opal would hate her reading such a faggot fantasy with nasty sex and violence—like it might ruin her or tarnish her soul. That was stupid. God made sense. People didn't. That's how come Eshu laughed at everybody.

"Who eats black cherry? We'll get some chocolate. You know

you like that." Opal had tears stuck in her throat. "Please, child, please."

"Black cherry was Sekou's favorite."

"Right." Opal's rough breath rattled into a cough.

Cinnamon hid her new treasures way under her bed beside Sekou's box of secret things—which she hadn't dared to look through yet. She piled more old sneakers for camouflage and blew dust bunnies about. She straightened the *Brother from Another Planet* and put a tack back in *Buckaroo Banzai*.

You got this, Sekou said. *Talk to you later.*

After two deep breaths, Cinnamon opened the door. Opal grabbed her, hugged so hard it hurt, then cried and got snot all over the pink princess PJs Cinnamon hated. They both cried. Apparently Redwood's spells to make Cinnamon a theatre person were good for everything. Cinnamon decided to start on the other seven hoodoo conjurations right after Opal's famous pizza.

Book II

Pittsburgh, PA, February 1987 & Dahomey,
West Africa, 1893

Perhaps all the dragons of our lives are princesses who
are only waiting to see us once beautiful and brave.

—Rainer Maria Rilke

We can sing ourselves
to the store or eternity as surely
as we were born into
this world naked and smeared
with blood and fight.

—Joy Harjo

Theatre CPR

The Monongahela Playhouse squatted on the riverbanks, an ancient shipwreck wheezing in a February snow squall. Wind tore at banners announcing the final shows of the season. Inside was cold and damp. Cinnamon shivered as evaporating sweat stole her heat and floated toward the gallery. Artists had rescued the old waste processing plant before she was born, but they never raised enough money to fix the rambling wreck properly. Hasty renovations threatened collapse. The Playhouse creaked melodramatically in every storm and smelled of sewage, especially in summer. In winter it was too drafty for foul smells to linger. Recent budget cuts meant the jacked-up furnace was set just above where the pipes froze. Stage lights and the audience kept actors warm. Everyone else (like young hopefuls trying out for the New Play Festival) stayed in coats and gloves. Cinnamon's jacket was soaking wet. She'd hung it by a radiator, willing it to dry out before she went home. Always a stupid optimist, even fourteen going on fifteen. Why else was she trying out for this no-name musical?

"You don't have a lobster's chance in boiling water." Opal read Cinnamon's mind. She did that a lot recently. "Theatre is a dying art. Dead already." She brandished a pack of Camels unfiltered and peered out glass walls at the storm. "Even if they would cast somebody like you, which I doubt, it won't get you anywhere."

"Uh-huh." Big and dark, Cinnamon was theatrically challenged.

"There's a bridge to nowhere." Opal wheezed. "If you jump, you don't break your neck on the river, you're just gone, away from here."

Opal was always staring out windows and talking about getting nowhere—since Sekou OD'ed. For over two years now, Cinnamon'd had to drag Opal off the floor and make her eat, get dressed, go to work. Cinnamon badgered her for days to wash clothes for a teacher meeting this morning and then get to this audition on time. She promised everybody to cut Opal some slack and not whine, so letters to Aunt Iris were filled with how things ought to be. She lied on the phone to Aidan and Redwood, and Aidan forgot himself and talked Irish or Seminole. Redwood didn't say what was on her mind. Iris never sent more *Chronicles* pages and wasn't even writing anymore.

They're older than the hills and don't have time for your young sorrows.

Water (condensation? leaky roof?) dripped from the foyer ceiling onto once blue and gold carpet. Bright green mold dribbled down brick walls and colonized the dampness in concentric circles. Not exactly promising, but, doing Redwood's spells #1 and #9, Cinnamon had found the Monongahela Playhouse walking by the river. It flowed inside her. It was her theatre.

"I need a smoke." Opal staggered out the glass doors. The heel on her right shoe wobbled like a loose tooth. Her puke-green coat opened to the wind.

Cinnamon turned away as Opal lit up. Ahead of her, at least sixty kids and their parents shook sleet from waterproof coats, snarling and jostling between the box office and the emergency exit, too eager to stand still. Behind her was the same hopeful chaos. The crowd smelled like wet dog and stale French fries. Half the noses were running. Parents shoved tissues or snacks at whiny brats who didn't know the first thing about patience. Cinnamon sagged. She was near the end of the line. She could concentrate for hours to get what she wanted. Opal liked that about her. *You didn't get patience from me, that's for damn sure.* Patience and discipline weren't the same as wasting time.

"Save my place," Cinnamon said to the bony girl beside her. "I gotta pee." Faking a bathroom run was better than *pointless waiting.* She dodged down a hall past a techie stuffing cold pizza into his mouth with grimy fingers. Techies never minded eating bits and jots of their work. They were grit and grease inside and out and could turn a pile of junk into a magical kingdom. She admired them.

A barrel-chested man, with silver Einstein hair and bushy eyebrows, rehearsed Prospero in an alcove. His swirling black cape ripped and roared like the Monongahela rushing up a ravine in West Virginia. His deep voice made the walls and floor vibrate:

> *And, like the baseless fabric of this vision,*
> *The cloud-capped towers, the gorgeous palaces,*
> *The solemn temples, the great globe itself,*
> *Yea, all which it inherit, shall dissolve,*

"Did I get that right? I'm still tripping on this cape thing." Prospero talked at an assistant stage manager hunched over the script. "I've told them twice."

"Long like that, your cape looks fierce and wizard-worthy," Cinnamon said.

Prospero smiled. "Not the most propitious moment for an interruption." Who said *propitious* out loud?

"Sorry." She ran to the main stage and peeked in on the rehearsal of Shakespeare's *The Tempest*. A mighty lantern swung across the proscenium and made her seasick.

"Shoo!" A hunky assistant, clad all in black and cute as an actor, chased her off.

Cinnamon dashed into the studio theatre. A muscular woman leapt into a chariot pulled by fire-breathing dragons and soared up over the audience. Euripides's *Medea*! Techies running the flies hissed at their pulleys, but didn't call for a hold. Medea cursed a man crouching over two motionless little boys in bloody tunics. Jason, the Argonaut. Stealing someone's Golden Fleece was very bad luck. What good was stolen magic?

Medea had thick ropes of black hair and silver streaks around fluorescent green eyes—a fierce hero and beautiful. Jason was supposed to be cute too. The Playhouse had brought him in from NYC where he did soaps and car ads: *Ride American, we've got dream machines!* Jason left Medea for another woman. Cinnamon didn't get it. How could you stop loving someone who could fly? That's what Aidan always said.

"Keep those kids out of here."

Cinnamon rushed back to her place in the lobby. The skinny girl scowled at her and flipped silky black hair, like saving a spot in line had been hard work.

"It isn't fair for you to run off like that."

Cinnamon shrugged. "Thanks."

Only forty kids ahead of her now. She counted. Twenty-two. Parents made it look like more competition than it was.

The skinny girl poked Cinnamon's shoulder. She didn't have anybody grown-up with her either. "You should have to go to the back."

"Why you stuck on that?" Cinnamon could squash this five-foot-three, button-cute wraith with one hand. "Who's going to make me?" She balled her fist, and a smile slid into a sneer at the pale white folks nearby. Five-foot-eleven and a hundred eighty-eight pounds was good for throwing your weight around.

Skinny scowled back, unafraid. Impressive.

"Coming through." A cart piled with fruit, nuts, cheese, crackers, and pop banged Cinnamon's side. She grabbed a fistful of crackers and cheese and stuffed it in her knapsack. She hadn't eaten since lunch—a thin bologna slice on a rice cake and a few apple slices. She'd sung that off in choir. In gym, she'd been too weak for basketball. Now she was running on fumes. After the audition, she'd eat in the bathroom so Opal wouldn't start in about dieting. Opal claimed she was helping Cinnamon lose that *extra baby fat she was laying in for the next famine.* Starving wasn't a diet.

> *Where the bee sucks, there suck I;*
> *In a cowslip's bell I lie;*

A handsome devil in high boots, tights, vest, and a jeweled turban blocked the food cart and spoke Ariel's lines with a tenor/alto lilt. As Cinnamon stuffed a fistful of cashews into her backpack, Ariel grinned and proclaimed:

There I cough where owls do cry.
On the bat's back I do fly

"She's come from far away to play Ariel in *The Tempest*," the skinny girl whispered.

"*She?* Really?" Cinnamon said. Gender wasn't the only slippery thing. Ariel had medium-pale skin and features that could have been Asian, African, European, Native, or some group Cinnamon didn't know—Aborigine, Māori? "How far away?"

Ariel bowed. "Alas, I am a slave to an old sorcerer's whims or else we could have our own adventure." Shakespeare's lines or something improvised?

"Why are you out here in costume?" A buzz-saw voice made Ariel un-bow and wink at Cinnamon. Brandishing elbows of steel, the production coordinator pushed through fans gathered around Ariel. She halted by Cinnamon. "Where'd she go?"

Ariel had vanished with no door, hallway, or stairs nearby. Magic.

"How did she do that?" Skinny's eyes glistened.

Cinnamon sighed. "Ariel's a magic spirit."

"Only in the play, stupid." Skinny was a realist. "You can't do special effects in a lobby."

Cinnamon shrugged. "All the world's a stage, right?"

"Yeah." Skinny scrunched her eyes at Cinnamon, surprised, impressed, wary?

The production coordinator barged through grown-ups and kids. "*I* didn't make this train wreck schedule!" She told the hunk clad in black. "You're *my* ASM. Be ahead of fuckups. Fix shit *before* I notice." Parents scowled at this language. "The foyer has to be *clear* for setup." She italicized a word in each sentence. "Donors *already* think they're throwing good money after bad. I didn't study *begging* at Carnegie Mellon."

"Sure." The hunky assistant stage manager nodded and hunched broad shoulders. As a college student, begging must have been one of his ace courses.

Cinnamon would study begging, carpet-mold, and how to fix a furnace. Theatre CPR. She shivered. Glass doors opened every few moments for folks coming or going with props, costumes, champagne, and buckets of shrimp. February wind off the Monongahela River blasted right in. Chattering teeth covered fearful whimpers. A hundred-fifty kids, and only five real roles plus ten in the chorus—

"Hopeless. Why does Hill do this open-call shit?" The production coordinator was halfway down the hall to the theatres. "I hate disappointing so many people. I *hate* it!"

"This audition is for show, stats for government grants." A peevish reply from a familiar voice—Medea? "Hill's already got the whole thing cast. Take a miracle to change his mind."

Cinnamon didn't believe in miracles.

The orca knapsack fell from her hands and spit a drawing from *The Chronicles* at her feet. She'd stuffed it in her bag at breakfast, for safekeeping. The scrolled artwork uncurled. Writing on the back of the drawing glowed, a fluorescent green, like Medea's eyes. Several paragraphs of notes were scrawled across the length of the page. These notes had not been there before. No way could Cinnamon have overlooked such a glowing green message. The Wanderer must be writing to her right this second—a propitious sign!

Skinny scooped up the parchment and thrust it at Cinnamon. "You're losing your shit."

Cinnamon snatched her treasure. "Thanks."

As Skinny studied the boy ahead of them, Cinnamon carefully unrolled *The Chronicles* page and read.

Acknowledgment for Temporal Gaps, Feb. 1987

Dear Guardians!

Pardon the less than propitious interruption. I'm on a bridge over the rippling Monongahela, balanced among swaying steel cables. I don't remember the climb up. This bridge is closed to traffic. No one would see me fall, except crows serenading an injured comrade. Above our heads, shooting stars drop from the sky. Crashing through the upper atmosphere, they burn to heat, light, and elemental compounds. Ash hisses in high clouds, a spray of dust to build a billion snowflakes. Irritable crows shit white globs, much warmer than falling snowflakes, and I dodge a spray of poop. The cold steel of the bridge is a shock to my feet and hands. Awareness also shocks me.

I'm grateful for your patience and perseverance. In *Chronicles* 8, I disappeared in the middle of a sentence. (Was I writing in 1983 or 1984?) You must think me rude or uncivil or callous. Actually, weeks, months, years go by when I'm lost to myself. I become somebody else altogether, several someones even—as when the armored bush infected me with its poisoned minions—coma, amnesia . . .

I do remember a few days ago. I was hunched on damp ground. A crow flew right over my hat into a shopping cart piled high with somebody's life—my life. The crow broke a wing on an empty picture frame and shat on my head. Instead of wringing the creature's scrawny neck (as a passerby suggested), I splinted the broken bones and wandered along the Monongahela River, pushing the cart, following the flock for days.

The wind almost took me apart. I sat down near this broken bridge. Raven Cooper gone, but not gone, who can blame Opal for being too mad to greet me? In that bar, swallowing a madman's bullets, the *aje* could have saved them both, saved us all . . .

The crow pecked at my self-pity, so I got up and followed the flock through KEEP OUT signs and gaps in wooden barriers. I climbed high. Now I hug icy steel and dance with the wind, bridge, and gravity. A humble witness, here's my challenge: distinguishing between what I merely *believe* to be impossible and what I *know* to be folly. A Guardian with an eye out for my story and an ear cocked to truth makes all the difference. Kehinde was always impatient with poor judgment and shallow faith. *What do you believe, Wanderer?* She would flick her fingers and speak Yoruba wise words:

> *When a door is slammed in your face, slide under the crack at the sill.*
> *When the road ends at a treacherous ravine, fly.*

Fly? Really? What is lush metaphor to a thirsty neophyte but muddy, tainted water?

I *believe* in doing impossible things. However, if a full-bodied being jumps out into thin air a hundred stories from the mighty Monongahela, gravity won't care. To fly you must control a force to counter the mighty forces dragging you into disorder. Take a stupid leap of faith and *splat*, you're a mess.

Since taking Abla's head, since the *aje* came back with the Taiwo-self, doubts about my story mission have grown exponentially. A true *Mission: Impossible.* According to the few legends I recall, when a mission is a bust, Wanderers scatter and scatter until, approaching infinity, they are nothing. Scattering is an elegant, indifferent fail-safe. Entropy. *Splat.*

The crows insist we move on before the blizzard swallows us. This bridge is creaking. Too many restless spirits roam the iron ropes.

> *Eshu is a brash child and a wise old man*
> *We are all blessed with contradiction*

Eshu is a shapeshifter
Pour libation to the master of masquerade
Everything at once, yet not any one thing

Dear Guardians, the emergency has passed. You are a lifesaver. Thank you for listening. I know you can fly. You have the energy of the spaces between things.

Never doubt this.

Urban Fantasy

"No way!" Cinnamon gasped. The Wanderer was there when Daddy got shot—another one of Raven's (*and* Sekou's) friends that her mom pushed away. Cinnamon peered out the glass doors. Opal was outside fighting with Star Deer—a silent movie melodrama. Stomping in snow, black hair frosted, Star made the forties look like power years. Opal was a zombie extra, sucking the embers of a cigarette, shivering on the wrong side of death. What was her problem? Star was the drama coach at Cinnamon's school; she belonged at the audition. Were Star and Daddy lovers? Or if Opal had something against Indians (like Uncle Clarence), why hook up with Daddy? OK, Star was Cherokee, not Seminole like Daddy, but . . . so what? If Cinnamon were rich, she'd take Star's advanced contact improvisation class. Star taught people how to fly!

The ASM called Cinnamon's number. Her chance of a lifetime had arrived. She whispered a prayer to Eshu, master of masquerade, no *suicide* for the Wanderer and also good luck for her audition. Maybe that was selfish. She shook off guilt and bounded up carpeted stairs to a broad landing that led to a photo gallery. Famous Monongahela players smiled, sneered, and winked at her. She hoped her picture would hang there one day. The landing functioned as audition space this afternoon. Musicians, tucked in the corner by the emergency doors, sawed violins, banged drums, and tapped a shrill upright piano. Were they auditioning too?

The director glowered at Cinnamon, as if she were worse than wayward rhythm and bad notes. The hunky ASM beckoned her forward. She almost bolted out the side door into ice and snow, but the crowd of eager young thespians blocked her exit.

"My mom had emergency surgery this morning or she would have been here." A story storm mugged Cinnamon. "Lung cancer, from years of smoking Camels unfiltered. Her chest is like a coal mine. Aunt Becca dropped me off. She went to the hospital to check on Mom who insisted I audition anyhow, 'cause I got the talent and dreams to rescue a dying art. Aunt Becca told me to do my best and make my mom proud. If I get cast, well, good news is like medicine. When you're hurting in a hospital room with death around every corner, good news can heal you." The ground was untrue, tilting away from her. Good news *should* heal you.

The ASM opened his mouth as if to object, then pushed her toward the stage.

"What can you do?" the director asked the boy in front of her.

Klaus Beckenbauer. He got cast in everything and was always terrible. Boys were precious commodities; so few to work with, talent didn't matter as much as not acting out and disrupting rehearsal. Beckenbauer was supposed to be cute too. He was pale, even for a white person. His veins showed, blue-green and red, and he had no lips. His nose disappeared between alabaster cheeks. She didn't get it. He was almost her height, but lean and athletic. His muscles probably made him cute, or maybe you had to be fifteen to get it. Perhaps understanding was on the other side of August 6, 1987.

Beckenbauer finished massacring a monologue from *Peter Pan* and winced. His mom glared at him. She'd hoped for miracles. Cinnamon handed Director Hill a recommendation from Star Deer. In a funk over Beckenbauer, he barely looked at Cinnamon. She did a Judy Garland speech she'd memorized watching *The Wizard of Oz* and an oldie Opal sang over and over, "Ain't No Sunshine When He's Gone." She imagined Sekou in a box underground grinning. They were still tight, even with him dead two years and three months. Her voice got big. *Public display* was fine for a song and everybody tuned in.

Skinny did a monologue from *A Chorus Line* about being short. Perfect. She belted a gospel hit that scorched nose hairs and eyelashes.

The ASM shoved sides from the new musical at Cinnamon. "I hope you can read."

"Since I was four," Cinnamon said. He didn't believe her. "I read music too. That's the truth—" Despite the monologue of lies she'd spouted before.

"Director Hill's got a lot of kids to listen to, so go."

"With them?" Cinnamon pointed. Beckenbauer was wooden and Skinny already hated her for no reason.

"You are number 129." The ASM talked slowly, volume on high, as if she was mentally challenged. "Isn't that between 128 and 130?"

"Great." She acted excited. What you believed onstage or off turned into reality.

"Ditch the backpack." He gripped the orca's dorsal fin and tried to wrestle it away from her.

"It's good luck." Cinnamon was stronger than he was.

"You think that ratty thing will help you?" Skinny smirked at Cinnamon.

"You can't audition with this!" The ASM was desperate. "I promise not to lose it."

Cinnamon beamed death rays at him. "You better not." She let go.

Skinny shook her head. "OK, you can sing. No big surprise, but a role?"

"Sure." One day she'd play Kehinde in a warrior woman movie and show them all.

Skinny leaned close. "It's 'Ain't No Sunshine When *SHE*'s Gone.'"

"Sounds good either way," Cinnamon said.

"Don't sweat the ASMs. They have zero power." Skinny rolled her eyes. "How come I get the losers?"

"Is there a problem?" Hill frowned, and they both smiled. "She's the Changeling. He's the Drug Prince, so you," he pointed to Cinnamon, "do Snow White. Wait." He waved at Beckenbauer. "Should we change the key?" He shook a curly mane of golden hair, figuring how to warp the show for Beckenbauer. Cinnamon pushed envy away. Envy was not your friend onstage. She could take envy to the bathroom and flush it. Musicians transposing to accommodate Beckenbauer gave her more time to prep the monologue.

She glanced at the cover. *Title Under Construction*—was that a clever way to say there was no title yet? Mr. Greg Diamond, the playwright, had an MFA from Carnegie Mellon and was excited to offer Pittsburgh audiences an urban fantasy—old fairy tales redone for today. The hobgoblins and warlocks were drug dealers and gangsters. Fairy godmother librarians offered wisdom and support. Or something like that.

Cinnamon scanned Snow White's monologue. She could memorize anything on the spot—lines, dance steps, melodies. Sekou was always proud of his whiz brain sister. *You're a natural for show business. Fuck you! You can do anything.* Snow White's speech made no sense, and the song was stupid, but whatever. It was urban fantasy. The accompanist played the melody in the new key. Cinnamon sang it back to herself.

"OK, Snow White, go," Hill said. The crowd snickered. Fat, black Cinnamon doing the ethereal fairy-tale beauty was a joke, even in the druggy ghetto version. Beckenbauer winced. Skinny looked miserable. "Let's go, Snow!" Hill snapped his fingers in Cinnamon's face.

"OK." Her voice wobbled, and she stumbled through the first few bars.

"These kids are a little high, not dead," Hill barked.

"Not dead." Cinnamon swallowed an ache in her throat.

"Hit the notes. Pick up the pace. You can do that, can't you?"

"Sure." Beckenbauer spoke for all of them. He was bright red under the pale white.

Cinnamon choked at the top of her monologue. Her jeans and blouse were new last October, but too tight already. Opal didn't have a budget *for fat girls stuffing their faces and blowing up another size every time you turned around.* So size 16 Cinnamon squeezed herself into an unforgiving size 14.

"Fuck that noise." She yelled Snow White's line at folks sniggering at her.

Opal came inside, cussing too—at Star Deer, who stomped off. Star didn't need to see Cinnamon botch an audition. A security guard waved at Opal's lit cigarette.

"Standing in the storm will kill me sooner than a damn cigarette," Opal said.

"Watch the language," the rent-a-cop woman said. "Please put the cigarette out."

Beckenbauer crashed into Skinny and knocked her on her ass. She chirped the last notes of her solo like a bird getting mauled by a cat. Their final trio was terrible. Cinnamon sagged. Her big chance was shot. Opal was right—a lobster in boiling water.

"Do it again." Hill helped Skinny up and mumbled advice or encouragement at Beckenbauer just loud enough for Cinnamon to catch the tone and not the words.

She never got second chances. What to do?

"Do it better." Ariel leaned a silver ten-speed bike against a pillar. Out of costume, the actor sported an African bohemian look: bold colorful designs, long duster robes, and fat pants that hugged the ankles. "Show us what you really got."

"Me?" Cinnamon gulped.

"Who else?" Ariel's eyes were familiar. Not the color or shape, but how they didn't line up or settle on anything. Ariel's smile reminded her of somebody too, crooked and sweet, a bit of the devil, as Aunt Becca would say. Opal was always ragging on Cinnamon for never remembering how people looked, for not looking in the first place. Had Opal sprayed Ariel with a hose once?

"The lizard that jumps from the high iroko tree says she will praise herself if no one else does." Ariel sang more than spoke, a resonant, full-chested, theatre voice. "That's a Yoruba proverb—from Nigeria." African wisdom to match the chic African outfit.

"Do you understand?" Hill shouted.

"Not really," Beckenbauer admitted.

"Don't comment on the character. Live the character. You must know somebody who's been tempted, who's succumbed to booze if not drugs. Get inside them."

"How?" Beckenbauer didn't care if everybody knew he was clueless.

People always assumed Cinnamon was dumb as dirt. She never risked confirming their suspicions by asking even intelligent questions.

"Dump your middle-class, *secret* baggage," Hill said patiently. "Slip over to how your character feels inside. That's art."

Beckenbauer went zombie pale again and hugged his belly. Middle class and all, did he have a junkie brother or sister? Sekou hadn't been anything like Mr. Diamond's play. He didn't angst over implications or fuss with elder wisdom. He just shot up bad shit one day. Cinnamon asked why all the time. He could never tell her. Twisting in a cold, dark box, Sekou whispered answers now:

> *It was cool. A dare. Friends. Curiosity. Opal was yelling at me about Raven. Shit, it made me feel good, better, best. No one could tell me anything. They already messed shit up worse than I could. Why save myself for nothing? Hey, at first, I could've stopped. I just knew I wasn't gonna get hooked, and then I was. Control is a fuckin' illusion. Raven Cooper in a coma was my fault, so why the fuck shouldn't I bliss my way outta here?*

"Bliss your way outta where?" Beckenbauer asked, ice-blue eyes bulging.

Cinnamon swallowed a holler. Beckenbauer heard Sekou ranting from the grave.

Skinny rolled dark eyes and snorted, "Outta this mess right here, right now," as if she was hearing Sekou too. She gasped. "WHAT THE FUCK?"

"Excuse me?" Director Hill's tiny nostrils strained to open wide.

"Sorry . . ." Skinny bit her top lip. "I'm . . ."

"Getting into the role," Cinnamon said. Being haunted by Sekou was no big deal for her, but realist Skinny twisted and itched, and Beckenbauer doubled over—not acting, in real pain. His mom yelled at him in German.

Hill cut her off. "OK, yeah, exactly. Use that." He steadied Beckenbauer. "One more time. Feel the words, the music. You can do it," he said warmly.

"All of you," Ariel said, even warmer. "Go with your hearts. Fly!"

Everybody telling her to fly . . . Cinnamon's heart beat against Redwood's Dahomean bead and Aidan's *mojo* bag hidden under her too tight shirt in the ravine between DD bra cups. The eagle feather tickled her. Turning fear into power was a basic hoodoo trick. She could do that at twelve. Sekou talking to Beckenbauer and Skinny meant something. *Words are a bridge.* "We got this."

"We do?" Skinny and Beckenbauer said simultaneously.

Cinnamon grinned. In sync ad-libbing was a good omen. "Yeah. Let's fly."

Medea halted by the dressing rooms. She shushed Jason. Prospero swept out of the men's room and halted too. Cinnamon let Sekou flow through her into Mr. MFA Greg Diamond's words:

Who you talking to with that lame just say no shit?
Oh, oh, us! Bad boys, bad girls
Too ignorant for words
Showing our asses to the whole world
Too stupid to know the history we're dying from
So stuck on ourselves—
Can't see the present we're dying in
Fuck that noise, Jack!
The R&B generation is so sure they done it all, invented every-thing twice—
Hey, you got my R-E-S-P-E-C-T
You done sat in, marched on, and overcome
That don't mean you know Snow White here
I'm naming this moment with my blood, not your tears
You're stuck back in the day

Jacked up on yesterday's news
We ain't thinking 'bout you
I'm now! This is my day!
Shit, I ain't even happened yet
I don't know me!
OK, yeah, we're as stupid as every other generation
But you're over and it's our turn now
So open my veins and bring it on

Cinnamon finished on the beat. Sekou was somewhere bright and open, grinning. Medea smiled too, and Ariel nodded. A sulky college girl perked up and shouted, "That's acting. Finally."

A parent in the back muttered, "Shit."

Prospero swirled his cape and roared, "Bravo."

Skinny answered Snow White's monologue with bring-down-the-house singing, a voice out of nowhere, belting, *"I ain't even happened yet. Watch out!"* Folks gasped.

Opal swallowed a cuss word for the security guard policing her in an alcove. She was missing Cinnamon's great moment at a professional audition over a cigarette.

"Beam me up!" Beckenbauer sang like his life depended on staying in tune.

They were high, not dead, exactly how Director Hill wanted. As their three-part harmony spun into a percussive improv, Cinnamon whispered, "Follow your heart," and bent back into a yoga bridge. Her fingers scraped gritty carpet, her empty stomach arched toward the grid. Beckenbauer boldly gripped Skinny's waist and lifted her as if she were feathers and froth. Skinny stretched her legs into a graceful split right over Cinnamon. The audience cheered. Skinny's skirt brushed Cinnamon's nose—lavender, sage, and peanut oil—a Chinese-food smell that made her mouth water. The musicians improvised a flurry of notes. Cinnamon pushed up to standing as Beckenbauer set Skinny down on the upbeat. Theatre magic.

An astounded audience held its breath. Hill was too stunned to compose his *I'm on top of everything* face. Beckenbauer was a done deal. Cinnamon and Skinny should make chorus for sure, maybe even roles. Now that would be something.

Ariel saluted them and pushed the ten-speed out into a fog of sleet. Only a crazy person or a wizard would bike Pittsburgh hills in icy winter. And wearing that getup . . .

Skinny, Cinnamon, and Beckenbauer did a spontaneous group hug, then scattered like an explosion. Terrified kids stared at the empty space they left behind.

"You all should give it up." The bold and brassy college girl swirled a long cape of silky hair and looked fierce like Prospero. "Go home and do—"

"Chanda, be cool." The ASM cut her off. He threw the backpack at Cinnamon. "Don't forget your killer whale." The orca wouldn't let her get lost. Raven gave her that.

"Next. Come on! Come on!" Director Hill went from impressed to irritable in two seconds. "I'm not going to be here till dawn."

Untying Knots

After a stellar audition, Cinnamon was flying high, but had to pee too, for real. She plucked her jacket off the cold radiator. It was still wet. She balled it up. Opal promised to take her to Goodwill to find a coat that fit, that kept her warm, that was purple or green or anything other than shit brown.

"Such a looong wait! Worse than Kennywood Park." Opal slumped into a broken chair by the radiator. "Pay all that money to stand in line forever, then the ride's done in a heartbeat." She waved an unlit cigarette in the security guard's face. "This audition is a scam."

"Mom!" Cinnamon grabbed her hand.

Phlegm in Opal's chest made her rumble like a big cat. "Just so the Playhouse can tell the National Endowment for the Arts that they let in a few colored people."

"People of color," Cinnamon said.

"Turn a few words around and call that progress? I'm not taking you to any more of these stupid auditions."

"Star Deer recommended me."

"She's a hope-junkie."

"She's the drama coach."

"Star Deer's a substitute math teacher, and you're smart. You do your homework."

"Yeah, well, we didn't pay any money."

"Time is money, honey." Opal coughed. "Time is all we have. Why wait around to hear no?"

Why go home to call if your phone's been turned off and you have to track down the lone pay phone that isn't jacked up? Opal squirmed at Cinnamon's loud thoughts. "I gotta pee."

"Hold up. Rebecca sent you a big-ass card for luck." Opal

rummaged through a bottomless purse. "I meant to give it to you before. Kevin drove to the bus depot to drop it off. Rebecca has that man wrapped around her—"

"Heart." Cinnamon pulled her magic-words journal from her backpack. She'd started journaling in December 1984—Redwood's hoodoo spell #4, one of the best. Actually, they were all great. She dumped backpack and soggy coat at Opal's feet.

Opal found the card. "A lot of good it'll do you."

Cinnamon stuffed the envelope in her journal and ran into the bathroom. Pee burned coming out. She wiped herself, gawking at the graffiti. So many penises in the ladies' room made her chuckle.

"Having fun with yourself in there?" Kids giggled and banged on the door. One girl poked her curly head underneath the stall.

"What's your fuckin' problem?" Cinnamon snarled. "I'm not done!" She growled for more effect. Feet scrambled back out to the lobby.

"What's going on in here?" an older, gruff voice demanded.

Cinnamon hastily pinned the busted seam on her jeans. The potty hadn't been a refuge since she was five. She should open her good luck card at a more *propitious* moment. She skulked out past a middle-aged, middle-class black lady, Mrs. Juanita Williams—a Golden Angel Donor, according to her name tag. Mrs. Williams smoothed a salt-and-pepper, dead straight bob and glared at Cinnamon, like she was too ghetto. *Fuck that noise, Jack.*

Back in the lobby, Cinnamon sank in a sturdy chair far from her mom's foul mood.

"Can I sit here?" Skinny plopped down before Cinnamon answered.

"Me too?" Beckenbauer sat in between them. He looked crushed-out on Skinny.

Beckenbauer's mom grumbled. This was the loser, people of color section. "They were the best, *Mutti,* that's all." Beckenbauer was so matter of fact, Cinnamon wanted to hug him. He didn't notice. He was sitting next to Skinny, not Cinnamon. No big deal.

Cinnamon wasn't sure she liked boys, even nice ones. Ariel made her cheeks burn. Was that a crush?

Mrs. Beckenbauer ranted in German, *nicht* this with a lot of consonants and *nicht* that with even more. She looked like a model—basketball tall, too red full lips, and sunken, blue-shadowed eyes. Beckenbauer ignored his mom and smiled at Cinnamon. He was radiant and defiant, a character she'd never seen him do. He laughed at the shock on her face. She wasn't good at masking emotion.

"I'm Klaus Beckenbauer. What's your name?"

"Cinnamon Jones."

He nodded politely. "Have I met you before?"

"Yeah." They'd been in four musical plays together. "Several times."

"Really?" Klaus rolled his eyes, searching his brain.

"I sang in the chorus. You . . . Wasn't professional, but—" He botched up big roles.

"Oh." Klaus scratched his jaw, drawing angry red lines from ear to chin. "I'm going to do better this time, if I get cast."

Of course Klaus would get cast. The boy competition was pathetic.

"Waiting for callbacks is the worst." Skinny smiled at him, totally in lust. Klaus didn't laugh at this emotion all over Skinny's face. He nodded politely. "Actually getting called back is higher hopes to dash." Skinny yanked her hair behind her ears, mad all of a sudden. She gawked at Cinnamon's popped buttons and busted seams.

"You've lost a few . . ." Klaus trailed off.

Sekou talking from the grave to this fool and to Skinny didn't mean Cinnamon could trust them. Making theatre magic didn't mean they'd all be great friends and *believe* in each other. It meant she had to watch out. Patty Banks and Cherrie Carswell had ambushed her twice, once onstage. Sekou was too nice—even dead.

Klaus turned from her scowl to Skinny. "Have we met before?"

They exchanged coy chitchat as the last auditioners fumbled

through *Oliver, Annie, Jesus Christ Superstar,* and tales Cinnamon had never heard. She jotted down lines from *The Tempest* and Ariel's Yoruba saying in her journal. A techie tripped over cables and knocked the last word off her page. Interns were setting up the donor reception, using scenery from an island paradise play. Wooden statues—exotic *people of color* deities—looked lost and forlorn in the shabby lobby. Interns covered streaky windows with a photorealist seascape. They suspended parrot puppets from the balcony and hung leis of fresh flowers on the half-naked gods and goddesses. Dimmers whined, and light-trees disguised as giant palms bathed the reception area in warm twilight. Bowls of tropical fruit peeked from the shadows. Dust sparkled in high-wattage beams. The hunky statues shimmered. In ten minutes, a bleak, moldy interior was transformed into wonderland. Cinnamon and Klaus hung their mouths open. Lighting design was going in her theatre CPR toolkit. Unimpressed, Skinny flipped open *Momo* by Michael Ende.

"I read that and *The Neverending Story,*" Cinnamon said.

Skinny smiled, then maybe remembered it was the competition talking and frowned. "I don't usually read fantasy."

"What a coincidence," Klaus said. "I read both in German."

"Am I supposed to be impressed?" Skinny asked.

"Why not?" He smiled. *"Kannst du eine Fremdsprache?"*

Skinny grinned at his Euro-chic style. He could have said she looked like a turd. Cinnamon hated watching people flirt. Her stomach throbbed. The snack she'd stolen was in her orca pack by Opal, who was cussing at the Sunday *New York Times* crossword puzzle that she'd fished out of their next door neighbor's trash. Forget going across the lobby to that. Cinnamon tore open Aunt Becca's padded envelope, wishing it was a loaf of garlic bread, crispy fried chicken, or mincemeat pie with cream cheese melting down the sides. She'd even take celery stalks. No luck. Nestled in plastic bubbles was a second envelope fashioned from hand-woven cloth—a checkerboard of purple and blue geometric shapes—Kente cloth. Iris had traveled to Africa to study fabric wisdom and sent slides and swatches to Cinnamon one Christmas, but she didn't remember what this pattern meant.

Proverbs from a loom in Ghana. Sekou confirmed her hunch. *I knew . . .*

"Shh, not here. Other folk might be listening in."

"Talking to yourself?" the ASM asked. Cinnamon glared death rays in his direction. He flinched and hurried off. "Sorry."

A message scrawled on a Post-it clung to the fabric:

> *Dear Pumpkin, break a leg. I'm not much for writing like your Aunt Iris is. She wasn't sure you were getting her letters, so she decided to hide in plain sight. She said you're the only one who can open it. Love, Aunt Becca.*

Iris had been writing her all along. The letters weren't getting through Opal! Cinnamon's fury was a fireball sweeping the lobby.

Klaus and Skinny flinched mid-flirt, mumbling, "What was that?"

Opal jumped up and glowered at the security guard. "Damn! Give me a break."

"What?" The guard furrowed her brow and scanned the room.

The scent of licorice and lily of the valley filled Cinnamon's nose, as if Aidan was hugging her and saying, *Don't let yourself get burning mad, honeybunch.* Cinnamon gulped cold lobby air. She'd just have to beat Opal to the mail.

"That storm off the river is ferocious." Cinnamon hid the envelope behind her back. "A miracle this ole theatre doesn't get blown over."

Klaus and Skinny giggled at some private joke. Opal shivered and sat down.

Aidan had fashioned the cloth envelope and Redwood hoodooed the fancy knot holding it closed. Cinnamon tugged the threads, making the knot tighter. She didn't have a clue how to untie it.

"Sorry," Cinnamon whispered. "I was ready to give up on you all." She faked a sneeze for cover.

"*Gesundheit,*" Klaus said.

Cinnamon coughed a few more words. "Thanks for not giving up on me."

Aidan said hoodoo conjurers heard underneath things. Iris could see your heart spirit wherever in the world you were. Redwood snatched lightning out of the sky, listened to ancestors on the wind, and talked to tomorrow. When Cinnamon was little, she and Sekou used to tell her magic elders everything, whether they were in the next room, up in Massachusetts, or across the ocean. It never seemed crazy, especially after Daddy got shot. It helped Cinnamon feel better, maybe Sekou too sometimes. Opal insisted that at almost fifteen, Cinnamon was too grown up to *believe backcountry hoodoo mess.* And not hearing from the elders for months, she'd stopped *talking out loud to folks who weren't there.* Distant souls had to listen for what she didn't say.

Squeezing the *mojo* bag between her breasts, Cinnamon peeked over the envelope's edge. Her mom chewed a pen and fussed with hard puzzle clues. This was her weekly IQ test where she proved she wasn't as stupid as her life. Klaus and Skinny mingled hair and soft giggles, stuck on each other for sure. Cinnamon slid her chair to the other side of the pillar out of view. Her stomach growled at bubbles of no-calorie anxiety. To open the envelope, she decided on Redwood's spell #5—*improvising magic words to conjure the world she wanted.*

"I'm a dream machine with a hoodoo spirit. I'll sing my own praises if no one else will. You better believe I can untie any mess. Watch out!"

The intricate knot shivered and tumbled open.

Letter from Iris Phipps,
February 1987

Dear Heart,

How are you? Those warp speed shout-outs on the phone are lively, but I can barely hear the fancy stories you're spinning with your stomach grumbling so loud. Are you getting enough to eat? I don't mean deep-fried death on a suicide bun—real food, fresh vegetables, whole grains, stuff you got to chew. I bet your stomach's squawking right this minute.

Oh my, I promised myself not to be an old scold. Sorry.

Folks might be standing by the phone, listening in, so you can't say everything you want. You write your letters in code too. What're you hiding?

We can still trust each other, right? You can talk to me anytime, anywhere.

I've written several letters full of bibble-babble mostly, so don't be mad if they went missing. Opal's got an eye out for that rogue train what's going to jump the track and ruin us. Who can blame her? She's afraid this mean ole world might break your beautiful spirit. Miz Redwood did a get-there spell to make sure this letter reaches you. She says, if I speak truth heart to heart, nobody but you can read it. I don't dare disbelieve Sister when she's hoodooing.

She and Aidan have been missing you and cursing New England, particularly the ice storms and standoffish manners. Aidan sounds too much like, well, somebody folks 'round here in Massachusetts don't want to get to know, so they don't. There's how he looks too—swamp man chic. Sister storms through town with lightning in her eyes—you know how she can do—scaring even the bravest souls away. She and Aidan get so terribly lonely. Theatre folk like to bunch together in a big crowd of good spirits and conjure another world. Nothing else like it—maybe a good book, where you play all the roles and do the set and costumes in your head. Instead of moping around frozen Northampton, Redwood's helping Aidan write down the tall tales, wild adventures, and hoodoo conjure they can remember—for you. They'd rather be telling you in person. Would you like that?

Opal's still mad at me for paying Sekou's funeral bill behind her back. I couldn't sit around and watch the creditors put you all on the street, could I? Pride can be too expensive. Now here I am writing to you on the sly.

Aidan wants to see you so bad, says it's urgent, but won't say why. The man wouldn't set foot in an airplane to save his soul, and he's talked himself out of taking another train—after one engine jumped the track in Hartford. This morning he said he'd walk the stars if he had to. Seminoles, when they die, walk the Milky Way to a City of Light. Don't you worry, though. Miz Redwood told him to haunt you later, see you live for now. Sister got him convinced that driving will get us to you fine. (Please don't tell him the safer-to-fly statistics!) What do you say? If I rustle up a chauffeur, could you stand a visit? Sister and I are dying to see you too. Too many days between us.

Good Lord, you're grinning a yes back at me already. You've been missing us as much as we've been missing you. That settles it. We're on our way.

I enclose a few gifts for your theatre CPR unit. The envelope is from the Akan people in Ghana—Adinkra cloth you haven't seen before. The patterns speak of patience and discipline, from the proverb: No matter how many red flames flicker in the eyes, the fire is from elsewhere.

Aidan has been weeks wrangling words to another song for you. Here's what I pried out of him:

Cinnamon
Sugar and spice, honey and ice
I'm your poem, your song
A simple conjuration
I'm your rhythm, your dream
A total dedication
The praise-house for your spirit
Truth you know when you hear it
I'm your poem, your song
A portal to your art
A shelter for your heart
Yeah, sing me in the morning
Sing me the whole night long
Sing me to the other side of pain
Sing me from crazy to sane
Sing me in life to death
Sing me with your last breath
Cinnamon
Sugar and spice, honey and ice

Stiff fingers and all, Aidan's bringing his banjo to play you his two new "Cinnamon songs" and also that praise song you wrote for Sekou. He claims the melodies could heal a broken heart. Sister and I haven't heard a lick. So you pester him. I dare that man to turn you down.

Redwood sends you a spell to sing the blues like her and Aidan. Nine is a hoodoo charm:

1: Stand still in driving rain or face a squall of bitter snow.
2: Stand still in the crush of a crowd or a roaring traffic jam.
3: Face a blare of speakers, screens, and story-sellers.
4: Feel the sun coming through you.
5: Snatch the rhythm of highways, great factories, a trolley train, the wind.

6: *Play your own rhythm on top or underneath the ones that you catch.*

7: *Go out and find stories nobody has heard or everybody almost forgot.*

8: *Sing with the voice of someone you love whose voice has gone quiet.*

9: *Sing, till you give everybody back to themselves.*

Sister's spells bring folks together. You are the light of our lives shining on.

Love, Aunt Iris, Granddaddy Aidan, and Miz Redwood

P.S. Thank your Aunt Becca for me. She and Kevin call up to Massachusetts every week to check on us. Kevin says we're the folks he always wanted. I know why Becca is still sweet on him. Two years and some change, that's a record for her!

P.P.S. I've tried to read ahead in The Chronicles of the Great Wanderer, *but since the eighth episode on the beach near Ouidah, when Somso was about to give birth and Taiwo was an* aje *spirit swallowing bullets to save Kehinde, the pages have been squiggles and blur. Thought I caught a glimpse of Raven Cooper once, flying through the air, grinning and waving at me, trying to catch something. The Wanderer throwing images or Eshu tricking my old eyes. These pages came loose today and dropped into my lap. The print was too tiny. I took that as a sign to pass them on to you.*

Notes (#3) to the Current Edition of the Earth Chronicles, Feb. 1987

Esteemed Guardians,

Eshu taunts me at the crossroads. One direction leads to regret, another to despair, and one is a bridge to nowhere. Going back the way I came is impossible. I have scattered into many different beings. Kehinde has gone on to dance with her ancestors and can't call me back together. You, dear Guardians, rescue me with belief. Like Kehinde, you call me home. You will guard my stories and tell your own.

Chasing lost memory, I have traveled this world, steaming to islands of fire, jetting to lands of ice, and walking the dust of many roads. Whatever country, tribe, or community I visited, it was clear from the condition of the storytellers who was on the rise, who was headed for a fall. If few storytellers carried the great epics into the next generation, if a community didn't bother to remember itself, disaster came. If storytellers were bought and sold and only a few free voices could be heard, if hardly anyone offered a challenge to greedy hearts or posed difficult questions, rivers dried up, mountains were eaten, and rain was toxic spew. If people spat on storytellers, gave them rags to wear, and forced them to live on the edge of ruin, these people, even in the fullness of their lives, faded into nothing, dragging their world into the void.

To kill a people without spilling blood, steal their stories, then feed them self-serving lies. Blood is nothing without story. You might think I exaggerate, dear Guardians, so look around and see for yourself.

A wise woman, tall and fierce, with lightning eyes and hurricane hands, once told me, *The most a person can do for another is believe in 'em till they come true.* Storytellers do this. I didn't understand at the time. The woman didn't seem wise. She made fun of herself on-stage and played a fool in picture shows. I didn't trust a masquer-ade. It was early in the twentieth century, in Chicago town, where all the trains met, where people from across this planet came and went in great hordes, with new tales they wanted to write, sing, and live. In a carnival atmosphere, the world upended, bold la-dies and fine fellows were flying west or running north. Promises flashed in their eyes, hope gushed from their pores, covering up the stink of train stations, factory smokestacks, and foul injustice.

From Dahomey to Chicago, I gorged on delicious humanity. Whenever I thought myself too greedy, Somso scolded me in her Igbo language:

Onye riri osisi oji kpaa ya nku ka o nwere ike: anaghi ari enu oke oji kwa daa.

If you're on top of the iroko tree, gather all the firewood you can: it is not every day that one scales the great iroko.

Gathering a good story and passing it on is redemption.

Chronicles 9: Coast of Dahomey, 1893—Demons

The sea raged against the jagged coast. Hot metal, cloaked in dead cells and fecal matter, made its way through twisty intestines toward my anus. Rather than swallow more bullets, I spat out the last few. Fire from my breath danced on the waves. My thoughts were scalded steam. An Igbo woman cowered in the sand. She had magnetic eyes, a dimpled chin, round cheeks, a moon face. Hugging her fat belly, she groaned. Yet another stolen woman from distant lands made into a traitor. Shadowy trees sighed as I readied for attack.

"Taiwo!" A warrior woman threw sand in my eyes.

My startled exhalation singed the fine hairs on her cheeks; poison from my tail dissolved broken shells at her feet.

"I am Kehinde—twin spirit. You held me in the circle of your being. Eshu laughed at us wandering desolate paths to royal cities with no names."

I reached sharp talons toward her heart, scratching rough cloth and scarred skin. Her blood glistened on the tips.

"I am your *stillpoint*! Eshu honors the oath we made never to betray one another. We are one road, one destiny." She flicked long fingers at my fire breath. "You hate the bitter taste of killing. You weep at every story's end." She gripped my poison-tipped tail, aiming venom at my eyes. "I have pledged to protect Somso with my life."

"Somso?" My words were smoke and sparks. "You brother's last word."

"Speak more and find yourself again." Kehinde pressed cool fingers against my throbbing temples. A shiver traveled from her nerves to mine. "Tell me who you are."

"Am I your Taiwo, the Wanderer?"

"Yes."

"Well, who *is* that?" Terrified, I glanced at the sea where I'd flung Abla's head and body. Would the *aje* also murder Somso? Kehinde slid her hands across my heaving torso over floating ribs to the end of my spine. She protected her brother's wife, but also saved me from myself. "I could scatter," I whispered. "What have I done?"

"Wanderer-Taiwo is who you mean to be in this lifetime," Kehinde replied.

I rubbed aching palms. "How do you live with so many murders on your hands?"

Somso cried out and stumbled to the water's edge. She squatted as muscles contracted. Frothy waves tugged at her feet. A stiff wind caught in her throat. Escaping my question, Kehinde hurried to her. After a great shudder, the placenta and baby came at once. The taste of new life, bitter and coppery on salt air, soothed me. I wanted to laugh or sing or roar at Somso giving birth to a girl in the sand. But my mouth burned from catching death on the fly, so I made no grand sound to welcome another daughter of Dahomey. The *aje* flickered at the edge of my Taiwo-self, stealing balance. Dizzy, I sank to my knees.

"Rejoice." Kehinde pointed to the curved blade of moon cutting through the clouds. "A beacon heralds the child's arrival." She rubbed the baby's back, urging her to breathe. "The afterbirth came with her. The Hausa people call such a child Melinga—someone born wearing clothes."

Somso muttered Igbo words and clutched her ragged insides.

Kehinde frowned at mother and child. "She might die." Whom did she mean?

Melinga coughed phlegm from her nose and throat and took a swallow of night air. New eyes blinked and teared as she named her first moments with high notes. The pattern of her being was strong. Kehinde held the baby toward Somso, who shook her head. Blood from her vagina drenched the sand.

"Too much blood," Kehinde said.

"A warrior knows well how we bleed ourselves away." Somso
groaned.

I bent between her legs and breathed the last of my heat inside her, searing arteries large and infinitesimal. She screamed and
writhed at the fire in her womb, banging my ears with bony knees.
I barely registered the blows. Close to a fleshy cave of life, sparking
with the aftershocks of birth, I wavered again between Taiwo and
the *aje*.

"No." Kehinde toed the hollow of my back.

Melinga distracted us with a high melody. Deep animal voices
answered the child. I managed a second blast of hot breath. The
last trickles of blood hissed in the heat. Nerves dulled to pain fired
less, and Somso's clenched muscles relaxed. I drank a final draught
of her and sweet Melinga before taking three steps back. My right
ear dripped blood and rang like a distant bell.

Somso inspected herself gingerly. "What have you done?"

"Should we watch you bleed to death?" Kehinde rocked Melinga quiet.

"Should I embrace demons?" Somso's words came covered in
spittle.

Kehinde turned from her and whispered, "The night is more
than half gone." She squinted at Melinga's round face and fat feet.
Most newborns were squishy and wrinkly. Brother-Taiwo's plump
child was a blade in her heart. "What will the sun see?"

"Melinga is our story," I declared.

Kehinde scowled at Somso. "How do you decide this?"

"Nothing to decide. The child makes sense of this world."

"But bringing treacherous Somso and a young one onto the
steamship or into Chicago town?"

"Melinga is your brother's child."

"Will she rejoice to know me?"

"Who saved Somso from death by my hand?"

"You would have regretted killing her."

"Ifa says, *What we look for is near us, yet we don't recognize it.*"

Kehinde frowned. "I dreaded finding Somso."

"She found us!"

Again, Melinga made strong music for one so little. Kehinde turned to Somso. "Your daughter calls you."

"*Ora na-azu nwa,*" Somso said. "A community raises the child. Who do I have?"

Kehinde held the baby toward her.

"How do you mend a rip in the sky?" Somso let loose a nerve-rattling hyena laugh. Startled, Melinga lost her song. "Somayina means may I not travel alone." Laughter turned to a wail. "I have no one." Somso was Igbo, another people from the east. She was suffering a great tragedy. We were too few to celebrate the birth of her child. No husband to make a fire, no women to feed and pamper her in the first weeks of her daughter's life. No family to sing praises to god for the gift of a daughter. No elders hovering between life and death to offer wisdom and guide Melinga to her personal destiny, her *chi.* Kehinde had schooled me in Igbo beliefs. The Fon learned the ways of their enemies to conquer them.

Escaping to a new world with your enemy was a different matter.

Kehinde thrust her niece and the slippery afterbirth against my chest. Grumbling, she stomped into the surf toward the European ship. Melinga's warm umbilical cord still pulsed. She nestled against me, soft and sweet, with spongy muscles and delicate bones. Her breath called complex, heady chemicals to my veins. Persuasive hormones cleansed my mouth of the taste of bullets and brought clarity to my actions.

"Will Kehinde abandon us?" Somso asked.

"Don't worry." I spoke too quickly.

Somso twisted her limbs into a knot. "Why not?"

"Kehinde and I searched through war and plague for you and your daughter."

"Disappointed?"

I dipped Melinga in the warm ocean and laid the child at Somso's breast. The pressure of milk surprised my flat breasts. An unfamiliar song touched my lips. I sang softly, words and melody I couldn't place. Music spirited away the pain of Abla's life cut short. I severed the umbilical cord with Kehinde's cutlass. Melinga tugged at a plump nipple and Somso moaned (pleasure and pain?). Her resistance faded as the baby fed. Even the waves settled down. Kehinde danced in the shallows to the suckling and gurgling. Her shoulders relaxed, her heartbeat slowed.

I caressed the baby's back. A life saved—redemption for a life taken? "Melinga."

"A good name." Somso leaned against a smooth stone.

"Yes. A beautiful name." I washed blood from Somso's legs with frothy sea water.

Somso flinched. "My husband . . ." Words died on her tongue.

"I met him only once, yet his story has stayed with me. I am Taiwo, the Wanderer, and am honored to share his name. May I live to honor his memory."

"You remind me of him."

"Ahh." Perhaps I'd come back from the *aje* more man than woman.

"How you look, how you carry yourself, so like him." She eyed me with more curiosity than fear. I was pleased, yet worried for the pain the likeness might bring.

"Why?" Kehinde tromped back to us. "Tell us." She stood over Somso as I gathered her niece's umbilical cord and dug in the sand.

"NO!" Somso shouted. "We must bury Melinga's cord in Chicagoland so she will be at home there."

"Why?" Kehinde demanded as the child sucked greedily.

"Chicago then." I wrapped the cord and afterbirth in Somso's veil.

"You know what I ask." Kehinde gripped Somso's chin and yanked her face up. "Tell us your story. Now."

Fire in the Eyes

Cinnamon paused. She didn't remember Wanderer-Taiwo swallowing bullets or Somso giving birth like that.

Still ready to believe anything?

She stared a hole in the theatre lobby back home to *The Chronicles* pages hidden under her bed. Keeping her promise to Sekou, she'd memorized every word.

Tall tale lies . . .

But, maybe Iris, an African scholar, not the Wanderer, changed the story, a story she made up in the first place. Lies were harder to remember than truth. Trial lawyer Clarence loved to pounce on lying fumblers and bring them down. Opal too.

Big as a house, but when you gonna grow up?

Opal's doubt smacked Cinnamon upside the head. Her mom didn't trust a soul, not even Becca, who loved her sister no matter what. One time Becca and Cinnamon walked in on Julian (Becca's boyfriend before Kevin) about to jump Opal's bones in the den. Opal said she was trying to prove how no account Julian was. Becca bought that story and Cinnamon had too. Since Opal'd lost Raven, she didn't *believe* in love anymore.

Cinnamon wiped sweaty palms on the moldy carpet and stared at *The Chronicles*. Fluorescent pages glowed in the dimness at the edge of the lobby. Half the bulbs along the back wall had blown out. Happy for shadows, Cinnamon squinted at handwriting so precise, it could have been typed. Not Iris's curlicue hand. Still, Cinnamon groaned. Opal's doubt had been messing with her mind all day.

It had started at breakfast. Cinnamon ran her mouth like a race-horse. She told Opal about wanting to play a warrior woman *ahosi* like in *The Chronicles*.

Opal sneered. "Iris probably wrote those tall-tale lies to cheer Sekou up. Got some homeless fool to play-act with her. Still ready to *believe* anything?"

"Uhm." Cinnamon gulped down slimy sardines on stale Ritz crackers without chewing. She never knew what to say when Opal talked like this.

"Big as a house, but when you gonna grow up?"

Cinnamon sucked water from the tap so as not to choke. "Aunt Iris—" always stood in Sekou's corner, loving him like blood family. So it was true; Iris would have done any good thing for him, but not *lying*. Iris simply used her West African studies to corroborate story details in *The Chronicles*.

"Who did the magic art illustrations?" Cinnamon said.

Iris couldn't draw a stick on the ground, let alone get pictures to move off the page.

"Your grandfather can carve anything come to his mind. Hear Raven tell it, Aidan can carve the wind."

Daddy was the painter. Cinnamon had never seen Aidan draw or paint.

"Raven *is* the painter, but you ain't seen everything."

Cinnamon hated Opal *reading her mind*. "So?"

"When you get old, things repeat, and there you are facing the same boring BS again and again. You wait." Opal always trotted out a long life of disappointment to justify her bleak outlook.

"That's not what Miz Redwood, Granddaddy, or Aunt Iris say, and they've lived way longer than you. You're only forty-one."

"So?" Opal mimicked Cinnamon's tone. "Don't go bothering Raven's folks."

A second can of sardines didn't want to open. Opal took a screwdriver to the thin metal, stabbing a bent edge. Cinnamon raced to her room and got a Wanderer illustration for evidence:

Kehinde danced with a snake in the *vodun*/orisha spirit cave. She ran back and stuck it in Opal's face, saying what she hoped was true. "This is Miz Redwood's favorite, because of the light caught on the page. A dark night, yet the water shines like day. Kehinde dances for *Mère d'eau*, Mami Wata we say nowadays."

Opal barely glanced at the waterfall spilling photons into their dreary kitchen.

"A source, not a reflection. Fluorescent or—"

"How can you spout physics at me and believe that hoodoo-voodoo nonsense?" Forcing the sardine tin open, Opal almost splattered grease on the spirit cave.

Cinnamon jerked away. "Physics and hoodoo are different realms, different *dimensions* of truth." The drawing blurred. Raven Cooper, tall and spooky, with smoky eyes and silky dreads twisting 'round a crooked grin, waved his arms in front of a gunman as two warrior women tasted tongues below a stained-glass Jesus. Cinnamon turned a gasp into a gag and rolled the drawing back up. The back of it was blank.

Luckily Opal didn't notice the drawing turn into a moving picture. "I paid full price, and the shit's gone bad." She tossed the rotting mess at the garbage can. "You shouldn't eat all that fat anyhow."

Nothing else to eat except Cinnamon's rice cake sandwich lunch, an old jar of stewed tomatoes, and a shriveled grapefruit with cottony white stuff covering half of it. The black cherry ice cream in the freezer was Sekou's. Shopping day was Friday, after the bus company paycheck. It was Wednesday. Opal sucked a breath. It sounded like stones were rattling in her lungs. She tossed the grapefruit.

"Where you been hiding that picture?"

"Nowhere." Cinnamon stowed it quickly in her killer whale knapsack and kept her mind blank.

"I bet Redwood put Iris up to this *Chronicles* scam. Damn alien fairy tales didn't do your brother no good." Opal blew smoke from one cigarette and stabbed the air with the embers of another. "Tall tale lies won't help you either."

How do you know? Cinnamon wanted to scream. *Look at how you messed Sekou up. Daddy wasn't his fault.* Reading her mind for sure, Opal crumpled into a chair. Cinnamon wanted to take her unkind thought back. Instead she said, "These sardines will stink up the house," and crashed out the screen door with the garbage.

Rain, the neighbor's attack Doberman, huffed a bark and trotted to the fence.

"It's rotten," Cinnamon told her, "I'll get you something good, I promise."

"Don't be feeding that mongrel!" Opal shouted.

Another bulb fizzled out in the cold Playhouse lobby. Cinnamon shivered, thinking of what she should have said to her mom this morning. No matter what anybody (including Opal and Clarence) thought about *The Chronicles*, a *true* story wasn't in a fight with facts. Plus, the elders couldn't have written *Acknowledgment for Temporal Gaps* on the back of the drawing this evening. *The Chronicles* and the Wanderer came from the spaces between things, touching this moment and many others. Iris had seen Daddy too, ghosting through the Wanderer's drawings. Sekou called that *coincidental affinity*: the universe lining up in your direction. Cinnamon finally understood what he meant—Eshu laughing his ass off, waiting to see if you were taking notes.

Cinnamon's magic-words journal slipped from her lap and fell open on the grimy carpet. She spied Redwood's hoodoo spell for actors. More *coincidental affinity!* The elders were probably cruising down the turnpike from Erie this very second, smiling at Pittsburgh hills leaping up out of nowhere. Cinnamon picked up the journal and spoke Redwood's spell out loud, to give it more power:

When you're onstage, give Doubt a comfortable seat in the wings.
Let Doubt watch you soar.

What worked onstage worked in the everyday too. Opal was mad at the world. She didn't want to *believe* in anything. Cinnamon wasn't like that. She had *different fire in her eyes.* The Akan weavers were part of her posse. So was the Wanderer and Aunt Becca and Kevin. She settled in for a good read.

Chronicles 10: Coast of Dahomey, 1893—Masquerades

Somso stared past suckling Melinga to the unruly sea. "You don't want my story."

"But we do," I said.

Somso turned to Kehinde. "After spying ghost Taiwo and his traitor sister in the market, Yao had everyone hunting you. Abla, a brutal warrior like you, saw that I knew something and threatened me. I told her, *I know my husband was shot dead and will never know his child.* Abla didn't care."

"How could you join forces with your husband's enemies?" Kehinde scowled.

"What are you?"

"Not his enemy or yours."

"So you say. Yoruba raiders from Abeokuta captured Igbo slaves too."

"Everyone takes slaves."

"After Husband-Taiwo disappeared, Abla threatened to kill me and his tomorrow in my belly unless I became her spy and helped track you."

"You're a traitor's wife ready to stick a knife in her at the first opportunity," Kehinde said. "Abla would have killed you both eventually."

"Why sell me to the impresario if she wanted to kill me?"

"You were useful. Abla taught me that a good soldier doesn't kill too quickly."

"Abla claimed you killed your own brother. I told her she lied. Did she?"

Kehinde's breath caught in her throat.

"Half a story is also a lie," I said.

Somso sneered at my feeble defense.

"What can I tell you?" Kehinde slow-danced in the receding tide. "My head belongs to the king, not to myself. If he pleases to send for it or my brother's head, I resign myself to duty. If my head is shot through in battle, this is honor. I'm gratified to kill or die in the service of my king. Brother-Taiwo was an enemy of Dahomey. He defied Béhanzin. He urged slaves on the king's plantations to revolt. So when I caught him at the head of the rebels, stealing the king's grain and killing *ahosi*, I didn't know him as brother. We *ahosi* warriors were outnumbered, fighting fiercely, but with little hope. I decided to make the most of death and send a rebel leader to the ancestors. As I aimed at Brother-Taiwo, a dying rebel fell against my arm and ruined the shot. My bullets lodged in the heartwood of an iroko tree."

"You didn't shoot him." I was relieved, as if Kehinde had aimed at my heart and missed.

"Taiwo had an easy shot," Kehinde said. "He hesitated. I quickly loaded my last bullet and shot a rebel charging in front of Taiwo toward me. One bullet took the rebel's life and also pierced Taiwo's thigh. *Kehinde,* he said, clutching the wound, *your aim is efficient, stopping us both.* As I drew my cutlass to take his head, he cried out. *Greet your twin brother. I went ahead to taste the world and send word back to you. Have the years erased my face from your heart?* Now it was I who hesitated. *Taiwo? No. You lie.* I said this even though I sensed he spoke truth. He didn't shoot as I approached, but dropped his rifle." The death dance sputtered on Kehinde's limbs. She stumbled to a halt.

Somso cried. Tears dribbled across her nipple into the milk. "Finish your tale."

Kehinde staggered about. "When I was first captive and Abla taught us the warrior way, I plotted revenge on Yao and the Fon invaders who'd stolen my life. I mouthed Fon oaths, yet swore to Oshun to be true to my ancestors, my family. I hid my hatred and lived a masquerade, miming loyalty. Now this fateful day had come. A wounded rebel leader, my twin, called me back to myself, urged me to set down the masquerade." She could barely speak. "Yet, what you rehearse, you become. I'd forgotten who I was or how to be free."

"No one forgets the taste of loyalty," Somso said.

"You know nothing," Kehinde replied. "Memory is a masquerade that must be performed or it can't live again. Kidnapped Yoruba, and Igbo girls too, were broken by Abla and so well trained, they resisted rescue by brothers, uncles, and even fathers. Abla could make these girls bring death down upon their families and clans. Witnessing their submission to Dahomey, I'd felt contempt for the loyalty they offered the Fon. Wise Abla gave me years of easy praise and valor. Now, facing my rebel brother on Béhanzin's plantation, a true battle raged inside me, and I understood Abla's powers. I'd become a proud, undefeated warrior, an inspiration for griot storytellers. I was loyal to the *ahosi* who fought with me. They were my family and destiny, not a Yoruba past I could barely recall; not a vanquished clan who offered poor protection against the mighty Fon. Should I honor the naïve oaths I made as a stupid young girl? Or did Eshu Elegba laugh at the foolish woman I'd become, a woman who had lost her true self?

"I raised my cutlass but shouted to Brother-Taiwo, *Run!* Pierced by a second bullet, he staggered into range of my blade and said, *You have not forgotten.* He fell against me, mumbling: Ifa *says, what we look for is near us, yet we don't recognize it.*" Kehinde glared at me, the Wanderer who had stolen her brother's form, who could speak his mind.

"What happened next?" I said, meeting her eyes.

"I would have dropped my weapons and fallen with Brother-Taiwo. But he wouldn't let me die. *Don't falter,* he said. *Your twin goes ahead to the land of the ancestors, but you must save yourself. When the Fon stole you away, I swore to free you. Because of you I became a rebel leader. I've been fighting for you ever since. Today Eshu offers a way, for you, me, and my wife. Somso. She carries my son, our tomorrow.* I knew of her. Yao, the spy who killed our father and raped our sisters, complained of a *Babalawo* protecting him from enemies and stealing his beautiful wife Somso."

Yao the murderer of dreams had been Somso's husband!

"Yao sold me." Somso spit a bad taste in the sand.

Kehinde grunted. *"Keep my Somso safe,* Taiwo pleaded. *I go on to our ancestors, so promise me, Kehinde, if you find her and my son, do this.* Impossible, I thought, yet twins share one destiny. I swore to Eshu to see Somso and his child through if I found them. At my promise, Brother-Taiwo's sense left him. He collapsed." Kehinde waved at me. "Eshu makes the road. Today I fulfill my promises."

"Did Husband-Taiwo die at your feet?" Somso trembled. "Tell me of his death."

Kehinde shook her head.

"I would hear this too," I said.

Kehinde gathered herself. "The plantation slaves fought with passion. We warriors had more skill and rifles. Seeing their leader fall, the rebels were thrown into disarray. Before they regrouped, before the *ahosi* warriors could spare energy to chase a traitor, I picked my brother up and ran. I slashed down anyone who tried to stop me. The air was thick with smoke and dust. Blood clouded many eyes. I stumbled to the empty *ahosi* camp and gathered what I could of my life. Eshu favored our escape. I carried Brother-Taiwo to a spirit cave. Dying, your husband spoke his love for you."

Somso's face hardened. "Did you really renounce your king for your brother?" She stroked Melinga's downy hair. "Perhaps this is the noble tale you recite now."

"Kehinde has never recounted these events," I interjected.

"What other tales has she kept from you, Wanderer?"

"Such stories are hers to share as she pleases, not mine to demand."

Somso sniggered. "How could Husband-Taiwo have such a sister?"

"How could he choose such a wife?" I asked.

"Once the Fon train a girl for war, they've broken her. She is never a woman again."

"What do you know of the Warrior and the Wanderer?" I hissed at Somso. Kehinde gripped my shoulder. "I faced the end of myself for Kehinde's trust, for all her stories."

"Love is blind," Somso said. "Kehinde, you say you carried your brother in one arm and struck down warriors with your other hand? That is a tale for a *gawlo* to flatter kings or manipulate villagers. Do you poison my mind and the Wanderer's with praise-singer lies and hope we'll trust a traitor, an oath-breaker?"

"I saw Kehinde balance her brother on the fulcrum of one shoulder. Kehinde has carried me too. She is the *stillpoint* of my wandering." I was shouting. Melinga paused from drinking. I lowered my voice. "A liar believes no one." Melinga suckled again.

"Who doesn't lie, Wanderer?" Somso said. "If you saw my husband wounded, why not heal him as you healed me?"

"I didn't yet know how."

"Why should I believe you?" Somso said.

"Why would I let Brother-Taiwo die?" To have Kehinde for myself. With respect to a *stillpoint*, Wanderers were ruthless.

Kehinde read me like an *Ifa* diviner reads a throw of palm nuts. "Don't doubt yourself, Wanderer." She circled Somso. "Were you so noble with Abla—resisting threats valiantly? Or did you volunteer what you knew? Perhaps you desired revenge. Did you love my brother or still long for Yao's caresses?"

Somso shivered at these suggestions. "What do you mean?"

"Did Abla promise you Yao's bed again? A French doctor to deliver a baby that wouldn't come?" Kehinde halted behind Somso. "Why should our honor be doubted when you led Abla to kill us? I saved your life, and Wanderer-Taiwo did as well."

"You are both sorcerers proffering polluted visions," Somso whispered.

"You'll betray us the first chance you get." Kehinde gripped her cutlass.

"So kill me now."

"The Wanderer has decided." Kehinde drew the blade across the sky. A burst of high frequency starlight scattered through the atmosphere, burning it blue. Morning. "You and Melinga are our story now." She made a gesture above my head, a knife thrusting from the crown of my braids into the clouds. "Eshu rides the Wanderer." Kehinde turned to Somso, calm and empty, the potential between a bolt of electricity and its target. My skin prickled. "We must trust each other. What is there for any of us in Dahomey? Our ship steams away soon."

To my surprise, Somso nodded. "Chicago will be Melinga's homeland."

"It is settled," Kehinde declared, even though nothing was settled.

Chronicles 11: Coast of Dahomey, 1893—Fire from Elsewhere

The wind carried melancholy melodies from the European ship. Sand flies, crabs, and birds scurried through the scenes of birth and death. Melinga dropped into sleep, a pebble into deep water. Her warm milk breath drew beads of sweat from Somso's skin. Kehinde gathered books, medicine bags, comb, and horsehair whip.

"Let's not miss the boat." She marched ahead.

I helped Somso up. We trudged toward the old slave hut and departure. My chest ached. Like the ocean tugging on the shore, Dahomey raked my heart. "Somayina who doesn't travel alone, did the Fon steal you from yourself?"

Somso's lip curled at my question. "I never missed Yao's bed."

"You are Igbo. Why did Brother-Taiwo marry you?" Kehinde asked.

Somso stepped over stony roots. Desolate gray seaweed tried to snag us. "I was never circumcised. My mother was a Christian and intended that I marry a Christian man who wouldn't mind."

"That isn't an explanation." Kehinde was relentless. "What else?"

"I wouldn't have gone willingly to a Yoruba man. They don't know how to treat a wife. Neither do the Fon. But Yao took me captive in a raid. Despite round hips and high breasts, I didn't give him children. What is a wife who produces no sons or even daughters?" She gestured disgust. "Yao's mother told everyone, *Somso isn't circumcised. She is barren and lustful. A man shouldn't keep such a repugnant wife.* I wasn't a warrior or a healer. So Yao sold me to the king's plantation where Taiwo toiled making palm oil." A smile caught fire on her face. "He never hid from the Fon. An *Ifa* diviner,

a great *Babalawo,* Taiwo wore the *ide Ifa* on his left wrist." She
held up a bracelet of opal beads anchored by strands of green and
yellow glass. "Everyone sought his counsel. Great wisdom can't be
subdued. Yao and his spies came seeking the secret of his power.
Taiwo recognized them easily. He warned them of a deadly destiny that could bring ruin."

"Why would a rebel-slave leader do that?" Kehinde asked.

Somso shrugged. "Where to hide from destiny? Unspoken,
blame the mouth; unheard, blame the ear. Yao, always prudent,
offered the necessary sacrifices. Change or die, yes? The other spies
ignored the verses Taiwo recited. Soon after, the *ajaho,* head of the
king's spies, accused them of treason. They lost their heads. Many
avoided Taiwo, but Yao greeted him with respect. Taiwo offered
Yao wisdom and Yao protected Taiwo from other spies. Our village had peace. We were happy to work the lands where Taiwo
made palm oil. Several foolish Igbo women warned against con-
sulting a twin, yet when no man would marry me, I asked Taiwo
to cast *Ifa.*"

"Warned you, why?" The twin reference made no sense to me.

"*True* Christians don't live by pagan superstition," Kehinde said.
The air crackled with irony and innuendo. "You're a Christian, like
your mother?"

"Yes." Somso fingered a crossroads talisman at her neck. She
sacrificed to the stringy-haired orisha who walked on water and
raised the dead. His followers ate his body, drank his blood,
and named Eshu the devil—a powerful, mysterious cult. "Your
brother liked my boldness in the face of superstition. He said,
Men always blame the woman. I was surprised to hear this from
a Yoruba man, especially a handsome one. *Yao has five wives,* he
said, *and can't make the grandsons his mother longs for. Could so many
women be barren?* This was honey talk. I said nothing, and he cast
Ifa."

"What verses did Brother-Taiwo speak?" Kehinde asked.

Somso recited:

Ifa says, there is no one to whom God has not been generous
only those who will say God has not been generous enough
Ifa says, see the blessing of visitors, the blessing of children,
the blessing of money, the blessing of a title.

"After offering this wisdom, Taiwo proclaimed, 'Surely you would have children with me.' He had no other wives. A bonded man was lucky to manage one. Our children would belong to the king. We were foolish to marry, but the whole village celebrated us. A wise *Babalawo*, what better choice did I have? Taiwo's talents didn't go unrewarded. The Fon weren't so stupid as to waste a capable person. They hoped to buy his loyalty. He humbly accepted Yao's goats, also glass beads from French traders, fine cloth from the Akan, and gold too. When I first lay in his arms, I felt rich. I didn't suspect that he was a rebel leader, sworn to die for freedom. Taiwo hid his hatred of Yao, but never forgot the taste of loyalty."

Stung, Kehinde looked away.

"We were happy. In a few weeks, I was pregnant. *Ifa* had guided us well." Somso's tears fell on Melinga's head. She cried easily. I marveled at her abandon. "Melinga was almost a year in my belly. Everyone said I would die giving birth and take the baby to greet his father in the land of the dead. My own fault, consorting with a twin."

"Save your tears. Twins are sacred," Kehinde said.

Somso wiped her eyes. "My mother's minister said one Yoruba or Igbo superstition is no better than another." Somso's magnetic spikes made my scalp itch. The tangle of emotions between her and Kehinde captivated me. "The villagers claimed that only witchcraft could save me and the child. Now I've given myself over to *ajo mmuo*."

"Evil spirit," Kehinde translated these Igbo words.

Somso grunted. "*Alu*, demon, abomination against Ani, earth goddess."

"Demons?" Kehinde sucked her teeth, as if I had never roared fire or dripped poison. "Your mind is in battle, Christian. Why consult *Ifa* or Ani if the wisdom of the ancestors is worthless *ma-amajomboo*[1] to you? Dr. Pierre insisted demons and orisha were unscientific superstition, but he knelt down to pray and ate the body and blood of his god. Christians come to conquer rich lands with machine guns and civilized lies. You converts are the traitors who have lost the taste of loyalty."

Somso's defiant electromagnetic spikes crackled in hot colors that no earthly language names. I understood Yao and Brother-Taiwo's passion. Who would not want to drink from Somso's well of power?

Kehinde made the gesture above my head again, a knife thrusting from the crown of my braids into bright starlight and clouds. "Eshu rides the Wanderer—a twin in this realm and others. Sacred."

"What do you mean?" I reached for her.

"You aren't broken yet." Kehinde hurried ahead. "We'll miss our ship."

Brilliant starlight splashed moody trees; a raspy breeze sang through the leaves; roots snapped and popped, tripping careless running things. Insects chewed the living and the dead, and shat fresh soil. Two hairy creatures slid into one another to create a new being. I was too troubled to appreciate these wonders. Somso shuffled along, leaning into me.

A marvelous journey across the great waters was upon us. A new world of stories beckoned. We had new life and needed to claim a new home. However, like the jittery people gathered around the jolly Italian impresario Captain Luigi and his sailors, I was anxious. I had murdered a great Fon warrior woman. Bloodlust defiled my spirit, erased memory. Kehinde was distant. Home had shattered into battlefield, last stand, grave. This journey was exile, a scattering . . . yet . . .

The ship, *La Vérité*, was a marvelous floating machine weighing many tons yet bobbing on the water. Smokestacks belched an oily brew. Rats, chased from the food stores, circled the laby-

---

1 Mumbo jumbo we say nowadays.

rinth of ladders and stairs to return to their haunts. Slave animals wailed in smelly cages. A broad array of humanity—as varied as on the streets of Ouidah—tromped aboard the ship. A torrent of languages washed over me. People escaping war-torn Dahomey jammed into tight little cabins.

I wrapped Melinga in Adinkra cloth, crafted by the Akan people in a distant land—a bribe from Yao to Brother-Taiwo. The Akan weave their wisdom. This cloth meant: *No matter the many red flames flickering in the eyes, the fire is from elsewhere.* Where did Kehinde's fire come from? Once on board, full of regret and shame, she avoided my glance, my anxious fingers. She mourned her broken past in solitude.

Steaming off for Chicagoland by way of Paris, *La Vérité* charged ahead of sailboats plying the wind. Storm clouds loomed in the north. Giant sparks flashed across the bowl of heaven. An unruly ocean tossed us toward saber-sharp rocks along Dahomey's treacherous shore.

Eshu roared through my ears and out my mouth.

Snowballs in Haiti

A terrible laugh gave Cinnamon goose bumps. The theatre lobby bounced up and down as if tossed on stormy waves. She felt seasick. Luckily, realist Skinny dashed around a bobbing pillar and gripped Cinnamon's arm, right there, right now.

"No callbacks!" Skinny's perfect pink and blue fingernails drew blood. "They're putting up a cast list. This minute!" She raced off.

"*Flugzeuge im Bauch,*" Klaus muttered. "What are you reading? It's glowing—"

"What does that mean?" Cinnamon stuffed *The Chronicles* pages into her journal. "*Flugzeuge im Bauch?*"

Klaus smiled at German in her mouth and leaned close. Boy perfume or zesty deodorant tickled her nose. "*Flugzeuge* are flying things. It means airplanes zoom in my belly."

"Sounds worse than butterflies."

"It is." He eyed his mother then whispered. "*Vati* will blow up if I don't get a really good role. *Mutti* will have hell to pay."

"Why would you not getting cast be your mom's fault?"

Klaus stared at Cinnamon as if a bug was crawling up her nose and flinched away.

"Whatever." The flying things were working her stomach too. "*Vati*—your dad?"

"Yeah." Klaus clutched his belly.

"Bad news, huh?" Vivid images popped in her head. *Colorless eyes and sausage fingers.* Vati, *taller and paler than Klaus, shot up evil shit in the garage then went off on* Mutti. *A fist print of broken blood vessels turned purple and green on her cheeks. A string of bloody snot hung from her nose. Mutti hid a bruised eye behind tendrils of red-blond hair. Klaus stood between his parents, taking a blow in his stomach, for* Mutti. Cinnamon gasped.

"What?" Klaus looked around.

"Uhm." The garage drug scene was a story storm. She hugged Klaus quickly, then punched his shoulder, how she used to do Sekou. "You'll get the lead. Watch." Klaus's face quivered. "Trust me."

The hunky ASM tacked a sheet on the callboard. Kids and grown-ups mobbed him. Skinny elbowed to the front. Mrs. Beckenbauer yelled German until Klaus sauntered into the fray. Cinnamon pressed Aidan's *mojo* bag to her heart. She willed her name to be on the list. A girl burst into tears.

"You're not on it either," Skinny yelled. Her almond eyes dribbled away into dirty streaks across her cheeks. One boy was so crushed at not being cast, he slugged his mom. A few kids jumped up and down beside parents who wanted to jump too.

"Are you sure?" Cinnamon barged through the crowd toward Skinny, fiercer than the production coordinator. "What's your name?" She surveyed the list.

"I told you. Marie Masuda. I remembered yours, Cinnamon Jones."

"Neither one of us made it, so who cares?"

Klaus beamed at Cinnamon. "You were right. I'm the Drug Prince, the lead." He punched her shoulder and whispered, "You should have been up there. Both of you."

"Don't tell me. Tell the director."

Panic streaked purple across Klaus's alabaster skin.

"Congratulations, my prince." A Jennifer Beals lookalike kissed Klaus on both cheeks. She could've stepped out of *Flashdance*. Tall and whipcord thin, she had big bosoms, hazel eyes, and dark curls, probably biracial like Beals. Cinnamon wanted to smash her half-white ass. "I got Snow White." The girl actually purred.

"That's great, Janice," Klaus muttered. He knew her!

Snow White smirked at Cinnamon and Marie Masuda before floating away.

"Janice," Marie said, as if naming poisonous vermin, "can barely read music. Flyer said you had to read music." Marie was as pretty

and skinny as Janice with a big gospel voice nobody would believe. Eshu was laughing at them. "It's not fair."

"My life's never going to change." Cinnamon sank to the floor by the mold.

"But we were outstanding." Marie sat down beside her.

Cinnamon leaned into Marie's bony shoulders.

"You two were better than everybody." Klaus's voice boomed through the lobby.

Even yelled out loud, the truth didn't help. Cinnamon gritted her teeth. It was a dumb play anyhow. Diamond couldn't even come up with a title.

Tottering on broken shoes, puke green coat pulled tight, Opal cornered Director Hill talking up a donor in glass slippers and a liquid silver gown. "That's my daughter." Opal pointed. "She was outstanding." Opal put an arm across the doorway and blocked Hill's exit strategy. "She's got more talent than ten of these kids." Opal's vocal cords were raw from smoke and sleet. "You saw her tear it up with Snow White. Everybody did." So Opal *had* seen her. "That little Oriental snippet was good too. Man, what's wrong with you?" Spit spraying from her mouth was flecked with red.

"What's wrong with *me*?" Hill chortled. "You need to calm down."

Opal hadn't raised her voice or done anything wild like the folks going off around her—no *public display*. "I'm very calm, sir."

Cinnamon leapt up. Calm and deadly.

"You have to admit they were outstanding," Klaus shouted.

Hill turned toward him. "Listen, you little—"

"Not the kid." Opal was up in the Hill's face. "Me." Opal coughed so hard Hill backed into the glass slipper donor still hovering at his elbow.

"Your mom?" Marie asked. Cinnamon nodded. "She got up out of the hospital to pick you up. My dad would never . . . I have to take a cab home. By myself."

"You must be realistic, Mrs. Jones." Hill knew her last name. He was good.

"Ms. Jones." Opal corrected him. "I'm very realistic. I drive a bus on these streets."

"Professionally, Cinnamon doesn't have a snowball's chance in Haiti of making it."

"Do you mean Haiti or Hades?" Opal said. The glass slipper donor snickered.

"I'm talking mainstream. Alternative work, OK, but anything popular . . ."

"You don't even believe the crap you're saying," Opal said. "Please. Spare me."

A third button on Cinnamon's blouse popped. Fumbling with her last giant safety pin, she hastily closed the gap.

Hill gestured at her. "There aren't roles for her . . . type."

"Not even in the chorus? With that voice?" Coughing caved in Opal's chest and twisted her face. "You're a coward."

The crowd gasped. The gutsy college girl cheered.

Hill looked ready to strangle Opal. "I'm no coward."

Opal grunted. "You lie to yourself, a lot."

Hill sputtered and turned purple.

Sekou writhed in his dark casket. *Cowards fight dirty. Opal needs backup.*

"Get out of my way." Hill tried to shove Opal aside.

"Don't push my mom." Cinnamon charged him with Marie at her heels. Tears dribbled down Marie's face making Cinnamon madder. "Both of us are good."

"Who said you weren't good?" Hill said.

"Outstanding," Klaus yelled, shaking his fist for emphasis. Silver blond wisps fell over his eyes. *"Ausgezeichnet!"* Maybe he *was* cute.

Other voices shouted about ghetto-itis and outstanding fat asses.

"Hold!" Hill hushed everyone. "Good as you are, I don't have roles for you in Diamond's musical."

"You changed the key for Beckenbauer, I mean for Klaus," Cinnamon said, "but you don't want to give us a chance, and we can really sing."

"In any key," Marie said. "We *read* music too."

"Admit it, Mr. Hill, they were better than you've ever seen." Klaus was smooth and sweet and cold as ice cream. "The best."

Hill glared at him. Golden boys should stick together. "Your little Mod Squad's cute, but no cigar."

"Mod Squad? That's really lame." Opal was laughing. "Are you stuck in 1968?"

"We're a professional theatre, not community service. We can't use everybody." His eye twitched. "In the real world talent gets wasted." The glass-slipper lady groaned.

"I hate the real world." Marie jabbed Klaus. "Don't you?"

Mrs. Beckenbauer clamped a hand over her son's mouth before he ruined his future.

"We make the real world, every minute, with every breath." Opal was wheezing, running out of breath to make her reality.

"Failing now is good practice for grown-up life," Hill said.

"They didn't fail. You did." A pale sheen covered Opal's brown skin. She teeter-tottered, ready to fall over nothing. "Coward."

"I've been patient with your disappointment—"

"How *good* are you, really?"

"Who the fuck do you—"

"Show's over." The production coordinator gripped a handful of Hill's shirt and pulled him into a throng of fancy donors. Two women spirited him away in a flash. The production coordinator herded parents and kids to the exit. "You all go home. Food is for invited guests only." She turned to the donor angels. "Eat the wafers. Mingle. We'll pop champagne soon."

The donors crunched and sipped on her cue except the glass slipper lady who watched Opal, Cinnamon, and Marie through slitted eyes.

"Wipe your noses." Opal shoved tissues at them. "You and your friends always got your hearts on your sleeves."

"Always?" Cinnamon didn't have any friends until this evening. She was a fat, geeky talkaholic. Other kids made fun of her. Sekou had to haunt her so she wouldn't be lonely. Marie blew her nose in sync with Cinnamon. Theatre magic was still holding them close, but how long would that last?

"OK." Opal kissed Cinnamon's forehead. "You three were special and spooky." She tried for gentle, for *nice* even. "Nobody's looking for that at an audition. You all were scary good, magic." *Nice* stole the last of Opal's strength. Her legs twisted, her arms flailed, then she collapsed on Cinnamon, who was glad for once to be a big girl.

"Just what I don't need," the production coordinator muttered.

Rust brown goo bubbled out of Opal's mouth. Her eyes rolled up in her head.

"Shit." The production coordinator waved at the ASM. "Help her."

"How?" he asked.

"Don't you touch her," Cinnamon roared before he even thought of moving. "Nobody touch her!" Everyone froze.

"Your mom should've stayed in recovery." Marie walked close, unafraid.

"It's my fault. I shouldn't have—" Cinnamon trailed off. Another story storm lie come true.

"Marie means we have to get your mom *back* to the hospital." Klaus stood close too.

They leaned against Cinnamon's shoulders, holding her up on the sly.

"Your mom's fierce, a hero," Marie said and slugged Klaus who nodded.

"OK, but, but, now, what?" Cinnamon said.

"Call your dad," Marie said. "He'd have to come for this!"

"He's been in a coma for four years and two months. Shot in the head."

That stumped Klaus and Maria. Opal's wheezing was louder than the radiators finally clanking to life in the lobby. She was getting heavier and heavier. Cinnamon's muscles protested. A flood of tears was a blink away. *Nobody wants to see that! You promised not to be a crybaby!*

Folks in the lobby started yelling—*infectious insanity.* "You can take the Negro out the ghetto, but getting the ghetto out the—"

Cinnamon screeched gibberish at them.

Sing with the voice of someone you love whose voice has gone quiet. Miz Redwood's spell #8b filled Cinnamon's mind. Spell #9b too: *Sing, till you give everybody back to themselves.*

Cinnamon tried Aidan's song, looking for the tune he was writing:

Cinnamon
Sugar and spice, honey and ice
I'm your poem, your song
A simple conjuration
I'm your rhythm, your dream
A total dedication
The praise-house for your spirit
Truth you know when you hear it
I'm your poem, your song
A portal to your art
A shelter for your heart

Klaus and Marie joined her with a sweet harmony after two times through. Everybody and her brother calmed down. Theatre magic.

Glass Slippers and
Golden Angels

A shelter for your heart

Sirens drowned out Aidan's song. Flashing red lights blinded Cinnamon. She shivered in the sleet on the Playhouse loading dock. Where were Klaus and Marie? Ominous heart monitors beeped off key in a forest of plastic tubes. Bloody gauze rolled into a wheezing pump about to give up the ghost. This emergency vehicle needed rescue funding. Two rickety stretchers crumpled before they were set up. Rusty wheels on the third skated across a treacherous walkway. Cinnamon skidded on glassy ice too. Black boots and folded arms blocked her. Lights on the ambulance spun like a merry-go-round as it raced away. The emergency room in Oakland wasn't far. The ambulance screamed and farted exhaust as it veered left. Wasn't the Tenth Street Bridge the other direction? Cinnamon must be turned around. The driver wouldn't go the wrong way, even if Opal came to and started working everybody's last nerve.

Time was wrong. Cinnamon stood in front of the Playhouse, holding Opal's broken shoes. The sky dropped needles on her woozy head. Fog tipis shrouded the streetlights. The roads were black ice. A stiff wind howled up the river, complaining about the sleet in its way. Nobody should be driving. She blinked away slushy tears and shivered. Her shit-brown coat was in the ambulance, twisted under the one functional stretcher.

"You can't see the ambulance anymore. Mmmoooovvve." How long had the security guard been poking a bruise in Cinnamon's arm?

Cinnamon almost fell off the curb. "Damn, lady."

"Watch your mouth." The guard shoved her toward the theatre entrance.

"I gotta get to the hospital."

"It's this way."

Cinnamon let the guard pull her into the lobby. She halted at the box office and dropped Opal's broken shoes on the counter. "You've done your job. Thanks. Bye."

"Excuse me?" Melting ice crystals on the guard's cheeks made her irritation sparkle.

"Ain't no reward for your suffering." Cinnamon did Snow White. "I got wheels. My aunt's cruising in with my grandparents and great aunt."

"Fine." The guard marched off.

Cinnamon scanned the crowd, slowly, so she wouldn't get dizzier. Klaus and Mrs. Beckenbauer fought in German. Marie Masuda smacked the pay phone, dumped coins in, and punched numbers. They didn't notice Cinnamon. Citing winter storm warnings, Prospero and Medea exited as donors mobbed Jason, the Argonaut from NYC. He offered a vacant smile and zombie eyes. Having zilch personality was an acting asset. Your own character didn't interfere with the roles you played. Cinnamon envied Jason. Folks made up their minds about her before she opened her mouth; she'd have to accelerate faster than the speed of light to become somebody else in their eyes—impossible in this sector of space-time. How would she ever find a ride to Oakland?

"Grants are minuscule; corporate giving is down. How is that Hill's fault?" The donor in glass slippers and liquid silver gown spoke to a clutch of angels. "He's a real genius. We're lucky to have him." She sighed, a woman in love. "You want vibrant art? Cut him some slack." She waved off hors d'oeuvres Cinnamon would've killed for. "Cutting-edge artists deserve our patience, our . . ." She smiled at Cinnamon. "Our forgiveness when the going gets rough." Cinnamon wondered what kind of car this rich white lady drove—maybe not four-wheel drive, but serious brakes and tires for sure.

"Bull, Gwyneth." A glowering platinum angel slung his arm around her waist. "Hill and his artsy-fartsy crew are ruining the Playhouse." He boomed over Gwyneth's protests. "New York tossed Hill out on his ass. Hollywood picked the bones before dumping him in backwater Pittsburgh. The guy's a loser."

Gwyneth rolled her eyes—right at Cinnamon.

Platinum burped champagne bubbles. "Why doesn't Herr Genius Director put on *Guys and Dolls* or *Oklahoma* or *The Odd Couple*? Something audiences want to see."

"Warmed-over warhorses can sink a theatre too." Gwyneth slipped from his grasp.

"*Sleuth*?" Despite his captain of industry confidence and Armani elegance, Platinum was clueless. Didn't need a detective to peep the triangle affair brewing. Damn! Cinnamon was ad-libbing like Snow White, even in her mind. She'd have been perfect for the role! Gwyneth smiled at her again. Certainly the number-one ride possibility.

Cinnamon walked up to Platinum. "Cutting-edge theatre isn't a moribund art form." She used dictionary words for Gwyneth. "It's effervescent."

Platinum grabbed more champagne. "Bullshit artists are always sticking their hands in my pockets."

"Harry! Be nice, now," Gwyneth said.

Harry threw back his drink. "What's nice get you?"

Gwyneth leaned close to him and whispered, "She and her Asian friend didn't get cast in Diamond's show. They were good too. Her mom checked out of the hospital to support her. Poor woman was so distraught, she collapsed."

"How do you always know these sordid stories?" Harry snorted. "It's a buzzkill."

Cinnamon dashed away from his mean mouth and her Opal-check-out-of-the-hospital lie. If she could go back and tell a happy *true* tale—the hero-on-the-bus saga, not a half-dead-in-the-hospital story, then . . . What? The elders conjured good magic. Cinnamon called up the twisted, dark fantasy, dystopia stuff.

Don't blame yourself. Sekou's words tickled. *Opal's lungs took up arms and revolted.*

"That's cold comfort, Bro." Cinnamon spoke full voice, not caring who heard. "I been begging her to quit. She lights up and says, *It's all I got left.* And I'm right there."

Opal is standing at the crossroads, and it looks like a dead end.

"I can't get her a fun job or turn myself into you. No fuckin' way can I wake Daddy out of that stupid coma. I can't even get a ride to the nursing home."

Trust me, Sis. You don't want to go see your dad rotting in that bed.

"Yes, I do!"

Nobody in the lobby noticed Cinnamon yelling except Gwyneth. Shaking a few blond tendrils from her French twist, Gwyneth marched over to Mrs. Juanita Williams, the Golden Angel black lady who thought Cinnamon was too ghetto. Gwyneth nodded in Cinnamon's direction as they conferred. Cinnamon cringed.

A cork exploded from a bottle. Dodging the lethal projectile, Cinnamon charged into the paradise set and tripped over a light tree. Swaying Fresnels and Lekos banged into a goddess and dislodged flower garlands. Cinnamon gripped the tree and steadied the instruments. Pink lily petals and a dusting of pollen collected on her braids. She hugged the metal pole and cried quiet tears. Not *public display,* but still stupid. Feeling sorry for herself wouldn't turn a lie around, wouldn't get her to the hospital. *Feeling sorry* wasted precious time. *All they had, really, was time.*

"Yeah, baby!" A throaty, familiar voice moaned.

Under cover of foam bushes, Chanda, the gutsy college girl, kissed the ASM. His hand groped under her shirt. She was writhing on his bulging crotch. Backlit by a shin buster Fresnel, her hair was a wheel of black fire. She looked like Kali, Hindu goddess, destroyer of illusion. Cinnamon gasped, covering her mouth too late.

"What're you gawking at?" Chanda yelled. "Wait. Why are *you* still here?"

"Shit!" The ASM pulled bushes in front of them. His eyes flew every direction, hunting more spies. "I told you *somebody* would see us."

"Don't be such a pussy." Chanda snorted. "A little danger spices shit up."

Cinnamon raced for the exit door. Mrs. Williams grabbed her before she could escape. She was two inches taller than Cinnamon and strong for a straitlaced, middle-class black lady. "What do you think you're doing?" she said.

"I'm walking to the hospital," Cinnamon replied.

"Have you lost your natural mind?"

"My pass doesn't work on this line." Cinnamon wasn't sure which bus to take. "I know the way." Or could figure it out. "I like to walk."

"Walk? Don't talk nonsense."

"Walking too ghetto for you?" Cinnamon flung Mrs. Williams's arm off of her. "Fuck sense."

Mrs. Williams bunched her lips together. *Fuck* probably drove her over the edge. Techies and donors hung their heads, too much *public display.*

"Walking is—" Cinnamon tripped over her tongue. "Safer than wheels tonight."

"You can't walk." Klaus escaped his mother and strode too close. Cinnamon shoved him. He didn't budge. "I've walked all around here." The Monongahela flowed in her. "I have!"

Marie ganged up on her with Klaus. "I'm not walking, and I'm going with you too."

"Not my walking shoes." Klaus kicked his foot high, a ballet move. "*Vati* is, he wasn't home. We can take the bus together." He waved a five-dollar bill. "I have fare."

"No. Buses have stopped running. Snow emergency. We'll all go in my car," Mrs. Williams declared, more five-star general than Golden Angel. "You two"—she dropped a hand on Marie and Klaus's shoulders—"keep an eye on her. She's not herself."

"No problem," Marie said.

"We got her," Klaus said.

Mrs. Williams glared at Cinnamon. "Wait here with your friends. I'm getting my coat." She stomped off.

"Mist," Mrs. Beckenbauer said, like a curse.

"Yeah, *Mist,*" Cinnamon said. "We've got to hurry."

Mrs. Beckenbauer frowned. *"Kannst du Deutsch?"*

"Sie kann ein bißchen. Hörst du das nicht?" Klaus said then whispered, "I said you spoke a little German." He held up her knapsack and a clump of *Chronicles* pages. "You dropped this."

"These too." Marie waved the moving picture of Dahomey and a Polaroid of hero Opal that had fallen from her journal.

Cinnamon's legs wobbled. "Losing everything—" She blubbered.

"I told you we shouldn't leave her alone out there," Marie said.

"Mutti was worried about getting home," Klaus said. "The guard said she'd watch her."

"You believed that?" Marie snorted.

"My mom is—I have to run interference." Cinnamon pointed at the Polaroid.

Klaus leaned closer to the image. "Is that guy holding a machete?"

"Knife boy!" Cinnamon said. "That's proof!"

"Of what?" Klaus asked.

"My mom almost got fired over Bonnie and Clyde."

Klaus and Marie shook their heads.

"OK, OK." Cinnamon flooded, "Opal supposedly yelled death threats at this glam gangsta couple, trying to cheat a ride downtown with last year's transfers. But the bus company couldn't fire her since right after Bonnie and Clyde, this white guy with orange hair and slabs of muscles jumped on her bus waving ten inches of knife like he wanted to kill somebody. And Opal just talked him down, telling him, you know, not to give up hope, 'cause opportunity was around every corner. She said, *Don't waste your life. I believe in you.* Knife boy turned into a fire hydrant gushing tears and snot. Opal hugged him, opened the door, and said, *Have a nice day!* He dropped the knife and jumped off. *Everybody all right?* she said and drove on."

"Really?" Klaus and Marie said.

"The bus company thought she was lying too, but she had Polaroid proof. And . . . and . . . Nobody at the hospital is going to believe Opal Jones is a hero. It'll be . . . *Angry Black Woman Collapses Before She Can Strangle Hunky White Director!*"

"Oh." Klaus hugged the orca.

"Wow." Marie tucked the Polaroid and *Chronicles* illustration into Cinnamon's journal. Lightning flashed over black waves in the Atlantic. "It's a . . . video."

Cinnamon reached drunkenly for her treasures. "Those pages come from a special book, *magic,* a book to see a person through tough times." She fell into Klaus who wasn't surprised by how heavy or out of it she was. He just caught her.

"Magic?" Marie rolled her eyes. Klaus shook his head. "OK. Fine." Maria slid the journal into the orca's mouth—no resistance. "Magic."

"I'll hold onto this for you." Klaus slung the orca over his shoulder. He dropped a luxurious black coat on Cinnamon's shivering frame. The inside was furry and smelled of his boy perfume—a fresh-baked bread and herb tea smell.

"You're freezing." Marie rubbed Cinnamon's icy fingers. Marie's lavender and sage mixed with Klaus's aroma and made Cinnamon's stomach gurgle.

"My crew." Cinnamon spoke this aloud to see how it sounded.

Amen! A perspicacious and intrepid crew, Sekou declared, in dictionary boy mode.

Klaus and Marie gasped. Eyes wide, noses quivering, they heard Sekou too.

Gwyneth swept into the lobby and jammed a furry cap onto her French twist. Behind her Harry tripped over the cloakroom doorsill and fell into Mrs. Williams.

She steadied him. "Too much bubbly, Harry."

"Why does everybody put up with drunks?" Harry muttered at Gwyneth.

Gwyneth thrust Harry out the streaky glass doors then hugged Mrs. Williams to her heart. They wore the same down coats, fleece-lined boots, and strained expressions—probably old friends who'd been syncing up forever.

"You better drive," Mrs. Williams said.

Gwyneth nodded. "Thanks for taking these kids out of your way."

"Thank you both." Marie smiled. "I couldn't persuade or bribe or even find a cab. My dad doesn't want to drive in the storm. He wanted me to wait it out."

"Yours too, huh?" Klaus said.

Some dads. If Raven weren't in that stupid coma, he'd come get Cinnamon in a hot second, weather be damned. Gwyneth heaved the glass door open. Whatever Harry was yelling got snatched by the wind. She glided out into the blizzard.

Mrs. Williams waited until Gwyneth dropped into Harry's car and then shouted, "Let's march." With the bearing of a commanding officer going to battle, she hustled them out into the brutal wind blasting the parking lot.

Perspicacious and Intrepid

Slogging through snow drifts made everyone breathe hard. On point, Mrs. Williams forged a path. Marie and Klaus sandwiched Cinnamon between them. Mrs. Beckenbauer brought up the rear. Commander Williams halted the troops under a busted streetlight by a flashy, silver Audi. The key wouldn't turn in the lock.

"It's iced shut. Do I need this?"

Cinnamon laughed. No one else thought it was funny. Mrs. Beckenbauer dug in her purse and pulled out a tiny spray can. As she spritzed the lock and handle, a flock of crows swooped across the parking lot. Bits of black plummeting through endless white made Cinnamon's heart flutter. "The night sky has shattered above the clouds and it's coming down on us now," she said.

"A poet, huh? You don't believe that stuff about crows and death, do you?" Marie said. "These particular birds are random."

"*Coincidental affinity.*" Cinnamon thought of the Wanderer's birds. "A flock flying in a storm means something."

Hovering at the gate of life and death, Eshu asks which direction you go take? Sekou said.

Cinnamon groaned. Opal, not Aidan, had one foot in the grave. "God wouldn't fire a hero. It wouldn't make sense," Cinnamon said. "God is a great spirit, not a petty one."

Klaus and Marie exchanged glances. Mrs. Beckenbauer shook her can violently.

"*Mist.* These are getting wet!" Klaus fumbled with the *Chronicles* pages. Words glowed green and blue as he stuck them in the orca's mouth.

"Fluorescent words. Cool," Marie said. "What's up with the magic book?"

Cinnamon hunched her shoulders.

"Tell us," Klaus said.

Cinnamon had been dying to tell *somebody* for over two years. Redwood's spell #6: *find a friend or two, and share secrets and magic out loud.* Friends had just been impossible to find. "Sekou gave *The Chronicles* to me before he . . . died. Sekou's my half brother, my best friend still. You heard him. He called you *a perspicacious and intrepid crew.*"

The stream of fog white from Marie's and Klaus's lips stopped. Cinnamon panicked. What if they *didn't* hear what she heard or heard bits and pieces of ancestor static on the wind—enough to raise the hair on your neck, but gibberish really? Or what if Cinnamon was crazy, talking both sides of the conversation, and they heard that?

"Verdammt!" Mrs. Beckenbauer said, a German *damn it* for sure.

"I got this." Mrs. Williams took the jammed spray can and attacked it with a tool from her purse.

Klaus pulled Cinnamon and Marie out of range of grown-up ears. "We heard your dead half brother?" He didn't mind asking stupid questions.

"Isn't that what I said, fool?" Cinnamon replied.

He frowned. "In our heads?"

"We hear everything in our heads." Marie swallowed the snow on her tongue.

"Right." Klaus rubbed slush out of his eyes. "We're saying that dead brother Sekou talks out loud, but most people don't hear him?"

"I'm saying it doesn't matter," Marie said. "The three of us heard Sekou, and we can't all be going crazy the same way. We're too different. Right?"

"I guess." Klaus's cheeks were cherry red. He had a shitload more questions. "Right."

"You all *believe* me." Cinnamon giggled. She could have cried too. "You're not mad about being haunted. Perspicacious and intrepid for sure."

"We shouldn't talk about this with anyone else." Marie glanced at the grown-ups. "If people don't hear Sekou, they'll think we're crazy. Our secret, agreed?" She stretched out her hands, palms up.

"Logisch." Klaus took one hand.

Nothing like logic. Cinnamon grabbed Marie's other hand and Klaus's too. They were a Mod Squad secret society with an oath and everything holding them together. They leaned into one another, bumped heads, and gasped a few nervous laughs. Cinnamon could taste their breath, warmer than the snowy air. They entwined their arms and tangled up their legs, becoming a single snow creature who toyed with balance and gravity on icy ground—contact improv. Cinnamon could barely believe how good it felt. Spontaneous choreography onstage wasn't a fluke. Laughing, the Mod Squad secret society tumbled to a halt and shook off clouds of snow. No getting around it, Cinnamon had to work happy alongside despair about Opal.

"Sekou wrote *The Chronicles*?" Klaus was a fearless questioner.

"No. Sekou was a Guardian. I'm backup." A story storm tingled on Cinnamon's tongue. "The Wanderer is writing as we go along. You guys are backup now too, so you'll have to memorize chapters with me. I got more at home. Pages come clear to my great aunt, and she sends them off. She and my grandparents are also Guardians. Every time we read, we keep the Wanderer from jumping off a bridge. The Wanderer is an alien from the spaces between things and needs us, like light needs an object to shine on or darkness wins. The Wanderer has broken into fragments and scattered, maybe into Ariel the actress. There's nobody believing in the whole Wanderer. *The Chronicles* is the spell to put the Wanderer back together. Believing can make a body whole."

Klaus and Marie stopped breathing again. Too much weird at once? Too fast? Even for a secret society posse? The scattered alien-from-another-dimension bit probably topped communications from the dead. Weird was hard to measure on an absolute scale though. For sure Cinnamon had taken them pretty close to flippin' freaky.

"Try it now," Mrs. Williams shouted and threw the de-icer to Mrs. Beckenbauer.

"Aliens *and* ghosts?" Marie shook her head. "Crossing the genre divide, aren't we?"

"Granddaddy Aidan, Miz Redwood, and Aunt Iris had fantasy. Me and Sekou got horror sci-fi." Diarrhea mouth was why

Cinnamon didn't have friends. Faggot brother, coma dad, and cigarette ash mom had little to do with it. "Whatever. I can't think. I don't want to talk about it."

Marie looked hurt. Klaus was confused. Mrs. Beckenbauer blasted the frosted locks three times. She took a deep breath and wrenched the door open.

Sweeping snow from the windshield, Commander Williams said, "All aboard."

They clambered inside, grown-ups up front, Mod Squad in the back. Mrs. Williams ratcheted the heat up to full. The fan sounded like poltergeists pounding the engine.

Mrs. Beckenbauer turned to her son. Klaus shouted over the racket, "Audi, a good *deutsches* auto, *Mutti*. No angst, OK?" He spoke German/English to them all.

Commander Williams had the engine in gear, spinning through slush. Mrs. Beckenbauer sputtered then turned back to face the road. They were away!

"It's glowing." Klaus held up Cinnamon's orca. He pulled out a few pages. "Words bright as day. Should I . . . ?"

"Of course!" Marie said. "Why do you think it's glowing? We're Guardians."

"Of course!" Klaus mimicked Marie's exclamation point and they laughed.

"Pittsburgh will be a great city when it's finished," Mrs. Williams yelled at a detour sign. A bridge was out. It was miles to the next bridge. She backed up slowly and turned around.

"You really want to read it?" Cinnamon couldn't get used to having friends.

"Are you kidding?" Marie nudged Klaus. "Go for it!"

"Listen first." Spewing a fast storm of words, Cinnamon filled them in on *The Chronicles* from Kehinde and Taiwo's appearance in a Mami Wata spirit cave to the dynamic duo boarding a steamship bound for Paris with baby Melinga and treacherous Somso. Klaus and Marie swallowed Cinnamon's storm of words as if each one was sweet and true and precious.

Book III

Pittsburgh, PA, February 1987 & Ocean Fog, 1893

I'm in no way an optimist. Optimism is a notion that there's sufficient evidence that would allow us to infer that if we keep doing what we're doing, things will get better. I don't believe that. I'm a prisoner of hope, that's something else.

—Cornel West

Chronicles 12: Atlantic Ocean, 1893—Monsters on the High Seas

The first two nights on the steamship, Captain Luigi, a thin man with ghostly pale eyes and a frizzy black beard, stood on the bridge and cursed milky air. He also heaped scorn on stars skulking behind the fog. Many steamships disappeared at sea—thirty a year. Fearing *La Vérité* would run against a reef and sink, Luigi cursed the engineer, his lazy stokers, and everyone else.

A turbulent sea wouldn't let anybody sleep. We were refugees of war headed to a masquerade carnival. I wanted to contain other selves, not put them on display. Wandering the foggy deck, I was forlorn, unmoored. In full warrior masquerade, Kehinde wouldn't let me touch her.

"What are these tears?" She flicked her fingers dismissively.

Wiping my eyes, I spoke half the truth. "I fear the *aje* might kill again."

"Some warriors get lost in a killing fever, but not you. *Ifa* says journey, sacrifice to overcome enemies and find peace." She narrowed her eyes. "Abla always gave *ahosi* warriors rum or palm wine, so they might sleep without dreams, march without pain; so that when they took a head they might blot out an enemy's last scowl. After my first drunken raid, I decided to see and remember what I did. When it came time for revenge on the Fon, I would know every way to kill—quickly without pain or slowly for agony. I would know myself." She gripped my arm tight enough to bruise. "Once, we defeated a village. The grown men and women laid down their weapons. At the edge of the village, a young girl charged me, brandishing an Eshu staff. I disarmed her easily. My cutlass was at her neck, but I hesitated. She didn't fear death and scrambled up, staring into my eyes with hope. I thought to let her run into the forest.

"Coming from behind me, Abla pierced her heart and said, *We'd never have tamed that one.* I asked, *How do you know?* Wiping blood from her blade Abla replied, *This girl would've broken her* ahosi *oaths and betrayed us. She'd have set gris-gris to poison our power. She'd have taken lovers, had babies, and assassinated us in our sleep. She wouldn't have lived for the glory of battle. But you will be a great* ahosi *general. I see your glory coming.*" Kehinde clutched the scar at her neck. "I sought glory, yet Abla isn't master of my destiny or yours." After this story, Kehinde slept peacefully every night, a knife in one hand, a cutlass within reach. No such luck for me.

The third foggy night on board, the bridge was deserted. Only a skeleton crew tended the steamship. Rich passengers from Europe snored on the upper deck. A tangle of rigging (for vestigial sails?) hung from slender masts thrumming softly in the headwind. Torn canvas covering the yawl boats rippled. Mist condensed on smoke-stacks and wandered through grime to form nauseating puddles at the base. As I vomited undigested tubers from dinner, a severed head rose out of cold fog and spat clotted blood and dead fish at my feet. Abla's rotting, bloated visage rode the surf toward me. My death blow had left jagged flaps of skin and a gruesome stump of spine. A tentacle from a creature nesting in her skull slithered through the cervical vertebrae and flung filth at *La Vérité.* I jumped back, disbelieving my eyes and the seaweed clinging to my chin.

"Watch out!" A sailor tossed me a rag. He was more substantial than the shadows, but barely. I couldn't see his face; his sweat smelled urgent. "The sea's a fickle wench, bitching her own beauty and loving you too."

I shook my head.

"English is what I've got."

He thought I didn't understand him. Actually I'd have welcomed Lady Atlantic playing a prank and dousing me with waste from our bilge. Instead, murdered Abla rode black water alongside the ship. Perhaps the sailor glimpsed this specter tossed about in unruly waves or reflected in my eyes. Rather than go on about his business, he drew nearer, leaning into my dangerous mood. His magnetic signature was as bold as his spicy scent. Abla spat at him. She shone bright as daylight, a hole in the dark water, illuminating nothing but herself. I wished for a cutlass. My empty hands slashed the rising mist. The sailor jerked back, not far, though.

"You've killed me already, Wanderer." Abla spoke Yoruba and displayed pointed, dagger teeth. "I won't die for you again."

"What do you want?" I spoke Yoruba also.

"You called me."

"Liar." I turned away.

Abla's head, relentless and bright, floated anywhere I cast my eyes. She laughed. "Wherever you go, Dahomey will live in you."

Her laughter recalled veins bursting and bones shattering. Blood oozed from the scar on my side. I groaned. The sailor offered me a scrap of fabric. I took it.

"You masquerade as a harmless wandering griot." Squid tentacles slithered through dead eyes. "Yet, I recognize the *aje* who comes to take our heads and eat our history."

"You confuse me with Fon spies." Fire bubbled up my esophagus and through sinuses into nostrils. I clamped it down. The sailor's hand hovered over my back.

"No girl ever resisted me, not haughty Somso or even proud Kehinde," Abla shouted. "I called forth the *aje*. Your head belongs to me."

I buried my face in the sailor's soft cloth, wishing I could wake from this nightmare to moonlight playing tricks on exhausted senses. The patient sailor stepped closer still, concern wafting from his pores.

Abla floated within reach. "*Ifa* says: *Don't use a broken rope to climb a palm tree. Don't enter into the river without knowing how to swim.* I am your history and your destiny."

I leaned over the rail. "We leave your realm behind and travel to a new world. You have no power there."

"You tell yourself lies you wish were true." Slimy creatures wriggled through Abla's teeth and got sliced to bits. "Soon you won't remember your true story." Tentacles reached for me.

I batted them away. *"Ifa* says: *This person should sacrifice so her eyes don't see evil where she is going."*

"You have nothing left to sacrifice. You will scatter to oblivion. Murderer." Abla sank into the water. Acrid bubbles drifted up and burst in the air.

Certain she would return to torture me again, I threw myself over the railing toward the bubbles, hoping to end her torment once and for all.

Chronicles 13: Atlantic Ocean, 1893—Light Show

I might have drowned this body, but faster than thought, the sailor gripped my hips. My torso banged into the prow. I arched my back reflexively and saved my head from slamming into metal and wood.

"Swim in the morning. The sea is restless tonight." The sailor spoke gently, but his grip on my waist was harsh. The wound in my side screamed pain. *Aje* fire smoldered in my lungs as he hauled me back on the deck, back to human. I yanked his left hand from my throbbing side. The sailor whistled. "You're a strong one." His right hand slid over my flat breasts then hovered with the left at my hips to catch any foolish move. "They say you Dahomean warrior women are men in disguise except the plump one with the baby." He was between me and the railing. "I would hear what you say."

Afraid to speak or look at him, I drank cold mist and doused the *aje*'s fire.

"Look." The sailor traced a glowing horizon line. "Dawn is coming. The sun, a jealous lover banished for the night, burns the mist away, burns the sky red, and the sea rejoices. Nothing like it on land, hemmed in by hills and forests or city buildings. Dawn is not crowded out here." The deck rocked under us, and I almost vomited again. He clutched my waist to steady me. "Do you understand what I'm saying?" The music of his speech and the shifts in his magnetic fields were different from Kehinde's, but he spoke English, a language she insisted I learn, a strange comfort to my ears. His rumbling chest was compelling. His skin smelled of fish, soap, and hot iron. I liked the taste of him.

"Do you touch women so freely where you are from?" I spoke his tongue. "Or only men?"

Shock sparked from his skin; his pulse jumped as he let go of me. "You meant to harm yourself. I—"

"Sought my breasts to save me?"

His shame smelled almost the same as Kehinde's. "I beg your pardon."

"Who are you?" My lips curled into a smirk.

His heart rate slowed. "No one you should talk to."

"Too late, friend." I leaned against his rough skin. His pungent surprise filled my nostrils. After a few moments his arms dropped gently against my back. In the circle of his being I fluctuated between man and woman and calmed the *aje*. "What's your story?" I smiled on his chest. "What adventure brought you to Dahomey?"

He shook his head.

"Surely not just dawn on the open sea." I drew his silent warmth into me until he shivered. "If not your story, tell me your name."

"On this ship, I am called Bob."

"Thank you, Bob, for holding on to me. On this world, I am Taiwo, the Wanderer."

I dashed below, so he couldn't snag me with a response or a question.

Many nights passed before I saw Bob's dawn. It was as he described—a true wonder. Black gave way to a pearly gray, then the sky caught the fire of the rising star. Bob hovered in the dark, a shadow. I ran around the boat to experience the light show from every perspective. As the mighty orb burned a hole in the horizon and made its grand appearance, Bob shielded my eyes, or the star's high energy rays would have scorched my retinas.

"Too much of a good thing, and you go blind." He pulled me deep into the shadows.

Dawn's afterimage lingered, dominating my visual field.

Bob headed belowdecks before my eyes adjusted to the dark, before I could catch the look of him, before I wanted him to leave. The day passed slowly as I waited to witness dusk on the open sea. I regretted missing such a spectacle even once. The steamship waded through cold fog. The star was a white disk; the sea rippled with unruly kinetic energy. Dusk was gray slop, and I was disappointed, forlorn. Captain Luigi and I cursed the weather together. That night, as I glimpsed Abla shining in the distance, Bob approached and gave me a bag made of soft material with a latent itch.

"It makes me scratch." A strange gift, I thought.

"Red wool," he said. "From sheep. Animals of the north, not a jungle creature."

"What is it?"

"A hoodoo medicine bag, *mojo* against whatever monster is out there in the water spooking you." He tied the *mojo* around my waist and stared out to sea.

I squinted at nothing; Abla had vanished. "What do you look at?"

"The past."

"Can you see it from here?"

"What I see is not long gone."

I widened my eyes. Sea and sky merged in smoky fog and blackness. "Tell me." Bob's face was close. The dark hid his expression as he examined me. I was more man than woman. Could he smell a rise in testosterone? "Should I beg you? Fall down and kiss your ankles?"

He scratched his neck. "Thomas, a regular on the night watch, was tormented by sea monsters, as you are. Leviathans, he called them, royal fiends from the mouth of hell. One stopped his heart right where you're standing. With his last breath, Thomas claimed that these beasties tracked sinners by the stench of their crimes. He was certain leviathans would never forget or forgive him."

"Where I stand?" Trembling, I stepped away. The cold wind was suddenly unbearable. "What great evil had Thomas done?"

Bob pulled me into the warm circle of his being. "Thomas never said. But I think, if there is a god, a heavenly father, he knows the temptations of his own creation. If he loves us as much as the preachers say, he forgives us our trespasses as we forgive those who trespass against us. Why make souls to burn in hell? God is not so wicked, or he is not God."

"You believe this, but what did Thomas believe?"

"In fallen angels, in leviathans patrolling the seas and devils walking the land. These leviathans hounded Thomas halfway 'round the world." Bob looked again into the past and shuddered. "I have keen eyes, Taiwo, but I've never seen any princes from hell riding the waves of sin, stealing souls, and fouling the waters. I too have sinned. Thomas said it was nigger luck keeping me safe." Bob shrugged. "The day before we left Dahomey, Thomas begged me to fashion a charm that very afternoon, to protect him from the princes of darkness. They were closing in to claim his tarnished soul. I repeated what I always said, *Even your god loves you*. I had no time to create a charm. *Mojo* isn't a grab bag of potpourri.

"That night I heard shrieking, a woman's voice, terrible enough to boil my blood. I thought it came from shore. Thomas's brother, Liam, made fun and said it was a banshee, warning the ship that one of us was about to die, family perhaps. Liam didn't think on his brother, but I raced around the ship and found Thomas clutching his chest on the upper deck. He pointed toward the coast and said a sea monster had bitten off the head of a woman warrior and flung her body against the rocks. The monster was coming for him next, for all sinners on board. *No*, I said. *Listen to me. Your god loves you.* Thomas was gone already. I don't know if he heard me."

I gasped at the image of that fateful night, vivid in Bob's words, unclear in my mind. Two lives the *aje* had taken. I was this *aje* still.

Bob patted my back, gently, as if I might break. "I don't know why I let you talk me into telling this ugly tale. It's not even my story."

"When you tell Thomas's saga," my voice shook, "it belongs to you and to everyone who listens."

Bob seemed embarrassed. "Keep the *mojo* safe. Hide it somewhere on yourself."

"What's inside?"

"Nine things: a broken chain, salt, goober dust from my momma's grave, an elephant's hair, sand from Death Valley, a pebble from every continent I've walked on, so three, and a rabbit's foot."

"Why a foot from a rabbit?"

"To drive evil far and keep it away. To be exact, I used the left hind foot of a rabbit shot dead with a silver bullet in a boneyard at midnight when the moon was new. It was the thirteenth of February, a Friday, and the fellow doing the deed was a cross-eyed, left-handed, redheaded, bowlegged colored man sitting astride an albino mule. That unlucky fellow is my no-good first cousin, who lies all the time, even to me."

"Sounds like Eshu rides him."

"That may be. Don't know Eshu. I do know I fixed the *mojo* hand with smoke from the ship's engine. Keep the *mojo* alive with a dab of this now and then." He handed me a little bottle of rum scented with herbs and flowers.

"Why do you give this incredible *mojo* to me? I'm a stranger to you."

"I've been watching you, trying to figure if you're one of the desperate liars pretending to be warriors to escape the war in Dahomey."

"What's wrong with escaping war?"

"Nothing." Bob took my hand. "There are people where I come from, the Navajo, who say:

I have been to the end of the earth.
I have been to the end of the waters.
I have been to the end of the sky.
I have been to the end of the mountains.
I have found none that are not my friends.

"Like *Ifa* verses." I was thrilled. "I hope to meet these Navajo someday."

"Navajo aren't *Ifa* Africans, and a poet isn't his people. Take care." Bob's sharp disapproval made me itch more than the *mojo*.

"I apologize. We write ourselves onto strangers, then see only who we've imagined."

Bob nodded, pleased by my bit of wisdom. "Folks forget themselves and become the lies other people, power people, tell on them." Had this gruesome fate befallen him?

"Kehinde worries, but we don't have to be the lies anybody tells!"

Bob snorted. "You say this and head for Chicago town to put on a savage carnival?"

I flinched. "We haven't given all of who we are away."

"You're soft-witted to believe that. They'll make what they will of us."

"No one has such power." I gripped his shoulders and shook him with the full force of my muscles. Startled, he stumbled backward. Momentum might have carried him over the railing. I leapt between his legs and gripped his waist. As his feet flew in the air, I dug in my heels, balancing him on the fulcrum of the railing. "You are a Guardian." The power of this word encouraged me. "They are invaluable to Wanderers. You hold us to life."

Bob peered into the black water below him. "You're a strange one." He laughed a little. "Guardian? OK, for Taiwo, the Wanderer, I'll do my best." He set his feet firmly on deck. He was close enough to drink my breath. "Happy?"

"Yes." Hugging Bob to my heart, I recalled why I'd wandered to this planet: for dawn on the open sea, for Bob's joy at my delight, for generous spirits and raging despair, for the woman, man, and *aje* in me roaring with desire.

Whatever else has been lost, this clarity about Wanderers has never deserted me.

"You haven't yet told me a jot of your story." Bob wagged a finger in my eyes. "What am I to guard? Who are you?"

My throat closed, and I couldn't answer. "OK. Don't trouble yourself. Tell me later."

I touched my lips briefly to his. They tasted of rum. I disappeared before he could respond. It was our way, leaving at the height of intensity, before the full light of day revealed other selves.

Roller-Coaster Ride

Klaus spoke the last words of *Chronicles* 13 like an actor so deep in a role he'd lost the here and now, and then he went silent.

"Don't stop," Marie said.

"There are more chapters." Cinnamon squirmed. "What's wrong?"

The Audi bombed down a steep incline, maybe Negley Avenue, and took a sharp left onto black ice. The wheels skidded into a three-hundred-and-sixty-degree whirligig. Mrs. Williams resisted braking, resisted spinning the tires. She turned into the skid, wore it down. Traffic on Fifth Avenue (Penn Avenue?) was mercifully sparse. Even a little snow turned hilly Pittsburgh into a disaster zone. This was a bona fide blizzard off the Great Lakes. The car spun to a halt, pointing in the right direction. Mrs. Beckenbauer sputtered a stream of German, *dumm* this, *fantastisch* that, and *mist, mist, mist.*

"You won't find a roller-coaster ride like that at Kennywood Park." Mrs. Williams exploded into laughter. "Safety inspector would close that bad boy down so fast, but suckers would still be lining up for a Boogaloo with death." Tension *exposed her nappy roots,* as Aunt Becca would say. "How y'all doing?" She glanced into the rearview mirror. Glassy eyes reflected headlights coming up from behind, slow but sure.

"Standing still is not a good idea." Cinnamon peered out the rear windshield.

Mrs. Williams shifted gears. "What'd the Playhouse put in the ginger ale?"

They sprang forward, escaping slushy drifts with a whoosh, and drove toward Oakland. Mrs. Beckenbauer shook her head. She wasn't feeling the *black* humor. Klaus and Marie squeezed closer to Cinnamon. Pathetic wipers scraped at windshields like broken wings flapping on an exhausted dragonfly. This afforded them only tunnel vision. Getting to Opal in the hospital was a real trick with snow-covered detour signs, disabled bridges, and one accident after another.

Mrs. Williams eased the Audi around a steaming truck whose nose was buried in somebody's hatchback. Two other cars had gone belly-up in snowbanks. Snowmen hugged themselves beside the wrecks. Beating their bodies for warmth, they waited for rescue that might be a long time coming. Mrs. Williams drove onto the sidewalk. Mrs. Beckenbauer bounced her head on the ceiling as they went over the curb. Back in the street, Mrs. Williams blasted windshield wiper fluid. The view got marginally better. Mrs. Beckenbauer rubbed her head.

"You three are too quiet. Story over?" Mrs. Williams yelled over the rattling heater. "I hope nobody minds music. It'll give the adrenaline something to do." She tuned the radio to an R&B station and pumped the volume on "Ain't No Sunshine When She's Gone."

"*Coincidental affinity.*" Klaus sounded too much like Sekou.

"This is like some kind of insane quest," Cinnamon muttered.

"Questing, we are questing." Marie was happy. "A night of adventure."

Klaus's cheeks were blotchy and hot. "We can drive in circles all night."

"Shit, that's it." Cinnamon wanted to punch herself. "I mean *mist.*"

"Mist?" Marie snorted. "What am I missing?"

"*Mist* means cow dung in German," Klaus explained. "*Mist* is polite word for shit."

"I don't want to get where I'm going," Cinnamon said.

"I could stay out all night." Marie's voice cracked. "My dad wouldn't care. He says I'm too mature to act foolish."

"And your mom?" Klaus's voice cracked too.

"She doesn't really count in our house."

Klaus grunted.

"At every road block and detour," Cinnamon said, "I pretend to be upset, but I'm relieved. Nobody can fool Eshu, though, master of fools and masquerades, guardian at the gate between life and death. Liar who speaks only truth, what is Eshu up to?"

Klaus and Marie shrugged.

"It's not Abla tormenting the Wanderer. It's Eshu," Cinnamon said.

"Well, that's a relief," Marie said.

"Seriously," Cinnamon said. "I know jack about reasoning with the master of fate."

"Master of fate?" Marie snorted then glanced at Klaus who looked miserable. "I'm sorry, who is that again?"

"Eshu, trickster orisha riding the Wanderer." Klaus had paid attention.

"What does that mean?" Marie sneered. "Don't act like you understand when you don't. That's not cute."

"Fine." Klaus sneered too. "She's worried about her mom, what she'll find at the hospital, that kind of fate. Don't get defensive when you don't know everything."

"What's any of that got to do with black ice?"

"Stop." Cinnamon was the calm force for once. "This isn't about *lethal weather* at the crossroads. What am I or what are you or what is anybody going to do? Eshu favors smart choices. *Who do you mean to be?* That could be a line in an Eshu praise poem."

That's good, Sis, Sekou said. A hoodoo light board operator faded him in on a ten count, right between Mrs. W and Mrs. B, who apparently didn't notice.

"Whoa." Cinnamon had never *seen* Sekou's ghost. Hunched over the gearshift, bouncing off the rearview mirror, he was backlit by a florescent orange spot. Reaching for him, Cinnamon's fingers passed through his knees, and a shock traveled up her arm. "What's up, Bro?"

Sekou's cheeks were hollow. Ribbons of light twisted in his short dreadlocks, tingeing his walnut brown hair with silver and blue. A thunderbird flapped its wings on his favorite Indian Power

T-shirt (which last Cinnamon knew was rolled up safe from Opal's purging mania under her bed). Raven had silk-screened that shirt for Sekou's sixteenth birthday. Sekou wore it the night Raven got shot, then he never wore it again, until now. The whale in the thunderbird's talon spit a stream of orange mist over the see-through fabric. Sekou's skin, bones, and organs were see-through too. He was a ghost with a still heart, flat lungs, and dusty silver bones.

Who do you mean to be? Sekou asked. *Which direction you go take?*

Cinnamon gripped Klaus's and Marie's thighs to the bone. Klaus cleared his throat. Marie twisted in her seat. Stevie Wonder's "Superstition" blared from the speakers.

> *When you believe in things that you don't understand*
> *Then you suffer*
> *Superstition ain't the way*

Sekou sang along, on the beat, off the key—not a singer really, even dead.

"Sekou's right." Cinnamon slipped her voice under Stevie Wonder's throbbing bass. "He's one of us, part of our posse."

"Uh-huh," Marie muttered.

"A brother from another planet, you know?" Cinnamon eased her death grip. "Don't get bent."

"Do we have any other options?" Klaus whispered. "I mean, do dead—" He eyed Mrs. W's and Mrs. B's bobbing heads and avoided the flashing orange between them. "Do half brothers just waltz into your conversation uninvited?"

Marie smiled at Klaus, totally in lust again. "Yes, how does this work exactly?"

Cinnamon shrugged. Maybe three folks *believing* made Sekou come in stronger. "My granddaddy said ancestors ride the wind, speaking to us. We just have to listen in."

Marie chuckled. "My grandparents tell me nonsense too. *From the old country.* Feudal Japan, practically. I haven't listened to them since forever ago."

"Granddaddy Aidan's part Seminole." That shut Marie down. Folks were more likely to believe *noble savage Indians* than *backward hoodoo Negroes*. "He says we're getting tone deaf, can't hear the spirit frequency. Hoodoo touches folks every day, but we deny it or don't notice." Out loud this sounded corny.

Knowing your own power is dangerous, Sekou said. *Most folks are fuckin' cowards and be ignoring their unadulterated awesomeness.*

"Be cool, Bro," Cinnamon said. "We got company."

The truth should have plenty fuckin' company! Sekou's lip curled. The thunderbird looked ready to take off. *Folks get stuck on stupid. Or ignore. That's the coward's way. I took it, didn't I? All the way to the last motherfuckin' stop.*

"We're company for your truth, aren't we?" Klaus said.

"Nobody's got the god's eye view," Marie said.

All right! Your crew ain't turning to zombies at sustained contact with the undead.

"Did your brother . . . How did he . . . uhm?" Klaus gestured.

Most people are cows, getting jacked up and herded into the wasteland. Mad cows.

Klaus stared at the fluorescent orange vision/mirage. "How'd you die, man? Cancer? Car crash? A bullet?" Rhetorical hollow questions. "What's the coward's way?"

I shot up a lethal dose of smack. Going down to the exit rather than cracking up and out.

Klaus furrowed his brow, blinked and blinked, as if he could make everything normal and clear again with the sweep of an eyelash.

"OK, Sekou. They can handle you, but why get mean?" Cinnamon said.

The truth is mean, not me. Sekou hit the beats with James Brown, revving up his rapper-nerd persona. *Who you see out there, fully claiming their superpowers?*

Cinnamon never called ghost Sekou on his shit for fear he'd quit haunting her, but he was being ridiculous. "We don't live in a comic book world."

"That's the truth." Marie backed her up.

"I don't know, maybe," Klaus mumbled. "The last few hours could have been frames from—"

"Don't be such a guy." Marie flipped her shiny black hair. "Even a big superhero dude with jet fuel in his veins couldn't turn the whole tidal wave of history around."

If the shit going down is so foul that even a superhero can't save us . . . Sekou's audio and visual faded a bit. Only the grin blazed bright. *We're fucked. That's why I checked out.*

"Instead of fighting back?" Cinnamon shook her braids, copying Marie. "Stupid."

"Was it?" Klaus and Sekou said in sync.

"Yes," Cinnamon and Marie replied.

Yo, dude! The girls are ganging up on us. Watch out!

"Maybe people together are like a superpower," Cinnamon said.

Papa ain't got no brand-new bag for that. Sekou hissed. *Get Mom to quit treating you like a baby. She's keeping shit from you still. Important shit.*

"What *important shit*? Tell me!"

OD'ing was my fault. Raven in the bar, my fault. It's what I believed before she said a word. She don't need to torture herself.

"Daddy getting shot wasn't your fault!"

Klaus clutched his stomach and gagged, like he'd been kicked. He doubled over.

"*Flugzeuge* zooming in your guts?" Cinnamon turned to him. "Airplanes or rockets?"

"Talk to us, Klaus," Marie said. "Use your words."

"I know about OD'ing and stuff," Klaus muttered.

Marie ground her teeth. "What stuff?"

"You mean stuff with *Vati*. Your dad?" Cinnamon said. "He didn't OD, did he?"

"Not yet." Klaus sat up and squelched a groan. "How do you know about him?"

"*Vati* does it in the garage." Cinnamon winced. "Your mom caught him."

"Yeah." Klaus's eyes were watery. *Vati* spooked him more than ghost Sekou.

Marie leaned over Cinnamon to reach him. "Your dad does drugs, really?"

"Shh!" Klaus hissed. He looked at the grown-ups.

"Don't worry." Cinnamon pointed to bobbing heads. "They're in oldie heaven."

As Martha and the Vandellas sang "Nowhere to run to, baby, nowhere to hide," another wave of pain knocked Klaus over. He gripped Cinnamon's hand. Marie joined Martha with a loud, high harmony. She belted Motown R&B like a natural.

"Where you from, girl?" Mrs. Williams shouted. "Sing it!"

"Marie's a shield," Cinnamon whispered to Klaus. "They can't hear behind her and the heater." She massaged his shoulder. "We're your Mod Squad secret society, your ghost posse. Don't be such a guy, like Marie said." She pressed harder. "I need a hammer and a chisel."

Klaus flinched away. "*Owa.* I didn't ask you to—"

"Your shoulders did." Cinnamon stroked gently. Klaus sobbed out a breath. She hesitated. He leaned into her fingers, his back begging for more. She hoped he didn't start bawling. *Nobody needs to see that!* "You done talking?" She spoke velvet tones instead of going off. "Come on, let it out."

Klaus chewed up words and tears and just about worked her last nerve.

"It figures," she muttered.

Why you pouting? Sekou said. *Don't like the dark fantasy twist?*

It figures that she'd have freaky friends with messed-up parents and lots of family drama. She snatched *The Chronicles* from Klaus's lap and, rather than confirm her dead half brother's suspicions, she started to read.

Chronicles 14: Atlantic Ocean, 1893—Warrior Dances

Captain Luigi was a seaman turned showman. In his troupe of Africans there was only one real *ahosi* warrior. Kehinde avoided the show-warriors and travelers from Europe—mostly mercenaries and cutthroats running from war-torn Dahomey. They were no different from Fon or Yoruba raiders or the Senegalese thieves in Ouidah who tried to rob and rape us. Kehinde kept to herself, stayed below, hiding her turmoil from me and everyone. I didn't want to argue over Chicago masquerades or speak of secret friends and Abla's head, so I avoided her and roamed the deck day and night.

Whenever the moon hid behind clouds or mist, Abla screamed at me, louder than the engines: "Abomination!"

"I don't believe in you." Holding up Bob's *mojo* bag, I chanted:

Homage to Eshu, the one who owns the road
Homage to Eshu, the one who holds ashe
Ashe—the power to make things be or not be!

Abla faded away then. Bob always found me, staring at empty black water, clutching his *mojo* bag, and whispering prayers to Eshu. I leaned into his warmth, and he put an arm around my cold shoulders. I gathered a collection of soft cloths from him to hold acid tears or blood from the wound that wouldn't heal. After dispatching Abla, I would shadow Bob as he prowled the ship on night watch. He spoke nonsense to restless caged beasts and passed treats through the bars. Gruff predators and hairy humanoids greeted him warmly, pressing a hand or paw through the bars. Was I one of his exotic pets? We shared the wonders of the dark.

Faint shooting stars streaked through the upper atmosphere. Beasts the size of *La Vérité* shot geysers of water at the moon and sent booming sound waves to the ocean floor. Unblinking eyes reflected the lantern light on the bridge. We climbed down a ladder once, and a behemoth drew near enough to brush against my naked foot. Its skin was sleek and cold, full of fat and brine.

"Nothing to fear," Bob said. "Whales heading north."

"Will the water turn hard?" I asked. "How will they manage?"

"They don't mind a bit of ice," he replied. "It's the steamship crashing you should worry about. *La Vérité* on ice."

One afternoon, when the bones in our ears had made peace with the rolling deck, Kehinde rehearsed warrior *ahosi* moves for the masquerade in Chicago town. Spellbound sailors and cutthroats crowded the railings as she stabbed shadow hearts and severed phantom heads. Squatting in a thick circle of rope, I grunted at her easy conquests. Kehinde thrust a cutlass at me. The blade burned my fingers, and I dropped it quickly. Kehinde swung her blade at my head, and I dodged, rolling over the feet of squealing spectators. Kehinde's blade sliced through the rope down to the filthy deck. With her free hand, she retrieved the weapon I disdained, twisted her hips, and let momentum carry her my direction— beautiful and deadly. I leapt around sweaty smokestacks and over yawl boats covered by rotten canvas. I slipped past caged animals who shivered and roared. Finally I flicked my fingers at our audience and stood still as an ancient iroko. Kehinde lunged. One blade halted at my heart; the other touched my cheek and drew a line of blood. A few in the crowd applauded. Horror and revulsion were easy to read on other faces. No one had ever looked disgusted watching the sailors engage in fisticuffs or wrestling.

"Is this who you fight for now?" I spoke Yoruba and pushed her cutlass aside. "You renounced your king for them?"

"I fight for one hundred francs. For the days of freedom the money will buy."

"Why rehearse what you want to leave behind?"

"Tell me what is wrong. What pains you still?"

Trembling and suddenly dizzy, I turned away.

"Is it Abla?" Kehinde's weapons clattered against the deck. She stepped closer. Waves of her heat lapped over me. "We swore an oath to each other."

"You don't understand." I should have talked about Abla. "I've forgotten so much."

"Nothing can be forgotten," Kehinde said. "It can only be hidden."

I stomped away from her and bumped into a sailor who wouldn't let me pass.

"What are you doing?" Bob grimaced. Bright starlight hurt his eyes.

"Why are you here?" I said. "It's afternoon."

"Liam said I had to see your . . . friend. Told me she's the real thing, not one of Luigi's con games. An honest to god Amazon." He grabbed my arm. "They think we're savages."

"We? You're not one of us. You don't make sense."

"Why perform this shameless display?" Somehow our warrior moves hurt him.

"I don't wish to fight for this or any audience," I whispered.

Bob was the friend who wandered dark, sleepless nights and disappeared at dawn. A familiar shadow, a welcome scent on the wind, I thought of him more as a creature of my mind than as a being in his own reality. Bob in full daylight was a revelation. He had blue/green eyes, like the Jesus orisha, and wasn't as pale as the other sailors who worked in daylight up on deck. His skin was the color of the beach near Ouidah. Pepper red hair curled close against his scalp. Splotches of darker pigment were splattered across his cheeks and arms, perhaps his whole body. He was a handsome man, appealing in so many ways. Later I would learn he shunned not light, but hostile eyes, curious about his spots. I touched a curved moon shape on his forearm and steadied myself. Men who looked like him had waged war on Dahomey with Colonel Alfred-Amedée Dodds. Perhaps Bob was a Senegalese fighting man and enemy of Dahomey. How could an enemy be a friend?

"Is Senegal your home?" I asked.

"No!" He was insulted. "I'm not African. America is my home. Chicago." He nodded at Kehinde as if we shared a secret about her. "The sailors want to wrestle her to the ground." Tears spilled across his splotchy cheeks. He caught my hand before I touched his face, and when Captain Luigi burst through a cabin door, Bob held my hand between us where Luigi couldn't see.

"Why are you so ashamed of us?" I asked. Bob dropped my hand.

Kehinde stood on guard, weapons ready.

"I don't need any more warrior lessons!" I disappeared into the bowels of the ship, escaping them both.

The warren of tight corridors belowdecks was hot and close. The engineer cursed his ornery boilers and didn't notice me lurking about. Trimmers lugged coal into the engine room from the bunkers. Soot-and grease-covered stokers heaved coal into the wide-mouthed furnaces. The fire required constant feeding. Many more dark men sweated in the fire's glow than roamed the dawn working the upper decks. When I grabbed a shovel, they made a space in their routine without comment. Above us, Kehinde stomped the last of her warrior moves. I wanted to run to her and beg for the past we'd left behind, instead I tossed heavy loads of coal until trembling muscles gave out at the end of the shift. The stokers thanked me with a bottle of rum. Kehinde was asleep when I returned to our narrow berths. I poured the alcohol into the sea to spite her or taunt Abla—I'm not sure which.

Chronicles 15: Atlantic Ocean, 1893—the Color of Love

And so it was. Each day, rather than tell Kehinde about Abla's head or the *aje* twinges that plagued me, I antagonized her. We fought over Bob, over everything, even the color of water. I insisted the ocean's blue depended on starlight caught by the sky. Kehinde said the algae, fish, and runoff determined the color.

Pointing at streaks of green and brown cutting across azure blue waves, I said, "At night these variations are swallowed in black."

"Nothing has color at night." She stormed away.

"You don't want to admit your error," I yelled at her back. "Water is colorless. Let it run through your fingers. What color do you see but your own?"

She halted. "Exactly! Blue sky will not turn a muddy river clear."

What did this matter? I wanted to ask her why Abla haunted me or why Bob from Chicago fascinated me, but instead I said, "You love ignorance."

"You warp your thoughts into knots." She jogged along the railing. Sailors jumped out of her way. "You're too much of a coward to tell me the truth."

"Who lied us onto this boat? What great journey is this? We float in the middle of nowhere! You might as well have left my body in the market at Ouidah or plunged a cutlass through my heart. Swift death is better than such a mangled life."

She tripped at my cruelty and limped away. Her broken stride almost undid me. What if Brother-Taiwo haunted her as Abla haunted me? The wound at my side throbbed. Love was a poison drip burning my vital organs.

Melinga rescued us. She ate and slept and shat. That was the rhythm of my hours. Somso always wept as the child nursed. The greedy mouth and fingers tugging at her nipples, fat feet kicking her ribs with joy, did this call Husband-Taiwo to mind? Leaving home for a blank future with a helpless daughter of Africa weighed on her spirit. Somso was content to pass Melinga to me. In full daylight, while Kehinde entertained bored sailors and mercenaries with death blows, I transformed into a seagoing creature, a gentle side to my *aje*. Melinga was untroubled by my fearsome countenance. Somso offered meager protest as I dove with the child into frothy waves. Nobody expected to see an *aje* with a baby in its talons. We were mist-phantoms playing tricks on their eyes.

Curious creatures, smaller than the behemoths of the night, gamboled behind our ship. Screw propellers churned up bewildered fish from the depths. These air-breathing beasts enjoyed an easy feast followed by exploration and play. They clothed us in spirals of bubbles and sang high-pitched odes. Melinga cooed harmony to their clicks and whistles. We leapt high in the air together. After wondrous frolicking, Melinga's ravenous weeping signaled the end of our jaunts. She was hungry most of the time, so I never swam far from Somso. Melinga's hunger kept me close to human.

"*Ora na-azu nwa*," Somso said these Igbo wise words again and again as Melinga nursed. "A community raises the child. What people do I have?" She wept.

"My niece drinks too many of your tears." Kehinde couldn't abide crying. "The Fon stole me away from everyone. Are Taiwo and I not your people? Be grateful."

"Is your husband dead?" Somso said.

"No. My brother, my twin died in my arms. I have no husband."

"You chose a demon companion. I didn't. Don't lecture me."

"You chose Abla who would have murdered us."

"What choice with a cutlass at my head and a knife at my belly?"

"You said there is always a choice. No one forgets the taste of loyalty."

Somso brooded. She would spend the day finding a proper retort. I was glad for their spats. Except for fighting Kehinde, Somso was listless. She ate little, and her milk was the fat of her body, melting away. A pain settled around her lungs. After a few spoken words, a dry cough would consume her. Blood coated her tongue. She too feared for her daughter, who must drink tainted milk and breathe spoiled breath.

"You're so full of life, demon," Somso said between spasms. "Why can't you heal me?"

I searched for invading creatures, a magnetic imbalance, the wrong smell in her urine, but found no sign of what plagued her.

"She doesn't get better," Kehinde remarked one chill evening. The north wind had routed travelers and sailors who took refuge in warm bunks. We had the sky and water to ourselves. The home star lay half under the sea and sprayed fiery streaks across the horizon. At last I experienced a dusk worthy of the dawns I had witnessed.

"How can I heal Somso," I complained, "if she won't tell me what is wrong?"

"You are the healer." Kehinde sighed. "She is my brother's wife."

"That makes her swallow hurt and nurse despair?"

"Yes. A diviner doesn't rudely ask what grave problem a person wishes to solve. Who shares torment with a stranger? The diviner consults *Odu Ifa* and speaks the verses. Using the insights of the ancestors a wise *Babalawo* clears confusion and offers people their own solution."

"Yes, *Ifa* says, *Initiate yourself again by using your wisdom and intelligence.*"

"What troubles you, Taiwo?"

"Nothing," I lied, ashamed of my fears and infirmities. "What troubles you?"

Kehinde pointed at a fat moon, low and orange on the horizon. Its reflection bounced in black water. "Does the moon, and the sun also, act differently in the sky here?" Red light streaked a purple storm cloud. Evening stars glittered underneath. "Does everything change as we steam north? Will the stars be different too?"

"The night, full of sparkling crystal beads and a carved ivory orb, is still a crown for the sea."

Kehinde touched my cheek. "The sea is a queen," she said. "*Mère d'eau*, Yemoja, a generous orisha whose name is really *yeye emo eja*, the mother whose children are like fishes. Yemoja changes her gown and headdress for the cold north."

I kissed Kehinde's fingers, enjoying the poetry of her mouth, of her sweat. She didn't resist. I took her other hand and twirled her. She spun several times before leaning her back against my heart. We laced fingers across her stomach. I pressed my nose and lips against swirls of hair that trailed from the nape of her neck down to her back. Magnetic spikes rippled from nerves just under her skin and were echoed in my energy field. The smell of her skin in salty sea air made my mouth water. Licking a bit of her onto my tongue, the blood pressure in the backs of my knees, fingertips, and groin spiked. Kehinde's sweet taste had changed. I was hungry to know why, but couldn't think what questions to ask. Holding her close I was dizzy and happy, flushed with the heat of desire. She was still my Kehinde, and I couldn't remember why we fought.

The star slid completely below the sea. Clouds fifty miles high, invisible by day, caught rays on their fluffy bellies and glowed bluish white. Kehinde rubbed her buttocks against my pubis bones. I traced patterns on her belly, grazing her breasts. Her nipples were hard and erect, like Somso's after nursing. We lingered in this embrace, slow dancing to the music on our breath. This was not a warrior's dance of death, but I whispered, "My head belongs to you."

Bright falling stars landed in the sea near the ship, burning and hissing in cold water. Abla did not dare show her murdered face, and I wondered if love was also *mojo* against night terrors.

"Take care," Kehinde said. "I don't know how to love."

Contact Improvisation

Chronicles 15 stopped at a meteor shower, like an old Hollywood cutaway to a roaring fire or billowing curtains. The Wanderer's words were a story storm taking over Cinnamon's mouth. *Hard nipples* and *pubis bones* made her want to melt into the posh leather seat.

Hunched over the brakes, Sekou sighed. *Frau Beckenbauer looks like zombies are about to attack.* He stroked a bear claw necklace that Aidan had given him. Was that under her bed too? Cinnamon had to quit being a chicken-shit and look through Sekou's secret stash.

"Verdammt, Vati wird uns umbringen." Mrs. Beckenbauer tapped her frosted window.

"What'd she say about *Vati*?" Cinnamon asked.

"My dad's going to kill us." Klaus still looked sick and pale.

A safety pin gave out, and Cinnamon's *mojo* bag, eagle feather, and mosaic bead burst through her shirt. *"Mist!"* She fumbled to put herself back together.

Marie pointed. "What is all that?"

"Mojo from my grandparents." Cinnamon got it hidden away. "Nine power things in the bag. Nine is a hoodoo number."

Marie slugged Klaus. "Is that cool or what?"

Klaus shrugged.

A plow blocked the road. Mrs. Williams turned down a snowy side street going 13 mph as "Walk on By" blared from the speakers.

"Talking's a cure. Singing's hoodoo too." Cinnamon surreptitiously nodded at Klaus's trembling lips. Sweaty wisps of hair curled in his eyes.

"I love this song." Marie sang along with Dionne Warwick.

"They were singing these songs before we were born. Isn't that wild?" Cinnamon stroked a strand out of his face. She did this when Sekou hid in his dreads. Klaus's silver blond hair was too flimsy for any real shielding. He jerked away as she brushed his forehead. Guys were black holes for attention sometimes.

"Close your eyes," Cinnamon said. "Trust me. Do it."

After a second he squeezed his eyes shut and let her pet him, long strokes, fingertips pressing into his scalp. Marie sang greatest hits with Mary Wells, the Temptations, and Patti LaBelle. She was all over the Staple Singers with *I know a place, ain't nobody crying, ain't nobody worried . . .*

"I'll Take You There" broke Klaus open. He whispered, "*Vati* won't stop."

Sekou leaned in close and whispered too, *Maybe he can't stop, Bro.*

"I'm not sure what he's shooting. Junk he cooked up? He's a biomedical chemist. Whatever, it's bad, and after overtime in the lab, he gets ugly. It's awful. I, uhm, wow, you know, I hate him sometimes."

Naw, you don't hate him. Sekou was gentle. *You just want to.*

"Tonight, he'll be crazy angry when we get home. He'll yell shitty things in English. *Mutti* wants me to translate. I say it's too hard, but she's not stupid."

How can you tell her? Sekou put a hand on Klaus's shoulder.

Icky images of *Vati* stormed Cinnamon. *Cock-sucking whore, you don't fucking fool me. I know where your mouth's been.* Cinnamon threw up shields. Sekou blazed a bit brighter, helping out.

Marie dropped out of R&B land and shook Klaus's knee. "What?"

"Out of a mosquito he is making an elephant." Klaus's Euro-chic accent was getting thick. "*Vati* takes all out on *Mutti*."

Cinnamon noted a bruise on Mrs. B's cheek, not totally hidden by hair or makeup. One eye was puffy. That fight happened tonight, before the audition. *Vati* whales on them in the garage; Cinnamon had seen him do it. She touched Klaus's stomach, wishing she could pull pain and throw it to the wind like Miz Redwood.

Klaus's eyes popped open. He stared down at her fingers and sighed.

"*Mutti* does nothing bad, nothing against him, nothing at all. *I wish I were with someone else,* she yelled tonight. And *Vati* . . ." Klaus's hands flopped around. "*Vati* is insisting she has some other guy. She, she . . ."

"Don't be embarrassed about your parents being sexual animals," Marie said.

"I'm not," Klaus said, but he was. "I'm not."

It's cool, Bro. Sekou punched his shoulder. *Nobody wants to think about their folks boning other people.*

"*Vati* flips out thinking *Mutti* likes boning some other guy. Nobody'd blame her. *Vati* is a total psycho nutcase. Where is this other guy? *Who* is he? *Mutti's* English sucks, and nobody does German. Nobody likes German. We're Nazis, you know, Jew killers."

"Nazis offed gypsies and homosexuals too," Marie said.

Whoa. Sekou beamed a weapons-grade sneer at her. *That's not very helpful.*

Klaus's shoulders seized up. "Yes, those people also."

"Stop that." Cinnamon shook this new tension out of him.

It's a theme. Japan raped Nanking. Zulus took out the San and Khoi people. White Americans did their best to eradicate Indians. Black Buffalo Soldiers were their scouts!

"OK. We get the theme," Cinnamon said.

"I hate people calling up the worst examples and claiming that's human nature." Marie was fuming. *So why'd she go on about Nazis?*

"Sekou's talking history, not nature, OK?" Cinnamon swept her hand over Sekou's ghost lips. "He hates people with *amnesia infirmity.*" She turned to Klaus. "So your mom's not the most popular girl in town, but somebody still might like her, even if—"

"*Vati* tracks her every move, following her without telling her he's there."

He spies on her! Sekou scrutinized Mrs. B. *No way!*

"He shows up in the grocery store, at the doctor's office. He could have been at the Playhouse tonight, lurking on a landing."

Marie froze. "Does he look like you only—"

"He needs help." Cinnamon cut Marie off before she said she'd seen *Vati*.

Klaus nodded. "He scares away anybody speaking German. She's in a German lit class at Pitt. *Vati* told me nobody talks to her except the professor lady. He sounded proud. Other than Pitt, she's home, being a good *Hausfrau*."

"I bet *Vati* doesn't know everything about her," Marie said. "Maybe you neither."

"*Vati* should split," Cinnamon said. "Why doesn't *Mutti* ditch him?"

Marie grunted. "Haven't you lost your mind over some hunk and made a total fool of yourself?"

"Actually I haven't," Cinnamon said. Why bother with love? Who'd ever want her?

"Wait. You'll see." Marie was so certain.

Sekou laughed. *Jaded Marie—the voice of experience.*

"Solid jade, that's me." Sekou's scorn rolled right off Marie.

"What the fuck am I supposed to do?" Klaus said.

"Survive," Marie said.

TURN HIS ASS IN—Cinnamon wanted to yell this. If she'd turned Sekou in maybe he wouldn't be haunting them. Maybe he'd still be alive.

"*Vati* almost, you know, we found him three times. Three! Like Sekou."

Naw. Sekou's thunderbird spit out a dead whale that dissolved into sparkling dust. *I wasn't playing around like your* Vati. *I went the whole way out.*

The fluorescent light in the mirror turned the corner behind them and disappeared. Fast, like a blackout, the ghost light show was over.

"Sekou's gone." Klaus looked out the back.

Marie touched her ears. "When he's here, it's like a buzzing, a rustling. That stopped."

"You're right," Cinnamon said. She never won an argument with her brother, even when he was dead, dead wrong.

"He'll be back." Marie was psyched by this prospect.

"We're a secret posse riding the *Geisterbahn,* spirit railway." Klaus tried for a smile. He and Marie gripped hands in Cinnamon's lap.

"On the ghost train. Questing, we're questing." Marie sang these words in a melancholic harmony to Smokey Robinson:

But ain't too much sadder than the tears of a clown.

Cinnamon quashed a wave of jealousy. She wasn't crushed on Klaus or Marie, right? Hopelessly crushed on two people would be stupid. She didn't believe in lust at first sight, except . . . Ariel had materialized in the Playhouse lobby and made her warm inside. Cinnamon could lose her mind over Ariel easy. Wild eyes, feline grace, thunderbird moves, Ariel believed in her and her whole posse. Ariel was probably too cute and too old, still Lexy went for jailbait Sekou. But nobody ever fell in lust with Cinnamon at first sight—too dark, too big, too smart . . . What about lust after contact improv? *The center of gravity is an erotic power zone.*

Her mouth went dry, and her cheeks burned. Hanging with Klaus and Marie was a contact improv intensive. Defying gravity, spinning through the air was tricky. *If you don't trust each other, everybody will fall flat on their asses.* Star Deer was always saying obvious shit like that. *Hear it once, forget it never* meant a lot of noise in Cinnamon's head. Star had promised to teach Cinnamon to walk a tightrope. *Bodies in motion, in flight, always a beautiful thing. Trust that.*

Streetlight bounced off snow and turned the road garish pink. Marie's teeth chattered; Klaus was dripping sweat. They looked ghoulish, cute in a horror movie way. Cinnamon let her hand drop on top of theirs, and they laced their fingers through hers. Electricity shot up and down Cinnamon. No denying it—she was crushed on three people. Damn. She finally got a hint of what all the fuss was about. The Four Tops were *standing in the shadows of love, getting ready for the heartaches to come.*

"I'm sorry." Klaus acted as solemn as a funeral director. "For flipping out on Sekou, on you guys too. Did I drive him away? Talking about OD'ing?"

"When did you flip out? I missed it," Marie said.

Cinnamon smiled. "Hey, Marie, I think you are right where you should be."

"Really?" Marie's face broke on a sneer she couldn't commit to.

"Yeah, Cinnamon's right," Klaus said.

The three leaned together, bumped foreheads, then swished hair into a tangle on account of Cinnamon's heavy beads. Unbraiding themselves, they giggled.

"You hanging on back there?" Mrs. Williams shouted. Wild eyes darted from the windshield to the mirror. "Hmm?" She turned down the music.

Mrs. Beckenbauer spewed loud German including several *Vati*s. She ended with *Verdammt!* Klaus answered in louder German. They argued. He threw in *Geisterbahn*.

"I have to go slow. Sorry," Mrs. Williams yelled. "We're a bad accident waiting to happen."

"Tomorrow this will all be funny." Cinnamon sounded like death working the Hallmark Cards shift.

"This is one of my favorites." Mrs. Williams ratcheted the volume up on an unfamiliar tune.

"Why don't we read some more?" Cinnamon whispered.

"I'll read this time." Marie snatched *The Chronicles* from Klaus's lap.

Chronicles 16: Atlantic Ocean, 1893—Dragon Slayer

Fallen stars, dead to the world, sank below the water's surface. Kehinde and I danced to our private rhythm on the rolling deck. Screw propellers and stately pistons added throbbing counter rhythms. Despite a bewildering cascade of electrical surges along my nerves, I didn't falter. My hand traced pleasure from the small of her back to between her thighs. Our limbs twisted and tangled until we made a braid of our bodies. Everywhere was delicious, but my tongue lingered on salty, smoky spots that made her sing.

"Take care," Kehinde said. "I don't know how to love."

"You do well with love," I said, savoring our connection.

"No, I have done terrible things," Kehinde whispered. "You make me remember."

"What are we without memories? Tell me your story." She hesitated. I kissed the scar on her throat and drew my tongue down along the bones between her breasts, nibbling at her navel. "Tell me, please. Your stories fill my empty spaces."

She stroked the nape of my neck. "Yao brought in a defiant woman. I liked her immediately. She had refused marriage to a rich man who beat his wives bloody. Yao thought she'd make a good assassin/spy. But she didn't want a warrior life and told me her escape plan. The next day, I betrayed her to Abla—to gain Abla's trust. I thought punishment would be a beating, no food, watchful eyes, but Abla made her part of the gate-opening force—warriors who lead an attack, the first to die." Kehinde blinked rapidly. "I can't recall her name or even her face."

"You share hard stories. Isn't that love?" I kissed her.

Two sailors beginning their late shift walked from the shadow of a yawl boat. One carried a lantern. He held the flame up for a better view. Kehinde pulled away from me.

"What difference do their eyes make?" I said.

"This you say, when you won't practice warrior moves in front of greedy eyes."

"It's Bob." I waved at Bob and another man from the night watch, a pale, brawny fellow with colorful tattoos on sunburnt arms. "You met Bob, when you challenged me to fight on deck. He disapproves of our show. Bob is a friend of sleepless nights."

Bob stepped back from Kehinde's wrath and raised his hands in submission.

Kehinde eyed him. "Only what you fight for will last."

"Are you jealous?" I enjoyed this spicy emotion rolling off of her.

"Should I be?"

After a rapid exchange of unintelligible English with Bob, the other sailor came toward us, curious, unafraid. Bob lowered his hands slowly. "Liam and I aren't armed."

Kehinde approached the tattooed man. "Englishman," she said, appreciating his brave spirit, "what can you say for the moon tonight?"

Liam barely glanced at the sky. The moon was overhead and smaller now. The orange hue had been abandoned at the horizon. "I'm Irish, milady," he said. "And the moon's a dim beauty compared to—"

Kehinde waved the knife at his neck and sauntered around the kitchen smokestack.

"You're lucky. Knives are messy work." I gestured at the Irishman's head. "Kehinde is in good spirits." So was I.

He clutched his neck and chuckled. "Yeah."

"Liam likes to play with fire," Bob said.

"That I do." Liam circled me.

"Liam? Thomas's brother?" Thomas whose heart I'd stopped from beating.

"Yes, Liam who never fears getting burnt." Bob's voice was a djembe drum of pleasure. "Why, Liam O'Rourke is so brave, he'd fly into the sun."

"Not a creature of the dark like you." I motioned at the lantern. "Liam O'Rourke carries fire with him."

"Kehinde is a volcano of a woman." Liam was in love.

Many sailors appreciated Somso's heavy breasts, moon face, and round buttocks. They turned to babes again, longing for the milk that flooded down the sack dress. These same men avoided Kehinde or noted her muscles and scars with discomfort. They ignored me. Captain Luigi forbade the crew from bothering royal performers. We were precious cargo, like the caged beasts, and not to be teased. No such sanction restrained us from engaging the sailors.

"Finish your praise song to the moon," I said. "I'll tell Kehinde your words."

Liam circled closer and leaned over the railing to watch the mist roll in. I stepped close to Liam and touched one of his tattoos. He flinched, but tolerated the curiosity in my fingers.

"Did you paint these adventures on your skin?" I said. "Is this part of your story?"

Liam held the lantern over arms and chest to illuminate his splendor. A blue demon slithered around his upper arm and spit fire at his neck. The demon had a scaly hide, craggy black belly, and long green tongue. People and animals raced away from the demon's gouts of fire into a forest that covered his chest and stomach. On the other arm, a similar demon coiled around a pale woman whose yellow hair framed full breasts. Her thick tresses were about to catch fire, but she was laughing. Blood or fire stained the yellow beard of a pale man who brandished a silver sword over the demon's head.

"Are you the brave slayer of demons?" I asked.

"Do I look like a dragon slayer to you?" He spoke to Bob.

"Who is this woman laughing in the face of death?" I asked. "Did you save her? Or did she have a secret weapon and that's why she laughs? Tell me."

Liam grinned. "You want to hear *my* story?" Did everything amuse him? "I'm nobody, your highness." Perhaps he made fun of me, but it seemed good-natured. "Nobody worth storying about, that's for sure." Bob had said something similar.

"In English, I have only read *A Tale of Two Cities, Frankenstein,* and *A Connecticut Yankee in King Arthur's Court,*" I said, forgetting *Sense and Sensibility.* "Why don't you tell me Nobody's story?"

Liam raised bushy eyebrows. "Bob told me you were an earnest one." He inspected me, as if he wanted to peel away clothes and skin to explore muscles, bones, and organs. "He didn't say you read books."

"For a story, I prefer a voice. I like seeing the body of a story or smelling sweat and electricity in the air. That is superior to dry words on thin paper."

"Just different," Bob murmured. "Reading gives you the keys to the kingdom."

"The biggest gun, the longest bayonet—these are the keys to the kingdoms that I have seen." Silence settled around us, bitter and cold as the mist. I sang a sea beast trill. Bob and Liam were delighted by my faithful imitation. The mood thus sweetened, I tried human language again. "Bob tells me nothing, Liam. He hoards his story. Please, tell me yours."

"It's Liam, is it, and not Mr. O'Rourke?"

I poked Liam's demon. "You tell me which it is." I've met few people who can resist an audience eager for their story, and those people, I don't remember well. Liam spoke too fast of things and places I couldn't imagine, but impressed himself in my memory. He had the strong smell of a young man, but wind and starlight had cut lines in his face. Hard labor had taxed his joints. Ship's food and rum had ruined his organs. The stories he told had marked him too. He had farmed unforgiving land only to eat dirt; he labored in coal mines to breathe poison dust; he worked shipyards to be beaten and robbed. The women he loved cheated him blind. He was not Fortune's friend. Kehinde hid in the shadow of the kitchen smokestack, listening to Liam's stories too. She understood and enjoyed what escaped me.

Liam slowed for his last few lines. "The dragons push back the invaders who have stolen the land from the rightful king, that bearded fellow on my right arm. The woman warrior is a witch, and she loves the dragons who fight for her and her king. I'm no dragon slayer, milady, but the dumb ass usually trampled in these high and mighty wars." He laughed at my wide eyes. "So I took to sea. I wanted to see the whole world, meet all the peoples, stand in the wild places with savages, warrior women, and wild beasties. I had to see the *maamajomboo* for myself. I have done this."

I was enchanted. "You are a Wanderer. We are alike."

This startled him. "Are you man or woman?" Liam reached for me.

Bob foiled his clumsy attempt to grope my crotch. "What's wrong with you?"

"It's an honest question." Saliva sprayed from Liam's mouth. "Afraid to answer?" In the flickering lantern light he had the savage look of a warrior or beast about to pounce.

"What difference does it make to you?" At that moment, standing close to Bob, I was more man than woman, but standing with Kehinde I'd been more woman. This was a poor answer. What would Liam understand? Bob glanced at me shamefaced. He'd groped me too when first we met. Was this the custom of Northern men?

"Eshu rides the Wanderer." Kehinde was at my side. She made the knife gesture above my head. "Eshu is the first and last born, old soul and newborn. Eshu opens the gates of possibilities. Much ashe—the power to make things be or not be."

"What about you, madame? Who rides you?" Liam dropped the lantern and moved to challenge Kehinde also—to show her breasts, perhaps.

Bob blocked this imprudent effort. Abandoning me, Kehinde leapt around Bob and put her blade at Liam's neck before either man could react. Liam was impressed by her speed and skill and foolishly attracted by her martial spirit. He licked his lips, confident that his brawn was a match for her skill. He wanted to wrestle her to the ground.

"Get out of here." Bob eased Liam away from Kehinde's blade.

"Captain will have your hide on a stretcher." He shoved Liam toward a door that led below.

Liam banged his hand through the rotten wood of a yawl boat's hull—a poor rescue vehicle. He sucked splinters from his flesh. His jumbled emotions were impossible to decipher. Bob braced for a battle he'd rather avoid.

"Taiwo won't fight you for fear of ending your story." Kehinde's knife glinted. "I'm not bound by this concern." She gestured at Bob. "He throws his spear with us. You're outnumbered, Irishman. Is this the day you taste death and greet your ancestors?"

"I meant no offense, milady." Liam bowed, snatched up his light, and trotted off.

Kehinde continued in English for Bob's sake. "Liam believes he's a dragon master who has not gotten his due. He thinks we should bend to a common man's will. Men in Ouidah looked at us the same way—men from everywhere. Is that what you all want?"

Bob shrugged. Kehinde looked to me for an answer as well. How would I know?

"My head belongs to me, not to king or husband." Kehinde tucked her knife away. "I've sworn an oath to my brother and the Wanderer. There is no one else." She stomped off.

I snatched Bob's hand and stole a bit of heat. The cold sea breezes cut through me too easily. "Do you throw your spear with us, against your dear Liam as Kehinde claimed?"

"Liam's not a bad sort." Bob slipped away from me. He crammed the hole in the lifeboat's belly with wood and canvas. He slathered foul-smelling pitch on the wound. "Someone's put him up to foolishness."

"Kehinde is not fire he should play with." I thought of Dr. Pierre. "She'll take his head if he goes too far."

"Liam's never been good at reckoning distance."

"Is he an old friend?"

"I met Liam in Chicago, where the Fair is."

"But are you his friend?"

"Liam is a street fighter. Chicago is a violent town. Don't go trusting strangers there. Don't go talking to strange men in the night like you do on this ship."

"This is how I met you."

"Chicago is the Wild West still. Everyone carries a gun. Hear what I say?"

"I threw my Lebel rifle away. I'm still very dangerous. *Aje* don't need a gun."

He talked over me. "Wild characters in Chicago—they won't know what to make of bold ones, such as yourselves."

"Are we bold?" I liked this word.

"I don't know how to say this other than plain. You're a knife in their heads."

"Yes." I made the Eshu gesture, a blade, a feather rising from my head. "A monster in the sea, a devil on land. I eat bullets and belch flame."

"Don't joke around. I'm serious. Men like Luigi, even Liam, they mock you and despise you and want to use you."

"Are they so different from you?"

"Don't you know anything? They smile for the profit you'll bring them, but they mean you harm, and there's no good end to that." He wasn't making sense.

"I'm not afraid."

"You should be."

"Why embrace fear?"

"Fear can lead to wisdom, caution. This isn't your world anymore!"

"America will be a new world."

"First there's France."

"Do you like France? Are the warrior women bold there? Do Frenchmen wish to wrestle them to the ground? Is it the Wild West?"

He shook his head at me. "French ladies are sweet. The men there make love with their faces so the ladies are happy to see one such as me come to shore." He laughed, a hollow sound. "What am I going on about?"

"I'm not sure," I admitted, thinking how I could make love with my face, wondering if Kehinde would like this. "Is it women you want in France? Or a man?"

Bob's nostril's flared, and many facial muscles went slack.

A beast roared from its smelly cell. Bob hauled me along his night watch. My question hung over our heads like a rusty cutlass. Bob wanted a man and a woman. This tormented him. Feeding his beloved pets, he was incautious. One hairy creature gripped his arm and wouldn't let go. The animal mewed and blubbered, a sad story. Bob listened patiently, and when the animal gestured to the stars and pounded the deck, Bob slipped from its grasp. Dawn was upon us; time to part. He drew me into the dark before I burned my eyes gawking at the rising star.

"Don't ask anybody else what you asked me. Sailors take advantage," he whispered. "Don't repeat any of our conversation." He clutched my hand then touched his lips to mine. "Do you understand me?"

"Yes," I lied—a bad habit now. "Yes."

Homeless Eshu

"We're almost at the hospital. Hallelujah!" Mrs. Williams hollered.

"Already?" Cinnamon held back a groan.

Mumbling the last *Chronicles* lines, Marie held up a drawing. Bright flashes made her squint. Ocean spray caught on Klaus's long eyelashes and trickled down his cheeks. Cinnamon wrinkled her nose at a dirty diaper smell. The moving-picture drawings captured every sense.

Taiwo, sporting pearly gray skin and a sharp dorsal fin, held Melinga above the waves. They surfed to a beat-up steamship. LA VÉRITÉ was painted on the prow, *Truth* in French. Taiwo transformed back and forth from grinning sea mammal to grim *aje*. Melinga nestled against a fin and then a claw. They landed on *La Vérité* and the video-drawing went still. Amazon Taiwo cradled Melinga. A red feather was tucked in Taiwo's crown of braids; a beaded bracelet dangled from a wrist. Melinga sucked Bob's *mojo* bag. Raven had done a painting like this of Star Deer holding baby Cinnamon. Beside Taiwo Kehinde brandished a cutlass. Beads circled her waist, ankles, and forearms. Somso leaned against a smokestack that stank of cooking oil. Akan fabric was draped over full breasts, belly, and hips. Her hair was a spiderweb of braids and metal trinkets. Unfamiliar Adinkra designs decorated the fabric and her cheeks.

Two sailors slouched in front of animal cages: brown-skinned, curly-headed Bob and pale, tattooed Liam. The tattoos were Polynesian. The dragon was about to fly off of Liam's arm. A lion nosed Bob's back. The men's faces were as unreadable as the Akan fabric. They looked with Somso toward a port framed by tall buildings and crammed with ocean liners, tugboats, and pleasure vessels. Sunlight blazed through stained-glass windows. Factories belched metallic smoke. The stench of industry mixed with salt air and steamship smoke. A severed head bobbed in scum lapping against the wharf: Abla. Her eyes were starfishes, her teeth from a shark's mouth. The whimsical, surreal style was unmistakably Raven's. Books let dead people talk from the grave. Books and drawings let you talk from a coma too.

"Bob likes men and women. Taiwo's perfect for him." Marie sounded excited.

"What about Kehinde and Taiwo?" Klaus was troubled. "Kehinde's jealous."

"I bet I know who did the illustrations," Cinnamon said.

"A primitive style," Marie said. "Like Gauguin or Picasso."

"Yeah." Klaus deferred to her.

"Primitive?" Cinnamon channeled Raven. "As if people of color artists were so stupid, style dropped from their fingers bypassing their brains. No. This is like Lois Mailou Jones or Chagall. Visionaries." Raven's and Sekou's favorites.

Marie cocked her head. "Chagall, yeah, for sure. I don't know Lois Jones."

"Me neither," Klaus added.

"I'll show you her stuff and my dad's," Cinnamon said. "Opal hid some, burned some."

Minnie Riperton hit notes higher than the stratosphere: *It is real if it is only in your mind.*

Marie stroked the drawing. The image shocked her fingers. "Freaky. This whole night, I mean ghosts and aliens—"

Klaus held a finger to her lips. *"Ifa says, Initiate yourself again by using your wisdom and intelligence."*

"Right." Marie thrust *The Chronicles* into the orca's mouth, zero resistance.

Mrs. Williams turned off the radio and made a wide, slow turn off Fifth Avenue. The University Hospital loomed up, a ghostly galleon barely visible in a sea of snow. Actually, it resembled a medieval fortress more than a ship. Klaus cracked a steamy window and leaned his hot face into the draft. The ground entrance glowed, pool blue mixed with a sick green. Emergency vehicles screamed as they came and went, fishtailing in black slush.

"We're finally here." Cinnamon was miserable. Knowing wasn't going to be better.

Marie petted Cinnamon's head. Klaus squeezed her hand. Mrs. Williams slammed on the brakes. The Audi skidded across an empty parking lot and halted nose to nose with a rusty shopping cart of African statues, cloth, and jewelry peeking out of crumpled newspaper. Ferocious creatures chased each other around the base of a carved African stool, which presided over the cart's lower shelf. Plastic bags full of cans banged against the rusty sides. A silky crow nested in the purse perch by the handlebar. A bedraggled right wing was wrapped in gauze.

"This crow is not random," Cinnamon said to Marie.

Behind the bird was a scrapbook stuffed with drawings. On the cart's side, a sign framed in Kente cloth, fluoresced: *Homeless Eshu: Will Do Magic for Small Change.*

"Eshu, like in *The Chronicles*?" Klaus asked the obvious question.

The engine sputtered and stalled to a halt. Mrs. Williams cursed under her breath. Everyone stopped breathing. An old man with uneven legs popped up five feet from the cart. He hobbled a strange dance in the snow. Scars crisscrossed his face; dark, shifty eyes refused to settle. He wasn't actually old, just beat-up. His coat was a patchwork of ski jackets and old fur coats held together with rusty safety pins and gray gaffer's tape. A green elf hat crowned his frosted hair like a knife bursting from his head. Flimsy polka-dot pajama pants were soaked through.

Cinnamon remembered him panhandling at Sekou's funeral!

Spewing foreign words, he waved a red pouch about and kicked snowdrifts with newspaper boots. He jumped up and flew five feet into the cart, which rammed into the Audi's fender. The impact burst a plastic bag, and a tattered sign landed on the hood: *Veteran, jacked up in the war. You got peace. Can you please help me?* The crow flapped its wings, hovered a few seconds, and bleated. The spell inside the car was broken.

"Close that window!" Mrs. Williams said.

The Homeless Eshu hobbled about picking up bottles and cans scattered in the snow.

"Pennsylvania doesn't even have a bottle bill," Marie said.

Mrs. W jumped out and threw the veteran sign at the Homeless Eshu. "Collect your rubbish somewhere else." She ran her fingers along the Audi's wounded chrome finish then turned on him. "You almost got us . . . Jesus!"

The Homeless Eshu gripped her fluffy down coat. "Big hole. No good going that way." Mrs. W dangled over a four-foot drop. The wind swept snow into the pit. The Homeless Eshu hugged her close. "I have you." Everybody jumped out of the Audi as he scrambled back from the crumbling edge with her. "You see soft snow cloud kissing ground. I see old wounds erupting, talking heads feeding us lies. Future look better the other direction." He had a strange accent, down-home country and also Euro-chic like Klaus. He talked on while Mrs. B patted Mrs. W's back. "Legba is old, old spirit, tired spirit, limping down dusty public roads, custodian of entrances and exits. Ancient, cranky, tired spirit." He pointed at a crane in the shadows. A sleeping dragon, its empty claw shovel was filled with snowy rubble. A deep gash cut across the width of the lot, a ravine that could have wrecked the Audi, totaled the passengers, or carried Mrs. W home to Jesus. Warning posts and yellow keep-out tape were tangled in snow drifts.

The Homeless Eshu had saved them.

"Thank you, sir." Mrs. Williams pulled away. "I can stand on my own."

Mrs. B stepped back. *"Sehr gut."*

He held up a bottle. "Massachusetts. Five-cent deposit."

"We can't thank you enough, sir, but"—Mrs. Williams hustled everybody toward the entrance—"we really must get inside."

Mrs. B hovered at the construction pit, toeing the edge of the hole.

"Other people might fall into the pit," Marie said.

Marie, Cinnamon, and Klaus arranged sawhorses and signs

around the hole. Mrs. W watched from an impatient distance. Sleet frizzed her hair into an irritable halo. The Homeless Eshu attached ragged strips of yellow keep-out tape to the sawhorses. Mrs. B secured the tape with fancy knots.

The Homeless Eshu bowed, his back cracking and popping. "Guardians, I salute you."

"You know who we are?" Cinnamon played cool.

"*Mojo* working here." His hand hovered above the hidden bag, bead, and feather. He held up a string of yellow trade beads identical to Cinnamon's.

"Those are from the Dahomey villagers at the Chicago Fair! You were there too?" He nodded. She pulled stolen bus fare from her pocket. "A sacrifice to Eshu."

Taking her money, his palm was sleek as sealskin. "Thank you."

"You look better than before." Cinnamon was enchanted.

"I do magic, for small change." He was blurry then sharp as a spotlight.

"Magic? You're serious." Marie dug in her purse. "Here." She placed a five-dollar bill in his hand. "Do magic for me too. Do big magic for us all."

"Please. We could use it." Klaus also offered five dollars.

"*Danke schön.*" Mrs. Beckenbauer added two twenties.

"Blessings on you as you fit grief *and* joy in your hearts." He placed a beaded wooden comb in Cinnamon's hand. "Oshun, wise orisha, she who wears a crown of peacock feathers, Oshun loves the hard edge of stone and the soft beauty of grass. Grace for grace."

"You can't give this to me." Cinnamon tried to hand the comb back.

He hobbled out of reach.

"What happened to your legs?" Klaus asked. "Was it the war?"

"No." The Homeless Eshu shifted crooked bones and stomped a turned-out left foot. His newspaper boots were from the December 27, 1982, *New York Times: Clutter in Space Might Stop ICBMs; Arafat to Meet with Kreisky; Whales Beach Themselves; An "Iron Curtain"*

Dividing a Mostly White Neighborhood from a Black Community on Chicago's South Side Has Been Torn Down. The words blurred. Cinnamon wobbled. Marie gripped her waist, managing gravity for her. December 27, 1982, was the day Raven got shot in the head.

"So peace twisted your foot?" Klaus made a vague gesture.

"Stop." Marie slugged Klaus. Reluctantly he swallowed a barrage of inquiry.

"That's how my legs are." Steering the cart through drifts, he headed out.

"Wait! *Coincidental affinity,*" Cinnamon sputtered. Klaus would have blurted out—are you the Wanderer? "We don't mean to be rude," she mumbled.

The bird fussed until the Homeless Eshu paused. He hunched his shoulders.

"I'm Cinnamon. He's Klaus, and that's Marie. What's your name?"

"I'm called Griot Joe," he yelled over his back. The crow cawed too.

"Thank you, Griot Joe," Cinnamon, Klaus, and Marie said in sync.

"I am with you. You are with me till we meet again." Griot Joe hurried off.

When the rattling cart and bleating crow were muffled by the snow, Marie turned on Klaus. "How'd your legs get that way? Did the war turn your eyes to slits? What's that accent? Where are you from? America? No shit! Really? Born in the USA! Bust my britches. Where are your parents from? How'd their legs get that way?" She shuddered. "You're German. I thought you guys were supposed to be polite."

"Who told you that crock of polite German crap?" Klaus shivered in his wet shirtsleeves. "Look, sorry, I didn't mean to—"

"Keep your sorry. Who means to be off the wall?" Marie ran ahead.

Klaus ran after her. "I asked what everyone was thinking. Griot Joe must get tired of answering leg questions, but—"

"Do you ask every stupid question that occurs to you?" Marie halted.

"No. Just the . . ." Klaus hugged himself. "Stuff slips out."

"That happens to me too," Cinnamon said.

"You don't get away with it," Marie hissed. "Do you?"

Cinnamon shrugged. She got away with other things.

Klaus's teeth chattered. "It's not my fault if everybody else was too chicken to ask."

"It's not about being chicken," Marie said.

Cinnamon jumped between them. "What are you so mad about?"

"I don't know." Marie pouted. "Everything."

"That can't be good for you," Cinnamon said.

"I don't have anything to complain about really," Marie muttered.

Images slipped past Cinnamon's shields. *Marie tiptoed in on a sleek older version of herself—sister?—shaking dark hair over a toilet. Marie froze as the woman gagged, finally sinking down and hugging the porcelain bowl. An older man—Marie's dad?—jogged up a twisty staircase. Marie locked eyes with the woman hugging the toilet then closed the bathroom door. Dad's mustache twitched as Marie blocked his path.*

"Can we go inside now?" Mrs. Williams tramped up the ramp entrance.

"Look." Klaus pointed.

Griot Joe sped down the empty main drag on his grocery cart, a tail of sleet wagging behind him. The cart didn't have any motor that Cinnamon could see or hear. They watched until he was swallowed in white.

"Magic," Marie whispered, without a question mark.

Hospital Blues

Opal wasn't in the Emergency Room. After a battery of tests, orderlies had taken her up high to spend the night, maybe a few nights, until results came through and doctors knew what was up. The receptionist, Ms. Allen, claimed she was resting quietly.

Cinnamon wanted to be relieved, but, "I gotta see her for myself."

Ms. Allen pointed at the wall clock. "Visiting hours end at nine." The clock stuttered at 8:45, banging and clicking. "Oh shoot. With the ice and snow, we lost power for a moment, and the generators kicked in. The clocks hate power interruptions." She was young and wore heavy makeup five shades too light for her dark pockmarked skin. Her hair was straightened to within an inch of its life and pulled back way too tight. She stretched cracked red lips over dull yellow teeth, but frowning eyes gave her fake smile away.

"Time is messed up. Go by the clocks. No rules broken," Cinnamon said.

"Nice. Like a bear pelt." Ms. Allen gestured at Klaus's coat. "This storm came out of nowhere. I only wore a jacket."

"Do I care—"

"We're immediate family." Klaus acted twenty-five and important. "I assumed we were allowed up anytime."

Ms. Allen sputtered. "Somebody's already—"

"The Joneses are quite a big clan, international in scope." Marie played an imperious rich kid used to buying her way into anywhere. "Renowned on several continents."

"That's right!" Cinnamon said.

Her bedraggled *family* dripped slush onto grimy carpet runners and held each other up. Mrs. B spoke in German to Klaus who gestured at the receptionist.

Ms. Allen got that he was blaming her. "You have to under-stand. This is a—"

"If you think we're going back out there without . . ." Com-mander Williams looked at the ceiling, trying not to come out her face at Ms. Allen. "You're dead wrong."

"Bitte, bitte, bitte!" Mrs. Beckenbauer sounded so sweet; she could have been melted sugar. She took Ms. Allen's hand. "Bad night. Mercy, yes?"

"Mercy, yes?" Cinnamon, Marie, and Klaus repeated, nailing her lilting accent.

"Fine. It's a zoo tonight. Go ahead." Ms. Allen waved them on.

Only one guest elevator was working. Grumbling about heart-attack snow and lethal cobblestones, a mob of white people squeezed in with Cinnamon's crew. Had Ms. Allen been talking trash about visiting hours being over? Cinnamon hated wondering if the dark-skinned receptionist was harder on colored folks. After rising seven floors, the elevator hovered a moment between levels as the motor fussed and the lights winked on and off. Cinnamon was ready to bust into the shaft and crawl up to Opal's room. Commander Wil-liams pounded the eighth floor button once, and they rose the last few inches. The doors clanged and banged before pulling them-selves apart. Cinnamon was the first one out. She raced across a slippery floor.

Miz Redwood, wrapped in a swath of purple and green che-nille, stood in front of an empty nurses' station. She was as tall, straight, and strong as Cinnamon remembered. A blue silk scarf flowed like a river around her neck. Bangles and beads at her waist jingled as she took in a breath and stretched her arms wide. The smile on her face filled the hallway. "Little Miz Woman! Look at you, growing into yourself."

"I knew you were coming!" Cinnamon ran into her full force.

Miz Redwood scooped her close. "We been coming back since the minute we left."

"I tried not to hope too much, in case you didn't make it."

"What you mean not make it? Aidan was ready to walk the stars to get here."

"Really?" Cinnamon's words turned into a jumbled mess. She babbled on about how hard getting to the hospital had been. Eshu was a fiend, testing her, testing everybody.

"We like a challenge. Convenience is overrated." Redwood's magic hands pulled pain and weary right out of Cinnamon. "Opal's goin' be fine. Doctors got X-rays, new rays, and whatnot, trying to figure out the mess she done made in her lungs. They put a drip in her arm for pain, to help her sleep too. After that she was flying so high, woman had the nerve to ask me to go buy her a pack of cigarettes. As if we come all this way in an ice storm to buy her some darned coffin nails."

Iris materialized out of nowhere. Her dry lips and cool fingers brushed Cinnamon's cheeks. She kissed Cinnamon's forehead too. "I couldn't keep them away."

"We had to see you, sugarplum." Aidan gathered them all to his chest. "Every morning I get up and you be on my mind, the only melody running 'round my mouth." He smelled of licorice and fresh cut wood, like always. "Iris wanted to jump on a jumbo jet." Aidan laughed. "That wasn't happening. Storm clouds had a dark look. Who need to go flying off into that? I made these ornery ole ladies drive from Massachusetts." The elders stepped back for a good look at Cinnamon and bumped into her international family. Aidan talked on to them too. "Clouds came chasing after us anyhow, spoiling for trouble. Bald tires were grunting and growling at slippery roads, but that storm hung fire till we hit Pittsburgh."

Commander Williams flinched at Aidan's Southern cracker accent then covered this with a cough. "Drive? In this weather?" She forced a smile.

"Been driving since before you was born," Aidan said.

"That's what the woman's worried about," Redwood said. The elders laughed.

Klaus and Marie gaped at her grandparents and great aunt as

if they were space aliens. Mrs. Beckenbauer did too. Commander Williams contemplated her watch and snuck peeks between sighs. Aidan wore jeans, a work shirt, and rubber boots. He had a thick white braid to the middle of his back and a walking stick with leather strands of beads cascading down the side. He could have been an ancient hipster or New Age cracker freak, but Miz Redwood was too elegant to put up with freaks. The crown of purple and green silk on her white hair told you that. Iris styled leather working boots under a dress fashioned out of Adinkra cloth from Ghana. The crosses and fat butterfly patterns meant: *the spirit never dies.* This was Iris's favorite wise word cloth. A banjo case banged Iris's back and twanged. They could pass for an antediluvian blues band.

"We couldn't leave the banjo home, could we?" Redwood whispered.

"I got songs for you, princess." Aidan flexed his fingers.

Cinnamon laid her cheek against the worn leather and felt the strings buzzing inside. Would she still like Aidan's hillbilly country music?

"Opal's thin as a whiff of smoke," Iris said. "What have you been eating?"

"Don't tell her. Sister don't really want to hear," Redwood said.

"When can Mom come home?" Cinnamon strained toward the corridor of doors. "Can I see her?"

"She's sleeping." Aidan held on to Cinnamon.

She was close to a tantrum. "I can watch her sleep."

"OK. I'll show you." Redwood gripped Cinnamon's arm with what Aidan called her storm hand. Supposedly she could catch a hurricane or stop a heart from beating with that hand. Feeling a power surge pulse against her bicep, Cinnamon didn't doubt it.

Redwood ushered Cinnamon to the first room on the left. She barely touched the handle with her *storm hand* and the door swung wide. The room smelled of industrial-strength cleaner, old coffee, and wet clothes trying to grow mold. Cinnamon swallowed a sneeze, and they tiptoed in. Opal lay in a forest of tubes and a cloud of sheets. Her skin was brown again, not gray, not drawn tight over her bones. Her eyes fluttered in a dream. Muscles twitched, hands and feet aching to move, but motion inhibited. It looked to be a good singing and dancing dream. Maybe Opal and Raven were doing the funky chicken in desert sand or hiking a canyon, singing the blues.

"Opal's not ready to leave us yet," Redwood declared.

Cinnamon turned to her grandmother and burst into tears. Twice in one night! Redwood's silk river scarf flowed across her cheeks and took the sting out of the tears, took the hitch out of her breath. Opal would get better, and Raven might come back from that coma too!

The other occupant of the room, an old white lady with a few less tubes than Opal, waved. "I'll tell her she had good company when she wakes up tomorrow."

"Can't we wait to tell her ourselves?" Cinnamon said.

Redwood pulled her out of the room. "They get the night to themselves." She closed the door and drew Cinnamon to the nurses' station. "We'll come tomorrow. I promise."

All eyes were on Cinnamon. "My mom looks better," she reported. "She's not knocking on death's door demanding to be let in. That's something."

Klaus spewed German at Mrs. Beckenbauer. She ran to Cinnamon and squeezed her hands, mumbling German. How long had this woman been in America without speaking English?

Aidan smiled and tipped a nonexistent hat at the ladies. "Introduce us to your friends." They hadn't done that themselves yet?

Redwood waved everybody over. "Come closer. We ain't goin' bite."

Cinnamon rattled off names and relations. Aidan didn't sound Native American but heavy Georgia cracker. He and Redwood were so country it made you itch, and Iris was so Afrocentric and Indian Power radical, what would anybody think?

Marie shook Aidan's outstretched hand. "I thought you'd be . . ." Black and Native, not Irish and Seminole.

"Pleased to meet you, Mr. Wildfire." Klaus covered the awkward moment.

"Klaus and Marie are music theatre people." Cinnamon bubbled on about talents and wonders. Motown Marie and Prince Charming Klaus blushed as she praised them.

"Theatre people." Redwood smiled approval.

"Hot dog," Aidan said, "you know we like the sound of that." Who says *hot dog*?

Iris whispered German to Mrs. B, who gushed at her. Iris waved a hand, and Mrs. B slowed down. Aidan put his arm through Cinnamon's, holding her up a little on the sly. He looked seventy-five, hale and hearty. He winked at her. They had come to rescue her, like always. Cinnamon wouldn't let Opal send anybody back to Massachusetts.

"I know nothing about Seminoles," Klaus said to Marie more than Aidan. "They don't teach us anything. It's only Winnetou stories in Germany."

"Winnie who?" Redwood wrinkled her brow. "Sounds familiar."

"Knowing what you don't know is a good start," Iris said.

"What you think you know that ain't so . . ." Aidan hesitated.

"That can make you a slave," Redwood finished the saying.

"Fellow from over there in Africa used to tell us that," Aidan muttered, dazed.

Redwood hugged him close. He was flying off somewhere. Redwood flew with him and stood her ground too. They soared and stumbled, a slow-motion jitterbug, sexy and bittersweet. Iris jostled the banjo on her back, so it twanged a drum rhythm.

"Where are you, Granddaddy?" Cinnamon took his hand.

Aidan found his way back to right here, right now. He tweaked Cinnamon's nose as if nothing strange had happened. "Ain't no memory, no dream sweeter than this moment with you folks."

Commander Williams cleared her throat. The chitchat died out. She offered to drive anyone home who was leaving right away. Cinnamon promised to pay everybody back for helping her. She tried to give Klaus his fancy coat. He wouldn't take it. Marie shoved a phone number at Cinnamon after making Klaus write his down too. Cinnamon didn't have a number. Opal's phone had been turned off.

"They got pay phones everywhere," Marie said. "You better call us." She tied her furry scarf around Cinnamon's neck. It smelled of lavender and sage. "Stay warm."

Cinnamon, ignoring Marie's protests, put Oshun's comb in her thick hair. "We can share." Cinnamon pulled her and Klaus into a three-way hug. Doing theatre made folks feel tight fast. Would anything be real in the morning? Would they remember how close they'd gotten? Marie turned away, hanging onto Klaus, probably 'cause she wanted to touch him or maybe so Cinnamon wouldn't see her face break apart into tears again. Marie didn't like being a wimp any more than Cinnamon did.

Klaus punched Cinnamon's shoulder. "We could run away together, get lost in the night and never come back."

"Are you serious?" Cinnamon said.

"Just kidding. Ciao," he murmured.

"Ciao." Cinnamon punched his shoulder and rubbed Marie's bony back.

Mrs. Beckenbauer nodded at Cinnamon and shook the elders' hands. Her eyes were red. *Vati* had her spooked too. A weary nurse returned to her station, glancing at everyone. Aidan and Redwood snagged her with an Opal query. Cinnamon's international family trooped to the one working elevator, and Commander Williams pounded the down button. Cinnamon turned away from this melancholy departure and edged toward Opal's room.

"Go on." Iris nodded in her direction. Nobody ever put anything over on her.

Not Over Yet

Cinnamon pushed open Opal's heavy door, hung Klaus's bear on a hook, and sat by Opal's bed. There weren't that many tubes—three monitoring devices and an almost empty bag dripping into her veins. Rapid eye movement indicated Opal was still roaming a dreamscape. Opal never slept this well anymore. She and Raven used to watch Cinnamon sleep when she was little. Cinnamon had considered this behavior boring parent weirdness. Watching the steady rise and fall of Opal's chest, Cinnamon was thrilled. Breath struck her as a miracle. She felt happier than she could remember.

Her stomach howled. She dug in her orca knapsack for stolen reception-snacks. The crackers were dust; ink from a pen had turned the yellow cheese green; only the cashews looked edible. She savored their salty, greasy taste then pulled out her magic-words journal. If she waited for morning to write the night's adventure-quest, she'd lose half of what had happened and think the other half was a wild story storm, truth but not necessarily fact. She used a purple Magic Marker for direct quotes. *What you think you know that ain't so can make you a slave* was a great line for her Eshu poem. The journal pages were thick; nothing bled through, and each sentence lifted her spirits.

Without meaning to she was singing "Ain't No Sunshine When He's Gone."

"Is that you, baby?" Opal murmured after the first two verses. She hadn't called Cinnamon *baby* since she was three. "You sound good." That was a lie. Cinnamon's voice was shot. "You OK?"

Cinnamon grunted. "You're the one we gotta worry—"

"I'm fine." Opal squinted in the fluorescent light. "Just, high as a space shot." Her face creased into a shit-eating grin. Drugged for sure. "I dreamt you got lost in a big snow ocean. You were on an ole-timey steamship floating in a sea of fluffy flakes."

"We were, sort of." Cinnamon smiled.

"You gonna give me a kiss, baby?"

Opal had never been a touchy-feely, cuddly mom. Afraid to hug too hard, Cinnamon gently scooped Opal close and kissed a sunken cheek. A cigarette smell clung to hair that had more gray than Cinnamon remembered. Opal's breath was syrupy sweet. Her skin was warm. Was this healing, or drugs?

Cinnamon sat back in the chair. "What are these?"

Two African statues, a female and a male carved from dark wood, stood guard on Opal's nightstand. Both statues wore knife-in-the-head headdresses. The female was kneeling and holding erect breasts, offering them. The male crouched and held a rigid penis, offering this too.

"A friend of Raven's gave me those," Opal said. "Joe? Yeah Joe."

"Joe?" Cinnamon stroked the statues. Static electricity shocked her. From wood? "Whoa."

"Joe and Raven were always talking AFRICA, always scheming and dreaming revolution. You remember Joe?"

"Not really." Cinnamon traced an Eshu feather and cut her finger. *"Owa."*

"You never remember anybody! Who do you get that from?"

"Myself." Both feathers were razor sharp.

"Maybe it's Junkyard Joe." Her mom's face was soft and open. The poker glare was tucked in a drawer somewhere with the rest of her regular Opal uniform.

"So what's this Joe look like?" Cinnamon asked.

"Brown-skinned, sad eyes. Crooked legs and back. He's got that wild bush hair and scars from the war." Opal paused. "But he never looks the same."

"He came to Sekou's funeral."

"Joe wasn't there. Only family." Opal groaned. "Your Uncle Clarence was—"

"Not inside the funeral home"—Cinnamon deflected Clarence—"in the parking lot. He was asking for spare change."

"Panhandling at Sekou's funeral?" Opal brushed cracker crumbs from the sheets with an antique handkerchief. "I wouldn't put it past him."

Cinnamon worked Redwood's spell #7—*say what you love.* "The funeral was a hard day. Griot Joe smelled like trouble. You were busy holding up the world."

"Joe was cleaned up today, gave me his handkerchief." She waved it. Embroidery around the edge ended in a *B,* for Bob? "He left those statues to keep me company in my dreams. A female statue's rare. I hope he didn't steal—"

"Naw." Cinnamon pointed at the feather-knives in their heads. "Eshu."

"Eshu, yes. I thought he was sneezing or high." Opal almost laughed. "He said Eshu threw a stone and hit a bird yesterday."

"Eshu's an orisha, force of nature, guardian of the crossroad."

"From West Africa, right?"

"Yeah, but Eshu belongs to the whole universe like, like black holes and sonnets, like electron clouds, honeybee dances, and the blues."

"Go on with your bad self." Opal actually sounded proud. She pulled Cinnamon close. "Joe, high as a satellite, visits your daddy, religiously. Star Deer too." She frowned. "Ms. Washington is back tomorrow. Star's substitute gig is up." She squirmed. "I can't get myself to that nursing home. What's the point?"

"I understand," Cinnamon said mildly. Opal had given up on Raven, but Aidan would take Cinnamon to see Daddy. If Opal refused to tell where the nursing home was, Aidan would still find it. Iris claimed he could track anything, even haints and wayward spirits. Aidan didn't need to be a ghost scout to find a man lying stock still in a coma, his one and only son to boot. "How'd Joe know you were here?"

"Everybody knows . . . Joe said Iris and your grandparents were

coming. He said don't be angry 'cause *love powers even a rogue ship*."
Opal furrowed her brow. "Joe looks like somebody else. He must
have a twin sister or . . . How do you say twin in Yoruba?"

"How would I know?"

"Professor Iris talks that Motherland mess to you. And, baby,
you don't forget anything." She reached for the water bottle. Cinnamon turned the straw to her lips. Opal drank it dry. She grimaced.
"Drugs. Dripping in my veins, but nasty in my mouth." Opal never
smoked weed, drank wine, or sipped a beer. Claimed she couldn't
handle drugs: *They handle me*. Once when she thought Cinnamon
was asleep, she told Aunt Becca, *Why I wanna scramble my brains and
spread my legs? Sekou was a marijuana baby. No more of that*. "Wait.
How did you get here? That's what I want to know."

The Mod Squad blizzard-quest gushed from Cinnamon's mouth
at hyper speed. She left out ghost Sekou.

"Slow down." Opal waved a spindly arm. "Life goes fast enough."
When had she gotten so splintery? Iris was right. They had to eat
better. Skinny folks had no backup energy source. Cinnamon
should get a job to help with bills, or—"What's your rush?"

Cinnamon snorted. "I hate slow." Fast people couldn't just decide to take their feet off a gas pedal. They were built fast. It was
fast or nothing, fast or utter chaos. If she didn't go at her speed,
she couldn't make sense.

"You arguing with me in your head? Before you know it, you'll
be old and—"

"Standing on a bridge to nowhere?"

"Yeah." Opal sucked on the empty water bottle. "God, I could
really use a—"

"You've got more than a cigarette to live for." Cinnamon snatched
the bottle and ran into the bathroom for a refill. "You're not over
yet."

"How did I get stuck with such a—"

"I'm not a stupid optimist." Cinnamon came back and slammed
the bottle down.

"So quit acting like one. Get in the real world."

Cinnamon waved at the tubes and monitors. "Is that where you are?" She cringed, wishing she could take the mean words back.

Opal wiggled a loose fang on the orca knapsack. "Aren't you too old to be dragging this ratty thing around?"

"Daddy gave it to me." Cinnamon stuffed the journal through the fangs. "After I almost drowned and got saved."

"It was a seal supposedly saved you, wasn't it, not a dolphin?"

"This is an orca." Cinnamon rubbed the soft underbelly against her cheek. She'd been talking to an orca at the aquarium, jumping up and down, and then she slid down a wall into a murky pool. She grabbed onto a musty creature who dipped in and out of icy water till they reached a sunny rock. The seal crawled off and Cinnamon clapped her hands like flippers. Everybody, seals and people too, were clapping and laughing. Raven scooped her up and hugged her tight, water dripping everywhere.

"No big lying like you always do." Opal yawned in more oxygen. "Did Raven make up a tall tale on this knapsack or did that shit really happen?"

"I don't know." Cinnamon didn't care. Her orca was full of memories and dreams. It had a mind of its own. Why throw that away?

"Raven loved to tell that story."

"You don't believe any of it?"

"No."

Cinnamon held up the Adinkra cloth envelope—*fire in the eyes.* "Aunt Iris wrote me a bunch of letters."

"Iris and them hoodoo fools 'llowed to tell you anything."

"Why have you been keeping *important shit* from me?"

"Watch your mouth."

"I'm no baby you got to watch sleep so I don't get hurt in a nightmare!" Cinnamon hissed. "I pick your butt off the bathroom floor every other day."

"OK. You so grown you can take anything?" Opal clutched the bars on the bed. "I told Sekou that he might as well have pulled that trigger—a selfish little shit out there chasing some faggot who was too old for him, Sekou dragged my beautiful Raven down in the gutter with him." Opal struggled for breath.

"Stop." Cinnamon didn't want to hear any more.

"Sekou took everything right to his heart. That's why he picked up a needle."

"Stop. I know that!" Cinnamon shouted.

The old lady roommate jerked awake and smiled at them. "Oh good, you two getting to talk." She drifted off again.

Cinnamon clamped her mouth tight. Her thoughts were loud enough. Sekou had a tough-guy-rapper act that fooled the masses, but when it came to folks he loved, he had zero defenses. If you loved him, you knew that. Scratch Sekou and he'd break out in a rash. Say something a little out the way, and he couldn't talk to you for months, years. He was always throwing up shields, but Lexy or Opal on a rampage could batter Sekou's shields to shreds in seconds if Cinnamon wasn't around for backup.

Opal's monitors sounded shrill. The squiggles were definitely agitated.

"I'm upsetting you. You're supposed to rest," Cinnamon said.

"Ain't nothing you can say that'll make me feel more like shit than I already do."

"Sekou would be mad at us. Daddy and the elders too, fighting and cussing."

Opal tracked shadows dancing over Cinnamon's head. "Yeah."

"Sekou blamed himself," Cinnamon whispered. "Not you."

"How you know that?"

"I know things sometimes."

Opal sat up a little. She read the magic truth in Cinnamon's mind. They weren't going to talk about that though. Opal pretended she didn't read minds. "Yeah." She sank back. Her breathing smoothed out. "Yeah, you do."

"Sekou told me to take care of you, 'cause you'd be too sad."

"Hmm." Opal held back tears.

"Griot Joe was looking out for Sekou. He gave him *The Chronicles*."

Opal gasped. "Joe was there the night Raven got shot, and Star too, having a drink, at a faggot bar. They all encouraged Sekou."

"Joe wears newsprint boots from December 27, 1982."

"No, maybe Joe wasn't at the bar. He came after."

The floor tilted under Cinnamon. A story storm engulfed her. "I think maybe Joe's the Wanderer, a sister, brother, *aje* from another dimension come to know this world, come to live in it and feel it on his skin, in his heart, come to taste pain and joy and everything in between. He's a patchwork of every story he's heard and lived."

"Aren't we all?" Opal frowned.

"But Joe's scattered. Stories are where he dumpster-dives, looking for the past he trashed. *Aje* fragments could be running amok. Dangerous, but Joe's an Imagineer, trying to call memory up from the void. An *aje*—"

"*Aje*? Damn, baby, we don't need to make up sci-fi demons to worry about." She poked Cinnamon's safety pins. "You're a mess, girl."

"I'm a size sixteen. This is a fourteen."

"Ain't no money for a fashion upgrade."

Cinnamon rolled her eyes. She didn't want to talk about her clothes.

"That's a nice scarf." Opal caressed it. "You're not shoplifting, are you?"

"It's a present. Look, Joe equals Wanderer is where the evidence points."

"My little scientist-artiste, believing in magic." Opal almost smiled. Clouds passed over her face. "What are you gonna do with me stuck up in here?"

Was Cinnamon at the mercy of Child Services? Cousin Carol or Uncle Clarence? They might as well book her a room in hell. *"Verdammt!"*

Born Two

"We got Cinnamon, Opal. Don't you fret." Iris talked from the doorway, backlit by the nurses' station. Aidan and Redwood were already in the room.

Aidan winked at Cinnamon as he fluffed a pillow under Opal's head. "I told Opal, ain't nobody talking 'bout dying," he said, "so no worry there."

"Doctors need time to do the best that they can." Iris filled the water bottle.

"That means we get to visit awhile." Redwood stood by the nightstand, admiring Eshu. Opal grimaced. "Better us than Clarence Jones, Esquire, to the rescue."

"What about Rebecca? Did you call her?" Opal asked.

"Just till they get you straightened out." Redwood didn't answer the question.

"What if they don't?" Cinnamon let a little panic slip.

"We scale that cliff when we get to it." Redwood wasn't afraid of anything.

"Rebecca got that spare room," Opal said. "Cinnamon wouldn't be in the way. Rebecca spends most her time at Kevin's."

"Think of the trouble Cinnamon could get into on her own." Redwood chortled.

"How are we doing? Empty, huh?" The nurse pushed through them to put a full pouch of clear liquid on Opal's IV drip.

"Sweeeeeet Jesussss," Opal said as the new dose flooded her.

"Sorry. She'll be in and out like this for a few days," the nurse explained.

Good. Cinnamon wanted to ask Opal about Raven's paintings when she was high. Cinnamon also had to persuade Star Deer (*Ms. Respect-Your-Elders*) to tell what Opal hid from her *baby girl*.

If Klaus and Marie were still her friends tomorrow, she'd get them to help. She'd do anything as a trade. Tracking down Griot Joe was a priority. She had a feeling he wasn't going anywhere far. Lexy must know the *important shit*. Too. Cinnamon would make him spill the beans, too bad if he still hated her.

"Your mom's a rogue hoodoo conjurer," Aidan said. "Getting stoned interferes with her magic."

"Don't fill her head full of nonsense." Opal slurred her words as the new dose kicked in.

"Cinnamon been knowing how to think for herself," Redwood replied.

"How'd you decide to come to University Hospital?" Cinnamon had almost forgotten to ask. "And get here so fast?"

"How you plan to answer that?" Opal sneered.

The elders looked angelic, doing hoodoo gestures, passing secrets, swallowing giggles, like adolescents putting one over on a clueless adult.

"Iris can see your heart spirit wherever in the world you are." Aidan bragged on Iris without explaining a thing.

"A nice young person offered us a ride," Iris added.

Aidan nodded. "The same one picked us up in '84."

"That was a young fellow," Iris said.

"I thought it was a girl." Aidan shut his eyes, concentrating. "She had a million skinny braids. Audra?"

Redwood chuckled. "That's young folks' style—dreadlocks, braids—everybody wearing that. Where you been?"

"Standing right next to you most times." Aidan laughed too. "Artemis?"

"I don't know about '84," Iris said. "Today was a young woman with family in Pittsburgh."

"Maybe they're twins," Redwood said.

"Snow didn't faze him *or* her a bit." Aidan squinted into the recent past. "A police person, used to emergency conditions, drove like a fiend. Aria?"

"Ariel?" Cinnamon suggested.

"Yeah." Aidan scratched his jaw. "Maybe she played a police-woman in a show."

"That was last time," Iris said.

Redwood nodded. "Carried us right to the emergency entrance."

"*Coincidental affinity*. Eshu laughing," Cinnamon mumbled.

Opal perked up. "What's twin in Yoruba, Iris?"

"*Ibeji*," Iris translated quickly. "Literally, born two."

"That's not the name." Opal fussed in the sheets, straining her tubes. "Damn it!"

Iris took Opal's hand. "In Yorubaland, regardless of gender, twins are named Taiwo, the first to taste the world, and Kehinde, the last to come, who is considered the elder. As I recall, Taiwo scouts out what life is like on Earth and reports back to Kehinde. Twins are children of thunder and share a soul; one is the spiritual aspect and the other, material."

"That's it." Opal was thrilled. "Taiwo. Joe looks like Taiwo."

Cinnamon was glad to be sitting down. So much probability magic. Griot Joe had to be the Wanderer from another dimension, living right now in Pittsburgh! Joe was one of her daddy's best friends. Raven painted scenes from the Wanderer's Earth adventures. Of course, Joe might have made up *The Chronicles* without living it. Circumstantial evidence, no matter how persuasive, was insufficient. She needed ironclad proof!

"Storm's backing off." Redwood pointed at dark windows.

Aidan peered out. Stars were twinkling. "Done enough mischief for one night."

"That's for sure." Kevin strode in, cowboy hat in hand, pointy boots slick and shiny. He'd braved the storm to rescue them. "Took hours to get here. Ms. Allen downstairs didn't want to let me up. I had to use my charm." He still had plenty of that.

"Who is it?" Opal blinked against the brightness.

"Rebecca sent that handsome cowpoke of hers to carry us home." Redwood tucked a wayward foot under the sheets.

"That's love for you." Aidan nodded.

"Roads are pretty clear." Kevin kissed Opal's cheek. "Don't you worry."

"Everybody telling me not to worry. Makes me really worried." Even high as a satellite, Opal managed to find her way to a salty mood.

Kevin smiled. "I can handle the wild bunch and Miss Space Cadet. You get better."

"She will," Redwood declared.

Everybody picked up the get well theme. Cinnamon didn't hear much. There was a riot going on in her mind. She couldn't wait to call Klaus and Marie and tell them her theories. Did Kevin carry her to the car? Good thing the man lived at the gym.

"You all right, sugar?" Aidan asked when he and Redwood settled in the back seat of the Toyota with her.

"Just being with her own self, I suspect," Redwood said.

Cinnamon was grateful for the understanding. She felt too shy to tell the elders her theories on the first night. Over two years of keeping secrets to herself, she'd lost the habit of blabbing everything at them.

The shocks in Kevin's Toyota were nonexistent compared to the Audi's tech. The beat-up station wagon bumped through potholes and around abandoned vehicles. Tucked in between Aidan and Redwood, Cinnamon felt every inch of the road. The frosted streets were deserted. Giant icicles dangled from power lines and tree limbs, growing longer as the car crept below them. An eerie tinkling of frozen branches and tumbleweed trash sounded like demons chuckling. A snow witch or sleet wizard had enchanted the hilly city. No sane mortal ventured forth.

"Cinnamon, honey, will you read to us?" Iris said from the front seat. "I've been dying to find out what's happening."

"Well, if Uncle Kevin doesn't mind."

"I was hoping for a little magic on this ride." Kevin glanced sideways at Iris.

Cinnamon took glowing pages from Iris's hands. This was

one of those theatre days that Aristotle praised, a whole lifetime jammed into twenty-four hours of conflict, action, and revelation. Do. Suffer. Know. Cinnamon certainly felt like a tired spectacle ready for a long dénouement. Redwood put her storm hand on Cinnamon's neck and pulled pain. Aidan gripped her chilly palm and hummed a warm melody.

"I don't have enough voice to read." Cinnamon spoke softly.

"Don't worry," Iris said. "When the story's raring to go, I bet *The Chronicles* can practically read itself." Talking a language that was as soothing as Redwood's river scarf, Iris spoke a spell that tugged Cinnamon headlong into *The Chronicles*.

The next morning, opening gummy lids was like lifting heavy weights. Cinnamon woke in her bed, too tired to move. She clutched *The Chronicles* pages in both hands, and they weren't one bit wrinkled. Bright light coming through her shade was altogether too loud. The orca lay on Sekou's desk, mouth wide open, grinning at her. A blue river scarf tumbled from the fangs to a sweetgrass basket on the floor where her eagle feather, *mojo* bag, shells, and Dahomey bead nestled together.

Sekou's time-bomb clock read 11:30 A.M. Cinnamon hoped the blizzard cleanup had shut everything down and school got canceled. Star Deer was gone. Cinnamon had done her homework before the audition, even the boring reading on *Liberté, Égalité, Fraternité* and the French Revolution. School was mostly stupid, and students usually made mincemeat of substitute teachers. However, Star's math classes were stellar. Kids acted right and aced their work. Nobody talked down faggot-Sekou or Cinnamon's fat black ass. Star had students turn proofs into sculptures lit by special-effects flashlights. Hip-hop kids, biting off Salt-N-Pepa's style, danced in this nerd art for the talent show. Star was the drama coach, too, and talked about doing plays: musicals, epic dramas, comedies, on no budget. *Despite what anybody tells you, doing art isn't extra,* Star said. *Thinking is the best show in town!*

With Star gone, Cinnamon would be getting into fights all the time.

Taiwo and Kehinde's latest adventures effervesced at the edge of Cinnamon's consciousness, a long dream that wasn't dissolving in the bright snow-light of day. Cinnamon didn't recall speaking a word of it out loud as Kevin drove them home last night. Maybe Iris had turned *The Chronicles* into an audio book, and the chapters played right below awareness. As Cinnamon read the new chapters again, each word on the page activated one in her memory dream.

Chronicles 17: Ariel and Abla

Dear Guardians!

I toss flesh for the crows to eat. The flock waits for a fellow traveler to trust wings and fly again. The crow sulks in the purse perch. I understand. Like my once-wounded companion, I am afraid of myself, of the *aje*, of flying, falling, and scattering. Somso regularly scolded me in her Igbo language: *Anaghi eji mgbagbu ghalu ogu.*

A person does not bolt from a fight for fear that someone might get shot.

The air is cold, and my hands won't stop shaking. Winter is not the season of my spirit. But, good news, I have proof. Scattering is as real as my coming together in a spirit cave ninety-five years ago in Dahomey. Battered shards of memory return. I write quickly before they flit away.

Wanderers have no fixed, eternal essence. Flux powers our spirits. Death is another transformation. Scattering is the Wanderers' greatest fear. A few legends speak of Wanderers who, with the aid of powerful guardians and *stillpoints*, drew as many as six selves back together. I can't imagine such a return. Why be one when you can be many? The first sign of scattering is many minds, and then you are splitting into two beings instead of becoming someone new. Sometimes, these beings refuse to remember one another or recall their shared past. Amnesia can be a blessing as well as a curse. From two, imagine breaking into so many pieces that all the king's horses and all the queen's women couldn't put you back together again. English does a beautiful rhyme on biology and the arrow of time.

Tonight, dear Guardians, braving killer snow from an inland sea, proof cruised right in front of my nose on a ten-speed bicycle. Beautiful to behold, dressed in elegant robes—Yoruba or Fon finery—

proof skidded into my cart near the old industrial plant perched above the Monongahela River. It's a culture house these days, doing masquerades. Actors called my scattered-self "Ariel" and praised last year's midsummer night's dream. In winter it's good to dream of summer's return. Now there were tempests to tame. Ariel swerved onto the sidewalk to avoid reckless drivers and didn't see me. We collided. Ariel wasn't wearing a helmet. Impact on the hard ground stole consciousness. I did what I could—my powers are greatly reduced. Ariel came 'round quickly though and jumped up.

"Thank you." Ariel brushed blood and snow from guarded eyes. Energy sparked between us. "Do you recognize me?"

"Should I?" Ariel checked the bike for damage. "Did we do a play together in New York? Chicago?"

Marveling at our similar magnetic signatures, I didn't know what to do or say.

"Are you a fan? What'd you see—*For Colored Girls*? *Midsummer*? That Alice Childress one—*Trouble in Mind*?"

"I saw you disappear onstage in every one." I smiled. "You're amazing."

"I'm not the characters I've played." Ariel balanced on the seat, put a foot in a pedal.

"Of course you are. Each character changes you."

"I can't even remember all the characters I've played."

"You carry them with you!" I clutched Ariel's sleeve. "I do know you."

"No, you don't." Ariel shook me off. "You've fallen for someone who doesn't really exist. A masquerade, a ghost." Ariel wheeled down the street into milky shadows.

I was intoxicated, immobile. My crow companion, desperately flapping a fragile wing, lifted up and pecked my head. Above us the flock urged me to move on. With the cart's power, I raced after Ariel, until I reached the University Hospital parking lot and lost the trail.

For eighteen seasons, I've been haunted by visions and ghosts who could have been me: a face rushing by on a trolley; a performer

hanging from a thin trapeze, twirling in the air, and vanishing; a
rogue with money-green eyes gloating over the latest successful
scam; a rescue worker dragging wounded people from burning
rubble; an actress giving old folks a ride to a funeral. Always I
was too far, on the opposite end of a broadcast, or breath-close yet
too jammed to read the magnetic fields. Eshu runs backward and
trips over herself. This time I'm certain. Despite being cloaked by
ground fog, by clouds of static and swirls of ice, I SAW MYSELF!

"Taiwo, child of the empty spaces, you *scatter* us all." Abla's severed head screamed at me tonight for the first time in fifty years,
in English. I've forgotten too much Yoruba, Fon, or Igbo for her
to torture me in those languages. Emitting a blue-green fluorescence, she floated in scum at the bottom of a construction pit in the
University Hospital parking lot. Sleet coated withered tentacles
coming through her translucent skull.

"You are *nzumbe*," she told me, "a damaged soul with delusions
of alien grandeur."

"You describe yourself."

"You have eaten countless African and American stories." She
spit tiny desiccated corpses at me. "Our histories explode your
belly, backbone, muscles, and skin. You fly off in a thousand directions."

I tore through my cart searching for Bob's bag. Chill air turned
my hands to clumsy claws. I wreaked havoc with drawings, altars,
minkisi—spiritually-charged vessels that I'd collected. Bob's red *mojo*
was nowhere. Tiny bottles of rum rattled in the bottom of the cart,
tempting me to drown Abla in alcohol. My crow companion pecked
my arms.

Abla laughed a foul wind. "Have you lost your slave magic?"

"No," I lied.

"Your *stillpoint* has deserted you. Come down to me."

I fell to my knees. "The mighty Monongahela begged me to lie
in her bosom and I refused."

"That river is a dead sewage drain. What people attend the
spirit of that water?"

"Why join you in a puddle of scum?"

"To dance your final destiny." Abla licked stone teeth.

"Only Eshu knows our final destiny."

"*Mère d'eau* has abandoned you."

"We carry the mother of water within." I teetered over the edge. "Change is always possible."

"Always? It's never too late?"

"Never."

"So, you're a coward not daring to change."

"I can sacrifice. I can let go of one self to become another."

"A man who risked all for you hovers at the gate between life and death."

"You dare speak of Raven Cooper lingering in a coma."

"What can you do for him, broken as you are?"

I spoke Kehinde's words. *"What is lost or cannot be found can be conjured."* I clutched my neck and felt Bob's hoodoo spell, a prayer in a bag, hanging on a thin cord. The wool was worn, and its red color had faded to rusty brown. The scent of rum clung to the threads. The *mojo* was alive. I snapped the string and held it over the pit. *"Ifa* is the path for everyone and no one." I waved the *mojo* at Abla's empty eye sockets. "I don't believe in you!"

Abla shrank away from the *mojo,* fading into the mud as you Guardians came barreling toward the pit in your silver charger. Propitious. Abla's infectious insanity churned my stomach. I did a warrior dance to calm my blood.

Guardian Opal was at the hospital looking for the bridge to nowhere. I told her tonight was not the night for flying over the edge. She squeezed my hand and remembered things I thought I'd lost forever. A true Guardian, she reminded me of who I had been. Hope harasses us all, and grace humbles me. I know where to find Ariel. The tempest play runs for many performances. With the offerings I've received, I have enough cash for a winter season ticket. Although shipwrecked in a storm, I see the light that could bring me together.

Dear Guardians, the telling draws us closer. Don't you feel this?

Each piece, each story is a bridge from nowhere over grief and pain right to Eshu's gate. Who do I mean to be? Oath-breaker betraying the ones I love or Imagineer conjuring the future?

I am in pieces, perhaps scattered across America. However, I am not over yet!

Book IV

Pittsburgh, PA, 1987 & France, 1893

Whoever undertakes to set himself up as a judge of Truth and Knowledge is shipwrecked by the laughter of the gods.

—Albert Einstein

I am not a religious person but I do believe in magic, mysteries and deals cut at the crossroads under the full moon.

—Pearl Cleage

Chronicles 18a: Paris Fables— *Océane* and the *Aje*

"Motes in the eyes of God," Bob proclaimed.

Traveling from one end of the Old World to the other, *La Vérité* steamed over three thousand miles of ocean, yet traced only a fraction of the Earth's voluptuous curves. The ship plunged into a foggy channel along a coast of France and, like light twisting through a prism, my story fractured into many stories. My eyes had been wrought from Dahomean mist, my skin from Ouidah sand. My mind was fashioned in Eshu's maze, so France was blurry, real and not real. In this version of my story, Luigi's troupe boarded a smaller boat, *L'Aventurier,* to glide down canals to the capital city of the Old World (or one of them—London was on the other side of the fog). The night before we reached Paris, no one slept. Wind off the shore tasted of mystery, danger, and novelty.

Kehinde traced wayward celestial bodies. "Has the dance of the stars changed?"

I smiled. "Bob tells me—"

"What do I care what Bob sees?" Kehinde said.

"He throws his spear with us."

"Bob drank no blood oath to us. He loves that rascal Liam as much as he loves you."

I was pleased to hear that Bob loved me. "Do you love me?"

The question irritated her. "I don't know how."

"Bob says the Earth tilts in the plane of the home star. It's a whirling top listing a bit askew. I've felt this. We sail into a spring sky, not winter. Twilight is longer now."

"Bob is askew. He'll betray someone." Kehinde spoke from bitter experience.

Nothing dampened my good mood. The *aje* threatened to zoom

across inky water and leap onto bustling docks. "We're about to arrive in Paris!"

"Why rejoice?" Kehinde clutched my hand. "France conquered Dahomey."

"You waste no loyalty on former Fon masters."

"I am impatient for a new world. I've seen enough of the old."

Melinga sucked honey from my fingers. I tickled her into chortles.

"You spoil that child." Somso chastised and praised me.

"You neglect her," Kehinde said. "Was it a son you longed for?"

"I wanted a natural child, not a demon baby, fat and old at birth. All her teeth have come and so much wild hair. No child babbles at this age."

Kehinde smiled at Melinga. "We have enough grief. Why mourn miracles?"

It was late afternoon when *L'Aventurier* finally dropped anchor in Paris. A gang of boats bobbed in murky water, scraping bottom in shallow water. Music from flutes and stringed instruments rode the breeze around drunken laughter, harsh commands, and friendly chatter. Horses tore muscles and sweated blood dragging cargo-carts. Land steamships made ingenious use of pistons, flywheels, and metal tracks. Chimneys belched vapors from burnt flesh and heavy metals. My nose dribbled mucous against poison gas barely diluted. A wall of houses framed the chaos. Glass windows glared the setting star into my face, a hundred red-orange eyes.

"Blessings to Eshu!" I was first to race across the gangplank.

Melinga cooed in my arms as I scooped up a pinch of Paris soil and rubbed it on my forehead and tongue. A thousand French people barged past us, bored by the wonders of their lives. A man, balanced on a hard seat between two wheels, wove through the crowd and whizzed past my nose. My heart ached to try his machine.

"Maman"—a little girl poked my thigh—*"qu'est-ce que c'est ça?"*

"What are you, the girl asks." Bob translated a language I'd learned from Kehinde. He smiled at the girl's mother(?). Was she one of the sweet French ladies tired of men making love with their faces? The woman snatched the child away as if we were poison.

"*Bienvenue* to Paris." Bob pulled a hat over his light eyes and, hiding in his own shadow, sauntered ahead.

Liam tipped his cap. "Watch your step, your highness. Unruly decks make still ground unsteady under delicate feet."

Kehinde snickered. "You watch your step." She flicked a finger at his grin.

After a short march, we came to a market—stalls, pavilions, and tables under umbrellas. Vegetables, animal corpses, cloth, wood, and metalwork spilled onto dusty streets. Melinga squealed as a man let loose a bouquet of colorful flying orbs. He reached for the bags of gas floating off. I leapt high on *aje* muscles and snatched a green orb for Melinga. I tossed the man metal earned at Kehinde's war masquerades aboard *La Vérité*. Bystanders gaped at Melinga gnawing the smooth surface of the orb.

"An offering to the war god." Kehinde pointed to a giant termite tower. "Let's not forget where we are."

Melinga released her colorful orb; it spiraled overhead. Clouds dark as dirt raced in and exploded. Balls of hard water pelted us. Kehinde caught a big one and, despite her ill humor, grinned as it melted on her palm. "What is this?"

"Hail!" Bob herded us into a pavilion.

The crowd turned into a mob, banging through narrow spaces, stomping one another. Somso shook hail from her crown of braids and smiled thanks at the owner. Enchanted, he prattled French. Somso spoke good Christian English. At the market's edge, a chestnut horse, rimmed in frost and carrying a sallow-faced man, galloped toward an oblivious crowd. The rider tugged reins and sputtered useless commands. A robust woman on a two-wheeled vehicle halted between the horse and the unsuspecting crowd. A brave soul.

"*Océane, ma petite,*" yelled a second woman on a two-wheeler. "*Non!*"

"*Oui.*" Océane spoke soothing tones. Slowing down, the animal slipped on frosty pavement and slammed into her. Océane sailed from her seat and hit the stone road with a gasp. "*Attention,*

Eloise!" Océane warned the friend behind her and scrambled to standing. She reached for the reins and missed. The horse trampled the wheels of her marvelous machine. A hoof grazed her thigh. Océane yelped. The confused beast lurched into her shoulder. Océane fell, hit her head on loose rocks, and passed out. The rider yanked the reins. Blood and foam dripped from the bit. Tiny Eloise dumped her two-wheeler and yelled for help as the horse pranced on Océane's stringy hair.

"The horse will dash brave Océane to bits." Tears spilled from my eyes. *Aje* head, heart, and tail strained against the Taiwo-self, and I/we raced to scoop up Océane. The *aje*, exuding the scent of a predator, clutched Océane. The horse reared, eyes bulging. The sallow-faced rider clung to its neck as the *aje* belched fire. The horse turned and galloped away.

Océane had no broken bones. Her brain had been shaken and patches of scalp were missing hair. Several gashes on her thigh and forehead oozed blood. The *aje* stopped the bleeding and cleansed wounds with tongue and tail. The tail kept vanishing. Eloise sat nearby, transfixed. The rain subsided, and the *aje* withdrew. Alert again, Océane clutched my free hand, human and sweaty now. Melinga grabbed Océane's long nose and babbled Yoruba.

"*Merci beaucoup, madame,*" Océane said softly. "*Vous êtes courageuse.*" She kissed Melinga's fingers, then mine.

"*Non, le cheval . . .* horse fears *aje,*" I replied. French was not my friend. "Not brave."

"*Si,*" she insisted. "*Vous êtes très brave.*"

A parade of sneering men with broken teeth and stringy mustaches stormed us. Rough arms snatched Océane. Several spit sour words at me, as if the cloudburst and wild horse were my fault—a trick played by *une Africaine sauvage.* The *aje* wanted to blast them to ash and smoke. Waving her cutlass, Kehinde pulled me back into the pavilion. Across the road under an umbrella, Liam whistled. He longed to see Kehinde's warrior dance. Captain Luigi had banned weapons on shore. He'd confiscated knives from a few men but hadn't searched Kehinde.

"You always cause a commotion." Somso chastised us in Igbo and smiled at the pavilion's owner. He gave her a bag of nuts. She offered him a brass bracelet. He wouldn't take it. "It's all I have." Somso placed the trinket on an altar at the center of the pavilion. An image of the Jesus orisha smiled down at her.

Outside, Eloise talked with several men spoiling for a fight. Océane was silent, dazed. My French was insufficient to follow the heated exchange. Kehinde brandished her cutlass and knife. I looked to Bob. He hung his head.

"Why are they so angry?" I peered at Océane. "Her mind is a little bruised. She should stay awake. Sleep is too much like death after a hard knock on the skull. A few tiny creatures attempted to make her cells their slaves, but I took some hostages and killed virulent ones. Brave Océane will be fine, I swear this."

Frenchmen charged toward the pavilion. Bob and Kehinde blocked their path.

Kehinde spoke Fon. "They are fools. You look ready to eat bullets and belch a gout of flame." Waving her cutlass, she distracted the smoldering *aje*. "Listen!" The startled crowd stepped back. Kehinde danced and sang in Fon:

> *Dagger in my mouth*
> *I climb the rock face*
> *I drive the wild pig*
> *Out into the open*
> *My tough skin is better armor*
> *Than the bristles of the porcupine*
> *If I have lost my ax, gun, or cutlass*
> *My teeth are sharp enough*
> *To tear my enemies apart*
> *My fingers are stronger still*
> *Iron claws to defeat you*

Kehinde severed spectral heads and stomped phantom hearts. She tossed a gossamer cloth and sliced it to ribbons before it hit the ground. She shaved a few hairs from Liam's curly beard. He laughed, and the mob became an audience marveling at the *Ballet Amazon* and *Voodoo*. Kehinde back-flipped over the battered two-wheeler and landed with her cutlass raised high. It glistened in now gentle rain. Mud-splattered men grumbled and dragged Eloise and Océane away. A red fruit splattered at Kehinde's feet. She skewered the fleshy remains as the audience clapped and dispersed.

"These people make no sense." Somso muttered my exact thoughts.

"They make their own sense, and we offend it," Kehinde said to me. "What did I tell you?"

"You're a fine doorful of a woman." Liam glared at the Frenchmen. "What would you expect out of a frog but a croak?"

Kehinde flicked the red fruit from her blade. "Are you so different from these frogs, Irishman?"

"Madame, you cut me to the quick." Liam clutched his heart and strode too close to her. "Is a dragon a seahorse?"

Kehinde poked his chest with the cutlass and drew blood. "Even a dragon brushing against thorns will tear its wings."

"You keep company with angels, milady." He kissed her cheek quickly and retreated.

"French victors still fear our pagan spirits and savage hearts," Kehinde said.

"No one will wrestle us to the ground," I said. "We will be bold here."

"They cut off the heads of bold ones with a guillotine, in a plaza not far from here." Bob gestured toward the center of the city. "The French mob begged for more blood."

"In Christian, civilized lands, we shouldn't speak of taking heads." Somso held up the crossroad talisman. "Many love Jesus here." She touched the talisman to my cheek. "I won't close my heart to Frenchmen. We agree for once, Wanderer, let's be bold."

The streets were an orderly stream of traffic again. Kehinde put away her blade. Somso strode ahead. Rainbows glistened in humid air. A swath of black lingered in the sky near the termite tower.

Lightning arced from the cloud's dark heart. Melinga clapped and drooled against my face. As a silver zigzag tore through the atmosphere to the tip of the metal tower, the *aje* longed to gather Kehinde, Bob, and Melinga into the circle of its being and escape Paris. We could spread through the spaces between things and discover the new worlds Kehinde desired. That was my last coherent thought before bolts of high voltage cloud electricity ripped into me.

According to Kehinde, giant sparks were headed for her, Bob, and Somso when the *aje* swallowed the white-hot spears. According to Somso, rogue bolts pierced the ground around us, and I used demon fire to shield everyone. Bob only remembered me shoving him to safety. Liam claimed he was blind and deaf in the lightning and thunder. He recalled cold claws throwing him down. In all versions, after saving everyone from a deadly strike, I emptied my stomach and fainted standing up, arms locked around Melinga, blue fire twisting from bloody nostrils. My skin turned cold and hard like polished river stone. Feverish sweat drenched my garments. The French mob gave me a wide berth. Only children, dogs, and half-wits stopped to stare at the African *aje*-statue who clenched a squealing baby in its talons. Kehinde kept these curious few at bay and whispered in my ear:

My teeth are sharp enough
To tear my enemies apart
My fingers are stronger still
Iron claws to defend you

I released Melinga and collapsed. Bob and Liam argued about what to do next.

"No French doctor," Kehinde insisted. She lifted me up, claiming I was light, airy, and sweet smelling, despite a stone statue appearance. Bob led us to a friend's house.

Hearing the lightning tales, Luigi applauded my devilish *Voodoo* and insisted I show off savage magic onstage in France and Chicago. I pretended not to speak Fon, English, French, or Igbo whenever he harangued me. Somso promised wild, savage magic for me. Perhaps this is why Luigi was loathe to abandon a sick performer immediately. He dreamed of the spectacle we could create and the bags of money he would make, if I survived . . .

Baron of Badass

Marie lounged on Sekou's bed with *The Chronicles* in her lap opened to the video-image of the Eiffel Tower in an electrical storm. Blurry or blank pages came after that. Marie chanted *if I survived*, eventually jumbling up consonants and vowels. Silver platform shoes, size 6 ½ and very retro, dangled from fidgety toes. It'd take the Jaws of Life to extract that girl from her tight black jeans. Her shirt was black quicksilver, hugging tiny breasts then flowing over seriously narrow hips and zero booty. Yellow letters on the front declared: A QUANTUM LEAP IS A VERY, VERY SHORT DISTANCE. Cinnamon chuckled reading this. Marie didn't do ornaments or jewelry except Oshun's comb, a crown of peacock feathers rendered from wood and blue-green glass beads that held waves of black hair out of her flushed face. That was a gift/share from Cinnamon. A bit of the Wanderer for them all . . .

"Wow." Klaus left his mouth hanging open.

He sat next to Marie, close, his leg, hip, and shoulder touching hers. Cinnamon vacillated from jealous to excited. Klaus wore a frumpy gray T-shirt and black jeans. Not wrinkled or dirty, just blah. Hunky guys got away with being blasé and anti-style. Klaus's muscles required no decoration. His hair was disheveled. Lank wisps curled over his eyes. His lips were as pale as ice. High cheeks burned bright orange and made Cinnamon feel warm. She'd never looked at people with her whole body. It was amazing what there was to notice.

"Wow." Klaus didn't mind repeating himself, didn't mind sounding stupid or too impressed. He got away with everything. "Griot Joe is Taiwo in 1890s Paris. How did he get so twisted up, hobbling around with a supermarket cart?" Klaus would definitely be game for solving the Wanderer mystery. Marie too. Cinnamon

simply had to ask them. Since when was she such a scared rabbit? "*The Chronicles* blows me out." Occasionally Klaus lost English
at the prepositions. Cinnamon didn't correct him. *Blows me out*
sounded good.

Marie moved her mouth, without saying anything or making
sound—trancing. Whoever read *The Chronicles* out loud teleported
through the spaces between things into the story world. You were
here and now and also there and then. At least that's what Cinnamon thought happened. Being in two places at once, inhabiting the
Wanderer's body and your own, was sexy in a horror-movie way.
Marie's dark eyes were spooky; her breath was shallow and wet, as
if she were sucking down an alien atmosphere. She combed the air
with rigid fingers then raked jet black fingernails across her cheeks,
leaving pink wiggly lines. They were all trancing—thinking deep.
Cinnamon never had friends to do that with except Sekou.

Klaus stared at Marie, worried. Alien contact didn't have to be
benign. What if reading *The Chronicles*, one of them got stuck in the
spaces between things? Mostly Klaus looked like he wanted to kiss
Marie's killer red lips. Or Cinnamon could be projecting. These
days she saw sex everywhere: full bosoms, sultry eyes, shapely buttocks, plump lips, well-placed racks of muscles, bulging crotches.
When Klaus hugged her, she felt his penis against her thigh, not
huge or hard or anything, just there. This could be the dreaded
hormonal shift to teenage sex zombie that Opal, Star Deer, and
everybody had been worrying about.

Cinnamon's period had arrived in sixth grade. That was forever
ago and no big deal. For the last few weeks, since the audition
actually, random body parts had been grabbing her attention, although nothing much had happened after that. At school, the in-
teresting body parts were always attached to kids who would have
tortured her if she were smaller, had fewer muscles, and broadcast
one-tenth the attitude, so who cared how fly or how sweet or how
fine . . . until Klaus and Marie came over tonight. They made her
hot and itchy, smiling at her posters, books, and Sekou's dictionary
collection.

Klaus was particularly impressed by the *Oxford English Dictionary* on its altar under the mirror. "What do you do with this?"

"It was Sekou's," Cinnamon replied. "You know, despite Hollywood pretensions, *bite the dust* dates to Homer's *Iliad*, and before probably."

What the hell was that about?

Then there was the three-way hug that went on and on, because if they let go of each other, they might drop off the planet into an abyss and burn up or . . . Did Cinnamon have to fall, hard, for her only two friends in the world? Sex was a big distraction. Why couldn't they just be friends?

Derailed by lust and dread, Cinnamon hadn't done one single thing she swore she'd do when Opal landed in the hospital. That one crazy night had gone on forever, and then two weeks passed so quickly, it wasn't even a blur, more like a blink. Every day Cinnamon showed up for ninth grade, advanced placement, visited her mom in intensive care, and went shopping with the elders. In between homework and chores, she'd done some scouting. Griot Joe and Bug-Man Lexy were MIA. Star Deer went off to do contact workshops in New Mexico. Getting *Ms. Respect-Your-Elders* to talk behind Opal's back about Raven would have been a miracle anyhow. Drugged Opal went in and out, ranting and rambling. Nobody could say if her mom was revealing deep secrets or talking crap, which meant no further progress on the *important shit*. Cinnamon scoured the attic, pulled up floorboards, and dug around under the back porch hunting Raven's paintings. Nada.

Big and bold, the baron of badass in her mind, yet Cinnamon hadn't asked Klaus and Marie for help. She'd have to explain the whole faggot thing. Their Mod Squad secret society had survived the ghost thing, an ambi-sexual alien thing, maybe even a trio thing. If Klaus and Marie freaked over the gay brother thing, Cinnamon would have to dump them. In fact, she ought to put them to the test immediately. But sex had her so turned around that for the second time in her life, not knowing seemed better than knowing. Angst over Opal had been a legitimate excuse for clinging to ignorance, but lust? She was terrified that rapper-nerd Sekou might drop in for a haunt and inadvertently broadcast his sex life before she was ready. Lust had shown Cinnamon to be a coward. Nothing to lose before. Klaus and Marie were a real test of bravery and she was failing.

Two weeks gone by, mucho heavy stuff coming down on her, and she told the elders nothing either. Everything she wanted to say sounded stupid. They were stuck up in the nineteenth century. Anything they said would probably sound corny and *so country, it made you itch*. Damn! Opal's crap had totally infected her. Cinnamon hadn't even asked Aidan to take her to see Daddy. It was disappointing and downright humiliating not to be who she needed to be.

"More clear words!" Marie yelled and read on. Thank God.

Chronicles 18b: Paris Fables—
Oshun's Comb

In this version of Paris, we arrived on a steam-powered train from Marseille. Bob took us on a tour: bridges, arches, spirit houses. Riding an underground train, we traversed the sewers. Boasting cavernous halls, waterways, and sidewalks, this sewer world was an ingenious city under the city. Somso and I were enchanted. My anxiety at the looming masquerade dissipated. Kehinde was distant. Bob suffered in daylight and wore a floppy hat and itchy woolen clothes; splotches of dark pigment on his hands were raw from scratching. Shadowy sewers should have put him in a good mood, but in his coat pocket, he found an old copy of *Household Words* containing a Noble Savage story by Charles Dickens.

"Not that tripe again!" Liam groaned. He groaned more when Bob dragged us to a dime museum to watch a savage masquerade—not by Dickens, but starring a friend. "You do this to yourself, laddie."

The crowd shrieked at a giant onstage, Raymond, a friend of Bob's. Raymond had a thick bush of hair, ruddy broken skin, and bright white teeth. He toted a broom handle spear and limped as if wounded. The crowd played Raymond's enemy. They pelted him with rotten red fruit, bananas, and coconuts. A warrior unencumbered for battle, Raymond wore only a skirt of rough cloth. Bones and bags dangled around his neck—*minkisi*, spiritually-charged vessels filled with power from the land of the dead. A short Frenchman in blue and red finery jabbed the giant with a dull sword. Raymond laughed at fake blood dripping from the parade warrior's blade. A woman swung in the air on what Liam called the trapeze. She shot arrows at straw men. Her bolts pierced their hearts and heads. Raymond leapt for her, but she was too high. A lioness yawned, bored, until they prodded her into big-cat acrobatics. Women in frothy white skirts kicked up their legs in a spirited dance. Liam insisted we leave before savages were shot from cannons and Bob got too angry for civilized folks.

We strolled along the river into a sudden electrical storm. Kehinde laughed at balls of hail, Somso grinned, and Bob's temper cooled. As in all versions, I risked scattering into the spaces between things to heal a stranger and save loved ones. Absorbing lethal electric charges, I passed out standing up with Melinga in my arms. Kehinde carried me to Raymond's dwelling. Transitioning to an *aje* during an electromagnetic storm was imprudent. What demon is not reckless? I was ill several days or weeks. But many Dahomeans fell ill when we landed in France. Luckily, Kehinde, Somso, and Melinga were immune to French maladies. Raymond offered me a dank room to recuperate in. His dwelling was near a spirit house that clanged its iron bells every fifteen minutes. We had no peace, no time of our own making. The spirit house claimed to shelter devotees of the Jesus orisha, but worshippers bowed in deep obeisance to their clocks, more than to Jesus's cross. God was the master of clocks, and his universe ran with angelic gears.

Once when I shrieked because of midday tolling, Bob gripped me and said, "You should go to Hamburg, Germany, on the North Sea if you want to meet God the Clockmaker and feel the heavenly tick-tock. France doesn't hold a candle to Protestant Germany."

"Hamburg?" I hissed. "Tell me Hamburg's story."

"If you promise to get well quickly!"

"There are in me always others waiting for an opening. I'm not sure I can be well."

"Nonsense." Bob dabbed my brow and drizzled a French doctor cure on my tongue.

Kehinde didn't notice. She poured libation to Eshu:

Eshu, guardian of the gate!
See! My legs are sturdy
Feel! My breasts are mighty
Let hungry rogue spirits find their way through me

She offered invading demons her body for mine.

"No!" I refused her sacrifice and flailed weak limbs. "The bells . . ." were quiet to their ears but vibrating still and breaking my heart. I passed out again.

Kehinde stood guard over my feverish body and wandering mind. Bob nursed me. Liam brought us food and drink; he would do anything for his dragon lady. Melinga fussed until Somso laid her against my swollen belly. The child cooed and pounded my flesh, occasionally calling me back from the strange stupor. Once I leapt out of sweaty sheets, dizzy and disoriented, Kehinde covered my face with kisses. Happy tears streaked Bob's cheeks. Even Somso looked pleased. I gulped a cool drink Kehinde offered me. She shooed the others outside.

"Don't leave me, Wanderer." Kehinde plaited my wayward hair.

"Tell me a story you don't want to tell. For love."

She thought a moment. "I lied to you about the woman I betrayed to Abla." Kehinde rested her forehead on my sweaty neck. "I do remember her face and her secret Yoruba name, Ekundayo. It means sorrow and tears become joy. Her mother was a Yoruba slave and taught her *Ifa* wisdom. Her Fon father called her something else. I've forgotten only that name. Ekundayo had planned to escape while we danced for *Mère d'eau*. Before marching off with the gate opening force, she gave me this Oshun comb." Kehinde placed a beaded ornament in my hair. "*Memory is the master of death*, Ekundayo said. *You love me. You'll keep me alive.* I tried to give the comb back. Ekundayo wouldn't let me. *Abla is suspicious of you. Be careful*, she warned as Yao took her away."

"Yao, who killed your family and sold Somso?"

"Yes. Ekundayo still trusted me, loved me. She was quick and foolish with love . . . I never saw her again. I dreamt once that she'd slipped from the battlefield and escaped. Abla had threatened to send us both to the front line, but spared me when I betrayed Ekundayo. If I loved her, why did I betray her?" She touched my forehead. "Your face creases like hers, when you think, when you're happy." She rubbed her cheek against my shoulder. "Oshun protected me through countless battles. Now the mother of waters protects you." Her arms circled my chest. "You know the worst of who I am and haven't yet abandoned me. Stay longer."

Feeling better, I stroked the cool glass beads in the Oshun comb.

Kehinde abandoned me in Pittsburgh. Why should I bear it? How should I bear it?

The painting is from a photo of the *Tour Eiffel électrique*. Kehinde and I are up high. I've lost the photo. This is recovered memory.

Hormones

"I'm wearing Oshun's comb," Marie said, near tears.

A spark of electricity leapt from *The Chronicles* drawing and zapped Sekou's time-bomb clock. The alarm went off: a giant explosion followed by shattered glass, walls caving in, and a siren whining—enough action-adventure noise to wake the dead and keep them from slipping back into the sheets for a snooze.

Marie gaped at the Wanderer's video-drawing. "That's the Eiffel Tower in a lightning storm," she shouted, "not a termite hill."

The Chronicles's trance-spell was broken.

"This is drop-dead cool." Klaus turned off the alarm.

"Is *drop-dead cool* German?" Marie said. "Say it in German."

"*Todschick*." He spoke a mouthful of sexy consonants. Marie repeated them.

"*Termite tower* isn't a literal description." Cinnamon felt an inexplicable need to defend Taiwo's intelligence. "That's how the Wanderer saw it, back in 1890-whatever, before checking out the whole world. Perspective is everything."

Marie rolled her eyes. "Of course." She patted the bed next to her. After a moment, Cinnamon plopped down, close. "Why do a painting of a photograph?" Marie leaned into Cinnamon and thrust *The Chronicles* under her nose. Cinnamon snorted a cloud of ozone. "Don't sniff it. Do that deluge thing you do."

Cinnamon pushed *The Chronicles* aside. She felt completely out of character. Could raging hormones make a bold person timid and cowardly?

"Yes. Why paint a photo?" Klaus looked as eager as Marie. "Please. A deluge."

"What?" Cinnamon played dumb.

"You know what," they said in unison.

Klaus and Marie seemed nice, but after one audition and a blizzard, Cinnamon didn't really *know* either of them. What if they
had joined forces to get Cinnamon to act crazy so they could make
fun of her?

"Don't be coy." Marie shoved her.

"I don't do coy." Cinnamon didn't know how.

Klaus punched her shoulder. "I've been waiting all day for—"

Marie narrowed her spooky eyes. "Why are you holding out
on us?"

"What?" Weren't aliens and ghosts enough? Why did Cinnamon tell them about—

"A story storm." Klaus's eyes darted about; his brow wrinkled.
"What else?"

Marie pursed her killer red lips. "You said the hidden truth of
The Chronicles comes to you in a firestorm of words, burning in
your mouth, until you spit them out, so fast the words smash each
other up."

"Yes. Deluge." Klaus sucked that word like it was finger-lickin'
good.

"Did I tell you all that?" Cinnamon swallowed slowly. "Both of
you?"

Marie smirked. "Klaus was at my house when you called yesterday."

They'd been hanging out without her! "Nobody told me."

"Don't get mad. I had to leave my house," Klaus said. "*Mutti*
goes volunteering every day at the Playhouse. *Vati* says nothing
against this." Klaus grinned. "Who argues with Commander Williams? And *Mutti* knows so much English!"

"I told you there was more to her." Marie grinned too. "*The Tempest* opens the first day of spring. That production could use mega
foreign aid."

Klaus licked dry lips. "Ariel gives me acting tips."

"Ariel's a scattered bit of the Wanderer." Cinnamon offered a
taste of her theory.

"No, really?" Marie said.

"Yes, Ariel is . . ." Klaus blinked rapidly. "*Mutti* goes to tea with the Playhouse Angels. Since our blizzard ride, she and Mrs. Williams are bosom brothers, yes?"

"Bosom buddies," Cinnamon said. "So explain why you were at Marie's."

"Oh." Was Klaus hiding something? "After Mrs. Williams picked *Mutti* up yesterday, *Vati* was . . . how he gets, so I tell him Marie promised to help with hard music for *Title Under Construction*, on a grand piano." Klaus sighed. "A big lie, but since the blizzard, I was going bananas and nuts. I was very lonely for you two. I knew where Marie's house was. Mrs. Williams drove there first after the hospital. Easy to take a bus and walk on by." He laughed, goofy and vulnerable. "I'm out there walking on by, many times. Marie sees me and says I must come inside. I walk in the door, the phone rings, and it's you. How perfect is that?" Klaus picked a scab on his knuckle.

"Stop that." Cinnamon grabbed his hand.

"*Vati* says it's a damn shame I got the lead. Irony too, Drug Prince. But I don't have to fall on my ass. I can drop out, next rehearsal."

"You can't drop out!" Cinnamon shook him hard.

"I'll help you with the music," Marie said. "We'll both help."

"Really?" When did klutz Beckenbauer get puppy-dog adorable?

"We're your crew," Cinnamon said. "You think we'd leave you hanging?"

Klaus had obviously thought they would. "I wasn't sure."

Marie touched the Oshun comb reverently. "All I do is think about you guys."

"Me too. Miz Redwood made me call," Cinnamon said. "I was chickening out."

Every day, Marie and Klaus rang Ms. Allen at hospital reception to check on Opal. They asked about Cinnamon too. Redwood stuffed coins in a pay phone and waited while Cinnamon dialed Marie's number. Who'd risk an encounter with *Vati*?

"So now we're here together." Marie tapped *The Chronicles*. "Do the storm thing."

Cinnamon gulped. "My mouth is a runaway train."

Marie flipped her hair defiantly. Cinnamon snorted at this cute girl move. "What's the big deal? It's not like getting naked."

"Yes it is."

Klaus flushed red-orange down his neck to his arms. He was having a naked fantasy. Cinnamon couldn't imagine getting naked with anybody. She tugged at the mud cloth outfit Iris bought her. The tunic fit, but the homespun fabric from Mali felt scratchy. Maybe raging hormones made her skin hyper-irritable. Blaming everything on creeping adolescence was stupid. She had to take responsibility. *Ain't no devil ever made you do nothing.*

Marie groaned. "We've already seen you do the story storm thing."

Klaus whistled. "You were talking full throttle, light speed." He liked how she was.

Marie did too. "We can keep up, you know." She sucked more blood into her killer red lips and gripped Cinnamon's arm. "We go that fast too."

"Well," Klaus squirmed, "sometimes."

"Of course." Cinnamon shuddered. Talking Opal into the emergency room had scared the stuffing out of her. "I'm worried about my mom." She lied with the truth.

Klaus and Marie looked baffled, the identical question marks on such different faces.

"OK. It's like this. Three times since she fell out at the Playhouse, my mom's gotten better. I'm talking get-up-out-the-bed, roaring-to-go better. Her blood tests are stellar; her heart is rocking; the gravel wheeze is a distant rumble. Doctors are ready to release her cranky behind, but out of nowhere, taking off her johnny, fussing at the nurse about a cigarette, or slipping on new sneakers—she relapses back to intensive care. What kind of bacteria, virus, or cancer would play like that?" Sekou had established her innocence vis-à-vis Opal's lung rebellion. Just in case, Cinnamon had thrown up shields against marauding story storms. No *slipping into darkness, taking her mind beyond the trees.*

"What else do you cogitate and not tell us?" Klaus wagged a finger at her.

"*Cogitate?* Really?" Cinnamon said.

"Cogitate. This is good English," Klaus replied. "Isn't it?"

"Come on, five minutes staring a hole in the wall." Marie looked mad.

"Only a minute or two," Cinnamon said.

"Brooding is not cute." Marie wagged a finger too.

"You were trancing too. Drooling ain't talking."

"Everybody trances reading *The Chronicles* out loud."

"I say everything twice, with a German accent." Klaus reached over Marie's pout and tickled Cinnamon.

"Oh, hell no, boy." Cinnamon tackled Klaus.

They pounced on each other on top of Marie, tickling their bad moods away. The three fell into a heap, giggling and bouncing so hard the bed creaked in protest. They halted abruptly. Awkward silence settled over them. Marie tugged one of Cinnamon's sleek new braids out of the topknot Redwood had done for her. Gold and blue beads at the end were from Iris's last trip to Ghana. Aidan made the leather ribbons holding the ponytail together. Marie undid that and all the braids tumbled down Cinnamon's face.

"Come on." Marie sat up. She was a bulldog with a bone. It was endearing. "You think we can't handle the hard stuff?"

Klaus set *The Chronicles* in Cinnamon's lap. He stroked the Eiffel Tower's sharp point. "This drawing set off a time bomb. Can you please explain that? Have mercy."

"Mercy, yes, please." Klaus and Marie nailed Mrs. B's heart-on-her-sleeves accent in two-part harmony. "Freaky mercy!"

Cinnamon howled, "Give me freaky any damn day!"

They bumped heads together and got tangled up in one another. Cinnamon still liked the taste of their breath, the warm and savory skin smells too: a woodsy herbal scent mixed with lavender and sage. Contact improv on the bed was a trick. Balancing and sharing weight, Cinnamon wanted to kiss somebody and get the taste of both of them on her lips. She wanted to get up and run out of the house.

Disastronauts and Glamazons

What if Klaus and Marie only liked her for the weird shit around her? They were gorgeous and sexy. She was a blimp, even in Afro-chic mud-cloth robes. Who'd blame them for grossing out? Cinnamon wouldn't fall for somebody who looked like her. What about Evelyn Powell, only an inch shorter than her and thirty pounds heavier? Cinnamon didn't get hot looking at Evelyn waddle down the hall, or Chris Hunt. He had flabby man tits and a girl's ass. Cinnamon didn't hate Evelyn or Chris. She never said mean things to their faces or behind their backs, but she didn't *lust* after them. Actually, she didn't *lust* after anybody either, except . . . Klaus and Marie dangled over the edge of Sekou's bed, clutching Cinnamon's thighs, balanced on a shared breath.

"Normal is so overrated," Marie said, sober in a heartbeat. "I hate the real world." Two weeks ago this child was a stone-cold realist. "The real world hates me."

Marie fought tears, fought *public display*. Dreaded hormones probably had her in their grips too. Cinnamon lost her breath and her balance. Luckily Klaus used the rogue momentum to take them through twisty rolls and a flip. Cinnamon and Marie landed on their hands and knees. Klaus was balanced on his side across both their backs.

"We're making the real world, right now." Klaus quoted Opal.

Taut as a steel cable, he pivoted his full weight on the fulcrum of Marie's pelvic girdle. Her arms trembled slightly, but she held him. Contact was dancing physics, not brute strength. Klaus tumbled and shifted so that he was balanced on Cinnamon's back, knees tucked to his chest. Marie pressed her belly against his slender feet. Grunting German, Klaus pushed his legs upward. *Gravity is my friend*, Cinnamon thought as their combined weight flowed through her arms and palms into the floor and to the center of the Earth. Marie spun like a top on Klaus's feet.

"Our Mod Squad crew is a force to be reckoned with," he shouted. "True, yes?"

"True, yes." Marie flipped onto the bed, floating through the air as if she controlled the wind. Aidan was right. How could you help loving someone who could fly? Marie held out a hand to Cinnamon and one to Klaus. "We should take our show on the road." They pulled Marie through a somersault onto the floor with them. "I think we need to hear your story storm before more *Chronicles* pages come clear."

"That sounds right to me," Klaus said.

"Ganging up on me, huh?" Cinnamon sighed. "OK, but only if you two help."

"Help you what?"

"Not call up the twisted, dark fantasy, dystopia stuff."

"You don't do that." Klaus leaned into her. "Do you?"

Cinnamon shoved him. "Why ask your ass for help, if the shit ain't fucking freaky dangerous?"

"Sorry." He snorted at her.

"Whoa. How fucking freaky dangerous is it?" Marie cocked her head, thrilled. "I'm not a wuss. Klaus neither. We got your back."

"OK, so he's Prince Charming and you're a fearless Glamazon." Cinnamon hid behind her braids.

"And you're not?" Marie smoothed each braid carefully into a thick tail.

"I feel like a, like a . . ." Cinnamon groped around for the leather tie, "like a stupid Disastronaut, you know what I'm saying?"

"No. You're not telling us everything." Marie squinted. "What're you looking for?"

Klaus pulled the leather tie from under his butt. "Glamazon? Disastronaut? Is this English?"

"English is whatever people who speak English understand." Cinnamon wanted to smack somebody. Was this her real self or more Snow White flashbacks?

"Marie's ten times more of a Glamazon than that waif Director Hill cast for the Changeling." Klaus tied the leather around Cinnamon's braids. "And you should be playing Snow White."

"Who you telling?" Cinnamon resented tears and snot dribbling out. Not getting cast *two weeks ago* shouldn't still hurt.

"I'm really terrible without you guys." Klaus tugged one braid free on the side. "Janice is always acting too cute, not fierce."

"Are you saying I'm a natural for the angry bitch?" Cinnamon aimed for mad and missed. She laughed through stray tears.

"No." Klaus sputtered. "*Fucking freaky dangerous* is a line in Diamond's play." He scratched his scalp. "You two can say it like you mean it."

"Who cares?" Cinnamon said. "Everybody wants cute. Janice is, is . . ." green-eyed, good-hair, flat-belly, stand-up-booty cute.

"Janice is a legend in her own mind," Marie said.

"She can't make Diamond's words her own." Klaus jabbed Marie's shoulder and Cinnamon's too. "There's no force in her field."

Marie balled a fist. "With Janice, you got to wonder, what marched up her ass and croaked. The three of us, we're, wow, we're dangerous energy in a freaky force field!" She kissed the tear on Cinnamon's nose and kissed Klaus's cheek too. They got very still. Marie grabbed *The Chronicles*. "Disastronauts, we gotta know the rules against us *and* for us. Disastronauts are the ones who navigate through the apocalypse."

"Right." Klaus nodded, touching his cheek at the kiss spot.

Marie set *The Chronicles* in Cinnamon's lap, as if it were the holy scripture of their secret society. "Check out the picture and say whatever."

"Like a theatre improv," Klaus whispered. "Look out, real world! Here come the Disastronauts and Glamazons."

He rubbed Cinnamon's shoulders trying to work out the boulders. He leaned strong, warm hands into each stroke, breathing moist air against Cinnamon's neck. Bony knees pressed up against her butt. Marie held Cinnamon's hand, squeezing it and stroking the palm. She tugged at the loose braid and rubbed Cinnamon's forehead with cool fingers. Cinnamon closed her eyes on the good feelings.

Maybe they did like Cinnamon the way she liked them. If she did a story storm, they'd all be dialed in so deep together, Klaus and Marie would have to help her with gay bar mysteries and the *important shit.*

"Pages coming clear!" Klaus shouted.

"OK, read first, then story storm," Marie said.

Chronicles 18c: Paris Fables— Spirit Houses

The Igbo say: *O bu mmuo ndi na-efe na-egbu ha.*
It is the deity that people worship that kills them.

I was deathly ill. Luigi threatened to abandon me. I was terrified. France seemed a cold wasteland where people built mountains to live in, covered the ground so it couldn't breathe, and left nothing green to hold hopes, fears, love, or regret. Few free animals kept company with the people. Comatose cows and crazy horses hobbled about. Promiscuous insects and rats were the bane of city dwellers' existence. Trees were not honored or even considered living beings. No wise old irokos stood in the light of distant stars, drinking ancient waters. Few living witnesses of life beyond the current life stood guard over French people's spirits.

Civilized people wore heavy clothes, ate too much rich food, and drank too much rum. Mouths rotted, hearts labored against constricted vessels, and bodies festered in old sweat and excrement. Chronic illnesses would claim many. The Paris air was thick with poison gas—so little oxygen for blood and brain. At night, workers in high boots and rubber aprons shoveled fermented shit from cesspits into horse-drawn wagons. The cesspools were vast colonies of creatures preying on human frailty. Marching past this foul-smelling work, I wondered, where were the mighty people who had defeated King Béhanzin?

I still carry yellowed newsprint where Dickens, the supreme English griot, accused us: *If we have anything to learn from the Noble Savage, it is what to avoid. His virtues are a fable; his happiness is a delusion; his nobility, nonsense.*

The French were strange to me, who knew too little. Without realizing it, I had come to view my scant experience as the measure of all things and my limited impressions as a full catalogue of life on Earth. After my short story, I presumed, as Dickens had, to be an expert on humanity and all the tales that could or should be told. This is a recipe for despair. *The deity that people worship* . . . Which one was killing me?

"Luigi will wait for you," Kehinde said. She snuck me out on day tours with the troupe. I've forgotten the places we visited. French names had no purchase on my body. The people greeted us warmly, smiled, and made singsongy exclamations. Crowds gaped, excited by our skin, muscle, hair, and milk-heavy breasts, as if having been born French, they were made of different stuff, as if they had never laid eyes on people before. Most who greeted us were pale, with stringy hair and bad teeth. Heavy clothes made it hard to tell what sort ventured close to watch us. In an open place with nodding, hobbled trees and whispering rank water, Somso sat on a stool with Melinga in her arms. Somso's health improved on still ground. Even in foul air, she was radiant. Show-warriors danced around her. Kehinde executed battle moves, taking the heads of phantom attackers. The French looked frightened. They were quick-witted and learned to respect her warrior *ahosi* nature. She spoke to bold fellows in their spicy snarl of a language, but none were clever enough to speak Yoruba, Fon, or Igbo. One man knew Arabic but refused to say a word. Dizzy and drained, I was unable to learn French idioms or gather stories.

Kehinde claimed the French had little to say for their world of wonders. They refused to explain—how the streets were made—what wives were worth—how cathedrals climbed to the sky—if twins were sacred or despised—what wars still raged—how trains charged down iron tracks as fast as ships raced through slippery water. None could tell her about Chicago, America; they couldn't say if the New World was what she had read in books, if the adventurers had lied or not, if it was *the land of the free and the home of the brave*. Audiences were too busy marveling at their precious language dropping from her lips to take her questions seriously.

"The French wish to see the defeated ones dance." Kehinde spit these words. "They clap for their victory, their power. It was the same in Ouidah. I danced for the Fon, and they stole my strength and ate my spirit."

It might be the same in the New World. I never said this out loud.

Audiences rejoiced at whatever mundane similarity they recognized between our masquerade and their lives. Most only spoke one or two languages. The world passed through Ouidah: Yoruba, French, Ewe, Mende, Portuguese, Ibibio, Chinese, Igbo, Arab, Bambara, Brazilian, Akan, Tuareg, Cuban, Hausa, Indian, Fula, English, and Fon. In the French countryside, we broke the monotony.

"They appreciate great spirits," I said. "Why else build mountains for their orisha?"

"They are in a contest with God," Kehinde replied.

We made sacrifices at spirit house doors to Eshu. Crossroad signs of the master of uncertainty were everywhere. Unfortunately Eshu was considered a devil and had to be worshipped in secret. An *aje* was an evil witch. Many celebrated Ogun of iron and war, creator of civilization, master of justice and oaths. But nothing compared to the wrought-iron altar squatting in the center of the city that could be seen from everywhere. We sacrificed often at the Eiffel Tower on the war god's green field, the *Champ de Mars*. The voluptuous exponential curve of the iron lady, its wind tolerance and nonlinear mathematical elegance thrilled me. A box climbed up and down, day and night, carrying passengers who had come to celebrate the warrior way. Kehinde sang praises to Ogun from a thousand feet above the ground.

Roaming Paris, we came across a mountain built to the god of Abraham and Moses, *La Grande Synagogue de la Victoire*. Somso pulled us away, insisting that it would be unwise to disturb this particular house of God. Walking on, we found no shrines to honor orisha such as Shango, Osanyin, Obatala, Oshoosi, Oya, or any of the Fon *Vodun*.

"No one praises Allah here," Kehinde said. "Strange."

"Have we traveled every street?" Somso smirked at Kehinde. "Spied every altar?"

Shrines to the Jesus cult were everywhere. Many fountains were anointed to *Mère d'eau*. The water woman, mother of us all, virgin girl-child greeted each day with mercy and grace, yet, "Why honor so few orisha and neglect the others?" I asked.

Kehinde agreed. "How can *Mère d'eau*, Ogun, and the Jesus orisha be sufficient for so many people?"

"Christians cleanse the world of paganism." Bob thrust Dickens at me: *I call him a savage, and I call a savage a something highly desirable to be civilised off the face of the earth.*

I crumpled the paper. "Throw this torment away and read *A Tale of Two Cities.*"

Bob struggled for words. I'd never seen that. "Civilization is a tight weave of ideas. Pull out the savage thread and it all unravels." Kehinde nodded with him. I didn't understand until—

Late one night, I rose from my sickbed and snuck out a window. I went sleepwalking in search of elder trees with the web of time braided in gnarled trunks and the future rustling through the leaves. Restless French builders had long ago razed their ancient groves. A tree might as well have been a tall rock. Frenchmen had learned how to abuse even the rocks! Kehinde tracked me to the *Champ de Mars* where I'd curled up in the bulging roots of a young tree. I was drenched in freezing dew. My ears throbbed from the trees shrieking nonsense at me. She carried me down lonely avenues. The forts in Ouidah were insignificant anthills compared to the mountain cathedrals and palaces lining boulevards that ran to infinity.

Parisians ignored our desperate escapade. We could have been ghosts, chimera in smoky gas lights. Kehinde paused to gather strength inside the cool gloom of *Notre Dame de Paris*. Light through glass tapestries enchanted her. The jeweled windows celebrated the Jesus orisha, *Mère d'eau*, and wise *Babalawo* and *Iyalawo*. We bowed our heads like everyone else. Buttresses flew above us, making me laugh in awe. I lit many candles for lives wasted. Drunk with wonder, I talked in tongues, then curled into Kehinde's warm, fragrant skin.

"Why won't you trust me with what troubles you?" she asked as we left the cathedral. I was still afraid to mention Abla's torment, Paris confusion, or scattering. Kehinde squeezed my arm. "Because I don't know how to love, like Bob?"

"You loved your brother."

"I killed him, didn't I?"

"No good solution." What else could I say? "Let's go high." We returned to the *Champ de Mars* and climbed the Eiffel Tower. Staring into the clouds, I admitted, "I don't know how to love either."

"*Si,*" Kehinde disagreed, sounding like Océane. "You risked death for me. You know who I am, what I've done. And still, you look at me with love."

I clutched her. "Never abandon me to Paris."

The Iron Lady

"Kehinde would never leave the Wanderer in Paris!" Marie declared.

Cinnamon squeezed her *mojo* and squinted at the drawing. A dreamy Eiffel Tower was getting struck by three bolts of lightning on a stormy night—how her daddy might have drawn it, real and not real. Cinnamon had never *looked* at the tower before. It was a tourist trap on the other side of the world. Nicknamed *la dame de fer*, the iron lady, it was constructed as a monument to the French Revolution and the Industrial Revolution for a world's fair in 1889. Mountain tall, just over a thousand feet, it was the architectural wonder of its day. Gustave Eiffel and his engineers had designed robust curves of wrought iron, flexible and strong enough to survive the blast of high winds for centuries. Eiffel had also engineered Lady Liberty. Engraved under the tower's first platform were seventy-two names of distinguished French engineers, mathematicians, and scientists. To have your name tattooed on the iron lady's hips was a great honor. No women were on this eminent list, not even Sophie Germain, a mathematician whose work on elasticity theory had been critical to the tower's very existence. Random factoids like this floated around Cinnamon's mind, but she'd never examined the iron lady's physical details or considered how the tower would fare in an electrical storm, how it would feel with a mega-current racing down its limbs.

"Story storm?" Marie said. Magenta letters on the back of her quicksilver shirt read RANDOMNESS IS DIFFERENT FROM CREATIVE UNPREDICTABILITY.

Cinnamon smiled. "This black-and-white drawing is photographic, like from an old horror movie or a dream. Paris is muddy shadows and ominous specks of light creeping toward the Eiffel

Tower, which is dark and dramatic, drop-dead cool, looming against a smoky gray sky that's so vague 'cause it's the near edge of infinity." Klaus and Marie nodded. "That necklace of lights around the lower platform, above the stocky tower-legs, is eerie, winking and signaling to the ones who can read the signs."

"The lights are flashing. Can you see that?" Klaus let his mouth hang open again.

"Yes," Marie replied. "We all see it, right?"

"Right," Cinnamon assured her. As the video-drawing pulsed brighter, her tongue tingled with too many words, coming at the speed of light. "Something weird is about to go down. Over there in the background."

"I see it." Klaus pounded a pillow.

"Me too." Marie bounced up and down. "Whoever cares about the background? The star, the important big shit, is always in the foreground."

"This is an unruly background." Klaus pointed at undulating dark shapes.

Marie smacked his finger. "Darkness breaking the rules, not sticking to the script—in my book, that's a good thing."

"Did I say unruly was bad?" Klaus said. "My book has the same good things as yours."

Cinnamon sucked up their excitement. "The *weird* over in the corner, calling down lightning, is fronting like it's background as usual for the real picture. It's whispering, *Don't notice me, don't notice me.* Quiet as it's kept, *the weird* is the real story."

Klaus did eerie sound effects, a door creaking, shoes squeaking, spirits knocking and sighing. Marie added a few high notes from the stratosphere. Cinnamon stroked a bristly patch of black in the lower left-hand corner. Static zapped her fingertips.

"A few spears of lightning are tickling these big gray hulks. What are they, a forest, factory, sleeping giant? Too big, too lazy to get up out of the storm? I mean, usually, a little lightning ain't nothing to those ole smug giants. They're grounded. But here comes *the weird from another dimension,* and what do sleepy giants know about that? They see what giants expect to see, how every-body does, and that's why things slip up on us, slip by even, a done deal before we notice. *The weird from another dimension* in the cor-ner is, is an inside-out black hole, a space between things. That's what the whole picture is about. *The weird from another dimension* is controlling that horizontal figure-eight lightning bolt, riding low in the sky just above *the weird*."

"Cloud to cloud lightning, caught in the act." Marie's eyes were huge enchanted pools again. She was trancing. Klaus was in the zone too.

Cinnamon's hand hovered over the Eiffel Tower. "The obvious spectacle is those three bright bolts slamming the iron lady's peak. They got enough megawatts surging from heaven to Earth and back to animate Frankenstein, his bride, and light up a world-class city. It's nowhere near enough power to wake Daddy up, though. Not yet." Cinnamon drooped. Why was she talking about Daddy? "I don't know. Maybe there's actually a power surge coming *from* the tower too. Eiffel built his tower for miracle moments like this, and the guy who took the photo must have been a wild obsessed artiste, braving the elements for a beautiful vision, you know? The Wanderer's a courageous artist too, drawing the iron lady in our world, in our universe, but also in the Wanderer space-place too. It's a big risk, but he/she went ahead and drew *the weird from an-other dimension* in the corner, in the shadows. So we've got Eiffel's power mixing with the photographer's and Wanderer Taiwo's . . ."

"And mixing with our power," Marie said.

"Amped by our power," Klaus said.

A rush of that amped power raced along Cinnamon's nerve network—not only sex, every power thing about them. They were hoodooing each other. "All that energy combined is bolting from the top of the iron lady. Definitely something that Eshu would orchestrate. *Ashe, the power to make things be, the energy of the spaces between things* . . . Eshu is trying to let us see what we can't see in what we always see. What?"

Marie was trembling.

"Am I losing you all?" Cinnamon thought they were right with her.

Marie huffed a ragged breath.

Cinnamon shook her head. "We got this."

"So keep going." Klaus put a finger to Marie's and Cinnamon's forehead, nose, and lips, then his own. He nodded at Cinnamon. She didn't know what he was doing, a theatre thing? A German thing? A Klaus thing? Her mouth tingled, from his touch, from all the delicious words and wild ideas too.

"This is blowing me out." Cinnamon gulped. "So the Wanderer's painting looks and feels and smells like a hellified electrical storm from 1890-something, but it's so much more than a memory of a photo. That figure-eight lightning bolt twisting between those innocent, fluffy layers of mega storm cloud, that sucker is, wow, it's uhm, a roller-coaster ride going in and out of the different dimensions, hitting the spaces between things, and then whirl-winding itself back to our side."

The figure-eight lightning bolt lifted up off the page, bursting through three dimensions or even more. Bright as a spotlight, it floated toward them. They gasped and squinted. Thunder cracked. Inner ears ached with the change in pressure. Not acting like a sane person, Marie stuck her right hand through the crossover point of the figure eight. Her hand disappeared up to the wrist. There was no explosion, flash, hiss, whine, or sizzle. Marie opened her mouth and grunted a thin stream of cold fog. Klaus and Cinnamon yelped, staring at the space where Marie's hand should be. The figure-eight bolt was getting brighter and brighter. It went way past too bright. Klaus gripped Marie's wrist and yanked her hand out. Cinnamon slammed *The Chronicles* shut. The figure eight got squished into oblivion.

"What the fuck?" Cinnamon dropped *The Chronicles* on Sekou's desk. It glowed around the edges. She threw her orca knapsack on top of it. "Are you all right?"

"Yeah, I'm, I'm, yeah." Marie sounded *wrong*. She pulled her hand away from Klaus.

"You sure?" he said as she inspected herself.

"What demon is not reckless?" Marie quoted the Wanderer.

Cinnamon sucked her teeth long and loud, the way Redwood did. "Please."

Marie cradled the dimension-traveling hand in her lap. The killer red color drained from her lips. Blood rushed from her extremities to her core. Her teeth chattered against her tongue. Her breath was cold fog, citrusy, limeade stuff, with a twist of ozone. In the home dimension, her exhalation should have been warm CO_2.

Waves of cold stung Cinnamon. "You're an ice cube, your whole body, colder than ice." Marie shivered agreement.

The front door slammed. It could have been a gunshot. Marie fell out on the floor like a beached sea mammal. Klaus and Cinnamon hauled her onto the bed. She clutched a blanket in trembling hands. Her knuckles were white. Downstairs the elders hooted.

"That boss-man figures if you ain't got no more sick days you should call in dead," Redwood said.

Iris tried not to laugh. "Be serious. She could lose her job over this." Were they talking about Opal? "What are we going to do?"

"It's not how deep you fish, it's how you wiggle the worm." Aidan was in Georgia-cracker mode. "Hey, we're home, sugarplum." He called up from the living room.

"What you all doing up there?" Redwood shouted. "Having a good time?"

Cinnamon didn't have any spit in her mouth. "Just hanging," she croaked.

Klaus and Marie had shown up while the elders were out.

"Come on down and say hello," Iris said. "My old bones refuse to take the stairs."

"Gal, what you talking 'bout?" Aidan laughed. "You young, sugar."

Redwood laughed too. "Baby Sister is goin' cook up some grub for you young sprouts and for us antediluvian relics."

"I'm not hungry," Cinnamon yelled. "Marie and Klaus already ate."

"Not my dessert." Iris rattled pots and pans. "There's music too. Redwood and Wildfire have been rehearsing." Wildfire was Aidan's Indian name. "'Course, anytime I try to carry a tune, I drop it at the first hint of harmony."

"If you're not too *busy* up there." What did Redwood think they were doing?

"We're reading *The Chronicles*," Cinnamon yelled. Her voice cracked.

"You OK, honeybunch?" Aidan came up a few stairs.

"Young people stuff," Redwood whispered, loud for Aidan's old ears.

"We'll be down in a minute," Cinnamon hollered.

Aidan stepped back down. "All right."

"Crap! Is it always arctic cold in your house?" Marie sounded like her snarky self. Cinnamon was relieved.

"I like cold." Klaus could wear a T-shirt in a blizzard. "Usually."

"Of course you would," Cinnamon said. "You're a furnace."

"Today is eleventh March. It'll be summer soon, and I'll be the miserable one."

"I can't imagine you feeling miserable about good sunny weather," Cinnamon said.

"That's a wicked draft, blowing through the walls." Marie's breath was still cold fog. "Don't you feel it?" She chomped her tongue. Her breath took on a tinge of pink. From blood? She went from shivering to convulsing. Klaus put an arm over Marie's shoulder and waved at Cinnamon until she slung her arm around Marie's waist. Klaus eased the blanket out of Marie's clenched fingers and threw it around the three of them. They huddled silently a long time, frayed nerves firing like crazy.

"Talk to me," Marie said, thickly. "That might help."

"I can't think of anything to say," Cinnamon said.

"Really?" Klaus didn't believe her.

"Tell me what's wrong with your furnace," Marie suggested.

Cinnamon screwed up her face. "My mom is cheap. She jacks up the thermostat so it can't ever go over sixty-three degrees. This is hot compared to usual. Opal don't want to pay for people walking 'round in shorts and underwear. She *ain't got money to burn*."

"Who has money to burn?" Marie said.

"What's the house like in the summer?" Klaus asked.

"It's a sauna. The next-door neighbors have stinky garbage that sits there, decomposing and farting fumes in our windows. We gotta go on lockdown until the garbage collectors show up." She should mention something nice. "It's not that bad. Opal takes it hard, as if stinky garbage is what they think of her. Most of the time it's fine. We get good cross breezes. The neighbors let Opal do their Sunday *New York Times* crossword puzzle." Cinnamon chuckled. "Actually, she steals it out the trash."

Klaus laughed with Cinnamon.

"Are we *not* going to talk about my hand disappearing?" Marie said.

Klaus frowned. "I thought you wanted chitchat."

"Me too." Cinnamon took a deep breath instead of coming out her face at Marie.

"I loathe chitchat," Marie declared.

"Loathe? Oh shit, excuse me." Cinnamon shot a desperate glance at Klaus.

"OK," he said, "so what did disappearing feel like?"

Marie held up her right hand. Black nails glittered now. "Bizarre."

"Do you think it's safe?" Klaus blew warm breath at Marie's icy fingers.

Cinnamon glared at him. "Why? You want to try it too?"

Klaus shrugged.

"It's probably not safe if I hung out for a long time." Marie shivered. "How should I know? I don't even want to *believe* it happened."

Cinnamon almost said, *You wouldn't catch me sticking my only right hand in no random hologram of extra-dimensional lightning.* "Can you wiggle your fingers?"

Marie did. They worked fine. Her hand looked normal except for the iridescent black fingernails. She huffed out a lukewarm, transparent, normal breath.

The killer whale knapsack tipped off Sekou's desk, tugging *The Chronicles* down to the floor. The heavy tome fell open. Pages fluttered in the draft blowing through the walls and settled after the Eiffel Tower image. New words glowed, crisp and clear. The orca grinned. On cue, the Squad crawled in sync over to the open pages. No image drifted up to tempt them.

"What if we read these two chapters to ourselves, not out loud," Cinnamon said. "No sticking our hands into alien other-dimensional orifices."

"OK," Marie said. "Klaus, you with us?"

"Sure, why not."

They murmured, *"What demon is not reckless?"* in three-part harmony.

Chronicles 18d:
Paris Fables—Masquerade

Bob's friend, Raymond Abernathy, rented rooms in Montparnasse from an enterprising Frenchman who charged stranded performers most of the money they earned for dank accommodations not far from *La Seine*. No one tended the orisha of this river. She gave off foul odors and produced sickly fish. Montparnasse was named for the home mountain of the Muses, Greek orisha of storytelling, knowledge, and creativity. The French disavowed pagan spirits, yet artists and scientists poured libation to the Muses. Museums—shrines to the Muses—were scattered around Paris. These were houses for profane spectacle.

Raymond was a forty-nine-year-old performer originally from New York, America. Seven feet three inches tall, possessing a massive head and hands the size of shields, he performed masquerades for carnivals and sideshows the world over. Raymond currently did a giant monster from wildest, darkest Dahomey, a savage Fon warrior who chopped off the heads of his enemies and ate their bodies, raw. Raymond carried enemy bones and heart gristle in a bag around his neck—gris-gris to protect him from evil spirits. Supposedly, these pagan *Voodoo* rituals made him *nzumbe*—living dead, insensitive to pain, and almost invincible. Audiences pelted him with rotten fruit and rocks to test this. Raymond bore many scars from previous shows and fresh wounds from the performance we had witnessed.

"Never yelp, no matter how it hurts." He schooled us in *nzumbe* masquerade in his front parlor.

Doubt crawled across Kehinde's skin and put her in a foul mood. I could smell it. "No one shall pelt me." She spoke precise English. "Here or in America."

Raymond shook his head. "I don't know about that."

Everyone else who'd gotten the fever had died quickly or recuperated. I felt better, but wasn't fully recovered. Captain Luigi was determined to bring the remnants of his savage troupe to the Chicago World's Columbian Exposition celebrating the four hundredth anniversary of the discovery of the New World by Europeans. Our troupe would head down *La Seine* tomorrow, en route to canals that fed the Lady Atlantic. *La Vérité* waited in the North Sea, but not for much longer. Luigi never knowingly brought sickness on board. Who could blame him? Last year cholera ravaged Paris. Luigi had reluctantly decided to abandon me to Paris, so Kehinde planned to stay too, with Somso and Melinga. Luigi threatened her with jail if she didn't get on the boat in the morning.

"I made no blood oath with you!" she told him. "And my blade is still sharp."

"Do I have to lock you on the ship?" Luigi replied.

"I'll make sure she's on board. Somso too, everybody," Bob said quickly and saved Luigi's head. Bob waved his *mojo* bag at Kehinde. He had an Eshu plan. She relented for the moment.

Leaving us to a farewell celebration with Raymond, Bob and Luigi marched off together to purchase supplies. Somso slept while Melinga nursed. Kehinde fumed, her hand on the cutlass in the folds of her robe. Liam downed a shot of rum with Raymond.

"A sailor could be shipwrecked in a worse bog than Paris," Liam declared.

"You'll stay too?" Kehinde lifted her eyebrows.

"You folks can find work here, onstage or off," Raymond said.

"No. Following *Ifa,* we head to Chicago," Kehinde declared.

"Without a boat?" I said. "How?"

"Cheer up!" Raymond grinned. "You'll make passage. Dahomey warring with France is headlines. Women like tigers, men fierce as gorillas. Audiences want to see danger, taste fear. At the museums, I've played Aborigines, savage Maori chiefs from New Zealand, and Kaffirs from South Africa. Different costumes, same gris-gris."

"I've been to New Zealand, mate." Liam clenched his fists.

"Maori men are brave warriors, not fools. The chiefs have tattoos carved across their faces. You've got a naked mug."

"Why do you do these masquerades?" Kehinde asked.

"I ain't never wanted to do nothing but step onstage and get the audience roaring." Raymond laughed. "I could play Frankenstein if he wasn't white, but a colored monster from New York City just ain't scary fun."

"So you decided on a Fon monster?" Kehinde was confused.

Liam downed more rum. "Ah, milady, you think Monsieur Abernathy should do melodrama?"

"What's your story?" I propped myself up in damp sheets. "Why not tell that?"

Raymond towered over me. "My mother and uncle run with me from slavery in South Carolina to the beggar house up north. Don't nobody want to see some poor soul shipping hisself to freedom in a box no bigger than a coffin, then when he get to freedom, the fool be emptying slop jars for two-bit whores. When Uncle Jared limp through that story, people do weep; or worse, they turn a deaf ear."

"This is a New World story?" Kehinde grimaced.

"But this—" Acting the Fon warrior, Raymond growled and grunted. "Audiences holler for more. I made that savage lingo up. A white man translates. He leaves out parts too harsh for the ladies."

Raymond rehearsed chopping off a head and eating a thigh. His eyes bulged from his skull. He stuck his tongue out. Saliva dripped from the tip as he thrust the gris-gris bag in our faces. Liam was disgusted, Kehinde also.

She spoke Yoruba. "The view of the slave is everywhere the same: down toward the feet." Her face was serene, her voice a honey drip. "Slave cur, what does he know of King Béhanzin's warrior *ahosi*?"

"What she saying?" Raymond smiled, always sweet for a lady. "She want more pie?" He offered Kehinde another piece of a fruit dish, still warm from his oven.

"Eat." I spoke Yoruba too. "He's our host. We're no better than he is."

"He is civilized." Kehinde grinned. "I don't wish to be."

"He is the New World you dream of."

"Eshu torments me." She shoveled a hunk of pie into her mouth.

"The pie is good," I said. "Kehinde wonders why you stay in the Old World."

"I messed up my ankle doing a death stomp and got a fever. Ship left without me." He jumped, twisted, and, favoring one leg, fell at Kehinde's feet. She laughed. "I'm only funny when I don't mean to be." Kehinde pulled him to standing. "You're strong."

"She's not hokum, like you," Liam said.

Kehinde leaned into Raymond with English. "I know warrior dances of death."

Raymond looked hopeful. "Can you teach me?"

Kehinde plucked an axe handle from by the fireplace and thrust it at him. When he reached for it, she danced to the side, spun around, and landed a blow against his broad shoulders that would have taken his head off.

Raymond almost matched her moves with his long limbs. "Do it again."

She did. Liam watched them, burning up inside.

Kehinde beckoned him. "Irishman, do a death dance with me."

How could Liam resist?

Kehinde was indefatigable, relentless. Raymond and Liam received many cracks on their backs. Sagging and dripping sweat, they never landed a hit on her. It was pitch dark outside when Raymond finally spun on the balls of his feet and hit Liam's shoulder. Spitting Irish curses, Liam snatched the handle and held it to Raymond's neck.

"Perfect," Kehinde declared. Her mood had sweetened. "This is what I will show the New World!"

Bob staggered in the door. His lungs labored against a sweat-drenched shirt. Gasping the foul air, he doubled over. "We better do this now."

Chronicles 18e:
Paris Fables—River Pirates

Bob's Eshu plan was a scenario for a derring-do masquerade. They wrapped me in herb-scented cloth, as if I were cheese, cured meat, or a tasty delight for first-class passengers. Melinga clung to my nose and babbled half-words from the torrent of languages she'd heard. When they pulled her away, she fussed in Somso's arms. The box they laid me in was bigger than a coffin. Pressing my fingers on the lid, I could pry it up easily; holes on the sides offered air and a strange perspective on the world.

"What if you die in that box, demon?" Somso said.

"Eshu rides the Wanderer," Kehinde said. I hoped that was true.

Raymond said a box-transport adventure would be boring, but my heart pounded, and my breath was short. My ordeal would be nothing compared to Uncle Jared's, who had mailed himself four hundred miles to freedom. My friends would be close. I had provisions: fruits, bread, water, and the useless French-doctor medicines that Bob secreted to me. The streets were deserted. The horses' hooves echoed on damp cobblestones as we clomped toward the river. The wagon swayed between the wheels, and I was lulled to shallow sleep. We came to a jerky halt. Bob and Liam argued above me. Spying some dastardly fellow, Bob wanted to abort. Liam insisted it was too late for second thoughts.

I peeked out a hole into gaslight dimness. A train of wagons was lined up at the docks with provisions for many boats. Powerful hands lifted me. As my shoulder crashed into the corner of the box, I wished for even closer quarters. Frenchmen joked with one another. The aroma of their exertion was as strong as the garlic, rum, and fish they consumed. Shouting insults, they dumped me. My back bounced against wood, and pain shot through my body. For a moment I couldn't see. When vision cleared, it was too dark to see. The workmen had departed with their lanterns. I tasted blood in my mouth. I had bitten my tongue.

Waiting hours in pitch black terror must have been the boring part of the Freedmen's stories that spectators wouldn't tolerate. I was surrounded by footsteps and curses. Boxes jostled against mine. Horses emptied their bowels. Foul odors jolted my nerves. Even flies buzzing close set my heart to thudding. What would Luigi do if he found a sick warrior smuggled in with his salt pork, pickled onions, and French wine? Would he punish Bob and Liam? Leave Kehinde and Somso stranded in a Paris jail? Perhaps this was a capital offense. Criminals in Paris faced a guillotine death. I thought of Abla's bloated head and gagged. Luckily I was too depleted for sustained worry. I tumbled into a healing slumber.

"*Merde!*"

Bright starlight trickled into my box with oily river air. I needed to urinate, but persuaded my bladder to expand. Something heavy and hard clattered to the ground.

"*Sacre bleu!*" Luigi swore in French, not far off.

I wanted to leap out, confess my crimes, and beg for his mercy.

"It's all shit!" Luigi yelled in English now. He smacked his wooden stick against the cobblestones. "Son of a bitch!"

Someone gave a soft reply, a deep unfamiliar voice.

"Do you know how much I paid for a boatload of shit?" Luigi raged on.

Another large object crashed to the ground and exploded. Splinters of wood hit my box. Luigi and his companion were close.

"River pirates," the man with the deep voice said.

"I can't afford delay. We must leave Paris tomorrow at the latest!"

Through a hole in my box, I spied Luigi's favorite coat, vest, and black stovepipe hat. His beard was streaked with sawdust. He brandished a wooden walking stick. A crowbar levered open a box across from me. It was filled with dirt and refuse.

"Prick-sucking bastards," he shouted. "I'll make them eat this shit."

Luigi shoved the refuse into my stack. I squelched a yelp as my box tumbled several feet to the ground. On impact, water and medicine flasks shattered, urine almost bubbled out of me, and the lid jiggled loose. I reached up to hold it in place, but sleepy nerves fired erratically and arm muscles cramped. Direct starlight made me squint. A man's head covered the home star as he peered in at me. My discoverer had a broken nose that had healed into a crooked line. His lips drooped at the sides under prominent cheeks. A black and silver mélange of stringy hair tumbled down to his waist. I held his dark-eyed gaze, not flinching or blinking. I thought of Raymond's brave Uncle Jared and tears flowed. The man swallowed his emotions then looked me up and down.

"A box of rags," he said and shoved the lid down. I was stunned.

"I'll kill those fuckers!" Luigi stomped off with his companion.

I waited until only water birds and unfamiliar humans chattered around me. Morning on the docks was noisy. Horses, boats, nearby trains, wagons, and workers banged about. I needed to vomit as well as urinate. My box rested on its side. Sharp pains burned through my shoulder. I pushed the lid off and rolled onto cold stone. I drenched the fabric wrapped around me with a gush of urine. The urge to throw up passed as I edged away from the filth in the open crates.

Bob's plan had failed. I had no idea what the future held. Too dehydrated for tears, I slithered into the road, spooking a horse hauling a wagon. The driver yelped and swerved his vehicle around me. Unwinding from the cloth made me too dizzy to stand. I crawled, scraping skin from hands and knees. Splinters wedged deep into my palms as I struggled to the edge of the docks. Vomit forced its way out of my dry throat into the river. Abla's head floated in rancid water, white eyes like boiled eggs bobbing in crumbling eye sockets. I had never seen Abla by day. She grinned as I dangled over the lip of rotten pilings, and fire bubbled up my esophagus into my nostrils. Immediately I felt strong and clear. To escape, I needed only to become *aje*.

Workers gawked at a savage ready to dive into *La Seine*—hostile?

curious? concerned? They made no move to intervene. Abla nodded
her head. The *aje* wanted to blast her from the water. Folly. The
living dead are immune to pyrotechnics. Abla hoped to trick me.
If I embraced the *aje* now, I risked losing the Taiwo-self and the
world I tried to love.

"You love me—that is why I return to you." Abla gurgled bubbles of river scum. "Love betrays you again and again."

"You don't understand love, Abla." I didn't either.

"Luigi will take them away." Abla's egg eyes gleamed. "You'll
never find them again. You'll never know if they love you, if they
would face death for your story."

I clamped the *aje* down and groped for the *mojo* bag around my
neck.

Eshu knows how easy it is to lose the way.

Secret Society Pact

Huddled together on Sekou's bed, Cinnamon, Klaus, and Marie trembled at the adventure, romance, and horror of *The Chronicles*. Still, the Wanderer had yet to explain the weird from another dimension swallowing Marie's hand. After "River Pirates," the pages had a rippling, milky surface, but no blurry images or illegible writing. Cinnamon didn't know what to make of that.

"We have to find Griot Joe." She closed *The Chronicles* and laid it on Sekou's galaxy pillow. "Joe can explain the weird from another dimension, and he needs us."

Klaus's chin wobbled. "What do we actually do for Joe?"

"He was up on a bridge, ready to jump," Cinnamon said, "but he didn't because somebody listened, because we believe."

"We're better than a bridge to nowhere," Klaus said, "still—"

"It's freaking impossible to believe"—Marie contemplated her hand—"that Joe was messing around in Dahomey and France almost a hundred years ago and right now he's some homeless dude pushing a shopping cart in Pittsburgh."

"Dude?" Klaus narrowed his eyes. "Did Taiwo scatter into different sexes? I mean into Ariel, a she, and Joe, a he, or . . . ?"

"Good question," Cinnamon said. "See, Klaus believes, don't you?"

"I didn't say that." Klaus worked a hangdog frown. "I'm am—ambi—"

"Ambivalent? Why?" Desperation gripped Cinnamon.

"Gender *is* slippery on Joe and Ariel," Marie observed, "so homeless *person,* OK?"

"From another dimension though?" Klaus shook his head. "Joe could be some weird, queer person without all the cups in the cupboard."

"Is that German mumbo jumbo?" Cinnamon groaned. "Sekou

said everybody is queer. But powerful wizards cast mega-cloaking spells so we no longer know who we are. We think we're who the wizards say we are. *Consensus Delusion.*" Oops. Cinnamon had to watch quoting Sekou on *this* topic.

"Consensus Delusion." Marie nodded. "I'll buy that."

"Oh, you will?" Cinnamon tried not to snarl. "Well, damn. Thank you."

"It means everybody lives in the same illusion, yes?" Klaus asked.

Cinnamon punched his shoulder. "Do you just front like you understand English?"

"No!" Klaus insisted. "No way."

"The lady doth protest too much, methinks." Marie quoted Hamlet's mother.

Cinnamon curled her lip. "Who the hell would side with that bitch?"

"You two are sounding more and more Snow White." Klaus looked wounded.

"I was standing up for you," Cinnamon said.

"I need a moment to put English together sometimes," Klaus said. "I'm not stupid."

Marie cocked her head at him. "Who said you were stupid? No, don't tell me. I already hate him." She sighed. "Here's my problem. Joe looks like a queer carnival bum, not an alien traveler from another dimension."

"Exactly," Klaus agreed.

"Oh, you both know people from other dimensions besides Joe and Ariel?"

"I thought the alien invasion was going to be a planet-to-planet thing," Klaus said.

Marie howled then caught herself. "You're serious, aren't you?" Klaus squirmed. "Have you read *Contact* by Carl Sagan?"

"I have." Cinnamon glared at Marie.

"Sorry. I'll read *Contact* too, eventually." Marie jiggled the orca's loose teeth.

"Quit picking." Cinnamon grabbed the knapsack. "We don't have to get mean."

"Yeah." Klaus looked miserable.

"We want to believe, but Joe could be scamming us, a bunch of naïve, gullible kids." She held back tears.

"Ain't nobody gonna put anything over on you. For real." Cinnamon wanted to hug Marie and kiss her nose, make her laugh. It was a friendly urge, not the *other* kind. But Cinnamon was too chicken-shit. While she pretended to reattach the orca's tooth, Klaus slipped his head past waves of dark hair and nuzzled Marie's cheek, as if it were no big deal. Cinnamon mimicked the move on the other cheek. Marie tried to pretend she didn't appreciate the attention but finally gave in.

Marie stroked Cinnamon's hair and Klaus's too. "What if Joe's a pervert or—"

"Pervert?" Acid fear bubbled in Cinnamon's throat. "Naw. He or she—"

"Could be writing sci-fi snuff porn." Marie talked over her. "Or putting psychotropic drugs in the paper, or, I don't know."

"That's why I didn't tell you guys my theory right off." Cinnamon edged off the bed. "I didn't tell anybody." She threw open a window, let in a blast of March, and shut it quickly. "I didn't even tell Miz Redwood, Granddaddy Aidan, or Aunt Iris."

Marie snorted. "I wouldn't tell anybody either. I mean, not grown-up people."

Cinnamon buried *The Chronicles* in the orca. "I like to tell them hard things."

"Caution is probably a good idea." Klaus nodded. "Although, theories get always better when you have to bounce them around other people. That's how science works."

"Proof. That's what we need," Marie said.

"Now you're talking sense." Cinnamon was thrilled, but played cool. "We can track down clues, interrogate the witnesses, get real proof."

Blood drained from Klaus's cheeks. "You mean, check out the scene of the crime? I suck at—"

"With two languages you've got double vision," Cinnamon said.

"I don't see in German!"

"Yes, you can," Marie said. "Scene of what crime?" Curiosity dripped from a smirk.

"December 27, 1982, at the Rain Forest Lounge," Cinnamon said. "It was 11:17 P.M. My father was shot in the head. He threw himself in front of a bullet meant for two ladies and smashed his watch falling down. Griot Joe was there. Sekou and Lexy were hanging with them and Star Deer too." Why hadn't Opal been there?

"Scene of that crime." Marie hugged herself.

"Star Deer saw the whole deal. We could sign up for her advanced contact workshop. Get our show together while hunting clues." Cinnamon scrambled for something persuasive. "Star is Cherokee and even keeps to some of the old ways."

"I hate history," Marie said.

"Really?" Klaus sighed relief. "I also hate history."

"Star's an urban Indian too." Cinnamon cringed at this ploy. Klaus and Marie exchanged glances, as if dreaded history was something they shared. Opal railed against dredging up a past that was better off buried. What about the good times—the nations holding together, coming through for the great events right now? "How can you hate history? It's way too big to hate."

Klaus pointed at the *Buckaroo Banzai* poster. "I prefer to look to the future."

"Yeah." Marie gave off a spooky, reckless vibe, like before she stuck her hand into the spaces between things. "Don't you just want to jump ahead into the next minute?"

Cinnamon shook her braids. "Time is an illusion. Now is all there is."

Marie rolled her eyes at physics. "I know. But we live in illusions."

"A proof is just something that convinces other mathematicians," Klaus said.

"Are we quoting *Vati*?" Marie snorted.

"I'm saying, there is no absolute reality," Klaus said.

Cinnamon threw up her hands. "We're not arguing. Look, if Joe's a scam artist or an alien adventurer, we'll track him/her down and get to a truth we three agree on. The future needs truth as much as the past does."

"It needs many truths," Klaus said. "Like Paris."

"I love Paris," Marie declared. "I've been there, down the boulevards, over to the Left Bank. I went up the iron lady."

"Me too." Klaus shrugged. "I was little though."

"You two got me there." Cinnamon hadn't been anywhere, except onstage, in books, and at the movies. She refused to feel bad about this. "Who cares? You're Prince Charming. You're a brave Glamazon. You can't chicken out on our Mod Squad. Together, we can handle Joe. Don't dis the crew."

"Yeah." Klaus's shields tumbled. "We swore a secret society oath. That has to count."

Cinnamon stretched out her hands, palms up. "Are we all on board?"

"Logisch." Klaus took one hand.

Nothing like logic. Marie grabbed Cinnamon's other hand and Klaus's too. They leaned into one another, bumped heads, and muttered, *"Logisch."*

Downstairs Aidan tuned his banjo. Opal claimed *a banjo sounds like a bunch of tin cans falling down the stairs.* Cinnamon had to agree with her this evening. The banjo didn't want to tune. It complained about damp March cold. Aidan cussed at moody strings and a wandering bridge. The aroma of cherries, peaches, nutmeg, cloves, and honey wafted up with the finger exercises. Cinnamon had told Iris that friends would be stopping by. Iris had her infamous cobbler ready to throw in the oven before the elders went off to see Opal at the hospital. Cinnamon had visited her mom alone before school. At first seeing Opal had been a big relief; now Cinnamon hated sitting there while machines beeped and Opal coughed in a restless, drug sleep, a Sunday *New York Times* puzzle balled up in a fist. Cinnamon fell out at the ass crack of dawn to poke through the neighbor's garbage for nothing. When Opal came to, she didn't explain the secrets she'd kept from Cinnamon or regret the trash she'd talked to Sekou. All she said was, *Damn, baby, you finally lost some weight.* As if Cinnamon not having any appetite was good, because she looked so cute starving to death.

Iris's cooking magic filled the house. The cobbler aroma made Cinnamon's stomach twist. "You want to go down and see everybody?" she asked.

"So we're not going to discuss my hand, directly," Marie said. "I'm just saying, so we're clear what we're avoiding."

"That's not all we're avoiding." Klaus edged toward the door and bumped against a poster of Redwood and Aidan from silent movie days. He stroked the title. "*Sorrow Mountain?*" He was dying to talk to Cinnamon's crazy elders.

"Cobbler's done. Come on down," Iris yelled.

"Cobbler, my grandparents and Aunt Iris, then we three can talk, about everything."

Marie groaned. "I have homework. Algebra. Word problems. Yuck."

"I love math. I can do algebra in my sleep." Cinnamon grabbed the orca with *The Chronicles* inside. The elders might make better sense of the new chapters.

"I have impossible music to learn." Klaus gritted his teeth. "*Vati* will check me. I have to sing well."

"We'll do a Mod Squad trade." Cinnamon nudged Marie. "Right?"

Marie stared at her weird from-another-dimension hand, shaking her head.

"Don't worry," Cinnamon said. "Miz Redwood's got a storm hand too." Marie's eyes got wide. Cinnamon dragged her and Klaus out the door. They wanted to go anyhow. "We'll do homework and music fast. And then we can tackle a serious detective mission worthy of Disastronauts and Glamazons."

Hillbillies and Country Gals

"Cinnamon's international family, hot dog!"

Cinnamon flinched as Aidan twanged the *o* into a long *aaww*. Nobody said *hot dog* anymore. Too late to tell him that or run back upstairs. The kitchen was cozy and warm from the oven's heat. It didn't look as shabby as Cinnamon feared. Iris had covered naked spots where Raven's paintings used to hang with African fabric and old theatre and movie posters. Aidan's animal carvings ran along counters and slithered up shelves. Eagles, osprey, water hens, and an ibis perched on the windowsills, peeking through dreary curtains. A hurricane mobile hung in the doorway to the living room—a snarl of black clouds flecked with silver glints. When Cinnamon was little, Aidan and Raven cut a hole in the wall by the door to make a kitchen island/service window. She'd helped with sanding and painting. The elders turned this counter into a hoodoo altar. Seashells and bits of glass glittered in the faint light of hand-dipped candles. A worn, once-red leather journal was nestled in a sweet-grass basket surrounded by prairie smoke blossoms, spiderwort, devil's claw, rattlesnake master, and gourds. Black shaggy acorns the size of grapefruits stood guard on either side of the basket. In the kitchen, mismatched chairs had feathered and mirrored scarves from Redwood's theatre collection hanging on their shoulders. Sitting down, Klaus and Marie oohed and ahhed.

Aidan put a mound of chocolate ice cream on top of the bowl of cherry peach cobbler in front of Marie. The ice cream melted on the warm crumbly crust. Aidan set cobbler in front of Klaus. Strips of leather coiled through his long white braid. He wore an Indian Power shirt that Raven had silk-screened. It was similar to what ghost Sekou had worn, but this thunderbird's wingspan went into the sleeves as it grasped a killer whale with bloodred talons.

As Aidan bent over with a scoop of ice cream, Klaus jerked as if the fierce bird clawed him.

"Cool shirt, cool braid." Klaus tried to recover.

"My son painted this." Aidan caressed the rough layer of color on top of smooth cotton. "That one too." He pointed to the shadow of a bird flying above the kitchen island. Raven had been shot before he could add colors and finish details. Opal had talked about painting over the sketch. She never did. "You know the tales of thunderbird?" Aidan flapped his shirt wings, almost lifting off.

"Not really." Klaus shook his head. "I know only *Winnetou* and—"

"Winnie who?" Redwood wrinkled her brow. "An Indian from that carnie show?"

"From Karl May. He wrote the Wild West from Saxony, Germany," Klaus said.

"Go out, find a thunderbird tale, and bring it back to me." Aidan clapped Klaus's back. "We'll see if it matches up to what I know."

Klaus was thrilled by the assignment. "Sure. I'm on this."

"Aidan is like the Wanderer." Redwood held up the journal from the altar. "He been writing down stories in this book since he was younger than y'all."

Aidan nodded. "Cinnamon's great grandmama, Miz Garnett . . . Storying was the hoodoo spell she gave me."

Cinnamon perked up. The elders never told tales on Miz Garnett, a powerful conjure woman from back in the day. Opal had banned old-timey hoodoo sagas when Cinnamon was a little girl. She'd be fifteen in August and had a mind of her own now. Everybody said so. "Are you going to tell us about Miz Garnett and her conjuring?"

"You know what your mama say on that," Iris replied.

"Opal had me believing in Santa Claus, the Easter Bunny, and the Tooth Fairy."

Redwood chuckled. "I don't know the Tooth Fairy."

"She trades dollars for baby teeth," Marie explained.

"Quarters." Cinnamon pouted. "Jesus walks on water, a holy dispensation from physics, so—"

"OK." Aidan was laughing. "Maybe I'll tell a tale or two for our scientist."

"Glad to hear it." Redwood thrust the banjo at him. "Ain't nothing like banjo music to carry a tall tale."

Aidan hadn't really played since he got to Pittsburgh. He'd fussed at the tuning pegs or halfheartedly strummed one hillbilly jig or another. After two minutes he'd put the banjo down, in a funk about *empty fingers*. Music came to his hands, not his ears. His hands looked full of music tonight. Cinnamon wasn't sure she wanted him to play. Not everybody loved hillbilly tunes, and what if it was tin-can clatter music? Aidan gripped the banjo neck gingerly; desire was in his fingers, love and fear in his eyes. Redwood's jaw twitched between a frown and a smile. Tears glistened on Iris's cheeks. Marie and Klaus gaped at the elders. Cinnamon fought mortification at ancient relatives tricked out like old hippies and silent movie stars. They'd traveled the world doing spells and other wild mischief. Who knew what weird from another dimension they might put on tonight? Aidan plucked a few tentative notes.

"You don't have to play, if you don't want to," Cinnamon said.

"He know that." Redwood cut her eyes at Cinnamon. "Don't need to remind him."

"Well, one of my favorite TV shows, *Hill Street Blues*—"

"Or give him an excuse." Redwood talked on top of Cinnamon.

"No idiot box!" Iris stunned them quiet. "We got company, theatre folks. I put my foot down." She muttered about *wasting spirit, the fool school,* and *learning to be nothing.* Tension in the air was thick. When sweet-natured Iris got mad, it felt like the end of the world must be nigh. Klaus and Marie looked as mortified as Cinnamon felt. "Advertisers get a season ticket to your mind. I'm not having it!"

"Sorry." Cinnamon hadn't actually wanted the Mod Squad to meet at her house. It was Marie's idea. She said Mr. and Mrs. Masuda always *hovered.* Marie's parents were both research librarians. A secret society meeting without Mr. Masuda snooping and asking research questions would be impossible. The Squad wouldn't

get more than a moment alone in Marie's room. Mr. and Mrs.
Masuda never met a book they didn't want to open up and read.
Marie wasn't bringing *The Chronicles* within a mile of her family. If
they got wind of ghosts, aliens, and hoodoo spells, they'd kill Marie. Opal wouldn't have approved of the sci-fi/superstition/magic
slop either, but Opal was still laid up in the hospital. Going over
to Klaus's house never came up.

"You goin' sit down and stay awhile?" Redwood was tracking
Cinnamon; Iris was too. They read her evil bitch embarrassment,
no sweat. Cinnamon panicked. Did they also notice that she had
turned into a teenage sex zombie?

"Take a load off," Iris said.

"OK." Cinnamon set the orca by the kitchen island altar and sat
in the one empty chair, an uncomfortable futuristic monstrosity,
what 1960 thought of 2000. Raven bought it as a goof for Sekou.
Nobody sat in it anymore. Where would Sekou sit?

Iris set baked chicken, quinoa, kale, and a whole-grain corn-
meal biscuit in front of Cinnamon. "You've got to eat some real
food before I let you at my dessert."

"Iris be a Rasta-fructarian macro-neurotic." Redwood laughed.

Aidan poked Iris. "She try to blame that on Northampton,
Massachusetts, *where the coffee is strong and so are the women*, but
Little Bit picked that up in Oh-high-oh."

"I'll *Little Bit* you. Y'all need to hush." Iris poured one of her
soy power drinks into wineglasses for everyone. "Can't have Cinnamon wasting away on us. What would your mother say?"

"She'd be happy." Cinnamon wanted the food, but also liked
the hollow hungry feeling that had claimed many pounds in the
last two weeks. "Very happy."

"Opal ain't always in her right mind." Redwood never bothered
to varnish the truth. "Half a chicken leg and a spoonful of greens
ain't too much to ask. Eat."

Klaus and Marie picked up their forks and shoveled huge globs
of cobbler à la mode into their mouths. Their faces crumpled

around the good tastes working together in great harmony. They guzzled the power drink and gasped.

"This is health food?" Marie giggled.

Cinnamon stared at her plate. She hated eating in public. In private, she didn't have to put up with folks telling her to push herself away from the table before she sat down, before she got something in her mouth. Even people who loved her ragged on how fast she was blowing up, how she'd never find anybody to love all that belly and booty.

Aidan kissed the top of her head. The banjo banged against his hip and the strings buzzed. Miz Redwood snatched Cinnamon's wayward braid and tucked it in with the others. Cinnamon pushed the chicken around the plate. It fell off the bone and gave off a compelling aroma. Wasn't nothing to do but put a piece in her mouth. She got a bit of biscuit and kale on the fork too. It tasted so good, she wanted to cry.

Aidan whistled. "Who care if Iris can't carry a tune? She write books and teach college better than she cook, and her cooking be a hoodoo spell, let you fly up to the evening star." He never got tired of bragging on Iris or anybody else he loved.

"Yes, that was delicious. Thank you very much." Klaus wiped at cobbler juice dripping from his chin. He had wolfed down his whole dish in four gulps. The boy wanted to lick the bowl. "Will you play for us?"

"I ain't played in a long while, Son. I got to have the feel for it, you know?" Aidan winked at Cinnamon. "Maybe when everybody's done eating."

Cinnamon chewed another scrap of chicken. Her stomach was so empty, swallowing food hurt. "I'm trying." She got a rhythm going from her plate to her tongue.

"Music would be wonderful." Marie savored each nut crumble, peach, and cherry morsel. She wasn't halfway done either.

"Hurry up." Klaus jostled her. "Do you need help?"

"No." Marie moved her bowl out of Klaus's range.

"That's not so bad, is it?" Iris put another spoonful of kale in an empty spot on Cinnamon's plate.

"That is cloth from Mali, yes?" Klaus pointed at Iris's tunic and skirt.

She wore mud cloth similar to Cinnamon's. "Why, yes it is."

"*Bògòlanfini,* handmade from fermented mud. *Vati,* uhm, my father, he did a chemical engineering project in Mali last year. He brought the cloth home for us." Klaus turned on Euro-chic charm. "For many centuries, *Bamana* people in Mali have worn *Bògòlan* during major life transformations. That's what *Vati*'s colleague in Mali told us. I mean, I don't really know but . . ."

"You got it right." Iris loved cloth and could talk for days about fabric from everywhere and how much it meant. "Cinnamon's pattern is *Basiaba,* for young women at the crossroads, the border is *ce farin jala,* a brave man's belt." Cinnamon didn't remember Iris telling her that. "I'm wearing crocodile fingers, a panther's skin, and the feet of a tortoise, along with the brave man's belt."

"*Ce farin jala.*" Klaus and Marie captured the music of the words in one try.

"Thank you, Professor Phipps." Aidan turned to Cinnamon, who was watching them anxiously. "I guess we're doing all right for old hillbillies and country gals. I didn't say nothing 'bout the fennel Iris put in the greens being good for farts."

Chuckling, Redwood sauntered in front of Aidan and plucked his banjo. "Quit cutting the fool. Cinnamon is almost done."

"I don't need dessert." Cinnamon swallowed the last bite of kale. "They can kill it."

Iris heaped the remaining cobbler into Klaus's and Marie's empty dessert dishes. "Seconds don't count, Aidan. You got to play for us. Quit stalling."

The rest of the chicken leg and a ball of quinoa appeared on Cinnamon's plate. Saliva filled her mouth. She felt light-headed. Her pathetic lack of willpower pissed her off.

"What you got for me, singerman, besides a fart joke?" Redwood rocked orange silk harem pants with beads and bangles at her

waist. Her hair was tucked under a Kente cloth head wrap. Clash-
ing squares and lines of blue, purple, yellow, and green irritated
Cinnamon. Nobody had told her what that pattern meant either.
And what about the sweetgrass basket with the giant acorns and
hoodoo herbs? Too much hidden meaning everywhere and no one
telling her what she needed to know. Before mad could bust out
all over Cinnamon, Redwood slid her palms along the armrests of
Aidan's chair and got all up in his face. She murmured *darling* with
a delicious Irish lilt and swished her hips. Talking Sea Island Gullah deep in her chest, she teased him in front of everybody. Klaus
and Marie exchanged excited glances while stuffing their faces.

"Come on, you old swamp dog," Redwood said, hot and sultry,
playing the shameless hussy in plain English. "Conjure me something real good. I want to shimmy shake these old bones."

Aidan's fingers flew up the neck of his banjo.

"Watch out now! Watch out!" Redwood shouted.

This music was on a different planet, in another dimension from
the fumblings he'd done the last two weeks. Cinnamon polished
off the chicken leg and ate a second biscuit without noticing. Her
stomach didn't growl or twist. Marie's lips turned killer red again.
Klaus's cheeks were splotched with orange as he tried to soak up
every furious lick Aidan played. Iris closed her eyes and swayed
inside the melody and rhythm.

Redwood was an elegant dancer. Not a single electron volt of
wasted effort. "This ain't a spectator sport." She pulled Marie and
Klaus up to shimmy shake with her. "You young folks are a tonic.
Get us up in the morning right." She spun and dipped with Marie
and twirled Klaus like a top. Her feet turned the floor into a drum.
"What I tell you, Aidan? You just needed to play. I knew the music
would come on back to you."

"Yes, ma'am, you did." Aidan had a shit-eating grin. "I was too
ornery to listen."

"Don't matter when you see the light, so long as you do." Redwood grinned too. "You still a conjure man with that banjo."

Aidan's fingers flew into another tune.

These were the magic hands Cinnamon remembered. When she was little, wound up, wired, a night terror for her parents, Aidan had promised to play her to sleep. Instead of Cinnamon drifting off after a song or two, they'd keep each other up all night, strumming, singing, and howling together, completely off the chain. In the morning nobody scolded or complained. Iris claimed a little night music was good for the digestion. Opal and Raven talked about dancing in sweet music dreams till dawn. Sekou usually woke up at 3 A.M. and joined in, playing rhythm. Good for nothing after that, he slept the next day away. Magically Redwood could always do the songs Cinnamon and Aidan had made up in the middle of the night. She'd say—

"Sing like your life depends on the next note, 'cause mine sure does." Redwood was saying that right now, with the force of a hoodoo spell.

"I got me some lyrics now." Aidan sang with a scratchy, sweet voice.

Tears filled Cinnamon's eyes and rolled down her cheeks. Happy tears for a childhood fairy tale come true. She didn't care if Klaus and Marie saw her blubbering. Redwood joined Aidan with a tricky high harmony that Cinnamon couldn't quite catch:

I see the light, a right bright ole light
A light at the end of the tunnel
It ain't the train, 'bout to run you down
It ain't the train, so don't turn around
It's the break of a brand-new day, hey!
I see the light, a burst from the blue
A spark in the dark for me and you
I say what you goin' do?
Get up off the ground
Quit messing around
I say what you goin' do?
Hold your head up high
Spread your wings and fly

I see the light, a right bright ole light
A light at the end of the tunnel
It ain't the train, 'bout to run you down
It ain't the train, so don't turn around
Say, it ain't the train, no way, hey, hey
Keep on going till you find your way
It's the break of a brand-new day

The second time through everybody sang the chorus. Cinnamon shook gourds from the hoodoo altar. Marie played silverware percussion. Klaus stroked pitches from the wineglasses. Iris hung onto the melody with folks harmonizing all over the place. Everybody ended on the upbeat, suspended, as if the song went barreling on somewhere without them, as if when it came back 'round again they could get on board where they left off. Marie and Klaus jumped up and down applauding wildly.

Before Cinnamon could beg for more, Aidan murmured. "That's all I got tonight." He set the banjo down carefully. His hands trembled. He rubbed the thunderbird on his chest, or maybe he was clutching his heart. "I ain't played much for, for . . ." He was falling into a deep hole. "Let's see, for—"

"For four years." Iris's eyes flew open. "Give or take three months . . ."

"Yeah," Aidan said. Cinnamon did the math. Since Daddy got shot.

"That was plenty." Redwood kissed his fingers. "Tomorrow, you can play more."

"Every day more," Cinnamon said too loud, a screech almost. "Not time for you to be . . ." spirit yet. She caught herself before blurting stupid crap. Good thing these folks didn't read minds, like Opal. "Don't be sad."

Aidan roused from his funk to smile at her. "All right, honeybunch, I got a good mood just for you."

Hearing Spirits from
the Other Shore

Iris dropped a bag of sweet potatoes in front of Aidan. "If you're not going to play any more music, you'll have to peel. My surprise casserole always tastes better if I make it up the day before."

"How's that a surprise?" Aidan said.

"I'll peel, singerman." Redwood grabbed the bag. "I know you like to chop."

"Can we come for dinner?" Klaus said.

Iris laughed at his lack of manners. "Certainly." She took a slice of mincemeat pie from the oven and set it by the empty cobbler dish in front of Cinnamon. A hunk of cream cheese was melting down the sides. "That's for you, if you still got some room."

Everybody watched Cinnamon do the calorie math. The pie would set her back several days. Rustling and buzzing from nowhere in particular interrupted her bargaining with herself over how many days of hunger the pie might be worth.

Eat it! Sekou said, all up in her shit, wearing his thunderbird tee. Iris's mincemeat was his favorite too. *You're drooling, Sis.*

"I am?" Cinnamon scrambled to clean her mouth off.

You're stalling, worse than Granddaddy Aidan.

"I don't mean to." Cinnamon took a bite of the pie. A sweet fermented taste exploded in her mouth.

It's not how deep you fish, it's how you wiggle the worm.

"Granddaddy said the same thing. What's that supposed to mean?" The rest of the pie slipped over her tongue and disappeared down into her belly. "Talk to me, Bro."

No reply, and the buzzing and rustling faded. Sekou was gone, before he'd checked in really. Cinnamon felt woozy or drunk even. On food! Marie and Klaus gestured and shook their heads at her, too slow, as if they were swimming in honey. The elders moved as if they'd stopped time while waiting for her to catch up. Redwood peeled a mountain of sweet potatoes and somehow picked up the pace. Cinnamon blinked, and a whole bag was done. The skins were curled up in bouncy ringlets. Wielding an enormous old knife, Aidan chopped the naked sweet potatoes into bright orange cubes and tossed them in a strainer perched over boiling water. Aidan wiped fifteen inches of blade clean.

"Is that uhm," Cinnamon had to concentrate to form words, "the Seminole heirloom knife that Uncle Clarence claims is pure Georgia cracker?"

It's a Maskóki hunting knife. Sekou was back, whispering over her shoulder.

"You're making me dizzy, whizzing in and out." Cinnamon didn't turn around.

"My daddy gave me this knife." Aidan tossed it from hand to hand. Did he hear Sekou? "He got it from a *Maskóki* man, a blood brother who died too young. His widow was my daddy's first wife."

"Miss O'Casey was Big Thunder's second wife," Cinnamon said. "They met in the Okefenokee Swamp, grassy water that rocks your sorrows away."

Now you're talking! Why do you listen to the BS Clarence spews?

Cinnamon hated to admit it, but, "Sometimes Uncle Clarence is right."

Not this time. Sekou was gone again in a flash.

"Wait! You want your chair?" Cinnamon stood up too quickly. Undigested food threatened to evacuate her tight tummy. She gulped down soothing saliva.

"What you chewing over?" Redwood said.

"I'm uhm . . ." Cinnamon sputtered.

Ribbons of colored energy shot from Redwood's storm hand. "You're what?" Redwood swept the curly potato skins into a pail and pointed the peeler at Cinnamon. "Just spit it out. Won't get easier later."

"Well, darling, she's sure to talk now, you being so diplomatic." Aidan sounded more Irish than Georgia cracker.

"Excuse me, sugar, I forgot." Redwood had a hand on her hip. "Irish diplomacy is telling a man to go to hell so that he looks forward to making the trip."

Redwood and Aidan laughed like the next minute they'd be jumping each other's bones. Had they always been this way, and Cinnamon was too young and dumb to notice, or was this more seeing sex everywhere? Marie and Klaus laughed too, washing dirty dishes. Opal refused to *waste money on a dishwasher nobody needed in the first place.*

Iris slammed a top on the pot of sweet potatoes and jolted Cinnamon. "Who moved the fennel?" Iris rummaged through a pile of onions, kiwis, and garlic cloves until she found the shaggy fennel and a mysterious plant with orange leaves and warts on its spindly stems. "That's the ticket." Iris liked to cook from scratch, from: send Aidan and Redwood out into the weeds to bring back hairy things with dirt clinging to the roots for a miracle-tasting casserole surprise. *Surprise* was what Iris always called the dish of the moment made from whatever good stuff was on hand.

"Everybody is doing something useful except for me," Cinnamon said.

Iris smiled. "Better hurry up and speak your piece, or I'll be in an ill humor, won't want to share my yam and goober surprise with anybody."

"If Iris be talking about yams and goober peanuts, you 'bout to miss a taste of Africa." Aidan smiled at Cinnamon as Klaus and Marie groaned.

"So what you got to say for yourself?" Redwood said.

Sekou dropped in again and hissed at Cinnamon.

"You know, dead folk always leave something," Aidan said, "a trail, a song on the wind. They ain't really lost to you."

Klaus froze. The big pot he gripped was dripping dark splotches on the floor. The dish towel trembled in his hand. Marie clenched the heavy lid, teetering at the edge of nothing. Everybody was eyeing Cinnamon, waiting for her to wiggle the worm.

"It's like this," Cinnamon said. "Sekou talks to me sometimes. To my friends too."

Klaus let go of the pot. Marie caught it, but the lid flew away from her. Redwood reached out with her storm hand and snatched the spinning metal out of the air, right before it would have hit Cinnamon upside the head.

"You two hear Sekou too, do you?" Redwood set the top on the counter.

Clutching the pot together, Klaus and Marie nodded. No point in denying it.

"Ancestors on the wind." Aidan skinned a ginger root with his scary knife. "Most folks don't listen. Getting deaf to the spiritual frequency."

"People are afraid," Iris murmured, almost to herself. "Maybe all they will hear are spirits. Or maybe they won't know who is a spirit and who is breathing still. That's a right reasonable concern." She dumped cooked sweet potato cubes into a bowl filled with wedges of butter that promptly melted. Aidan shaved in ginger root and mystery weed until Iris raised a hand. She splashed lemon juice and added a few dollops of molasses before beating the sweet potatoes to orange fluff. A dusting of cinnamon, nutmeg, and cloves was followed by a drizzle of maple syrup and a spray of chopped fennel. Iris never measured anything. *You can't go by the numbers, got to go by the taste.*

"You don't have more to tell us than that, honeybunch?" Aidan worked a French whip on half a dozen eggs.

"Talk up a storm when you want to," Iris said.

Sekou wrote Iris anything—even letters about mean boyfriends dumping him. What was the matter with Cinnamon? Iris folded the frothy eggs into the sweet potato mix and blended it to a smooth texture. She poured thin planes of an herb peanut concoction between thick layers of sweet potato fluff into a deep casserole dish, finishing with dots of butter, peanut dust, fennel flesh, and tiny pink mushrooms.

"You worried 'bout Sekou talking to you?" Redwood held the oven open. The blast of heat felt wonderful as Iris set the casserole on the middle rack. "After my mama . . ." Redwood closed the oven. "After Miz Garnett died, she used to talk to Aidan."

"That she did. Like to drive me wild." Aidan looked wistful. "Actually it was my own torment working against me, not Miz Garnett."

"I see Sekou too," Cinnamon admitted.

"How do he look?" Redwood said. "Worse or—"

"Good," Cinnamon admitted. "He was wearing the T-shirt Raven gave him."

"The thunderbird one?" Iris said.

Aidan hugged his own version. "He wrote Iris about wanting to burn it."

Cinnamon shook her head. "Bug-Man Lexy said Sekou was a drama queen, mostly big talk, until he OD'ed."

"Do we know about Bug-Man Lexy?" Klaus said.

"Is he dead?" Marie painstakingly wiped down the forks. "Did he OD too?"

"Ah, no, Lexy is, uhm, he was uhm, he and Sekou were tight, were . . ." Cinnamon sputtered to a halt. Everybody stared at her. If Iris knew the scoop, Redwood and Aidan knew too. The elders didn't help her out though. The casserole gurgled in the oven, spitting sweetness that sizzled on the oven floor.

Marie broke the silence. "I get it."

Klaus looked baffled a second and then said, "Oh, Sekou, *er war vom anderen Ufer.*"

"What's that?" Marie asked.

"A figure of speech," Klaus explained. "He was gay, *from the other shore.*"

Cinnamon tilted her head at him, a Marie move. "Lexy is still very much with us, on this shore."

"Hey, this shore *is* the other shore," Marie said. "And we're hearing spirits."

The gay-boy truth was out, and no meltdown.

"When I was eighteen, nineteen, after Redwood's mama had been . . . taken away from us, I . . ." Aidan gazed into the past and shuddered. Back in the present, he fixed Cinnamon, and Klaus and Marie too, in his eyes. "After a posse of white men raped and lynched Miz Garnett, after they set fire to her in a Georgia pine that didn't burn when she did, Miz Garnett come on back to keep a lookout on her children and on me too."

Klaus and Marie were transfixed. They didn't mind this history. Cinnamon was furious. This was *important shit* Opal didn't want her to know. "Keep going, please."

Aidan looked away. His jaw twitched. "I felt like a low-down worthless coward."

"Nothing you could've done, a boy against a posse of grown men," Redwood said.

Aidan took hold of her storm hand. "But I was set on drinking myself to kingdom come. Now, even dead and gone, Miz Garnett wasn't having none of that. Bold as you please, violet orchids growing in her hair, swamp stink on her breath, Miz Garnett sat in a broken rocking chair on my front porch and scared me sober."

"You don't drink." Cinnamon was confused. "Ever."

"Not anymore. But I was worse than your Uncle Dicky."

"Too many folks be erasing themselves with booze, smack, or cigarettes." Cinnamon couldn't imagine Aidan falling down, stupid drunk. "Why would you do that?"

Aidan shivered. "I thought I'd lost most everything, tried to drown the last bit of myself in a jug. Walking the coward's way."

"He wasn't the only one." Redwood sighed. "I was up in Chicago town, cooning, so I could forget my own hurting self."

"Cooning?" Klaus asked. "What is cooning?" Cinnamon was too stunned to explain. Marie whispered something about black folks acting stupid in minstrel shows to him.

"Like Raymond Abernathy in Paris?" Klaus said.

"Every night and twice on Saturday," Redwood said, "getting drunk on a crowd of folks laughing at me and mine, tearing us down, bringing us low."

"I can't believe it." Cinnamon shook her head. They let her imagine glamorous stage adventures.

"Don't listen to them," Iris said. "Aidan come back from the dead to save me. Sister opened the doors to my tomorrows. She was tearing up the stage in Chicago town."

"You were just knee high to a sprout, hair like a dandelion gone to seed." Aidan tweaked Iris's nose.

She smacked his hand away. "Sister knew how to strut her stuff onstage! She was a headliner with that Persian dreamboat."

"Saeed," Aidan said, sounding almost jealous.

"Saeed was definitely from the other shore." Redwood smiled. "Found him a sweet Union man."

Iris grinned. "When Saeed danced he made your heart leap. Aidan was busy working his banjo hand, like tonight. He was a matinee idol in the moving pictures." Aidan tried to protest. Iris shushed him. "This is my story. Aidan had women swooning in the dark over his brave warrior escapades. Sister flew through the air on everybody's dreams and put on her own picture shows, Sea Island romances: *The Pirate and the Schoolteacher* and *Sorrow Mountain*. She and Aidan lived happily ever after in that one. Now that's how I remember it. Everybody was doing the best they could. They saved enough money to send me from Oberlin all the way to a PhD. We had hard times for sure, but plenty of grand times too."

"Amen to that." Redwood dispersed the memories with a flick of her wrist. Grief and joy washed over them, but did not linger. Redwood took a breath and looked ready to fly. "We have to stay on track. Sekou is a good spirit."

Iris nodded. "He won't tell you anything wrong." She headed for the sink.

"Wait! You not goin' rinse that down the drain." Redwood grabbed the mixing bowl, scraped sweet potato fluff from the sides, and sucked it off her finger. She scooped the last dab for Aidan before passing the bowl to Klaus to wash. Aidan sucked her finger to the knuckle. Redwood shivered at his tongue tickling her thumb. Old as they were, still acting bad, in front of folks too. How did anybody stay in love that long?

"If Sekou tell you something out the way . . ." Aidan paused. "You gotta trust . . ."

"Trust your heart spirit." Redwood finished his thought. "You'll know the truth."

"How?" Cinnamon, Marie, and Klaus asked in unison.

The elders exchanged looks and unreadable hand signs. "Who can tell you what you got to figure for your own self?" Redwood glowered at them. "Life is finding the way and having a good time doing it."

Cinnamon thought of Kehinde and Taiwo guzzling poison water or dying of thirst. "Are you kidding, offering fortune-cookie wisdom when we're facing impossible shit?"

Redwood laughed. "Fortune-cookie masters steal from the best minds."

"You're all for doing life your own special way." Iris had a devilish half smile. "You'll figure how to make that *way out of no way*." Maybe she *could* read minds.

"Cinnamon was an ornery cuss even as a little baby." Aidan squeezed her nose. Nobody else would have dared. "She spit carrot baby food in my face, ready to go hungry rather than eat slop."

"I still hate cooked carrots," Cinnamon declared.

Iris pulled the casserole dish out of the oven. It was done already. Time was messed up. "Babies know what they want." She held up a spoon of her sweet potato *surprise*.

The aroma made Cinnamon swoon, but she'd gone over the limit. "I'm too full."

Redwood muttered Sea Island Gullah and shook her head. Klaus gobbled the surprise gratefully. Laughing, Marie had a taste too. The March wind howled outside, blowing a sudden storm against the windows. Wind chimes clanged on the porch as clouds swallowed the last bit of daylight. Hail pelted the roof. Lightning flashed nearby. Lightbulbs dimmed out for a second.

"So, little miss woman, is that all you got to say for yourself?" Redwood demanded.

"You guys had fantasy; that was easy. We're in the twentieth century. We get science fiction too."

"Is that so?" Redwood's tone was deadly.

Cinnamon flinched. Lynching, easy? Thunder shockwaves shook the foundation.

"What about trancing out to *The Chronicles*?" Klaus licked Iris's spoon.

"That's nothing." Marie displayed her hand "What about—"

A flurry of sparks arced from her jet black nails, crackling and frying dust motes, zinging metal pans and doorknobs. One bolt blackened a wooden eagle's eye. Cinnamon and Klaus jumped and hollered. Marie trembled as more sparks surged from glowing fingertips. Aidan dodged sparks and wrapped his banjo in Kente cloth. Light fixtures got zapped and blew out. Iris squinted in the bursts of bright energy and grabbed a stepstool. Candles died and hissed smoke. Crazy shadows danced along the walls. The acrid smell of ozone stung their noses. Redwood strode to the hoodoo altar, stretched out a long arm, and opened her storm hand. Every zigzag of electricity raced toward her. Marie's hand spit a final trickle then went dim. Sparks gathered in Redwood's palm, spiraling into a white hot ball. Grunting, she closed her hand into a tight fist. The kitchen was pitch dark. Iris clomped up the stepstool and screwed a bulb into the overhead. Warm incandescence filled the kitchen.

"Did that just happen?" Klaus said.

"Before you go flying off on a wild tear," Redwood spoke calm into the jittery room, "you have to know what's goin' bring your behind back down to Earth." She opened her hand. The palm was empty and clear.

Ear Worm

Redwood's storm-hand display was what Cinnamon, Marie, and Klaus needed. Finishing each other's sentences or talking over one another, they explained the last *Chronicles* episodes in hyperspeed. Marie gave a graphic account of her hand getting swallowed by the weird from another dimension. Cinnamon offered the Wanderer Taiwo is Griot Joe theory. Klaus mentioned Ariel doing magic blocking that no one could explain. The elders absorbed this barrage without comment. Exhausted, the Squad tumbled onto the worn couch in the living room. Three people hadn't sat together on the poor thing in years. It caved under their behinds and gave off a dusty, musty odor.

"Sometimes I say things." Cinnamon did a solo turn. "I mean, I make up things, or, a deluge of words comes to me. It could be tall tales, but mostly what I say turns out to be true. I said you all were coming here after Opal fell out at the audition."

The elders stood framed in the kitchen island window. Iris relit the candles. Redwood set these spears of fire by the acorn guards. Aidan opened his worn journal and pulled out a dried orchid. The elders huddled close to one another, flickering and mumbling in the candlelight, a silent movie without the titles.

"Do you have any words of wisdom?" Cinnamon said. "What should we be doing?"

"Hell if I know," Redwood said. "All we had was fantasy . . ."

"Who's cutting the fool now?" Aidan chuckled. Iris did too. It wasn't funny.

The orca slipped off the kitchen island and spewed out *The Chronicles*.

Iris picked up the heavy tome. "A new chapter has appeared, beyond 'River Pirates.'"

Aidan squinted at tiny handwriting. "Wanderer wants us to read nineteen together."

"It's too late." Klaus struggled up from the collapsed cushions. "I must go home."

"Me too." Marie jumped beside him. "I have homework I better ace or else."

"Or else what?" Professor Iris said.

"My parents want a doctor in the house, not another worthless, starving artist." Marie rolled her eyes. "Roaming the streets with a tin cup would be such a waste."

"*Owa*," Klaus said.

"Like your sister?" Cinnamon spied a sleek version of Marie hugging the toilet bowl.

"How do you know about her? Did I tell you—"

"I feel her on you," Cinnamon said.

Marie shrugged. "You and Klaus have *real* issues."

Bullshit. Quit fronting. Sekou wavered in front of her.

"No, it's not a big deal." Marie insisted.

I'm on to you, sugar.

Marie glared at a ghost who was hardly there. "My parents don't get it, Sekou. I love science, so why am I singing Whitney Houston, Madonna, and Prince? Mega parent angst—what if I cut my hair like Salt-N-Pepa? What if I'm not smart enough for the real world?" Cinnamon and Klaus snorted. "If I get a B in algebra, can I be a doctor?"

Sekou came in brighter. *Algebra comes from* al-jabr *as in* Kitab al-jabr wa'l-muqabalah, The Book of Restoring and Balancing *by Al-Khwārizmī, a Persian mathematician.*

"What's with the drive-by shootings, dictionary boy?" Marie said.

Writing recipes for the unknown as a function of the known, you're all over that. Logic and patterns. Sekou was gone before the *s* had faded.

The elders didn't say if they saw/heard Sekou or not. They hit the other problems. Marie had no real difficulty solving math mysteries. Unreasonable expectations and poor sentence structure in the crappy textbook sapped her confidence. Figuring out the logic trick without second-guessing herself was key.

"Is this cheating?" Marie asked.

"You're doing the work," Professor Iris declared.

Aidan was a conjure man with his banjo. He played music from *Title Under Construction,* and in no time Klaus could sing his part regardless of the wild harmonies they threw at him. Redwood hoodooed the phone with her storm hand and called the Masudas. Mrs. Masuda, despite not wanting her daughter to run away to the theatre, was thrilled to talk to a silent movie star. Redwood worked her *mojo* on *Vati* too. He was expansive and invited everyone over for dinner, Saturday in two weeks.

Klaus drew a finger across his neck, as if slitting his throat.

"We'll protect you," Marie whispered, full of algebra and Glamazon bravado.

Cinnamon picked up the receiver. The line was dead.

Redwood clasped Marie's hand. "Cinnamon tells me you're a great actress."

Surprise darted across Marie's face. "You told her that?"

"Feel your hand now," Redwood said. "Feel every bit of you while you're at it."

"That's a theatre game," Klaus said, "feeling self with self."

"Right." Marie closed her eyes to do this. "I got this. Wow."

"Believe in how you feel right now." Redwood let Marie's hand go.

Concentrating, Marie strained her muscles.

"Relax." Redwood stroked away tension. "If sparks start to fly, *act* like ain't nothing happening. You two practice this too."

Cinnamon and Klaus were already doing it.

"Now feel your power together."

They opened their eyes, clutched hands, and touched their heads together.

"What you call yourselves? Mad Squad?"

"Mod Squad," they said in unison. "How did you—"

"A conjure woman can hear underneath things." Aidan lifted

the violet orchid from the altar and held it in the center of their circle. Close up, the flower seemed fresh, alive. "Miz Garnett left this flower on my busted rocking chair." Aidan leaned over Cinnamon. A shadow fell across his face. He looked older than grizzly hills at sunset. "I'll take you to see Raven tomorrow, if you still want to go."

Pain darted through the room, zapping everybody, worse than the sparks from Marie's fingers. Miz Redwood lifted her eyes to the thunderbird shadow flying over the kitchen island. Klaus and Marie held their breath and squeezed closer.

Klaus hummed Aidan's song:

I see the light, a right bright ole light
A light at the end of the tunnel
It ain't the train, 'bout to run you down
It ain't the train, so don't turn around
It's the break of a brand-new day, hey!

"It's an *Ohrwurm*, a worm stuck in my ear, sorry," Klaus said.

"Sure, I'll go see Daddy," Cinnamon mumbled.

"*Ohrwurm*," Aidan said with a Georgia drawl. "Yeah." He pointed the orchid at Redwood and Iris. "Nobody else want to go with me. They got their reasons. I understand, but—"

"I said sure, didn't I?" Cinnamon shouted.

"All right then." Aidan nodded at everyone, light back in his spirit. He pressed the orchid into the middle of his journal pages. "Let's get to the tales of the great Wanderer. See what them Dahomey folks got in store for us tonight."

"Yoruba has one pronoun, *oun*, for he and she." Iris smoothed down a folded corner on the new *Chronicles* pages. "The Wanderer is *oun*." She put plaid glasses on her nose and read *The Chronicles* out loud. Nineteen was her favorite prime number.

Chronicles 19: Carnival Visions

All versions of Paris converge on one ending. I was sprawled on the dock in hot starlight, uncertain of truth, of a path to take; Abla floated in the Seine, yelling:

"Kehinde is a coward who betrays everyone. She sent Ekundayo, a woman who trusted and loved her, to face guns with no protection. Now you wear Oshun's comb, a desecrated trinket. Bob has terrible secrets too. He will betray and abandon you! Wanderers and warriors should disdain sentiment. Love is folly."

I closed my eyes on Abla's torment and dreamt. Kehinde and Bob wrestled, half-naked on the war god's field. The iron lady was referee. They wore short skirts with beads at their waists and throats. Bob's hair was as red as flame-tree foliage. Inky, iridescent splotches dribbled across his face and arms and down his chest and legs. He was the Spotted Man in full light. Kehinde's deep purple lips curled over knife-sharp teeth. Her nipples were also dark violet. A red feather was tucked in the crown of her braids, for Eshu. She was *La Femme Sauvage,* warrior *ahosi* stolen from herself, feeling nothing. They lunged at each other. Lightning arced from black clouds and lit up their bodies. Bob pinned Kehinde's shoulders; she wrapped muscular thighs around his head. A ghostly ringmaster smacked a fiery whip against their ribs. Sparks got caught in tight ringlets of hair. Silver smoke snaked around rippling muscles. Bob and Kehinde broke apart and circled each other.

The *Champ de Mars* hosted a dime museum carnival. The field was jammed with giant warriors, tiny cannibals, men with piebald skin, broad-chested dwarfs, two-headed Amazons, tree-dwelling ape people, and water women with fused legs and webbed feet. These freaks put on mock battles in between spears of lightning. Ten thousand spectators hung from the Eiffel Tower and shrieked. People too poor or too timid to venture far from civilization were much entertained by the regrettable but inevitable demise of noble savages and freaks.

Kehinde drew her cutlass, and Bob seized a bayonet. The crowd roared and tossed metal and paper offerings for a fight to the death. Kehinde and Bob scrambled to scoop up the tribute, slashing at each other. Ribbons of blood decorated their bodies. I screamed at them to stop. The *aje* roared fire. Clouds burst and smothered the *aje's* breath with water crystals. A snow horse charged out of collapsing clouds and zigzagged down a white-hot bolt. Iron hooves stomped other acrobatic freaks to pulp, and the mob applauded. Kehinde and Bob were the last ones standing. The horse charged them. Shouting, waving my arms, I lunged into its path, not as *aje,* but as my Taiwo-self. The horse slammed into my chest and shattered. Kehinde held a cutlass to Bob's neck. He had a dagger at her heart. I choked on balls of hail.

"We can't give up," Kehinde shouted in English.

"Of course not," Bob replied. "We sacrifice for Taiwo."

The dream dissolved. Crusty eyes parted—

Night had fallen at the water's edge. The last glow of the home star turned a few clouds the color of bruises. *La Seine* reeked. My arm dangled in refuse. I was thirsty and achy, but illness had left me. I stood up and fell on my face. The fever had taken the strength of my muscles when it departed.

"Taiwo must be here, somewhere," Kehinde said nearby.

I scanned the docks. A tiny man held a lantern at a giant's thigh. A bearded woman with thick hair covering her arms poked into broken crates. A two-headed man (fused twins?) on a white horse looked backward and forward. I blinked, hoping to banish phantoms. The dream had been fluid, an edited spectacle. What I saw now was disjointed and random. A young girl, sleek as a fish, pulled herself from *La Seine* as a two-headed woman marched up the boardwalk with a lantern in each of three hands. A fourth hand held a leash on a long-eared dog who sniffed the air. The water woman shook stringy hair and sprayed droplets of slime about.

"Watch it!" a soprano and an alto shouted as a lantern sputtered. Not identical twins.

"It's too dark to find anything down here except trouble." The water woman scratched the dog's ears. "Isn't that right, Floppy?"

"Eshu taunts us." Kehinde's voice again. I could finally see her.

"Sorry, ma'am. I don't like saying this." The piebald man wagged his head. "Anything could have happened to your friend."

"Taiwo is near." Kehinde held up Oshun's comb. It had fallen from my braids.

My throat was too constricted for sounds. Shadows concealed my presence. How would they ever find me? I crawled toward Kehinde. Foul-smelling containers blocked a direct path. I dragged myself around obstacles and across the filthy road. Time dragged also. Kehinde conferred with the piebald man and furry woman. Floppy licked my face, slapped a bushy tale against my ribs, and barked at the alto.

"Is that you?" Bright eyes and white teeth in two dark moon faces smiled. "We come out here in the middle of the night to rescue you and here you've found us."

I rolled into Kehinde. Clutching her thighs, I pulled myself to standing and fell into the circle of her arms. She offered a flask from her belt. I sucked down the sour brew then whispered, "I worried that you, Bob, and everybody were gone upriver to the Lady Atlantic, and I'd never see you again."

"Why would I abandon you?" Kehinde hugged me.

"You've abandoned others." I drenched her shoulders with forbidden tears.

"That isn't our fate." She poured libation to the master of uncertainty. "I praise Eshu, the wonder-worker who makes a whistle from the head of a serpent and calls you to us." She stroked my damp face and put Oshun's comb in my hair. "Eshu offers only the challenges we can meet." We tasted lips and tongues too briefly.

"I'm no longer ill. The fever has fled. I can walk, if you let me lean on you."

"What foolishness!" She had hired a coach to carry me back to Montparnasse. "Raymond throws a party to celebrate our voyage tomorrow."

A horseman rode ahead to spread the good news. The coachmen eyed my soiled, raggedy clothes and wrinkled his nose, yet refrained from putting up a fuss. The ride to Montparnasse was longer than I remembered. When we stumbled in the door, the front room was packed. Raymond had asked other giants, spectacles, and defeated ones to search for me. His colleagues (friends?) lived nearby, many in the same building he lived in. After a long day of masquerading, they had prowled the docks for hours, interrogating anyone for word of *une Femme Sauvage*. Now they gathered to celebrate the return of the Lightning Eater. In their versions of Paris, I had saved a whole crowd from the lethal bolts on several occasions.

"We are here because of you," they shouted.

"I don't recall these heroic deeds," I stammered.

"After swallowing all that lightning, of course not." The two-headed singer let Floppy lick me again.

Praises were shouted to Jesus and the saints, to Allah and the God of Abraham, and to Eshu and Oshun. Musicians picked up stringed instruments, drums, and flutes. Worn-out masquerades put on their dancing shoes. Trays of food floated by, filling the air with delicious anticipation. I held in a torrent of tears for Kehinde's sake.

"You need a bath, demon," Somso said. "What have you been wallowing in?"

People I didn't know hauled buckets of hot water so that I might wash away the filth of my ordeal. Melinga enjoyed the luxurious warm tub with me. Kehinde plucked out splinters, rubbed my body with rough cloth and fragrant oils, and dressed me in a silky gown from the East, a cool night breeze against irritable flesh. I was too exhausted to sit up on my own. More sleep was out of the question; this party was in my honor, and I wanted no dreams. Kehinde propped me up on pillows in a cavernous chair where, as honored guest, I might watch everyone drink rum, sing, dance, and tell what they called war stories. Luigi breezed in and out, relieved that my fever had passed.

"Where is Bob?" I asked. I didn't see Liam either.

Kehinde massaged my head. "Did you really believe Bob or I would abandon you?"

I wanted to lie, so I remained silent.

"You think so little of us?" Kehinde braided my hair into tight rows. "Bob would never leave Paris without you. Neither would I!"

"Bob and Liam still search for you," Somso said. "Kehinde sent Raymond to collect them. Otherwise they'd be out all night."

"Bob loves you. I swore a blood oath." Kehinde stormed to the banquet table.

"You're right to doubt her. Warrior life ruins a woman." Somso tapped her feet to the drums. "All day, the child hollers for you. When you are returned to us, she sleeps quietly." Melinga nestled in my lap, snoring under the music and loud talk.

"She changes faster every day, a dependable miracle," I said. "Go enjoy yourself."

Somso eyed a dark woman with a stripe of pink flesh running from forehead to neck, across a shoulder, and presumably on to the pink bare foot she tapped. Somso leaned close. "These horrors should have gotten tangled in their umbilical cords and strangled. Sane people don't celebrate deformity or abominable twins."

"Audiences come to see a spectacle. I don't know if that is celebration."

Somso grunted at me and Melinga. "The company I keep, who am I to talk?"

"Are we all monsters to you?"

Bob and Liam burst through the door, holding each other up. Raymond came behind them, a keg of spirits in his arms. Bob almost dropped Liam when he spied me. He propped the Irishman against a wall near Kehinde and stumbled close. I tasted rum in his breath as he sank to his knees and laid his head against my shoulder.

I kissed his forehead. "I'm well. You won't need to sneak me aboard in the luggage."

The two-headed woman sang a duet. Raymond tugged Somso's hand. Resisting his enormous smile and the infectious music proved impossible. Somso stomped into the center of the dancers. Kehinde scowled at me from the banquet table. This too, I decided, was love.

Bob clutched my thighs, breathing into my neck. He was one drink away from drunk. Another man hesitated in the doorway. His stringy black and gray hair was braided into a heavy rope down his back. He wore clothes for celebration. A smile overtook his face. I recognized him.

"He was on the docks this morning," I said to Bob. "He didn't betray me to Luigi. I owe him thanks."

Bob waved at him. "Ghost Dog was the alternate plan."

"I don't understand." I nodded to Ghost Dog who returned the gesture.

Liam was several drinks beyond drunk. "Gentlemen and fair ladies!" He cracked an imaginary whip. The guests grew quiet. "Here is the Ghost Dog, a full-blood Oglala Sioux Indian from the Wild Wild West, farther west and more wild than Chicago!" He drew Ghost Dog into the room. "This rough riding, hard shooting, fearless brave will join our august company as we traverse the seas heading for the New World. Captain Signor Luigi is eternally grateful to Ghost Dog for foiling dastardly river pirates who tried to cheat him out of the profits *Les Femme Sauvages* made for him. As reward, Luigi offers Ghost Dog a berth aboard *La Vérité* and moments of glory on the Chicago stage." Liam pulled off a boot. "Luigi, God bless him, is about as Italian as my big toe." He wiggled it. The crowd howled.

"Why is this funny?" I said.

"Luigi is Walter Williams, late of Toronto, Ontario." Bob leaned against my legs. "He changed his name to spare the family. *Luigi* has more show business flair."

"Ole Walt could lie the sweet out of sugar and sell his mother's bones to the Devil." Liam sniggered over Bob. "Why'd you change your name, Bobbie boy? Didn't want to be Bamidele, the Spotted Man from that lost tribe in Abyssinia, anymore? Tired of cooning so now you're the happy shepherd to wild beasties?" Bob shoved Liam away.

"You were a masquerade in a freak show?" Abla was right about Bob's terrible secrets. "Why didn't you tell me?"

"He did private shows too." Liam leered at him. "For lusty ladies and gents."

"Shut your ugly mug," Bob said.

"Bamidele is Yoruba for come home, come to the West with me." Liam planted a sloppy kiss in Bob's tight curls. "Or is that a lie you told to win my heart? So I'd play the prince and rescue you?"

"You're drunk." Bob punched him in the gut.

Liam flailed. "You want to go outside and wrestle?"

My head spun. Would they fight over the past Bob wanted to hide?

Kehinde pulled Liam away. "You're too angry, Irishman."

"Somebody ought to be angry," Bob muttered.

"Not tonight." Kehinde danced with Liam. "We celebrate. Eshu opens the doors from this universe to every other. Tomorrow we journey to a new world together."

"Eshu demands sacrifice." I was still worried. "You must be willing to die in order to live—especially to reach a new world."

What would our sacrifice be?

Book V

Pittsburgh, PA, 1987 & America 1893–1971

Come celebrate with me that every day
something has tried to kill me and has failed.

—Lucille Clifton

Hold All of Me

Raven Cooper had shrunk. Three or four inches. Most of his face was sliding off high cheekbones, leaving a monster brow to jut out over half-slit eyes. Slack lips formed a sneer around yellow teeth, and cloudy spit oozed down his chin. Tubes sprouted from his face and arms. Cinnamon froze in the doorway, afraid of this monster, afraid of herself. She swallowed whatever was rising up from her gut into her throat. She dug her fingers into Aidan's thigh. He gripped her hand, and they took tentative steps across the scuffed linoleum floor. Sun shone against peach cement-block walls trying to give the room a first-day-of-spring glow. Ragged begonias strained their leaves toward a blotchy window. Flower deadheads nodded in the heat convection between window and radiator. Cinnamon stopped five feet from her daddy. Aidan halted also. Pink chairs with sagging seats and rippling backs did not invite them farther in. The imprints of friends and relatives lingered on the cracked fake leather. Cinnamon hated the yellow stuffing that poked through.

"It's too hot in here," she said as sweat curled under her arms. "And it . . ." stank. Aidan nodded. Why was he so quiet? Maybe standing in this room was as hard for him as it was for her. Probably harder for Raven.

Since they'd told Cinnamon that her daddy was shot in the head and lying in a bed, lost in his own mind, unable to reach this world, all she'd wanted to do was get to him, touch him, rouse him. She'd secretly thought that, despite what the specialists and experts said, despite what Opal and Sekou feared, despite the elders insisting they knew no spell, no conjure to bring their son back, she, Cinnamon the Great, would be able to wake her daddy up. Opal couldn't stand to visit him, said she never went, and flat

out refused to tell Cinnamon where he was. Sekou too. *Trust me on
this one, Sis. Lingering is worse than gone.* The elders weren't telling,
and Aunt Becca claimed she didn't know. Cinnamon couldn't find
a single clue, no bills or letters or anything. She was certain that if
Opal and everybody would stop getting in her way, stop treating
her like a baby, if they'd just let her go see him . . . Didn't they
want Raven back? Didn't they want a miracle?

The monster on the bed made a gurgling sound. Cinnamon
took a step back and to the side. She used Aidan as a shield. Sekou
didn't have shit to say to her now. Snow White blasted her though:

> *Too stupid to know the history we're dying from*
> *So stuck on ourselves—*
> *Can't see the present we're dying in*
> *Fuck that noise, Jack!*

As the smell of poop and disinfectant twisted in her nose, the
wake-up-Daddy kiddie fantasy played in her mind.

Raven, a jaunty turban-bandage around his head, lay
in billowy white pillows and sheets, as peaceful and beautiful as an angel. Cinnamon snuck away from Opal and
their sad house, rode the bus to East Liberty or maybe
out to Monroeville. She tore up the stairs to the fifth
floor of a grand nursing home. She easily outran the lame
guards at the door who were supposed to keep naughty
children out. Nobody had to tell her which room. Daddy's door glowed. She burst in, singing his secret name—
Gilidinehuyi, Cherokee for lightning—and Raven's eyes
popped open. She stopped at the foot of the bed, waiting
for all of him to open up and come back. After a long
sleep, after weeks and months and years of dreams, a person would need a few moments to realize he was awake,
to realize she wasn't a dream angel but his magic hoodoo
child, who knew the spell to call him back to himself.

Raven rose slowly from the cocoon of sheets and tugged at the turban-bandage until it unraveled. A round scar at the scalp line had healed forever ago. He tapped it, remembering his last conscious moments with a shudder. Cinnamon kept whispering his secret name, and Raven shook off the lingering effects of a bullet to the brain. His dreads whirled about his head, a dark storm of hair, like Kali, mistress of time, destroyer of unreality. He laughed and flexed muscles up and down his body. Cinnamon blinked, and he was dancing through the fab '60s moves he and Opal loved to do: Funky Chicken, Mashed Potato, Boogaloo . . .

"Cinnamon! What you doing way over there? Come here, girl, let me see how you've grown." He waved her close, hugged her tight, a bear hug with growling and grumbling, and then said, "I've been waiting on you, spice child. I've been dreaming 'bout you. I knew you'd come to rescue me. I knew you'd believe in me till I had to wake up. Go get your mom. Tell her don't be afraid to come see me. Tell my love I've been dreaming 'bout her too."

The fantasy was old and embellished over the last four years and three months, a trusty friend always running in the background. Without realizing, Cinnamon rode the bus with this fairy tale, ate every meal with its sweet promise, and took the *all's well that ends well* vision to bed with her. It never occurred to her to give up hope until...

Soft yet insistent gurgling from Raven made Cinnamon turn away. Two empty beds waited on more patients. Clusters of beat-up chairs hunkered nearby, ready to catch any pathetic loved ones who dropped by. Thank god Raven was alone this afternoon, no other coma-ghouls or sad-sack relatives. Aidan leaned into Cinnamon's back, not much weight, just a touch of him. He smelled of the wood he'd been carving on the bus and black licorice. She squeezed her *mojo* bag and forced herself to turn around.

Raven looked wrong, older than his ancient father, a prisoner in solitary confinement. Mind locked up and flesh wasting away; what was the point of holding him or anybody in this
stupid room? Why not let him go on his way? Kehinde insisted
a quick death was mercy. So true, because then, nobody, Cinnamon, Aidan, nor Opal, would have to come watch and wait in a
smelly, depressing nursing home. Raven could be dancing Boogaloo with the ancestors. Cinnamon closed her eyes to see his
fancy footwork in a city of shining ghosts. Another child of God
come home, he'd be welcomed with music and light. Cinnamon
opened her eyes to truth:

Raven would be better off all the way dead.

"Iris take everything to her heart. Can't get her within a mile of
here." Aidan's cracker-twang grated. "Redwood ain't one to hover
'round like an ole buzzard for her only son to be dead flesh. She'd
help him go out, if that's what he wanted."

"Uh-huh." Something even Iris and Redwood were afraid of.
That was a first.

"Can you blame them? It took you and me two weeks to get here."

"Yeah." A bruise at Cinnamon's temple throbbed. Sore ribs
ached. Ever since Star Deer had stopped substitute teaching, Cinnamon was punching someone out at school and getting smacked
herself. Aidan rubbed her locked-up shoulders. He murmured
Irish or Seminole. What was wrong with English? Tears Opal
would have hated rolled down her cheeks. Cinnamon scrubbed at
the stinging wetness with the heel of her hand. She was tired of
crying and so mad she wanted to scream. How much hope had
she wasted? The shrunken body in the bed was a thousand times
worse than the dead dust stand-in tucked in the casket for Sekou's
memorial service. Opal was right; Redwood, Iris, and Sekou too.
Visiting Daddy was the worst idea she'd ever had. Nothing to see
here better than a memory. She wanted to bolt.

Aidan sucked a breath and sang a few notes. "Is that the right
key?" he asked, as if she knew the damn song he wanted to sing.
"What you think?"

"How would I know?" she muttered, pissed at him for dragging her into a hellhole.

"Help me find the key, honeybunch."

Cinnamon shook her head.

"Selfish of me, not wanting to come alone." Aidan's fingertips grazed the bruise at her temple. He kept sucking deep breaths till his cheeks were rosy and hot, till his eyes glowed iridescent green, and then he was singing. Corny, hillbilly music wasn't on the same planet with the sounds he made. True, his mouth was full of banjo twang, and his chest had caught a rumbling washtub bass but . . . the physics of sound bested her. Muscles resisting comfort resonated sympathetically with arpeggios and pounding bass. Aidan's music was bone deep, *spirit sweet*. It wrung the anger right out of her. Daddy used to say, *Redwood and Wildfire can sing a moment from dark to light. They can sing you to heaven and back.* Daddy didn't exaggerate. As Aidan cruised the melody, lyrics materialized out of *heya bobs* and *na na nas*:

Not just what you thought,
But what you can't see
Not just my hand
Hold all of me
Not just what you need
What if I can't be?
Not just what you want
Hold all of me
Now or never, once and forever
Hold all of me
Not just what ain't right
Not just what look bright
But what you can't see
Not just 'cause you should
Not just what feel good
What if I can't be?
Hey baby, hey baby

Now or never, once and forever
Not just my hand
Hold all of me

Cinnamon sobbed and howled with Aidan. She never found the right key or a decent harmony. Reaching was good enough. Aidan slipped his arm through hers and slow-danced her right up to the bed. Blurry oscilloscopes kept a rhythmic vigil: heart rate, blood pressure, and an incomprehensible line or two.

Raven's left side was exposed, as if he'd shrugged off the psychedelic covers during a fitful sleep. He had thin, pale sticks for legs; swollen toes poked out of the swirly sheets, each nail like the blade of a shovel. Cinnamon brushed her fingers against his silky dreads. Well-groomed and thick, they were white at the scalp with salt-and-pepper tips: somebody was taking good care of his hair. Fat tendrils snaked across his shoulders to a chest that looked caved in compared to what Cinnamon remembered or compared to the photographs she'd been staring at since he got shot.

External memory hidden in the *OED*: Raven and Opal, sweaty and muscular, dancing under a desert moon; Cinnamon huddling next to Raven as he paints her scary dream; Raven and Sekou toting heavy tomes up the back stairs; Raven in a bright snowfield, throwing baby Cinnamon high in the air, the elders laughing in the background; Opal with her head in Raven's lap, smiling in her sleep; Raven painting the Eiffel Tower elevator and three tiny figures on the platform. Sporting Kente cloth and crowns of braids, the trio had to be Taiwo, Kehinde, and Somso brandishing jewel-handled knives.

A nagging oscilloscope bleeped louder than before. Cinnamon wanted to kill the awful person who snatched the life in those photos from her and Opal, stole it from Aidan, Redwood, and Iris too. The gunman had aimed at those two women, but shot her whole family—one suicide, one dead to the world, and the rest critically wounded.

Aidan hugged Cinnamon to his chest. She was a mountain of fury about to erupt, but Aidan held all of her.

Eleven (on a Scale of Three to Fourteen)

"Was that you singing?"

A chunky young man in blue scrubs stepped out of the bathroom, talking over the loud flushing noise. Aidan and Cinnamon jumped at the sound and sight of him. Cinnamon hid behind her grandfather, not ready for *public display*.

The attendant(?) scowled at them. "Who are you? Who let you in here?"

"Who are you?" Aidan's face was as wet and snotty as Cinnamon's. He dragged a sleeve over his cheeks and pulled his mane of white hair into a ponytail. "I reckon you got a civil tongue in that head, and I'd sure like to hear you use it." He sounded so hillbilly cracker. Why not do the Irish brogue thing or a Seminole lilt? Maybe not Seminole, his costume was too New Age Indian on a vision quest.

"I'm a volunteer." The young man gaped at Raven then Aidan, disbelieving a likeness that even a mean coma couldn't erase. "What're you two doing here?"

Aidan sputtered at the rude question.

Cinnamon gathered herself and stepped forward to speak. "We're—"

"Family." Panicked, the volunteer eyed her up and down.

"What you looking at? You know me?"

Blotchy hives broke out on his chubby cheeks and neck. "Oh, shit."

Aidan and Cinnamon spoke at once, saying *my son, my daddy* on top of each other.

"I see that." The volunteer looked like he needed to go back to the bathroom. Big brown eyes roamed around his head. He scratched tiny bumps popping up on his hand—probably not expecting Raven to have a white-cracker father and a black Glamazon daughter. "*She* didn't come again today, so I gave Mr. Cooper a shave. He doesn't have much of a beard. The nurses who turn him and stuff don't bother to shave him. *She* told me he liked a smooth chin." He shoved agitated hands under an oversized hospital shirt. "Thanks for singing. I play music for Mr. Cooper. Gets his eyes going, gets a few muscles to twitch, like he's dancing. But some A-hole jacked my car last weekend, got my equipment. I usually spin the old R&B."

"He'd like that," Aidan said.

"How do you know?" The volunteer's blotchy skin made Cinnamon scratch too.

"We're family," Aidan reminded him, calm as a brick. He should tell this fool to disappear and let the *family* have Daddy to themselves.

"Haven't seen you before, and I thought I knew everyone who comes."

"He gets a good bit of company?" Aidan asked.

"My man is real popular."

Aidan was thrilled, Cinnamon envious.

The volunteer waved at Cinnamon. "Come 'round here. On a good day, he moves his left hand a lot." He lifted Raven's wrist gently. "Today seems like a good day."

Butterflies, helicopters, and jets fluttered in Cinnamon's stomach. She wasn't sure about touching a half-dead hand.

"Go ahead," Aidan said. "That's his painting hand."

"Oh." That got her to the other side in a flash.

A female and a male Eshu crouched on the bedside table. Carved from dark wood and sporting knife-in-the-head crowns, they were from the same family as the pair Griot Joe gave Opal. Cinnamon whispered greetings to the master of the crossroads.

The volunteer startled. "Eshu, right." He pressed Cinnamon's palm against Raven's cool, smooth skin. Her fingers brushed bony knuckles. "Squeeze," he said. "Not too hard, just so he knows somebody is here."

Cinnamon squeezed. Raven's cracked lips trembled. Dull eyes roved under slack eyelids. Muscles twitched across his cheeks. Perhaps the sun coming from behind a cloud made him squint. A reflex? He gurgled bubbles of spit, choking, or was he saying something? She was on him now, looking for a sign.

"No ventilator. That's big." The volunteer smiled at the rise and fall of Raven's chest. "He's ten or eleven on the Glasgow Coma Scale. He does sounds, like just now, maybe words, and flexion or withdrawal to painful stimuli. He'll open his eyes and look right at you. Dr. Elliott says that's a long way from vegetable matter."

Cinnamon squeezed Raven's hand again. "Star Deer says, *Breath is a doorway between the conscious and the unconscious mind, a direct connection to all of our selves.*" She dabbed drool from Raven's lips with a towel tucked at his neck. "What's this scale?"

The volunteer scratched his bushy Afro.

Aidan strode next to Cinnamon. "Go on man, explain it."

The volunteer took a deep breath. "Three is dead."

Cinnamon flinched. Two was deader, one deadest? "Yeah."

"No eye movement, no verbal, motor response to sound or pain. Fourteen is totally awake, with it."

Cinnamon's heart raced. "Eleven is close to fourteen."

"Breathing on his own steam means the brain stem is looking good, and after four years." The volunteer was very proud of this achievement. "His eyes track movement, and that hand, sometimes I swear that hand is talking to me." He cleared his throat and glanced at Aidan. "Black male, gunshot victim, they don't always get a high level of care. Why waste resources on a gangsta, you know?"

Aidan grunted at this injustice. He should tell this fool he was Seminole and Irish.

The volunteer grunted too. "*She* is on the case and gets him mucho stimulation, quality physical therapy. And Star Deer never misses a day."

Opal couldn't afford that. Star must be working for free.

"Dancing your muscles builds the brain," Cinnamon said.

"Nobody expected eleven though. *She* always believed Mr. Cooper could do it."

"*She* who?" Aidan was suddenly impatient.

The volunteer shrugged and scratched.

"You were all over us," Cinnamon said. "And you don't know—"

"Well, see, *she, she*—" The volunteer pawed his mouth, mortified.

"Spit it out!" Aidan shouted. He rarely lost his cool like this.

"Uhm . . ."

Raven's ring finger tapped Cinnamon's palm. "Whoa." She resisted screaming, jumping, or doing anything to overwhelm him. Her heart thudded against the *mojo* bag. Aidan, calm again, studied her with a question in his eyes. Blood pounded in her ears and banged at her bruised temple. She held her breath and waited for another hand sign, for any kind of move. A full minute of beeps and Aidan and the volunteer wheezing, but from Raven—still hand, still eyes. No muscle twitch. Nothing. Even the gurgling had stopped. One tap had been exciting, yet she needed more. Several taps would be communication, a *code*, not a random nerve firing or wishful thinking. "Daddy," she said. "Was that you or me?"

"Talking's good," the volunteer said. "You know what he wants to hear."

Aidan nodded. "Go on, sugar. You're a world champion talker."

Cinnamon's mouth tasted terrible. She had no spit to clear it out. "Hey, Daddy, it's me, your spice child. I'm uhm. We're, Granddaddy Aidan and I, Mom is, is, she's smoking too much, see and, and, you know about Sekou, right?" The volunteer flinched. Cinnamon ignored him. "Maybe Mom didn't tell you. Sekou's spirit now, talking to me from the beyond." Her tongue was leather. No story storm in sight, only bad news. She looked to Aidan. "What should I say?"

"Tell him the good things, your new friends."

Nothing "good" was coming to her. She had a mouth full of nasty.

"Doesn't matter what you say." Aidan leaned close, vital and strong, looking so like his son before the bullet, Cinnamon gasped. "Trust your good spirit, honeybunch."

She was no bundle of sweetness, but acid Snow White in a ghetto fury tale. "Hey Daddy, we miss you. Every day. Mom's sucking down ashes and running for a bridge to nowhere. Sekou's riding the ghost train. And I'm, I'm, I wish, I do wish . . ." She turned to the volunteer. "Eleven, huh?"

"Out of fourteen. That's high. Eleven's hope."

She stared at Aidan. "Say what*ever* comes?"

Aidan's green eyes clouded over a second then blazed bright. A flash of his pain struck her. She needed to hold all of Daddy for him too. Daddy had a spark of life. Who was she to give up on him? Who was she to snuff him out?

"You felt him move?" Aidan said.

Cinnamon nodded.

"Say whatever you got."

Cinnamon spoke softly in Raven's ear, to elude Aidan's ancient ones. "I'm sorry, Daddy. This is what I got—'cause we really love you and miss you, so I wish that gunman never took a shot, never even took a breath. I wish you hadn't jumped in front of his gun and saved the day. Those two women were your friends, sure, but we're your *family*. That bullet hit us too. How could you throw your life away? Weren't you thinking about us? Sekou's haunting me, and Opal's in the hospital sick to her heart and breathing blood, from a bullet in your head. I wish you'd been a split second too late and the bullet flew by. Those two ladies are probably off some-where loving each other, living a happy life. The gunman wanted to shoot down their love, not you, not us. It's mean, but I wish any-body else was laying up in this bed, some stranger. Let him and his family be all torn up. What would I care? If the bullet really had to get somebody, I wish one of those ladies had ended in a coma or died instead of you."

Death was the meanest wish Cinnamon ever had, but it was too late to take it back. Taking it back would've been a lie anyhow. No way to unthink evil thoughts. Raven didn't respond. What use was

evil talk to him? That's what she had. Cinnamon laid his hand on
the psychedelic sheet and backed up toward the bathroom. From the
gentle expression on Aidan's face, her nasty rant went undetected.
Eshu was on her side.

The volunteer looked dismayed. Nothing wrong with his hearing, he probably caught every word. Served him right, standing
around eavesdropping on private business. He glared at Cinnamon,
trying to make her ashamed of death-wish thoughts. Who was he?
Cinnamon glared back until the bruise at her temple throbbed. Nobody ever won a stare-down with her. Today at school she'd tangled
with kids hopped up on raging hormones or drugs. Suckers hurled
faggot/dyke jokes, curses, and death threats. She never broke a
blink. The trash-talker that smacked her upside the head got an
elbow in his mouth and one less hour of consciousness.

The volunteer shuddered and looked away. Lumpy hives raised
skin up his arms. Cinnamon refused to hunt down generous feelings. *Nice* was a target painted on your heart. *Nice* landed you in
the hospital, in a coma, or dead. Cinnamon didn't want to be *nice*
ever again. She just wanted this clown to leave them alone with
Daddy.

"So, you be coming here regular, looking out for Raven?" Aidan
sounded so warm and loving. "What you say your name was, Son?"

Relieved, the volunteer turned to him. "Well, sir—" It was sir,
now was it? "Maybe your granddaughter doesn't remember me.
I've put on some weight."

Cinnamon never remembered important people, why would she
remember him?

"I'm planning on medical school when I graduate Pitt."

"Seeing a bright tomorrow." Aidan smiled.

"I'm acing my classes."

"Good for you." Aidan had the nerve to chitchat about the idiot's future.

"Don't you have other patients to visit?" Cinnamon said.

Aidan snapped his head at her. A strand of white hair whipped
across her cheek. The volunteer looked down at the floor. His feet

were small for such a big frame. He had a neck full of ingrown hairs and more hives he'd scratched raw. He mumbled.

"I'm not deaf, Son." Aidan eyed Cinnamon. "But nobody's ears are good enough to make out what you be saying there."

"Since you're family, I wonder if you might know about *her*. What's happened?"

"What's her name?" Aidan's tone was sharp. He cleared his throat and the next words were gentle. "You ain't ever asked her name?"

"No, sir, I, I . . ."

"He didn't ask our names either," Cinnamon interjected.

"She comes by all the time. At first I didn't want to ask who she was. I didn't want to scare her away, and she was so fierce. Then we got used to each other. Why upset that? I haven't seen her for weeks. She always tells me if she has to miss. I hope nothing bad has happened. We're stretched thin as it is."

"Why would we know who comes by?" Cinnamon snarled.

Aidan scolded her in Irish, Seminole, or maybe it was Georgia mule talk.

The volunteer sputtered. "You're family. She used to come every day, hold his hand, fuss over his hair. She'd tell raunchy jokes. *A brassy redhead with a great dye job gets naked and her man complains, the rug ought to match the drapes . . .*" He trailed off. "Sorry. You haven't ever seen her?"

"I'm from up Massachusetts way," Aidan drawled. "Don't get here as much as I want to. How she look, young, old?"

"She could be thirty-five or forty-five. Black lady, well, she looks black." He paused. "She's good for him, that's how she looks."

"How do you know she's good for him?" Cinnamon asked.

"A feeling I get." He crossed his arms, fists under his biceps, a familiar tough-guy stance. Who used to do that? "Look, I gotta bounce. A report due for class. If you see her, tell her Mr. Cooper misses her. Everybody misses her. She's good people."

"I'll tell her," Aidan said. "Nice of you to volunteer here. Thank you."

The volunteer gulped. "Least I can do." Rushing out, he hopped over a furry orange squiggle crawling across the floor. Caterpillar? Millipede?

"Mom never comes," Cinnamon said. "She can't bear to be here."

"You ain't the only storyteller in the family." Aidan picked up Raven's left hand, his painting hand. "It's me, Son." He curled Raven's fingers around the sculpture he'd finished on the bus. "That's a windy ole storm—Miz Redwood's idea." His voice cracked. "She sent a hurricane to keep you company. It come right out the wood at me. You always talkin' 'bout me carving the wind." He choked up. "The funnel touches ground, pulls pain out the Earth, and whirls it up into the sky."

Cornball. Aidan got away with country hoodoo crap constantly. Cinnamon rolled her eyes. The mirror in the bathroom blasted an ugly reflection at her. She jerked away from the expression—so Snow White, or so like—

"Opal ain't told nobody, not even Becca, how she be coming here," Aidan said.

"You don't know it's her."

"Yes I do, sugar. Her love is still in the room with us."

They walked to the bus stop in a funk. Maybe Aidan had heard the nasty Cinnamon had spewed or felt the evil still fresh in her heart. Every time she looked up, he was boring a hole in her. She lost these staring battles, no contest. On the bus Cinnamon opened *The Chronicles*. Nothing new had appeared in weeks. Griot Joe was key to the mission, and he'd gone silent. Was everything impossible, hopeless? As the bus pulled out, blurry fluorescence turned into crisp paragraphs. Demon words were coming to the rescue.

Chronicles 20: Father
of Mysteries

"The wind is free."

Luigi chanted this to the rhythm of *La Vérité*'s heaving pistons. Lazy machines devoured a coal mountain, roared, and spit fire, yet provided little steam. The captain and Somso strolled through fog lapping the deck, as a violet sea swallowed an orange behemoth. In the wind shadow of a smokestack, Melinga and I watched the Earth rotate. She giggled. I felt desolate. Bob sat hunched against a broken lifeboat. Liam was passed out beside him. They smelled of rum and blood from a fight.

"My profits burn to ash," Luigi grumbled.

"Your profits?" Somso laughed. "We earned this money."

The closer *La Vérité* steamed to America, the more we twisted our stories. In the tall-tale versions, Luigi never planned to abandon me. A bolt to the head had addled my brain. Bob erased Spotted Man memories with rum and fisticuffs. Liam denied hopeless love for Bob and Kehinde. How could love be hopeless? Somso grumbled about Melinga spending too much time with rogues, heathens, and an *ajo mmuo*—evil spirit. Still, she dumped her daughter on us at every opportunity. Bob even carried Melinga on his night watch. Kehinde pretended Raymond's war stories hadn't poisoned our faith in America; we would be free, like the wind.

"Stuff it," Luigi yelled at homesick, seasick animals rattling their cages.

"You waste energy on anger." Somso spoke crisp English learned from her Jesus cult. "The wind is bound by the land, water, and mountains too. Nothing is free."

"I never know what you'll say," Luigi said.

"Why should he be able to divine Somso's speech?" Kehinde materialized out of the dark, speaking Yoruba.

Luigi circled Somso. "I'll make a spectacle of you from coast to coast."

"Men have talked nonsense to me since my twelfth year," Somso said. "You remind me of my first husband, Yao, a very rich man with many wives." No mention that Yao was a scoundrel and assassin, a dead-end man who had no sons or even daughters.

"I'll take that as a compliment." Luigi bowed. Kehinde curled her lip.

"You don't trust him," I whispered.

"Or Somso," Kehinde replied.

"What's Somso got in her trick bag?" Bob said.

The ship rocked over choppy water, and Somso stumbled. Luigi offered his arm.

Kehinde pointed toward land I could not yet see. "The New World."

Bob whacked Liam, and he woke with a growl.

"America," Bob said.

I held Melinga up. "Here is where we shall bury your umbilical cord and find out who we are called to be."

Somso halted with Luigi in front of us. "Wanderer, you have taken Taiwo's place. You should have this." She displayed the *ide Ifa,* a beaded bracelet worn by a *Babalawo,* sign of a father of mystery. "My second husband always wore it, except for his last day. I never understood why he left it on our bed." She stroked opal beads that anchored strands of green and yellow. "You share his name, his destiny. Go on, take it."

"I'm not wise enough." I glanced at Kehinde. Her face was a cool warrior mask.

"Nothing precious, cheap glass beads," Luigi said. "Right?"

"Exactly. What are pagan trinkets to me? I'm a good Christian, and Melinga will also love Jesus." Somso dangled the *ide Ifa* over the rail. It reflected the last rays of the home star into my eyes. "Do you want me to throw it away?"

Melinga reached for the dangling treasure and protested when I pulled her to my heart. "Why discard what doesn't matter to you?" A flick of flame escaped my nostrils. "Lady Atlantic holds the truth of all her children. Her many beads of wisdom color the rippling waves that are her garments. We can make a better offering."

"Such poetry." Somso retracted her arm. Blood flooded her lips and cheeks; electricity buzzed around her head, as if she'd been caught hiding stones in a packet of bullets for sale.

"I will keep the *ide Ifa* safe," I said, "if you like."

"One day, you will be wise enough to wear it." Somso dropped the bracelet into my hand and hurried on with Luigi. Melinga squealed and mouthed her father's beads.

"Somso probes for weakness," Bob said. "She plays a long game."

"In Somso's story, her husband's blood stains us," Kehinde said. "We are her enemies. Abla would slit Somso's throat and claim Melinga." Another flick of flame flared from my nostrils. "No fear, Wanderer, I'm not Abla."

"The *aje* doesn't possess your restraint," I said.

"We have our own story," Bob said.

Kehinde nodded and stroked Melinga's thick hair. "To live is to hope."

Liam curled into a knot on the deck. "Life could just be a bad habit."

"You don't *believe* that." I slipped the *ide Ifa* into the folds of my robe.

I hope Ariel has it still.

Who Do You Mean to Be?

The bus driver careened around a corner, almost smashed a cab, parked and minding its own business, and then scraped the finish off of three cars. Nobody called the driver out. Opal would have lost her job behind that kind of stunt.

Cinnamon slammed *The Chronicles* shut. More chapters appeared, but she had zero patience for aliens, Amazons, and clueless sailors in 1890-something. She was here and now, not then and there. Who gave a holler if Somso was a royal bitch planning to trick Kehinde and Taiwo? Melinga would be the one to suffer, growing up in the disaster adults made. Then Melinga would make a disaster too. Hadn't it been going down like that for eternity, or for two hundred thousand years of *Homo sapiens sapiens* history?

"Don't feel like reading on?" Aidan nudged her.

"No." Cinnamon usually read until the words ran out. Blank or blurry *Chronicles* pages were a cruel disappointment. Everything was a cruel disappointment. No one told kids that growing up. Who'd bother with a second decade?

Actually, Opal put out warnings. Cinnamon never listened.

"Eleven." Aidan repeated this like a country fool. He was ready to tell random folks standing in the aisles. "Ain't that the best news?" Passengers cut their eyes at him. He was oblivious. "What you got to say to eleven?"

"It's cool," Cinnamon replied.

Aidan frowned. "It's a damn sight more than cool. What's wrong with you, gal?" He wanted the stupid optimist act.

When Cinnamon had been little, she'd felt invincible, immortal, and almighty. A true believer just this morning: if she put her mind to it, she could learn or be anything; if she worked hard enough, she could do anything; and she had all the time in the world. Opal was always tired and depressed, but not Cinnamon. Bring on the danger, fiends, and zombies. She was Cinnamon the Great—upbeat and indefatigable. But she'd left Cinnamon the Great on the scuffed nursing home floor. Who was she now?

Hillbilly Aidan would have zip to say about that, so she kept her mouth shut.

The ride home took forever. Actually, despite a spring snow squall, an accident, and two roads under construction, it only took forty-five minutes. When they got off the bus, Patty Banks and Cherrie Carswell were hanging on the corner. They gaped at Aidan's beads and flashy walking stick, then smirked.

"Ain't you goin' introduce me to your friends?" he said.

"They hate me." Cinnamon touched the bruise at her temple.

"How do?" Aidan could smile at anybody.

"Hey." Patty and Cherrie snorted. Big lies would sweep school tomorrow.

Climbing the hill to her street, Cinnamon walked behind Aidan, slower than old man slow. Maybe she'd lost her mind at the nursing home. The next-door Doberman yammered at her for dragging by without a scratch, tummy tickle, or treat to supplement the starvation diet that supposedly kept her lean and mean.

Cinnamon growled, "No, Rain. Go sit."

The dog dropped onto her haunches. Aidan glanced up to Opal's porch. The twenty-three steps could have been Mt. Everest. He leaned into the climb. Cinnamon sat down halfway from the top. Rain barked.

"You can get up. I'm too tired."

Rain trotted to the fence eyeing Cinnamon with doggy concern.

"Who is that cracker they got up in the house while Opal's at the hospital?"

Cinnamon snapped around to face neighbors talking shit. Aidan kept trudging up the steps. No one in sight to fight with— was she hearing things? On the porch, Redwood and Iris hugged Aidan as if they hadn't seen him since forever and a day.

"How do he look?" Redwood asked.

A skeletal Raven Cooper squatted in psychedelic sheets and mouthed words, scolding Cinnamon silently. She read his lips. Folks wishing death on strangers was how he landed in that stupid coma.

"Eleven on a scale of three to fourteen," Aidan said. "What you ornery women got to say to that?"

"Hope hurts sometimes." Iris sighed. "You pick your days for hope."

Redwood squeezed his shoulders. "Did I fight you on this?"

"Will you go see him?" Aidan replied.

"Everybody can't worship at the same altar." Redwood looked stricken.

"He's our son, not a monster."

"Was our son."

"Wait till he's dead to bury him," Aidan shouted. Redwood waved her storm hand. Aidan turned to Iris. "Eleven is a prime number, right?"

"It is indeed." Prime numbers were Iris's favorites.

Redwood yelled at Cinnamon. "Did those few steps wear you out, young as you are?"

Aidan bent close to Redwood and Iris, muttering and pointing at Cinnamon. She ran the last eleven steps. By the porch her shields were tissue paper and eggshells.

"What's wrong with you, child?" Iris read the death wish in her heart.

"I gotta lie down." Cinnamon squeezed past the elders and dashed up to her room.

More Good News

Cinnamon almost got her door shut, but Redwood held it open with her storm hand. She walked in without an invitation. Cinnamon dropped *The Chronicles* on the *Oxford English Dictionary* and pouted.

"Marie called over to the hospital for you." Redwood had her hands on her hips. "Klaus too. I think that German boy's sweet on you."

"You don't know the half of it."

Klaus wore his heart on his sleeve. Marie kept hers under heavy guard.

"So tell me."

"Romance instead of nursing home disaster?"

"Why not? You can tell me anything."

"You a nosy old sinner like Granddaddy, poking and prying and hot diggity dogging?" That came out too bitchy even for Cinnamon's foul mood. "Sorry."

Redwood flashed a shameless hussy grin. "Aidan's Aunt Caitlin tried to make him a good Catholic. She failed. Baptist and holy rollers never snagged me either. Aidan and I run off together into the Okefenokee Swamp. Church couldn't hold our spirits."

"Oh." More *important shit* she needed to know.

"It's all in the book we're doing for your birthday."

"That's not till August!"

Redwood reached through the foul mood and pulled Cinnamon to her heart. "So, Miz Woman, what you know good?"

Cinnamon should have told Daddy about her secret romance. He'd have understood the trio thing. The elders raised him to be wild. "I don't know how to begin."

They were all sweet on each other. Cinnamon never understood the big fuss about kissing until Marie. Girlfriend did this tasty, flirty dance with her tongue that made Cinnamon weak in the knees. Klaus had magic hands, on her neck, by her ear, strolling down her arm. She was twisting and tingling, and they hadn't gotten down to anything.nasty. Fine as they were, what were Marie and Klaus doing with Cinnamon?

Redwood held her at arm's length. "What are these faces you're making?"

Klaus and Marie might be doing a con, some twisted scam. Cinnamon didn't go out hunting pale blond hunks or five-foot Glamazons who could sit on their hair. They'd come after her. She was hanging by herself after the audition, not thinking she wanted anybody like that. Marie was fifteen, Klaus almost sixteen. They had the jump on her in the romance department. Every day was torture, waiting for her best friends (only friends?) to cut her loose and do each other. She even considered cutting them loose first. Romance was overrated. With Opal wheezing her lungs away and Raven shriveling up, wasting away, why was Cinnamon doing a trio weird thing?

"It can't be that bad," Redwood said.

"Unless I'm suffering acute wishful thinking, we're all sweet on each other."

Redwood poked her and winked. "That's more good news, right?"

"No." Cinnamon dropped down on Sekou's bed.

"They're on their way here."

"I don't want to see anybody."

"Iris never goes back on a dinner invite."

"I feel like roadkill."

"They rustled up tickets for *The Tempest*. Tonight is that special preview."

"*Mist!* We planned to test if Ariel was from another dimension, then get her—it?—to unscatter with Griot Joe, and *voilà!* The Wanderer would be whole, with a full mind and, and . . ." Every night before falling asleep, Cinnamon imagined unleashing the whole Wanderer on Daddy's coma. Weird science had to be way ahead of human medicine. She was hardly conscious of this new wake-up Daddy fantasy. Telling Redwood would be admitting it to herself. "Fairy tale, comic book, kiddie crap."

"Tonight's an early show," Redwood said. "You gotta be fit for human consumption in an hour."

"Everything's too hard. Impossible."

"You climbing *Sorrow Mountain*?"

"Granddaddy's song? Ha. I'm doing Fury Mountain."

"Your muscles are cramping and burning up."

They were.

"Your heart's pounding a ghost back beat. Talk to me."

"Granddaddy was so sad this morning, and now he's fine. I can't do that."

"Who says you have to?"

"Daddy drooled in that stank room, didn't even look like himself. Eyes were rolling around in hollow sockets. Dead eyes."

Redwood looked stricken again, like on the porch.

"OK, sorry, not dead, but unfocused."

"Aidan don't want to let Raven go." Redwood stumbled over nothing. Cinnamon broke her fall. Redwood's heart was doing the ghost back beat too—dead and not dead, her only son.

"Wait, people crowd in to see Daddy regularly. They're not giving up. They do live music jams on drums and saxophones. DJs spin R&B and world music sets. They dance Daddy's muscle mind. Moving to a groove is the best physical therapy. And Daddy has a stack of wild art PJs and stimulating sheets. It's a, a changing art exhibition. Forget hospital-bleach white. People sneak in puppies and kittens to lick and purr on him. They bring flowers and smelly things—so much memory in your nose. Fresh-cut wood, green tea, orange peels, candy bar wrappers, cigar stubs. Smells call up a whole world, even with a bullet scrambling your brain.

"Griot Joe smuggles in his crow to sing jazz riffs with the poets dropping verses. Poem for cement block blahs, poem for the sweet smell of germs dying on an alcohol high, poem for salt-and-pepper dreads, and poem for taking your own sweet breath, no ventilator. A parade of rapper nerds in there every week, freestyling about what's wrong with the world and how they're fixing it and what's right with the world and how they're relishing every tingle and taste. You know Daddy loves a good rant, a good ode to joy. Folks bring him gossip, news, bad jokes, and urban legends. He has visitors and volunteers doing his hair, trimming his nails, and acting like the family should recognize their chunky behinds."

Redwood smiled at the word deluge. "Aidan didn't mention any of that."

"The story's in the room. It storms into my mouth. I talk it out."

"Who you telling?"

More images tingled on Cinnamon's lips. She gulped them back.

"Don't swallow that. Spit it out."

"The flabby attendant had to be Dr. Bug-Man Lexy. He jumped over a millipede instead of stomping it."

Redwood shook her head. "Doctor who?"

"Sekou's Lexy, rapper nerd DJ, medicine man on the case." Cinnamon banged her head against the wall. "I never remember people. Lexy blew up seventy-five pounds since Sekou's funeral. I was too busy being evil to recognize this chubby cheek version. Lexy's part of the mission. *Mist!* He probably thought I recognized him and hated him still." She banged her head again. "I never hated him. It's pointless anyhow. None of our comic book tactics will help Daddy."

"I don't know about that." The river scarf at Redwood's waist was a torrent pounding the floor. A wind from nowhere rattled the windows. Mist, the foggy English kind, crept under the doorsill. Cinnamon closed her eyes on hoodoo flourishes.

"You're not sulking in your room tonight," Redwood said.

"Why not?" Tears snuck out of Cinnamon's eyes. "You never even go see him."

"No. I don't."

Cinnamon buried herself in Sekou's galaxy pillow. "Quick death is better."

"For who?" Redwood pulled the pillow away.

Cinnamon quoted Kehinde. *Who wants to linger in pain and humiliation?*"

"Everybody's dying, honey, but I'm taking my time."

"I'm tired of sitting up in stank hospital rooms, waiting on nothing."

"You've been dealt a difficult hand."

"I haven't faced lynching, I know."

"Raven's still with us, and Opal's alive and kicking."

"What's Mom got to say to me but 'yippee, you're getting skinny' and 'don't let the elders snooker you into more hoodoo mess.'"

"See? Opal's spirit is fine. Still herself."

"When do I get to be me?" Cinnamon was hollering.

"What you doing right now?"

"Mom hates who I am." Her throat hurt. "She wishes I OD'ed instead of Sekou."

"No. Opal wish Sekou was still with us, and wish Raven was all the way here too."

"Mom hit that nursing home, visiting Daddy every day, and lied about it."

"So I hear tell." Redwood sat down next to Cinnamon.

"Why does Mom have to lie?"

"Opal want to shield you from pain."

"She treats me like a dumb little kid. I've been old since Daddy got shot."

Redwood slipped her storm hand between Cinnamon's head and the wall. "I'll go see Opal with you, get this straightened out."

"No more hospitals. No more funerals either. People are dying like they ain't got nothing else to do."

"Quoting Opal? She ain't goin' be in that hospital much longer."

"Doctors have been saying that forever."

"Checking out tomorrow. Still need watching, so she's going to stay with Becca."

Cinnamon gasped. "Wow."

"Opal be steering clear of us ole country fools trying to run her life."

"No, it's me." Cinnamon's head throbbed, bruise up front, bump on the back. "Can you hoodoo me into acting right?"

Redwood drew pain to her fingertips. "You got that kind of power, not me."

"I used to think you all could do anything." Cinnamon curled into her. "I wanted to grow up to be you."

"A singing, dancing hoodoo wonder." Redwood hummed a melody Aidan had found during a sleepless night. When Cinnamon hit a sweet harmony, Redwood stood up. Heading for the door, she was sooty winds and black clouds, a whirlwind. Around her, red, blue, and silver sparks burst from the spaces between things. What good were carnival tricks if Redwood couldn't call Daddy back from a coma?

Cinnamon sputtered. "Wait."

Redwood turned and held out her storm hand. Sparks gathered over her palm and morphed into a bright white spiral. "I'm listening."

"Today I was up in that stank nursing home wishing people dead and meaning it. In the mirror I looked evil, not like me."

"I seen that look out on the porch."

"If I could find Daddy's paintings, if I could uncover the *important shit* Mom's trying to keep from me, what you wild elders did and what happened when Daddy got shot . . . that'd be a spell to make me and everybody better. Maybe I could help Mom too, and she'd want to come home instead of running away."

Redwood closed her hand around the spiral of sparks and clutched it to her heart. "You lose something, Iris be the one to help you find it." She headed downstairs. "Get ready. Klaus and Marie arrive in fifty minutes. They're both sweet on you too. Any fool can see that a mile away."

"Really?"

I called it. Sekou whispered after two weeks of silence. *Didn't I? Everybody's queer.*

"You were always exaggerating. How could I believe you?" Cinnamon replied.

You were always snooping on me and Lexy, hearing what you shouldn't.

"You're snooping now."

What else I got to do? He was gone as quick as he came.

"How about rest in peace?"

Changing into the jeans Iris had bought for her bold, womanly figure, Cinnamon felt ugly. Pulling her braids into the side waterfall looked silly. Forget smearing on makeup. That was Iris's money wasted. Maybe Marie could use the expensive goop. Aidan's knotted silver buckle was a bit of Celtic flash, but trying to look cute was pointless. Cinnamon threw up her hands and knocked *The Chronicles* off the *OED*. She caught the heavy tome before it hit the ground. Light pulsed from the spine. Pages fluttered to a video-drawing of Redwood and Aidan wandering through a fantastic city. They gaped at giant balloons, moving walkways, and a crystal palace of electric lights.

"No way." Cinnamon whistled.

Her grandparents were young and movie-star beautiful. Why hadn't Cinnamon inherited their good looks? The Wanderer must have met them when they time-tripped off to the Chicago Fair. Two chapters came before this moving-picture drawing. Cinnamon was behind! With forty-five minutes until Marie and Klaus arrived, she sank down, lost in the words before her butt touched the floor.

Chronicles 21:
American Dreams

When *La Vérité* docked in New York, I fluctuated from man to woman to *aje*. France had made me leery of the unknown. Entering a land where ancestors dissolved in fog and the future was unmoored frightened me. What was this rush of atoms and light without history? A robust woman on a two-wheeler waved at ships on the waterfront. Her magnetic signature seemed familiar. A wound on her head had recently healed—brave Océane? Or had Abla stolen Océane's face?

I turned to Lady Liberty, grand orisha guarding dark waters. She held a book of laws and a torch of wisdom. A broken chain circled her feet.

"*Iwori Meji*," Kehinde said. "Sacrifice and journey, who argues with a cure?"

"The patient who suffers and dies." Bob embraced his foul mood.

Liam suggested a tour of the New World capital. "Tomorrow we ride the rail to Chicago. Let's make the most of this evening. Bobbie knows the best New York sights."

Waiting for a telegram from Chicago, Luigi let us go without protest. America had river pirates cleverer than he, eager to cheat him. Ghost Dog said as much and joined our excursion.

The air in New York was lifeless, the ground unyielding. The streets were clotted with buildings, and people were thick as flies on a corpse. I raised warrior shields and tried not to feel. Few Americans frowned at Yoruba and Igbo words or stumbled over exotic flesh. Even so, the *aje* was ready to spit fire at three gawking youths.

Ghost Dog distracted me. "We're a traveling spectacle." He had played Wild West Shows across America. "You will get used to this."

"Transforming alien ground into home soil requires much sacrifice," Kehinde said.

"I'm Oglala Lakota." Ghost Dog kicked the dust. "This land is my home soil."

"You're from the Wild Wild West." Somso pointed. "We shall bury Melinga's cord in your country, and she will be home."

"Ha!" Bob led us down an alley to a river. "You're foolish and a bad Christian if you believe sticking rotten afterbirth in the dirt will make America home for your daughter."

"What you fretting over, Bobbie boy?" Liam threw an arm around his shoulder.

Bob shook him off. "The animals sense danger, even if you good folks won't."

Somso flicked her fingers, smiled at Ghost Dog, and spoke Fon. "This white man is handsome and doesn't smell. His robes are beautiful. Is he rich, with many wives?"

"Ask him yourself if you're in such a hurry for a husband." Kehinde also spoke Fon. "Luigi has rebuffed you?"

"Don't scold me," Somso said. "Is no man worthy of you, only demons?"

"They're talking about us," Liam said.

"Not you, Irishman." Kehinde spoke English. "The Wild West man."

"Ghost Dog keeps the story of his country secret." Somso spoke English to flirt.

"What would you like to know?" Ghost Dog said.

"You're an old friend of Bob's from Chicago," I said. "Tell us what he fears."

Bob stepped breath-close to me. "I'm about to sell my friends to misery and pain."

"Your caged beasts? Your *femmes sauvages*?" I stepped back as Bob sputtered.

Somso sashayed up to Ghost Dog. "Tell us how you came to Paris."

Ghost Dog drank her smile. "It's a short tale. I was performing battles from the Great Plains when my horse fell and broke both our legs. Wild Jack and Lonesome John shot the horse, a swift death for happy spectators. French doctors put my leg back together, but too slowly. Wild Jack shipped his show home without me."

"Why do you do vile masquerades?" I sneered. "Look how they abandon you."

Ghost Dog held up a pouch. "I send the money Wild Jack pays to my family. Digging in dirt is another man's path. Telling the story of brave warriors, of successful raids and days of glory, I can do this. And I have seen much of the world."

"Yes." Kehinde looked at me. "We can do this."

"I hope to find a path to tomorrow," Ghost Dog said, pleasing Kehinde even more.

"They've shut the way to tomorrow for the likes of us." Bob scowled at a construction site blocking our way. We halted at a fence.

"We still got a toe in the door." Liam poked Bob.

Bob poked back. "Maybe you do."

"Men who only mourn their losses shut themselves off from tomorrow," Ghost Dog said.

"If a door is slammed shut, slide under the sill." Kehinde rolled under the fence.

"If the road ends, fly." I jumped it.

Ghost Dog lifted Somso over as if she weighed nothing.

"I've no wings." Bob walked around. "Don't lecture me with noble savage wisdom."

"I refuse eight hundred miles of foul temper." Liam followed him.

A man lighting gas lamps gaped at us and fell from his eight-foot-high two-wheeler. Bones shattered on impact, and he howled. I made no move to aid him or a companion he knocked senseless. The *aje* was wary of aiding strangers after France. Ghost Dog joined the crowd gawking at the broken men close up. We left him and hurried to the Brooklyn/New York Bridge. Hanging from graceful curved cables and grounded in solid bedrock, it was the longest suspension bridge in the world, a sight as impressive as Lady Liberty or the *Tour Eiffel électrique*. I gave a squealing Melinga to Kehinde and ran out on the walkway into a forest of steel. Bob chased at my heels. We halted at the second set of towers. The East River gurgled a hundred thirty-five feet below us. I put my ear to a cold cable to hear its song.

"The bridge sways," I said. "Do you feel it?"

"No." Liam huffed to a halt behind us. "Wouldn't that be dangerous?"

Kehinde tapped Liam's chest. "A swaying bridge survives the storm that snaps a rigid one." He gripped her fingers. She allowed this intimacy. Melinga clapped for their good spirits. The wind sprayed moisture in our faces. Maroon clouds floated overhead, and below us, island cities were patchwork cloths thrown at the sea.

"Thank you for this view." I kissed Bob's mouth before he could jerk away.

"People were afraid to walk out here at first." He pulled me from the railing.

"Afraid I might jump?" I teased him.

"Jumbo led a parade of fellow elephants across the span to show how sturdy it was. Imagine twenty beasts marching along, Jumbo trumpeting *glory be*."

"Elephants?" Liam chortled. "Of course, you'd be telling that."

"A year later," Bob said, "a train rammed that bighearted elephant into the next world. P. T. Barnum scattered Jumbo all over. His heart went to Cornell University; his bones sit in a New York City museum. Barnum stuffed the hide for show then donated it to Tufts." Bob displayed a blue *mojo* bag. "A fellow from Barnum's circus sold wiry elephant hairs supposedly plucked from dead Jumbo's head. How could I resist? A bag of tall tales and misfortune soaked in rum . . ."

"That's not the story of the bridge." Liam ambled ahead to Kehinde and Somso to watch sailboats glide downriver.

Bob put away his *mojo*. I leaned back into his chest, pressed dew-damp braids against his cheeks, and pulled his hands around my belly.

"Taiwo," his voice was rough, "you're a torture and a joy."

"That is life on Earth." We leaned against the stone tower. "Tell another bridge story. Not a scattering."

"Washington Roebling had just begun building his father's design when caisson disease left him paralyzed, deaf, and mute. Emily Roebling stepped in as chief engineer to finish the bridge. She shared her husband's passion for building impossible things. Many doubted her womanly mind and clamored for a man. Mrs. Roebling worked twelve years till she could tramp from one shore to the next. Some say she channeled her husband's genius. Others say she was the great mind behind the great work."

"Women plant and build and go to war. Men pretend they have never seen this," Somso said. She waved at Ghost Dog striding in our direction and ran to him.

"Come on, you two, the sun is low." Liam turned around. "Damnation!"

One moment Bob and I touched our cheeks to warm stones, the next we climbed up the tower and balanced on a fat cable bundle. The wind whistled, ready to blow us away. I gripped Bob's waist. He was feverish hot. The curved moon spot on his forearm was bloodred. The crowd below us shouted many languages.

"Come away with me." Bob's breath tickled my ear.

"It's so romantic," a stranger yelled.

"Naw," another shouted. "They're jumpers."

"What reckless demon rides you two?" Kehinde spoke under the babble.

Liam gripped her and Melinga.

"We're a spectacle," I said. "Luigi would collect coins."

"The Chicago Fair is a circus museum." Bob laid his cheek against mine. "Rotten tomatoes in your face, like Raymond. Let's escape before they run us down and stuff our hides. That's how the carnival masquerade always ends, I know."

"Since Paris, you've barely talked to me, touched me. What am I to you?"

His calloused fingers traced my collarbone, lingering in the cleft at my throat. "I'd be scared of that question on the open sea with stars shooting overhead and whales singing ocean hymns. So for damn sure, I won't find out in Chicago."

"But you see, I ran through an armored bush. I swore an oath."

"To play their savage?"

"For Kehinde. For love."

"You love me too. We'll disappear in New York and find another ship."

"Luigi expects to make his money back—"

"He won't find us. We owe him nothing. In the wind and water, we'd be free."

"You sound like him, romancing Somso with tall tales."

"Chicago isn't what you dream. It's no better than France or here or anywhere. We can swear oaths if you like." Bob kissed me. My nerves spiked. "I can't leave Kehinde, even for love of you. I won't." I glanced down. Kehinde's face was a warrior mask.

"She'd follow you," Bob pleaded. "Liam throws his spear with us."

"I refuse to abandon Melinga to Somso," I declared. "Kehinde won't steal her."

Bob was desperate. "Somso might give Melinga to you."

"Never," I realized. "She'd give her to you, perhaps." I touched his belly. "Chicago is where your umbilical cord is buried. Why not find tomorrow there?"

Bob glared at the East River. "In Chicago, they tossed my cord in a trash heap and left my family bleeding and burning in the streets."

"That was yesterday. Every dawn on the ship you run from tomorrow into dark—"

"You don't know what I run from."

Kehinde slipped Liam's grasp. "Bamidele, I know your story. It's also mine." She strode with Melinga into the weave of cables and halted below us. "Raiders always come in the middle of dreams. They steal us from ourselves, eat our spirits. *Nzumbe*, living dead, we sing their praises and take heads at their command. At the masquerade fair in Chicago I'll give up the traitor-warrior to become someone else."

Bob snorted. "So you think now." He pulled away from me and slid down a cable.

I followed and grabbed him before he could escape. "Tell me what you run from."

Bob warred with himself, but finally relented. "I worked a circus brothel in Chicago for King Willy. He bought me, 'rescued' me from the trash heap for himself and special clientele. I thought I loved King Willy. Liam came often, always the highest bidder, paying top dollar for the Spotted Man and Frieda, a dwarf woman, for the whole night. One Sunday, Frieda ran off with Liam's money. King Willy came after me with a horsewhip. He said he'd flay the spots off my ass, kill me, for one night's wages. He jammed a gun in my mouth. I pissed myself. How had I ever loved him? I knocked him down. I stomped him. King Willy never got up. I was gibbering. Liam hauled me away. Ghost Dog let us stay with him, till I got right in the head again. So you see, I have no love for Chicago." He searched my face. "What do you say?"

I was more *aje* than human with only fire in my mouth. Bob raced off to Brooklyn.

Liam took my arm. "Let him run. He'll come back before the engines are stoked."

"We don't have to be who we've been," Kehinde said.

In the long hours from dusk to dawn, I paced along the train cars waiting for Bob. When the home star appeared, Luigi smacked the cages with his walking stick, terrifying the animals. I snatched it from him. Bob grunted behind us.

"You're late," Luigi said.

"The train ain't left." Bob loaded unhappy beasts into boxcars.

"Got no answer to my cables." Luigi grumbled at him.

"Nothing I can do about that." Bob turned to me. "Chicago will be your fault."

Words failed me again. Should we have run off to sea as he said?

Kehinde poured libation to Eshu. "We're at the mercy of many-headed change."

To avoid Eshu's laughter, to avoid Kehinde and Bob, I slept all the way to Chicago.

Trying Times

"*The Tempest* was over an hour ago. It's hopeless," Cinnamon said. "Impossible."

"It's not." Klaus tried to cheer her up. "I'll wager Mrs. Williams will help us get Ariel and Griot Joe together."

"You'll wager that, will you?" Marie mocked the fake British accents running around the Green Room. She was in a sour mood too. "How can Ariel be a no-show?"

Soggy carrots and anemic celery languished on the decimated buffet table. No VIP was desperate enough for these cookie alternatives. They sipped champagne and oohed and ahhed over the actors and designers. Prospero swooped through the crowd in his cape, wizard-worthy on- and offstage. Critics proclaimed it a privilege to get seasick as the mighty lantern swung across the proscenium to a gamelan orchestra. Director Hill was declared a genius, but the most buzz was for Ariel and her impossible disappearing acts. Marie walked the set, hunting secret scrims, mirrors, or trapdoors. She found nothing like that, but her weird hand tingled. Proof. Ariel vanished through the spaces between things and reappeared anywhere. Fifty hot snots, or maybe fifteen, insisted it was the most magical production of *The Tempest* they'd seen. VIPs whipped out checkbooks. A five-figure donation slid into a platinum-donor envelope. Ariel brought in big bucks. Director Hill was an asshole taking credit for somebody else's magic or weird science. He probably stole the gamelan idea too, from some production he'd seen.

"You don't know that," Klaus said. "He—"

"Hill's a shark." Marie shut him down. "He is using our Mod Squad blocking for his ghetto fairy tale, but not me and Cin."

"Yeah," Cinnamon snorted, "what's the genius in that?"

"You want to be mad, so you're unreasonable." Klaus punched her shoulder. "*You* told me not to drop out. You both did."

"That was before we realized Hill was a rip-off artist." Cinnamon pouted.

"Why should *they* get everything and my role too?" Klaus had a point. "*Vati* was so sure I'd fall on my ass and ruin another good production. I'll show everybody."

"You better," Cinnamon said.

"Yeah," Marie hissed, "the only acting Snow White Janice knows how to do is flirt."

"Are you worried?" Klaus's question smacked them both.

Janice was slender curves and bouncy curls. Marie was flat as a boy up top and no hips either. In three-inch platforms she was still really short. Cinnamon was half an inch taller than Klaus and only fifteen pounds heavier since recent weight loss; yet, Janice won the beauty contest. Klaus could shut them down too.

"Janice flirts with me to piss out her new boyfriend." *Piss out* was a Germ-English keeper. "The assistant stage manager dumped Chanda, a college girl, for Janice. Chanda's mother is from India. Her name means moon."

"Moon?" Marie grinned. "You would know that."

The ASM was the cute rogue doing the Kali girl (Chanda?) in the island paradise set at auditions. "He better watch out," Cinnamon said. "Janice is jailbait. No nooky in the bushes." They laughed so hard strangers joined in. It wasn't that funny.

"Somebody ought to warn Janice." Marie sounded concerned. "Lover boy is *into* exotic colored girls, high school or college."

The blood drained from Klaus's cheeks. "Do you think I'm like this?"

"Would Marie and I be with your pale ass if you were, fine as we are together?" Cinnamon chomped her tongue too late. She'd declared their Squad a sex item out loud. Nobody denied it. Klaus bit a celery stalk and sprayed juice on a tipsy platinum angel.

The woman giggled and patted Klaus's arm. "Celery is just

stringy water. Don't look so serious, young man. You're almost cute. It spoils the effect."

Cinnamon and Marie pulled Klaus away from bad adult behavior.

"We got a special three-way thing." Marie dropped her full weight onto them, a contact improv move. "We do the weird from another dimension."

"*Ja. Ja.*" Klaus gripped Marie's hand and Cinnamon's too. "I don't know who I am up to, in to? on to? This is first time. You two, are first real thing."

Cinnamon nodded. "Me too."

"You guys are shitting me," Marie said.

Klaus and Cinnamon hunched their shoulders, embarrassed.

"Wow. I've been crushed out on somebody steady since I was twelve. A parade of losers, breaking my heart."

Klaus tensed up. "We won't break your heart." How could anybody guarantee that?

"Promise?" Marie sounded pathetic.

"I promise," Klaus said and slugged Cinnamon.

"Cross my heart." Promising was hard. What if she fell down on them?

"How did you kids crash this party?" Director Hill stood by the buffet ruins in Armani wool. Glass-slipper Gwyneth hugged him from behind, her chin on his shoulder. She wore a liquid gold gown and transparent heels filled with gold sparkles. Their styles matched. Gwyneth had ditched Harry. "This is a private affair." Hill leaned over the empty punch bowl and shook golden boy curls. Cinnamon caught a whiff of marijuana. "Not the time to swipe free cheese, dear."

"Klaus's mother is a volunteer," Marie declared. "We have VIP tickets."

Cinnamon waved the stubs.

Recognition dawning, Hill backed up. "How's your mother coming along?"

Cinnamon's tongue knotted up. He probably thought she was stupid.

"Ms. Jones is going home tomorrow," Klaus said. "We are very pleased."

Gwyneth squeezed Director Hill. "Tom and I stopped by the hospital last week." First Harry, now Tom, all she needed was a Dick. "Ms. Jones was looking so much better. Wasn't she?"

"Yes." Hill came around the table and squeezed Cinnamon's hand, then hugged her. "Give Ms. Jones my regards." They headed off, leaving Cinnamon in a daze.

"Hill knows how to mess with your head," Marie muttered.

Klaus snagged the ASM. "Have you seen Ariel?"

"Ariel took off on a bike," he replied. "In this storm!"

"Some homeless dude has been stalking her," an intern bagging trash said. "Time for you kids to leave. Nothing to steal, everything's locked up."

"Excuse me?" Cinnamon did a full-body, black-girl scowl. "What?"

"Oops." The ASM ducked out.

The intern got up in Cinnamon's face. "A gong disappeared Wednesday and a leather jacket walked out of the Green Room last night. That's what."

"You have a death wish, motherfucker, talking this shit at me?" She shoved him at the buffet table. He fell over and banged his head on the plastic punch bowl. Her hand squeezed his throat; a knee jammed his groin. "Do I fit the description of the thief?"

Marie chuckled. Klaus shushed her.

The intern was bleach white. "Sorry. I didn't mean anything."

"You don't piss on my head and call it rain. I should kick your sorry ass."

The intern flailed. "I was . . . taking precautions?" Carrots rolled onto the rug.

"I could break you with a thought."

"Not right now," Marie said. She and Klaus dragged Cinnamon out into cold drizzle to wait for Kevin to pick them up. Marie banged her hips against Klaus. "Admit it. That was Glamazon cool."

"OK, yes, I enjoyed it too." He grinned.

"Really?" Cinnamon sagged. "I don't need to be fighting. What's wrong with me?"

Klaus stroked her face, pausing at the bruise. "Prince Charming says: *These are trying times.*" He and Marie kissed Cinnamon's rage-hot cheeks. She swooned.

"The night is still young!" Marie said.

Sweet Revenge

Kevin drove the Squad to Opal's, chewing their ears about Aunt Becca. She was bartending in Shadyside and sticking to the job like she was sticking to him. Kevin hollered, "Be good, y'all," from the bottom of the steps and hurried to pick her up. The elders had gone out; the house was empty. The Squad could do whatever they liked.

Opening the front door, gloom greeted Cinnamon. The naked overhead light blasted cruel photon torpedoes. She switched it off. The air tasted ashy. Stale cigarette smoke wafted from the coatrack. Down the spooky hall, paunchy walls leaned into each other. The rug was pretty roughed up. The ancient refrigerator wheezed in the kitchen. It'd be dead before the month was out. Aidan's wooden animals had disappeared from the shelves—running for cover. Their house had been *off* for four years and four months. No wonder Opal refused to come home. Cinnamon sank with Marie and Klaus onto the couch in the dark. Nobody was sure what to do next. Iris had hidden the TV. She wasn't giving advertisers a season ticket to their imaginations, even for *The Cosby Show*.

You want entertainment? Do it yourself.

"So, Klaus, what happened with *Vati*'s big dinner party?" Marie said. "Last weekend, remember?" Klaus closed his eyes, too shy or too ashamed to speak. Marie groaned. "Please talk, without making us beg."

"We should each tell something hard." Cinnamon thought of Raven drooling in the nursing home and her wishing death on strangers. "I'll go first if nobody wants to."

"No, I'll go first," Marie said. Klaus's eyes popped open. Marie arched her left eyebrow theatrically. "What? You don't think I have anything hard?"

Images stormed Cinnamon. *Marie's sister spewed in a toilet. Marie held off frantic parents. Her sister burst out the bathroom door and into the street. Five-toe footprints in melted slush led down a hill.* Klaus furrowed his brow at Cinnamon. Did he feel her trancing?

"Tough girls also get the blues." He did another Prince Charming line.

Marie stood up and paced around the coffee table. "No interrupting, and if you don't know what I'm talking about, go look it up later or something."

Klaus shrugged. "Sure."

"This is like getting naked. Let's do it upstairs." Cinnamon hauled Klaus from the bottomless cushions. "Sekou has dictionaries and encyclopedias and history tomes."

The bedroom smelled of books, hair oil, and Sekou's candle collection, not *off* like the rest of the house. Cinnamon lit the Arabian rose tapers. She'd been saving them for a special moment. Klaus fell out on Sekou's bed. Marie hung in the doorway. Cinnamon grabbed *A People's History of the United States, Funnybook Physics,* and a stolen social studies reference guide from the shelf over Sekou's bed. She plopped down by the galaxy pillow. Klaus put his head in her lap.

"You ready?" Marie said softly.

Cinnamon stroked peach fuzz on Klaus's cheeks. He did a baritone cat rumble.

"My mom's parents were in a Japanese internment camp in Gila River, Arizona."

"What? Wait!" Klaus jumped up.

Marie stomped around the galaxy rug while he flipped through articles on Japanese Americans, over a hundred thousand US citizens ripped from their lives and thrown into camps during World War II. Gila River was an Indian reservation, home to Pima and Pee-Posh folks opposed to the camp. US government officials missed the irony and ignored the outrage. Indians were overruled. A few German and Italian Americans got interned too. That was news to Cinnamon, and Sekou had kept her schooled on reasons to riot.

"Ready?" Marie hovered in the doorway, her proscenium arch. "I don't have to—"

"Over before you've started?" Klaus quipped and Marie looked ready to bounce.

"Let me braid your hair," Cinnamon said.

Marie flipped dark waves out of her face. She'd wondered if Cinnamon could do heavy, slippery hair. "While I talk?"

Cinnamon waved her close. Candlelight made anything seem possible. "I won't do real skinny braids. That takes forever."

Marie dropped to the floor by the bed. Cinnamon leaned her face into Marie's lavender aroma, dragged a comb through slippery snarls, and braided. Klaus eyed her fast fingers. She let him attach beads at the end of the first braid. Cinnamon massaged Marie's scalp before doing a second and third braid. At the fourth, Marie sighed.

"Mom's parents lost everything but survived Gila River, a harsh desert camp. Dad's parents had come to the US through New York City. Immigration put Chinese on their forms. Who cared till Pearl Harbor? The white hicks where they lived never really asked. Maybe they were happy not to know. There was one other Japanese family, the Unnos, an older couple, good Buddhists in their sixties with a grown son who went to fight in Europe. They kept my grandparents' secret. Mr. Unno asked Granddad to look after their farm. So my grandparents learned farming and went through the whole war, pretending to be Chinese farmers in very good English.

"After the war, when Dad was born, they moved to San Francisco and never talked about those years. Dad's older sister slipped him the dirty family secret when he turned eight: no Santa Claus, and by the way, the 'rents saved their skins with Chinese lies. His sister worried that if people found out, catastrophe! Dad wasn't born till 1946. How were Chinese lies his fault? The camps were crazy. People froze to death in the desert. Why not get around that? Dad told Mom before they married. She still loved him."

"Of course," Cinnamon said.

"Natürlich," Klaus added in passionate German.

Cinnamon wove a hidden streak of dyed blond hair in a side braid. "You got more?"

Marie chewed a lip. "Mom told me and my sister. She thought we should know. Dad is furious. He claims it's his secret, and Mom should let the past stay in the past. Dad's only got daughters, but in America, *we* can be his legacy. My sister's a real genius at math, debate. She got into Amherst College, so I was off the hook. She only dabbles in theatre. *I'm* the actress. I sang Dad around to believing in me. But according to her, I'm a banana." Yellow outside, white inside? "My sister put up this one-woman show, telling the whole family drama at a hole-in-the-wall over in Shadyside. It's World War Three at my house."

Klaus muttered in German and fussed over a green bead without a hole.

"Stop that." Marie smacked his hands. "Say something."

Only lame crap came to Cinnamon: *This is America. Everybody be passing.* "That's rough."

"My parents are threatening to disown my sister. This is 1987, not feudal Japan." Marie's lips trembled. "My sister's got the hots for some revolutionary Latino dude. She's eighteen, so she stormed out of the house to his place."

"In her bare feet," Cinnamon said. "I could see that coming."

Marie flicked her weird hand. Sparks flew. "Maybe she won't go to Amherst next fall. Mom and Dad are dropping hints. I have to be the big doctor of their dreams now. Theatre has become criminal activity, so I lie. They trust me. I could—" Shoot her sister? "OK, you guys tell something, quick."

Klaus threw the defective bead in the corner.

"You already heard my shit," Cinnamon said. "Can we finish your braids?"

Marie blinked rapidly. Cinnamon took that as a yes and braided the second half in a blur. Muttering in German, Klaus did an ombré bead pattern—dark blues to pale greens with an occasional flash of silver.

"Look in the mirror," Cinnamon said.

Marie halfheartedly swung her braids. "Later."

"We should do a hoodoo spell for family high dramas . . ." Cinnamon trailed off. Sitting on Sekou's bed, candles sputtering, an empty house creaking, they could have indulged raging hormones and MADE OUT, instead of whatever they were doing.

"You've been silent or in German for an hour." Marie tugged Klaus's scraggly hair.

"Yeah." Cinnamon squeezed his tight shoulders.

"Ariel would do anything for the Golden Angel Donors," Klaus said.

"Non sequitur." Marie punched him. "Explain?"

"The angels are like your fairy godmothers," Cinnamon said.

"This is about canceling the dinner party, isn't it?" Marie sprang up.

"Talk to us. Don't be such a black hole." Cinnamon dug into knotted muscles.

"*Owa.*" Klaus flinched. "Ask me questions. That helps."

Groaning, Cinnamon and Marie coaxed the story out of him. Glass-slipper Gwyneth, Commander Williams, and the VIPs invited themselves to Klaus's to brainstorm the Playhouse fund drive. Mrs. B saw it as a rehearsal for *Vati*'s dinner party. She served cake and coffee and talked bad-English-getting-better. She knew more than anybody realized. Medea blew through, a surprise to pump their spirits.

Meanwhile in the garage, *Vati* was shooting up nasty crap. He nodded out on his tools and made a terrible racket. The angels had to go see what was up. Mrs. B couldn't stop them. Klaus didn't want to. The ladies barged in on *Vati* drowning in his vomit. A few heartbeats later, he would have croaked. The ladies shipped him to the hospital, and the hospital shipped him to rehab. Commander Williams and Gwyneth helped Mrs. B take care of business. Luckily, *Vati* made his own drugs. The family bank accounts were still intact.

"That was two weeks ago." Marie was pissed. "Why didn't you tell us sooner?"

"Why didn't you tell sooner?" Klaus replied. Marie shook her braids.

"Shame," Cinnamon blurted. "And wishing death on somebody."

"I'm evil like that, but"—Marie pointed at Klaus—"you?"

Words stormed Cinnamon. "If *Vati* gets clean and sober for a second, he could talk Mrs. B out of her right mind. She'd take him back without being sure he was cured—"

"Should she story-storm on?" Marie took Klaus's hand, kissed his palm.

After an eternity, Klaus mouthed *"Ja."*

"Watching *Vati* choke, you imagined him taking a last breath, imagined light frozen in his eyes, so you and *Mutti* would be free." Cinnamon's throat ached. "Who'd want to talk about that?"

"Certainly not in English," Klaus said with perfect comic timing. They laughed hard, rolling and choking. The house groaned. A draft blew in from the hall, and shadows danced. Naked, with their clothes on, the Squad fell into each other and held on tight. They listened to the house rock on the edge of a cliff and not fall over.

Klaus touched Cinnamon's bruise. "Your turn."

Her palm tingled where Raven had tapped it. Why keep that secret? The whole nursing home saga tumbled out. When she finished they were nuzzling and kissing, sort of making out. Cinnamon's and Marie's braids got tangled up.

"Wait!" Klaus undid the knot.

The spell was broken. They looked at each other, sheepish.

Cinnamon shivered with so many good, new feelings. "This must be—" SHY.

"*Oma*—Grandmother—used to say: *Verzeihen ist die beste Rache*," Klaus said.

Cinnamon and Marie practiced the phrase until they nailed it.

"Translation please?" Marie asked.

"*Rache* is, is . . ." Klaus sputtered.

Cinnamon jumped up and grabbed Sekou's German-English

dictionary from the foreign language row. "Spell it, the whole phrase."

As Klaus rattled off letters, Marie stretched limbs gone to sleep. She flipped through *The Chronicles*. "New chapters! We're behind!"

"Forgiveness is the sweetest revenge." Cinnamon said. A note was tucked between *zücken*—flare up and *zünden*—ignite. "First I read this missive from my ghost brother, then you guys do new chapters out loud. OK?" She refrained from mentioning that she'd read *Chronicles* 20 and 21 without them.

Note from Sekou,
December 9, 1984

Sis,

I love you, kid. You're the one. Get out there and run some-thing big or write a vast epic or act the hell out of great, juicy roles. Be sure to star in your own life while you're at it. Do every wonderful thing you do for me too.

Please look after Opal. Mom's shields got blasted. Her soul's leaking out. I know that's real.

If you see lover boy, you'll figure what to tell him. Last couple weeks I been feeling lower than low, which has nothing to do with Lexy or Opal, you, or anybody but me. My man bought me this German-English dictionary yesterday, an early birthday present. What the hell? Lexy used to crack on my collection. Sit-ting on my bed, getting high on my weed, he was always saying dictionary geeks weren't sexy. N!$$#& got hot when I looked up words, really hot when I found something unbelievable. I mean he loved this geek.

(Opal doesn't want me forcing the n-word on you. Or queer sex. Like you don't hear that shit everywhere.)

Geek is an old word. Geeks were worthless fools in 1876. In 1919, geeks were snake charmers and carnival degenerates bit-ing off the heads of chickens. The obsessive student thing started in the 1950s: somebody ranking on people who wanted to know too much. That's wrong. Ain't nothing bad about being greedy for knowledge. That's why you picked up this dictionary. What are you looking up? What are you greedy to know?

I must be dead. Sorry about that. If I don't do it soon, the drug will have my soul, and I won't be able to do it at all.

Lexy wrapped the dictionary himself, instead of making his moms do it, in little-boy paper with planets, stars, and galaxies on navy blue-black. Lexy loves this SF geek shooting my mind to the stars. Bad analogy. Sorry. Lexy looked for a Chinese dictionary, but couldn't find one. German's not Chinese, but a real fucking challenge too.

Once upon a time, I wanted to learn ten languages by age thirty and fly around the world and talk to everybody. One of those pathetic kid dreams, before you realize that half of everybody hates the other half for no good reason. OK, there are reasons. Whatever. I'm depressed. You're not. Do your story. Learn German if you want.

Lexy was so excited yesterday. He bought me a bucket of fried calamari and stashed a quart of black cherry ice cream in the freezer—a chaser for the rubbery sea-bug. I ate the whole bucket myself. Lexy got the jump on everybody and celebrated me all to himself. I'll be legal in two weeks. Eighteen years, a man, like magic. No more jailbait blues for him. That doesn't mean we'd be kissing on Fifth Avenue. Maybe we'd stop slinking off behind washing machines. The different cycles were supposed to cover the noise. You were too smart to think we were back there separating the dark from the light. Too cute, prowling around in your comet nightie, twinkling and talking to yourself, then catching us doing the nasty. I wasn't mad. I was glad you saw us. Relieved. Lexy was scared, hollering scared. Cut him some slack. He'll be hurting, doing a butch act, fronting the unsentimental macho. You know, crying on the inside, like Opal.

Lexy calling me a geek . . . I first saw him escorting a gravid ant queen across the avenue near Carnegie Museum. I walked behind him, helping to divert her to grass. We didn't acknowledge each other until the dinosaur room. Doing that do you flow that way, do you like me two-step under a T. rex. He dragged me to the bugs and butterflies talking warp speed, like you do. Drawers of death on a pin, trapped in a vacuum so we humans can appreciate our genius, our superpowers. Lord and masters of the Earth, we can stick anybody on a pin. Lexy is into bugs, dead or alive.

He said studying ants, bees, and butterflies was communion with God. Dr. Bug-Man! He got down on the floor to show me an ant trail and stole my geek heart. An entomologist in the making and this n!$$#& called me a weirdo for being a dictionary demon?

I'm rambling.

When you run into Lexy, improvise one of your good stories. Let him know how much he meant to me. I love everybody. I can't stand myself, almost too fucked-up for words. My mind ain't right. That's the scariest thing, losing my soul and my mind. I freaked on Lexy. He tried to drag me to that nursing home. I got there once. But twice? No way. So I went off on him, talking shit I didn't mean. Lexy's been making himself scarce since the tirade.

I'm too sad . . .

Griot Joe gave The Chronicles *to me the night Kehinde died and Raven got shot in the head. They were stone-cold heroes— saving us from a crazy man aiming a gun at love. Kehinde and Taiwo were too beautiful for him. What the fuck? Griot Joe says that ripped some pages from his book, still, he's writing the whole story down, from Africa, from the nineteenth century at least. Somebody else—Aria?—be holding the twentieth century.*

The past might as well be another planet.

Joe works the spaces between things. Words magically appear on the page. Memorize what you can so it doesn't get lost again. I'm counting on you. You're a Guardian, in charge of tomorrow. Keep your shields up against bullshit torpedoes.

Love,

Your Own Brother from Another Planet

Bathroom Refuge

The *Brother from Another Planet* poster was hanging crooked and had faded, or Cinnamon was dizzy sick. "Hold up. Can we take a break?" She staggered down to the narrow bathroom, a second-floor afterthought when the outhouse came indoors. She bashed her shoulder on the door. Vessels broke, and a bruise blossomed. She dropped onto the toilet. Hot piss burned coming out. She wiped herself and stood up. Pulling on her underwear, she almost fell over.

Wishing somebody dead didn't make her responsible for a psycho gunman shooting at Kehinde and Taiwo.

"*Mist!*" She washed her hands.

Marie pounded the door. "What are you doing in there?"

The potty stopped being a refuge forever ago. Cinnamon broke out in tears.

"There are so many new pages," Klaus yelled.

Cinnamon wanted to burn the damn *Chronicles*. Nobody needed to know every stupid thing that went down from 1892 till now. Marie's dad was right. Opal too. They should let the past stay in the past. A hundred years was too heavy when you only had fourteen and a half of your own. The door banged open into her thigh.

Marie stuck her head in. "Are you in here moping about Sekou?"

That would be righteous. Cinnamon was mostly feeling sorry for herself. "That gunman shot my dad *and* Kehinde."

"Come on, we have you, and you have us." Klaus tugged her away from the sink. "We'll read to you. This shall let your mind soar elsewhere."

Cinnamon didn't deserve friends like this. But how could she get rid of them now?

Chronicles 22: Chicago Dreamland

How could Bob say Chicago was my fault? Kehinde and I were bound to Somso. We loved Melinga; Bob loved her too. Running off to sea with Brother-Taiwo's child would have poisoned the future. Chicago was nobody's fault.

The World Columbian Exposition was a celebration of a new world conquered. Refugees and renegades called on honored ancestors to inspire future greatness. At this grand carnival masquerade, Xavier Pené, a French river pirate, outwitted Captain Luigi. With French government blessings, Pené imported Fon warriors from Dahomey to Chicago for a primitive spectacle. He set up a village at the end of the mile-long Midway Plaisance, an open-air entertainment museum. Dahomeans cavorted around ugly thatched huts. Plump women, naked to the waist, drank rum, brandished long knives, and danced mock battles with half-naked men. Spectators paid a quarter to stroll beyond civilization into the heart of darkness. Curious crowds claimed disgust at heathen carryings-on, but, as in Paris, were enchanted. Pamphlets advertising Pené's show proclaimed slavery a blessing. American Negroes had been saved from heathen savagery! Bob howled to read this. Luigi wept. He had too many debts, no profits, and a troupe of useless savages eating through the last of his money. He thought to sell his African masquerade to a traveling Wild West Show. Buffalo Bill was set up at the edge of the fairgrounds. Rumors flew that Bill, Wild Jack, or somebody needed Indians, black cowboys, and even African warriors for another tour of the Old World. Somso was disgusted. She encouraged Bob and Kehinde to take Luigi's head. I was against this. Luckily, Liam threw his spear with me.

"This is homecoming," he said.

"Tomorrow we ask welcome of Lady Michigan." I waved at distant water. "Fresh blood from rash deeds might offend this Indian orisha."

"You speak wisdom, demon," Somṣo said as Bob fussed about cutthroats and desperados.

"Let's visit the Fair," I suggested.

"Before spilling blood, eh, Bobbie?" Liam said. "You warrior ladies better look smart." Liam slapped Bob's back. "You too."

Kehinde also appealed to Bob. "Let us write our own story."

We donned fine cloth, hung polished metal from our necks, arms, and ankles. Kehinde slung a cooing Melinga on her back. Liam wore a tall hat and a clean waistcoat. Bob relented and put on Yoruba robes. He covered tight red curls and hid pink spots to become Bamidele, a merchant *Akewi*, storyteller, from Yorubaland.

The fair was a spectacle of moving walkways, moving pictures, talking discs. The Krupp Weapons Building had a 248,000-pound gun bigger than a railroad car. Edison stuffed electricity in a bottle—for night-light. Ferris's giant wheel spun 2,164 people through the air. As we toured the fairgrounds, dark-skinned Americans complained about Africans "acting the monkey and bringing the colored man low."

Bob pretended he spoke no English and responded in patois: *"Cut your chains and you become free, cut your roots and you die."*

Liam took off with Ghost Dog for the Wild West Show while we explored the White City—Greek temples, fountains, and great halls. Plaster and wood masqueraded as marble and stone. A twin sister to Lady Liberty presided over a lagoon. Electric lights sparkled in dusty twilight air. Desert people, snow people, travelers from island paradises and mountain retreats laughed, told tall tales, and ate delicious food. They sported costumes invented for the night or worn by humans for a thousand years. Skin was tattooed and scented or simply star burnt and wind etched. Musicians serenaded us, playing strings, gourds, reeds, and gut. We laughed for no reason but good spirits.

As we marched beyond the lagoon, the air twisted and broke apart. Kehinde gripped my hand. Two people glided through the spaces between things and stepped from a future place into our moment. They smelled of rainstorm, woodsmoke, and decayed leaves. She had a purple flower stuck in fat braids. He had a colorful turban wrapped around stringy black hair. Redwood he called her, and he was her Aidan. Gawking at the open-air museum, they almost stumbled into us. We made a space to let them pass. Aidan gaped in my eyes. Redwood nodded a greeting. Kehinde and I nodded back. Oblivious, Somso chattered about a surprise to come; Bob, still in a foul Chicago mood, brooded. Redwood took Aidan's arm and ambled away before I could ask about their mode of transport.

"I bet they're royalty from Africa, Dahomey or Abyssinia," Redwood whispered, delighted by us. "They came from their castles in a great ship 'cross the ocean."

"What if they're regular folk just come to the Fair?" Aidan said, dazzled also.

"You mean same as you and me?" Redwood smiled and mimicked Kehinde's warrior *ahosi* stride for Aidan's wide grin. "Can't believe your eyes, huh?"

"Of course I do." Aidan scooped up a bead that had fallen from my waist. He stuffed it in his pocket as he and Redwood hurried off.

"When you first appeared, the air twisted so," Kehinde said to me. "Who are they?"

"The future," I replied. "Eshu favors us with tomorrow."

Kehinde considered them. "Eshu never reveals the whole truth in one glance. Who's to say if they're a good sign or bad? Eshu favors no one. Only a fool thinks otherwise."

Just after bumping into the future, we collided with the past. Yao the incorruptible had shipped with Xavier Pené to perform African savagery and primitive derring-do in the Dahomey village. He jumped from the basket of a giant hot-air orb. I didn't recognize this muscular Fon warrior with scars over his heart striding toward us. Eshu had been riding me the day he attacked us in Ouidah. Kehinde thrust me behind her. Bob stood shoulder to shoulder with her. Somso ran into Yao's arms. Surprise! She'd met him earlier and planned this rendezvous. Kehinde drew her cutlass.

Thus ends the best Chicago memory.

Heroes

"This is from Taiwo's waist beads!" Cinnamon displayed the mosaic bead Redwood and Aidan had given her.

"Wow." Klaus passed the bead to Marie as if it were a sacred artifact.

Marie rolled it around her weird hand. "Time travel, really?"

Klaus smiled. "Can they still do that?"

On cue, Redwood boomed at the front door. "That fool bus dispatcher be looking up his behind for yesterday and tomorrow. Why feel sorry for him and not me and Opal?"

"She got her job back," Iris said. "Bus company couldn't fire a hero-mom."

The elders laughed on the porch as Commander Williams roared up in her silver Audi. Mrs. B was riding shotgun. It was past midnight—no time to read about Somso and Yao's dastardly scheme. Marie hitched a ride with Klaus and put the ten-dollar cab fare in the Squad's emergency fund. High on each other, they danced down wet, slippery steps. At the bottom, Cinnamon pulled them into a three-way hug. Her heart ached. Commander Williams threatened to honk the horn. Marie kissed one cheek and then another; Klaus did the same—a Euro-chic cover for young lust.

"Sunday brunch is at eleven," Iris called from the porch.

How would Cinnamon last until Sunday? "We'll read *Chronicles* 23 together."

Klaus and Marie nodded and said, "Ciao!" as the Audi sped off in a cloud of drizzle.

Cinnamon hurried to her room. She squeezed the flames of flickering candles. Pulling on wildcat PJs, she was itchy and tingly. Punches, kisses, and a tap from Raven echoed across her skin. Too weird and wired for sleep, she ran into the hall and bumped into the elders, coming to tuck her in.

"Mom won't get better at Aunt Becca's," Cinnamon declared. "She's running."

Iris sighed. Aidan and Redwood sang:

Running won't set you free
Yeah, a man could still be a slave
On the loose and-a acting brave
In shackles he just don't see
No—Running won't make you free

They had a song for everything, but she wasn't a baby anymore.

"Did you two meet Griot Joe in 1893?" Cinnamon climbed under the covers.

Aidan shrugged. "Opal's famous, made it in the papers."

Redwood dropped an article from the *Pittsburgh Press* in Cinnamon's lap. Gwyneth Fraser, the glass slipper lady who dumped Harry for Tom, had written a story on Opal:

STAGE MOM A TRUE HERO: Making the World Real With Every Breath.

Hero Opal Jones set knife boy on the right track, stood up to coke dealers, and got out the vote. She put her older brother through law school, showed up for her man in a coma, and believed in her daughter's theatre dream when no one else would.

"Is this true?" Cinnamon was shocked. "Helping Uncle Clarence?"

"Viet Nam nearly wrecked him," Redwood said. "Opal had to do something."

"She never let Clarence tell anybody," Aidan said.

"Wow." Cinnamon read the article again. "When did this come out?"

"Two weeks ago. Opal hates *public display*. Especially since she lost Raven to that coma . . ." Iris's face lit up. She slipped into the hall, down the stairs, and up again.

Redwood watched her. "Following a hoodoo trail."

Cinnamon yawned. "What trail?"

Aidan winked at her despite what a bitch she'd been. "Get some rest."

"OK, fine, don't tell me." Reading the article again, Cinnamon fell asleep.

Early Saturday, Kevin stopped by to pick up clothes for Opal. Cinnamon was ready for him. She jumped in the front seat and buckled up. "I'm coming with you."

Kevin rolled his eyes and put the Toyota in gear. They drove twenty minutes in uneasy silence. Subtext crackled. Becca lived in Highland Park, a nice neighborhood near East Liberty. Wilted crocuses dribbled color on muddy ground in her yard.

"A *liberty* was common land right beyond the city," Cinnamon said, cheery and sweet. "Look, the pussy willows have buds. I'm missing spring."

Kevin grunted and parked. "No mess, you hear me?"

"Right." Cinnamon snatched the garment bag and followed him in through the side door.

Becca hugged Kevin and kissed him deeply before noticing Cinnamon. "What are you doing here, baby girl?" Becca took the garment bag.

Cinnamon shrugged. "Can't I—"

"Who turned the music off?" Skinny Opal straggled in from the kitchen wearing baggy pants and flip-flops. Her skin was ashy. Twists of hair broke out of an oily scarf. She clutched her purse and pressed buttons on the cassette player.

"Hey, Mom, how you doing?" Cinnamon smiled.

Bob Marley wailed "Redemption Song." Opal leaned against

the mantel over the fake fireplace. "Since when are you up so early on Saturday?"

"Since I read that article." Cinnamon stepped inside Opal's battered shields and hugged her. The smell of hospital disinfectant mingled with coffee. "You're a hero."

"Naw." Opal grimaced and pushed Cinnamon away. "That's your daddy."

"You too. You shouldn't keep that to yourself. I only knew the knife-boy story."

"Reporter dragged that crap out of me when I was drugged."

"They brought you some clothes." Becca held up the garment bag.

Opal waved her hand. "Nothing's going to fit."

"Elastic waists, good and tight," Cinnamon said.

"I don't need anything squeezing me." Opal snatched the clothes from Becca and shoved them at Kevin. "Take 'em back." Kevin blinked at her.

Becca grabbed the bag. "What'll you wear?"

"New clothes," Opal said as LaBelle sang *Voulez-vous coucher avec moi?* "I love this song." She bumped her butt in everybody's face.

"Medication is still making you dopey." Kevin did a few moves with her.

"Free at last! I can have a cigarette without a damn alarm shrieking." Opal riffled through her purse. "Where are my cigarettes?"

"No smoking in my house," Becca shouted. "You know that."

"Yeah, kill yourself out on the street," Cinnamon said, "on that bridge to nowhere."

Opal crumpled, as if a bomb exploded her insides. Her wheezing was so loud—Cinnamon couldn't think or breathe or take her mean words back. Becca dropped to the floor with Opal, talking softly. Kevin dragged Cinnamon to the car.

"I told you, no mess." He blasted Michael Jackson's *Thriller* and drove too fast in pounding rain. She gripped the dashboard for fifteen tense minutes and banged her knees when he jerked to a halt. "Getting out?" He left the motor running. "Or do you plan on messing up the rest of my day?"

"Sorry." She stepped out on wobbly legs. "I haven't been right for a while."

"What you goin' do about that?" Driving away, Kevin splashed muck on her.

Secret Stash

Cinnamon hid in her room the rest of Saturday. She did three weeks of math, wrote a paper on the Yoruba, Fon, and Igbo for world history, finished *To Kill a Mockingbird*, and started *1984*. She fell asleep on Opal's hero article. She woke to a warm and sunny Sunday. Forsythia had blossomed overnight. She stared out the window, panicked. No more chores, homework, or bad weather to blame for being evil.

"Go get some sun before brunch." Redwood shoved her out the back door.

The neighbors were at church. Cinnamon unchained Rain and let her jump the fence. She sat on a rock with Rain's head in her lap. "Doing the evil attack dog all day must be a drag." Petting the Doberman, she missed her Squad's arrival in the front. Klaus brought a Passamaquoddy thunderbird story for Aidan's collection. Marie had found a Quillayute one. This celestial bird had graced Indians from Washington state to Maine. They wouldn't tell Cinnamon these marvelous stories. She had to find her own tale first.

"Go look under your bed," Aidan said.

"It's time for brunch. I'm hungry," she said.

"Iris say Sekou left you a treasure trove." Aidan squeezed her nose. "Go on. Your friends will help."

Cinnamon's stomach flip-flopped when they charged upstairs to her room.

"You have a box from Sekou under your bed all this time?" Klaus tugged her braids.

"I can't believe you didn't look." Marie peeked underneath.

Cinnamon shrugged. "I want to look now, OK?"

Marie and Klaus pulled the bed away from the wall. They pushed aside ratty sneakers and an old gym towel. Dust bunnies made everybody sneeze. Marie dumped newspapers from December 1984 on the desk chair, and Klaus dragged out a cardboard box wrapped in crinkled paper—planets, stars, and galaxies on navy blue black.

"Go on," they said in sync.

Cinnamon made herself open the box. There were nine things, a hoodoo number:

> *1: The thunderbird T-shirt Raven silk-screened on top of*
> *everything*
> *2: A bear claw on a leather thong that Aidan sent for Sek-*
> *ou's eighteenth birthday*
> *3: A stack of letters from Iris wrapped in Redwood's river*
> *silk*
> *4: The mix tape of Sekou's last jams with Dr. Bug-Man*
> *Lexy*
> *5: A purple owl butterfly with wings that mimicked owl*
> *eyes*
> *6: A broken banjo string looped through three tiny keys*
> *7: A manila envelope with thirty dictionary-boy words on*
> *poster board*
> *8: A Rain Forest Lounge Exhibition list—thirty words*
> *paired with dimensions*
> *9: A T-shirt at the bottom:* WE'RE ALL MOSTLY SPACE AND
> THE FORCE TO HOLD IT TOGETHER

Dazed, Cinnamon handed Marie the thunderbird tee. Marie slipped it on. Cinnamon thrust the bear claw at Klaus. He shook his head. Marie grabbed the thong and tied it around his neck. Cinnamon sank to the floor. Klaus waved the MOSTLY SPACE tee in her face. Marie tugged off Cinnamon's sweatshirt and with Klaus's help got the iridescent green and purple tee over her DD sports bra. Cinnamon shivered, too out of it to be embarrassed.

"What's the *Rain Forest Lounge Exhibition?*" Klaus picked up the list.

"I don't fucking know!" Cinnamon regretted yelling. "Sorry. The box was like Sekou hiding under my bed. Opening it, it's like he's gone for good. Stupid, huh?"

"It's cool," Marie said.

"*Mallemaroking?*" Klaus handed the list to Marie. "Is this good English?"

"Probably." Cinnamon glanced at it. "Like *Douroucouli* and *Magniloquent.*"

"*Adumbration* is number one, but the list isn't alphabetical." Marie tapped a word. "*Xenophilia.* That's the opposite of xenophobia."

"Sweet potato pancakes. Hot dog!" Aidan shouted from the hall.

"We have to find him a new happy phrase," Cinnamon said.

Iris appeared in the doorway looking devilish and spritely. "Cilantro and black bean patties too." She dropped a handkerchief on the floor. Squawking and flapping her arms, she lifted a leg, bent down, and gripped the handkerchief with her teeth. Marie, Klaus, and Cinnamon fell over mimicking these backcountry moves. "Mr. Buzzard takes practice, but he never lies to you," Iris said. "Tucking treasure under the bed runs in the family. Opal told Sekou to hide those keys. Let's see what they open up."

Redwood and Aidan were staying in Opal and Raven's room. Bright rectangles marked the walls where Raven's paintings used to hang. Carved animals scampered on the shelves through pictures of Sekou and Cinnamon. On the dresser, a half-smoked cigarette butt stood at the center of an ashtray sculpture. Broken lighters, burnt matches, and ashes spiraled around the cut glass pyramid—a hoodoo altar.

"Redwood wants to give that mess to Opal," Aidan said. "I persuaded her to wait."

"She won't like it any more next week," Redwood said.

"Maybe she'll laugh though," Iris said. Cinnamon laughed now.

"What are these?" Klaus asked.

Two cedar boxes with padlocks sat on the rag rug. Aidan hauled a third box from under the bed. His back popped when he stood up. Cinnamon tossed Marie then Klaus a key. The locks opened on their first try. They lifted the lids together.

"Daddy's paintings! Mom didn't burn them." Cinnamon hopped around the room like a little kid. She twirled the elders and gyrated with Marie and Klaus. She halted at the center box. Her hands shook as she unrolled canvas #16. Gasps erupted at Kehinde dancing with moonlight in Dahomey.

"That's the image at the end of *Chronicles* 1," Klaus said.

"Daddy's colors are more vivid," Cinnamon said.

The landscape was more playful, and Kehinde looked even fiercer. Klaus unrolled #3: the *aje* riding silvery waves and baby Cinnamon clutching seaweed hair. Raven had used her as a model for Melinga. Marie held up #27: Taiwo hugging a great iroko tree.

"Everybody should see these," Marie said.

They covered the bed, floor, and walls with twenty-three canvases. The paintings glinted in the gloomy light. Some pictures were unfamiliar, telling stories they hadn't yet read in *The Chronicles*. Cinnamon unfurled a galaxy image and squealed.

"Let's do an exhibit right downstairs, with good lighting. We'll hang this star-scape on the ceiling and we'll do a, a performance for Daddy's birthday at the nursing home: contact, poetry, and music. Me and Granddaddy can write a blackbird song for crows and Ravens. Everybody has to come and be stimulating. A hoodoo spell. " She tugged at Redwood and Iris. "You too. Please. It'll be for all of us."

Aidan held his breath. Iris nodded, and so did Redwood. Klaus and Marie cheered.

A timer went off in the kitchen. "Anybody hungry?" Iris said.

After brunch Cinnamon and her Squad entertained the elders in the TV alcove with the continuing saga of the Wanderer from another dimension. Redwood and Aidan chuckled over their appearance at the Fair and lit candles for the next chapter.

Chronicles 23: Chicago Nightmare

"Yao the incorruptible wants Somso to run off with him." I translated Fon for Bob. We headed for Buffalo Bill's masquerade just outside the fairgrounds. The deserted field at twilight's edge was ominous. "Yao promises to protect Somso and Melinga from a fate worse than death with American showmen." Melinga fussed. I plucked her from Kehinde's back and threw her high. She sang a sea-mammal song. Somso flinched.

"I'm a man of honor," Yao declared, "not an oath-breaker who pierced his brother's heart." He watched me fly up to catch Melinga with blood in his eyes. "Decide."

Kehinde slashed creeping mist with her cutlass. Cannons at the Wild West Show roared, and horses shrieked. Cowboys, Indians, and the cavalry played life and death. Liam and Ghost Dog were to meet us after the stagecoach raid. I hoped they came soon, before Kehinde or the *aje* squandered Yao's lifeblood.

"Kehinde's betrayal cost many *ahosi* warrior lives." Yao spit disgust at her feet.

Appalled, Bob halted. His Yoruba robes fluttered in the wind. We all halted.

"What do *you* know?" Somso pulled Yao out of cutlass range. "Abla said you were at the river."

"I know what happened." Yao carried no visible weapon, yet aimed death at Kehinde's heart. "Listen to the true story."

"So says the master spy." Kehinde sliced phantom heads and pierced ghost hearts.

Yao smirked. "Kehinde fired her elephant gun at a rebel-slave leader. Her bullets couldn't pierce a father of mysteries. She ran from the battlefield without taking his head. Coward."

"He's a nasty rascal." Bob spoke English. "What's he saying?"

I translated as Yao continued. "Taiwo consulted *Ifa* and knew the direction coward Kehinde ran. *Ifa* warned of a deadly trap, but the verses only offer wisdom; a person must choose which action to take. Taiwo loved his sister. Yoruba believe twins share one soul—perhaps that is so. But Abla had made Kehinde *nzumbe*. Her soul was only good for obeying Abla's will. A great Fon warrior, Abla defeated them both. Kehinde fell upon Brother-Taiwo from an ancient iroko tree and knocked him senseless. She dragged him to a spirit cave and plunged her cutlass through his heart. Taiwo was a sacrifice to Yemoja for saving Kehinde from hungry sharks so many years ago. Who better than a twin to take her place in the land of the dead?"

"Yemoja would not ask for this sacrifice," I said.

"I found Taiwo in the spirit cave, his heart pierced. He clutched Kehinde's staff."

"You lie. I was there. Taiwo was riddled with bullets. There was no staff."

"Kehinde was always happy to kill. Abla saw the warrior she would be."

"Abla saw what she wanted to see." I turned to Kehinde. "Tell him."

Kehinde's heart rate doubled. Blood shifted from gut to muscles. Yao watched her as he filled the air with lies. "Eshu tortures the oath-breaker with an *aje* who loves the child as a father might. The *aje* killed Abla, who knew the truth. Somso, you saw the murder and told everyone. The crossroad *nkisi* from the Jesus orisha protects you now, but for how long?"

Whispering prayers, Somso clutched the cross at her neck and stepped behind Yao.

Kehinde drew Yao away from us. "In Pené's troupe, a Yoruba woman recalled you stealing her family to get rich from their sweat. She told me your boast, Yao. You said you'd drink from my heart and kill the *aje* or anyone who threw his spear with us."

Yao drew a hidden blade and lunged at Kehinde, faster than I'd ever seen anyone move, thrusting at her neck with such force

he could have taken her head. The *aje* roused too slowly to intervene. Bob leapt to Kehinde's aid with bare hands. He was too far.
Somso screamed as blood spurted at the sky. Kehinde's neck was
not where Yao's blade landed. He had sliced her shoulder. She'd
twisted and jammed her cutlass upward, and the ferocity of Yao's
attack drove her cutlass through his breastbone, heart, and out
the flesh of his back. Yao lost grip of his blade. He and Kehinde
dropped to their knees, cheek to cheek. He spit blood in her face.
The *aje* blasted fire above their heads.

"You're right, Yao. I carry my brother's rebel spirit," Kehinde
said. "When I was a girl, you brought rape, murder, and treachery
to me." She released her cutlass. Yao's body toppled into the dust.
"Take your curses to the land of the dead." Somso grabbed Yao's
blade and sprang at her. Kehinde smacked it away and gripped
Somso's throat, choking her. Somso struggled, clawing at Kehinde's bloody arm. Kehinde released her suddenly. "This is a new
world," Kehinde said. "I don't want your death."

Somso collapsed in the dust. The *aje* aimed its poison tail at her.
Bob stepped in and shielded her. Melinga clutched my seaweed
hair, clicking and whistling.

"Please, we're free now." Kehinde gripped *aje* talons and cried
silver tears in the moonlight. She had never cried before.

The *aje* turned from Somso and burned Yao's body and Kehinde's cutlass with the next fire breath. Using the last of this
heat, I seared Kehinde's wound. Melinga covered her face with
kisses. Fairgoers exiting the Wild West Show smiled at our colorful group clothed in ash and sparkling static. Liam and Ghost
Dog appeared, joking about Buffalo Bill's spectacle. Baffled by
blood, tears, and gibberish, they brought us to Luigi's camp. We
explained nothing. Who could talk?

Nobody slept that night except Melinga, nested in my lap.
Somso snuck away in the dark. Bob followed her. Melinga woke
once, crying. A woman in our troupe fed her son, then Melinga.
Kehinde lay huddled against hard ground muttering *no more death*.
She wouldn't let me touch her. The bandage on her shoulder was

soaked with blood and pus. Liam sat vigil over her. In the morning, Bob slunk into the tent and hid in shadows.

"We don't have to be who we have been." Speaking Yoruba, Kehinde struggled up with Liam's aid. "Yao ran into my blade and killed himself."

"The *aje* would kill Somso to prevent Somso killing you," I declared.

"No!" Kehinde struggled for words. "My Taiwo . . . starlight eyes, hair smelling of sea greens, sometimes you're no more than the bright edge of a shadow." She smiled. "Your breath is a sea breeze or a firestorm, but you hate the bitter taste of killing. You weep at every story's end. You'd regret killing Somso. We'll make another story."

"Beautiful poetry, but the *aje* doesn't think as you do, or as I do in human form."

"We're not Abla." Kehinde's eyes clouded. "Today we bury Melinga's cord and pour libation to the orisha of Lake Michigan." She trembled.

Liam steadied her. "What're you going on about? Talk English. What happened?"

I told him of Somso's treachery, Yao's death, and the *aje*'s fury.

"You're between the Devil and the dead sea then?" he said.

"Probably. Every choice breaks me apart."

Spying Bob in the dark, Liam cursed. "Scoundrel, when were you going to tell me?"

Bob ignored Liam's anger. "Somso says she forgives you."

"That's Christian charity, to forgive the people you tried to kill," Liam said.

"I stole both her husbands," Kehinde murmured, then her mind wandered elsewhere. Liam laid her gently on fabric bedding.

"Somso!" I hissed—a curse word now. My rage woke Melinga.

Bob scooped her from my lap. "Somso trusts you with Melinga."

Liam snorted. "She has no love for her daughter."

"She rejects a demon child of a twin." I spoke as if I understood Somso.

"Neglect is also poison." Bob tickled Melinga. "We could steal the child and travel the world." He gazed at me, calm and clear. "What do you say?"

The plan thrilled Liam. "Let's do it."

"Kehinde was stolen," I said.

"My father sold me to a circus brothel when I was twelve." Bob spoke softly. "King Willy said he loved me, but it was all lies. I enjoyed killing the lies, but hear me now: killing is a moment of pleasure and a life of regret."

I knew what he said was true, but what choice did I have? "We might persuade Kehinde to run off with Melinga, after the taste of Yao's blood has left her mouth."

"We might not." Bob grimaced.

"Kehinde swore an oath to stand by Somso and the child."

"Somso thinks the child is a monster." Bob hugged Melinga. "No good solution—we steal her for love, when Kehinde can't resist."

"We bury the cord and then see." I was adamant. "Deception isn't love."

Bob and Liam concocted a simple plan. Somso was to meet us at the lake to bury Melinga's cord. Ghost Dog would take Luigi to talk with Wild Jack about selling his African savages while Liam procured a wagon, and I gathered the few possessions we'd brought to the New World. We knew no one to say good-bye to. Bob put a silky blue *mojo* around my neck containing hairs from Jumbo the Elephant and pulled me to his heart. "You're the sea demon who rode dark waves and scared a man to death," he said.

"How long have you known?"

"I suspected that first night . . . You mean to kill Somso once the ceremony is over. Kehinde will hate you for this. You'll hate yourself. I can't allow that."

"My Guardian." I stroked his tight curls. "But we'll make Kehinde understand."

"Yes." Bob kissed me, long and deep. "If we do a sacrifice for . . . Eshu." I nodded as he mumbled incomprehensible French at Kehinde.

Her eyes flickered bright at *les sacrifices*. I should have been suspicious, but she waved me close, to heal her wound. I thought only of banishing tiny creatures who would steal her life force.

It was a chilly, damp afternoon. Bob bundled Melinga up. She fussed at him and reached for me, sparks on her fingertips. I barely noticed, too busy bringing Kehinde's fever down. They departed before us. Finally Kehinde was stable, and Liam drove us to a secluded shoreline in a wagon pulled by a tired horse. As the roar of the Fair faded, Liam chatted and joked with his dragon lady. She patted him occasionally, soaking up the passion he had for her.

Lake Michigan was a freshwater inland sea. Waves rippled across the surface, splashing froth against golden sand. Bob and Somso were late. Kehinde leaned on me, and we strolled up the beach. Liam stayed close to the horse. I talked of future travels, of possibilities. The home star slid to the horizon. Distant stars became visible against a velvet void. I suggested we steal Melinga and go off with Bob and Liam. Somso had no love for her daughter and would never find us. The *aje* need not kill her. Kehinde agreed.

"Since coming to America, you've been distant," I said. "Today you're reasonable, a poet, a lover, speaking of starlit eyes and the bright edge of a shadow. Why?"

"Warriors and cowards are afraid to trust." Kehinde stumbled away from me. "Bob knows how to love, to sacrifice. I should have released you from your oath."

"I can love you both."

"I don't know if I can love anyone."

"Hush." I gathered her into the circle of my being.

A north wind lifted moisture from the far shore and dropped it on us. We waited hours, getting drenched. Bob and Somso were too late, but I told myself lies: they've lost their way sneaking around Luigi's thugs. Melinga was hungry—they stopped to feed her. The horses stumble through mud. They will come soon. Dawn approached, and a west wind blew the clouds away.

"They aren't coming. Bob has abandoned us." Liam staggered to the lake's edge and fell on his knees in cold water. He howled at the fates for doing him wrong yet again. "If Bobbie and I had started off better, there might have been a chance."

"Bob running off with Somso—it makes no sense," I said.

"Eshu has many heads," Kehinde replied. I wouldn't understand these words until years later. "Always look for what you can't see."

I buried Melinga's cord by the lake. She would be of this land. Fire scorched my nostrils and heated acid tears. Bob and Melinga were gone. My heart was in several pieces. I almost scattered then and there for lost love, but Kehinde's breath was shallow, her shoulder was hot and full of pus. She could barely stand. I held her up. This was also love.

The home star was high in the sky when Liam said, "You'll catch your death." He heaved us into the wagon and drove to Chicago.

We stayed with Ghost Dog's masquerade friends while he and Liam searched for Bob and Melinga. For a year, they searched far and wide. Kehinde and I did savage masquerade. We ate the dust of many American states. Liam drank too much and raged at everyone who ventured close, except Kehinde, or perhaps that was me raging. Kehinde never loved Liam as he loved her, but she was his friend—a comfort, a knife in his heart. One day, Liam refused to search anymore. He went off to get drunk and never came back. We were in a desert place. I was ready to let Abla tug me into the abyss when Kehinde demanded a story I didn't want to tell. I told her of Abla's torment and Bob's *mojo*, of fractured Paris, of *aje* rage and scattering. We drew close and drank each other's breath.

"I can hold all of this and more." Kehinde tugged at Bob's blue *mojo* with Jumbo's hair. "What is lost or cannot be found can be conjured. We make our own story. Is that not love?" She raced through sharp cacti and beckoned me to follow. "We're not dead. We can search for Bob and Melinga. Would they abandon us? We must search for them and find love."

And so we did.

AC-DC

"That's a killer ending."

A week passed, and *Chronicles* 23 still haunted Cinnamon. Canvas #25—*Xenophilia*—was a black lake filled with broken bits of starlight. Liam calmed a horse as a demon moon wept misty tears. Kehinde caressed Taiwo's face. Why *did* Bob run off with Melinga and Somso? Cinnamon blinked away tears. She was too sentimental.

The ASM proffered a tissue with a used corner. "I told you, a killer ending."

Cinnamon sat in the back row of the studio theatre with him. "Yeah," she lied. "It is." She'd snuck in to watch a tech rehearsal of *Title Under Construction*. The script was stupid, but the actors were doing a good job, even Snow White Janice. Klaus deserved an Oscar. He acted totally into Janice's every pout and prance, right up to her death. Strung out on bad drugs, Snow White wasn't too high to take a bullet for sweet love. Every main black character died—OD'ed or got shot, and white Prince Charming was a better man for it. The playwright sat next to Director Hill with his head in his hands for the whole show. He jumped up applauding now, shouting *bravo, brava*. Cinnamon was over not getting cast. Better plays would come along.

"Your boy's good." The ASM sounded surprised.

Cinnamon pointed at the playwright. "My boy?"

"No." He leaned close enough to steal a kiss. "Klaus."

Cinnamon jerked back. "Oh. Right." If this dipstick knew they were together, why was he flirting? No one ever flirted with Cinnamon. What was wrong with him?

"You'd have been great." He poked her orca knapsack. "Fierce attitude."

"Maybe." Cinnamon hurried away from his cute-boy leer.

Klaus had no idea she was there. The Squad was supposed to hook up after Director Hill gave notes. Star Deer was back in town. Klaus had tracked her down and signed them up for a ten-week contact improv class. Cinnamon had been saving money, but was one hundred dollars short, even with Squad emergency funds. Borrowing was out of the question. She'd tell Star today. Klaus and Marie could take the class and teach her the moves.

Cinnamon slipped out to the lobby. Interns were setting up an urban fantasy landscape for a reception. Fairies clustered on fire escapes, bad witches popped out of chimneys, good witches made books come to life. In the bathroom, sopranos and altos harmonized over the stalls. They were so yummy-chummy, Cinnamon wanted to gag.

"I thought Hill was giving notes," Cinnamon said at the sink.

"He told us to rest up for the opening—and that was it."

"Rest?" Cinnamon splashed water at her face. Klaus would be doing contact every afternoon after school. Star Deer worked you till muscles refused to defy gravity.

"You're Klaus's friend?" a vaguely familiar curly-haired girl asked.

"Yeah." How could everybody know? "So?"

"Nothing." The girl sneered.

Cinnamon hated teen melodrama. She escaped to the box office. Klaus and Marie weren't there. The Green Room was empty and dark. Nobody was in the studio theatre except downtrodden techies bitching about idiot actors. The Squad had forty minutes to get to Star's studio by bus. That was cutting it close. Star didn't do colored people's time. Cinnamon raced up to the gallery of the stars. At the landing, Klaus was hunched under a picture of Medea riding a chariot to the stars. Cinnamon swallowed a cheer. Klaus radiated distress. Seeing Cinnamon, he clutched his belly and glanced across the landing. Loud voices got muffled by a mound of velour curtains in the center of the gallery. Cinnamon recognized Marie's R&B bellow. Extracting an explanation from Klaus could take forever. She bounded around the dusty velour, and—

Marie was kissing Janice Fucking Snow White.

A long sweet kiss—Cinnamon knew exactly how it tasted.

"Both of you?" Janice smirked at Cinnamon over Marie's shoulder. "With that big ugly dyke?

"Shut up about her!" Marie didn't see Cinnamon.

"I don't believe it." Janice shook bouncy curls.

Cinnamon missed what Marie said next. She imagined pounding the cute out of Janice's smirk, but her heart was breaking and her muscles were soggy. She stumbled back toward the stairs. Klaus blocked her escape. Given her weakened condition, he was as strong as she was. She feinted around him.

"Wait," Klaus sputtered. He knew what was going on. He was a part of it.

"You too, huh? Why?"

Busted, Klaus almost fell down the steep steps. Cinnamon grabbed him before he broke his stupid neck. He clung to her, his heart pounding.

Janice barged past them. "I don't do crowds. Too freaky deaky for me."

"Hau ab, Arschloch!" Fuck off asshole—Cinnamon cussed at Janice in German.

She hurried down the steps. "Fuck you too!" The fear in her voice was thrilling.

Klaus pushed Cinnamon back to the gallery. Marie sank down in a puddle of braids under a photo of Ariel in a kitchen-sink drama. Cinnamon stomped around the heap of black velour several times. The hormone drip was frying her brain. Time was herky-jerky. Would she have kissed Ariel in a secret alcove? Maybe. It never came up.

"Why aren't you saying anything, Cinnamon?" Klaus had to ask.

Her heart was broken. Everything could be broken. Why speak?

"I don't think I can do *us* anymore," he said solemnly. "The three of us."

Marie rolled her eyes and snorted. "Is that supposed to be noble?"

"No."

"Janice wasn't interested in me until she thought there was an *us*," Marie shouted.

"I kissed her too," Klaus confessed.

Cinnamon snorted. "I figured that out already."

"Kissing her does nothing for me." Marie rubbed her weird hand across her mouth and got a shock. "*Owa.*" Served her right.

Klaus shuddered. "It's no good with Janice."

"I spent a year crushed-out on that Snow White bitch. Since I heard she was AC-DC."

"AC-DC?" Klaus scowled.

"Alternating current. She likes boys and girls," Marie explained. Klaus groaned.

"Why?" Cinnamon did a melodramatic dead-person fall into the velour.

"I went crazy for a moment." Marie crawled toward her. "You never go crazy?"

Cinnamon snarled at Marie who stopped crawling just out of range. "Quit moaning, Klaus." Cinnamon hugged her orca. "You two broke my heart. Not the other way around."

"Janice told Klaus guys aren't my thing," Marie said. "That's why he's mad."

"Not only that," Klaus said. "I—"

"I made an exception for you."

"*Danke schön.*" Klaus dripped bitter German thanks at her.

"You happened to me, Klaus, and I didn't fight it." Marie hid in her hair.

Klaus glared at Cinnamon. "Were you making an exception? Only girls for you?"

"I don't usually like anybody," Cinnamon shouted. "It was better that way."

This startled Klaus. The wild look drained from his face and cheeks. "Are we breaking up over Janice Fucking Snow White?"

"Janice will tell everybody." Marie sounded panicked.

"Is that all you're worried about?" Cinnamon shook her head, disgusted.

"I'm not a coward, but Janice knows my sister," Marie muttered.

Cinnamon hissed. "And you're the good daughter."

"Janice won't tell," Klaus said. "We know her AC-DC secret."

"She doesn't have to tell. People see us and make up their own minds." Cinnamon smacked the velour. A dust cloud brought on a sneezing jag.

"Gesundheit," Klaus said. "We were trying to warn her about the ASM."

"Yeah. You think you know yourself, then you're kissing someone you don't even like anymore. How is that possible?" Marie stared at Cinnamon.

"Why ask me?" Cinnamon stood up. "I was thinking of ditching you both before you ditched me for Janice or somebody cute or just did each other."

Klaus stood up and handed her a tissue. "You've been waiting for us to—"

"Betray you." Marie jumped up next to him.

"I see how you watch us. Since the audition." Klaus did Cinnamon's full body scowl.

Marie nailed it too. "Yeah."

"I was right." Cinnamon tried to walk around them. They blocked her.

"You never wanted to trust us," Klaus said.

Cinnamon backed up. "But I was right."

"Were you?" they said in sync.

Cinnamon sputtered.

"We can't be late." Marie pulled them out the emergency door. It shrieked at them running along the loading docks to the bus stop.

Flying

Star Deer's studio was spare—hardwood floors, mats, mirrors, and a high ceiling. Windows in the rafters offered natural light. The focus was bodies in space. Star was tanned a deep brown from a trip to New Mexico. Tumbling and flying, she looked fierce and beautiful. She and Daddy had been so close. Cinnamon wondered if Opal was jealous of Star. Jealousy had been a vague notion until this afternoon. If people squandered your trust, what should you do if you still liked them, if you still *lusted* after them in tight leotards and baggy crops?

Star tolerated their late arrival, offered Cinnamon a discount payment plan, and smiled as they fell on their asses. The whole class fell a lot, so the Squad fit right in. Did Cinnamon have a Squad anymore? Klaus and Marie fronted like everything was hunky-dory. Cinnamon should never have come. And why the hell was she running on to Star about the hoodoo spell she wanted to do for Opal, Raven, and everybody—a spell she was no longer sure she could pull off. "Everybody's stuck on stupid. How can I undo the bad magic if I don't know the *important shit*? Like about Daddy getting shot."

"A healing ceremony?" Star arched her eyebrow like Marie. "And you come to me because?" She wiped a towel across her face.

"We found each other doing contact," Cinnamon replied. "It didn't look like that today—"

"We're usually better," Marie said. Klaus shook his head, agreeing.

"You were distracted." Star blinked slowly, jetlagged. "Focus. You'll be fine."

"So, you'll help?" Klaus grinned. Did he think she was cute for an older lady? Another fascinating colored girl? The class was full of black and Indian girls—

"What does Opal say?" Star was *Ms. Respect-Your-Elders.* "Is she feeling better?"

"Mom's driving bus again. I'm meeting her after work." Cinnamon had almost chickened out, but Redwood wouldn't let her. "Mom's on my side these days." She hoped.

Star's eyes crinkled, tiny lines of joy radiating from a warm smile. "OK."

"Before we go"—Marie tugged Cinnamon's braids—"let me catch you. Come on."

"From me to Marie and back." Klaus bounced on his toes.

Even in a good mood, Cinnamon preferred throwing and catching people to being tossed. She hated flying at anxious, skinny dancers with her hundred-seventy-pound mass. Mad, she had to weigh two hundred pounds. "What're you two trying to prove?"

"It's gravity, balance, not size, not brute strength." Marie took a wide stance. "If we focus, we can do it. Trust me."

"We're not breaking up until after," Klaus said. "After the celebration."

"Who says?" Cinnamon said.

"We're not petty," Marie declared. "We've got a mission."

"Yes," Klaus said. "We do right. Two votes to one."

"Since when is love a democracy?" Cinnamon almost laughed.

"Verzeihen ist die beste Rache," Klaus said simultaneously with—

"Forgiveness is the best revenge," Marie said.

Star pretended not to follow their exchange.

"This is a conspiracy, right?" Cinnamon ran before they could answer. Klaus lifted her. She flew. Marie caught her for a breath, whirled her over a shoulder. Braids and beads snagged. They both faltered for a second. And then Cinnamon was flying again toward Klaus who tumbled with her through a string of forward rolls dissipating their energy.

"Again." Star pulled them up. "Tie your hair back. It's exactly the move you need."

After ten times, muscle fatigue halted the rehearsal.

"What's your fee?" Cinnamon asked. "Artists should get paid."

Star laughed. "Let me show you what I got at Opal's infamous tag sale." She led them to a back room filled with fabric and sculptures. Tapestries covered the walls. The rugs were master artworks too. Four of Raven's paintings—an open-air museum in Paris, Redwood and Aidan at the Chicago Fair, a Wild West Show, and Opal and Raven in a desert flash flood—hung around a giant aluminum foil sculpture.

"Joe made this sculpture altar from junk he dumpster dives." Star touched a three-legged bench. "Toilet paper rolls, dead light-bulbs, broken furniture, and busted TVs. He wraps stuff in foil or coats it with silver paint. For Eshu, he says, and the spaces be-tween things."

"Griot Joe?" Klaus asked.

"He's a good friend of Raven's. He and his crow have been crashing here while I was away. I'm a sucker for hard luck stories." Star folded her arms over her chest. "He told me Guardians might be looking for him. You three fit the description."

"We want him at the celebration," Marie said.

"Can we use these paintings in the Home Exhibition?" Cinna-mon said.

Star put an arm around Cinnamon's shoulders. "Opal threat-ened to burn what didn't sell. I bought them for you. Dr. Bug-Man bought two."

"Oh."

Star sighed. "Raven was painting a science-fiction epic—an alien meets the orisha kind of thing. He painted his friends into the major characters. Sekou turned the Rain Forest Lounge into a giant graphic novel, *The Chronicles of the Great Wanderer.* I danced at the opening, but . . ." She paused, swaying, unsteady on her feet.

The Squad caught her, defying gravity with their shoulders. They clumped together, holding her up.

"I didn't see what happened," Star stammered. "I was in the bathroom. I came out after the shooting was over. Opal can't for-give me . . . I get it but . . . Sorry, sorry, uhm, Lexy saw more than anybody. Get him to tell you."

Star had no idea when Joe would return. Klaus wrote him a quick invitation. Marie splurged on a cab to get Cinnamon to her rendezvous with Opal on time. Redwood had suggested that she and Klaus go along as backup. They piled in the cab, being so sweet—feeling guilty? Weren't they always like that? New *Chronicles* pages glowed in Cinnamon's orca. Instead of awkward conversation, they read *Chronicles* 24 silently as the Ethiopian cabbie sang a love song to someone half a world away.

Chronicles 24: Tree of Forgetfulness

One gunshot at the Rain Forest Lounge pierced Kehinde's heart, and left me without love. The bullet slammed into Raven Cooper's head, and I lost my mind. I scattered. One bullet stole most of the twentieth century from me. Years smear across my memory.

I want to blame that bullet for everything, but actually, after we lost Bob and Melinga, America was a chimera, phantom stories . . . People danced in the streets. Poets turned shadows into praise songs. Bridges arched across rivers and rocky ravines. My gnarled fingers remember working on the railroad or in mines, ravaging the ground for coal to burn and gold to hoard. Kehinde sang for our supper. I disappeared for tips. Chicago exploded every night. It grew taller, wider, louder, sweeter. Buildings climbed on my back and over the treetops, crowding the stars, shifting the wind, and banishing daylight. People burst in from every direction and dimension. Leaving their stories behind, they became night watch on other people's glory. Underground railroads no longer carried freedom fighters, but day laborers, horn players, revolutionaries, robber barons, and jazz singers. A cacophony of attitudes, smells, and beliefs rewrote my nerves. Everywhere a different truth was spoken. I don't know who to remember, what to forget, who to believe. So much joy and suffering, it was terrible and beautiful.

Writing now, I imagine who I might have been. I make a whole cloth of the fragments. Akan weavers unravel the threads of foreign fabrics and reuse the silk threads to make their cloth stories. The Akan say:

Don't let me die in the day,
Don't let me die at night,
Don't let me die at all,
But let me die.

Knife Boy

Klaus and Marie sauntered into an ice cream shop to wait for Cinnamon. Opal parked her bus in a tight spot, like slipping a hand into a glove. She was shaky on her feet coming down four steps to the ground. A few days on the job and she looked wasted. Seeing Cinnamon, Opal smiled broadly and hugged her so tightly neither one of them could get a breath. "You look beautiful. What're you wearing?"

"Iris can make anybody look good."

Opal fussed over her braids and Celtic buckle. "You styling the world, huh?"

They went to the deli Daddy used to take them to after Opal finished a shift. The loud traffic faded behind thick glass walls. A ferocious waitress hurled quips at regulars and charmed or scared away newcomers. Cinnamon and Opal sat in a quiet corner. Opal ordered corned beef on rye with hot mustard and a pickle. Cinnamon got a bagel smothered in garlic-and-chives cream cheese. They were both on good behavior.

"I haven't been here since before." Opal wanted a cigarette. She chewed at the pickle.

Cinnamon had so much she wanted to say, she was suddenly weepy.

Opal handed her a napkin. "Talk to me, baby."

A young white man pushed through the grimy front door. His bright orange hair was a mess. He blew a crooked nose. The waitress barked at him. He pointed at Opal's back. The waitress shrugged. He strode over. Opal turned and gasped. She knew him.

"Sorry," he sputtered. "They told me you come here after work." He held up the HERO MOM article. "I had to find you." He threw his arms around Opal. She hugged him back. It was knife boy, in the flesh.

"You're real!" Cinnamon hugged him too. Secretly, she suspected that, despite the article, Polaroids, and long knife in Opal's closet, the bus tale was wishful mythology—like swimming with seals or having two people like Cinnamon the way she liked them. *Proof* made Cinnamon's nerves tingle. Knife boy and Opal chatted. His girlfriend had ditched him—not the end of the world. He had a job and was doing graduate work at Pitt. He ate a grilled cheese and guzzled a pop, glad to see Opal looking good. She was glad he was doing fine too. When he left, Opal's eyes were wet. Cinnamon pretended not to notice and handed her a napkin.

"Your grandparents, your great aunt, they're good for you," Opal said.

"So are you."

"Look at the weight you lost and all A's."

"I always get all A's."

"I'll be back. When I'm a fit mother again."

"You visited Daddy every day. Why didn't you—"

"Driving that bus, I get tired out. There's peace at Becca's."

"You said you burned Daddy's painting—"

"I said a lot of crap." Opal waved at the waitress. "Can we have more pickles?"

"Did Daddy cheat on you?" Cinnamon drank scalding tea.

"What?"

"With Star Deer or some fancy lady?"

"No."

The waitress approached with a stack of pickle spears.

"Did he cheat on you with a man?"

"Hell no. Shush." Opal snatched the plate. "Thanks."

The waitress laughed. "You're paying for 'em. Don't thank me."

Opal waited until the waitress walked behind the counter. "Your daddy cheated on me with his art." She looked out the window. "Star kinda helped us get together, out in the desert." She grabbed Cinnamon's hands. "I wish you knew me before, when I was . . . I wasn't always a mess. People aren't only the worst things they've done."

"I know. We're fixing up the house, hanging Daddy's paintings, and clearing out the bad energy, so you can come home. When you're ready. I'm not telling you what to do or anything." Talking a mile a minute, Cinnamon told Opal about the exhibition and birthday party. Calling it hoodoo would have upset her. "Lexy has two paintings. Star had four. There were twenty-three under your bed. Sorry for going through your stuff. We're only missing one painting from Sekou's list. That's good, isn't it? My Squad is doing a show at the nursing home for Daddy's fifty-eighth birthday."

"Redwood says you three are something else."

"You'll come, won't you?"

"Don't beg me, baby, you know I hate that."

"You have to come. It won't be the same without you."

"We'll see. Aidan loves the song you're writing. You want this last pickle?"

Kevin drove Opal back to Becca's. Marie called another cab for the Squad, supposedly so Kevin wouldn't have to drive all over creation. Actually, she and Klaus wanted a report and maybe a little more time with Cinnamon. Doing penance?

"My mom's cool. She'll be there." Cinnamon wanted this to be true. After five minutes of awkward silence she said, "Let's read *Chronicles 25*."

Chronicles 25: Flash Flood

From Chicago to San Francisco to Pittsburgh, from 1893 to 1942 to 1982, Kehinde and I searched for Bob and Melinga, for love. We never gave up. As Melinga grew older, we looked for her children. Finally, we searched for grandchildren. A good life.

A clear memory: we first met Raven Cooper and Opal Jones in desert moonlight, kicking sand at the stars. It was 1970, or 1971, in New Mexico. Slogging by adobe houses at twilight, my mind was blank as hot sand. I carried a heavy pack—a few precious possessions, bedroll, food, and water. Kehinde complained about tired blood and achy old joints, yet kept pace with me. Her small pack weighed nothing. The *aje* modulated poisons to keep Kehinde fit and spry. Praising the dry heat and her stamina, I made a stupid joke on flash floods as we passed the umpteenth warning sign. Kehinde wasted no energy laughing.

Star Deer, a dancer friend, had scrawled a map to her cabin on a napkin and given us a key. We could use the place, even if she wasn't there. Our money was low. It was a good option. We'd walked miles; Star assumed we'd be driving. Stumbling over rocks and prickly cactus, I got us lost. The home star was heading for the horizon. The moon rose and clouds rolled in. Ozone tickled my throat. Flash flood warnings weren't a joke anymore. As the clouds got deep, we scrambled through scratchy ankle growth that turned into a cactus patch. Desperate for an overview, we climbed up to a ledge.

Internal combustion engines with poor mufflers echoed in the ravine. A stampede of angry machines approached from several directions. We thought to climb down and flag a vehicle when Kehinde spotted a shotgun poking from the window of a pickup truck. The occupants yelled nonsense in a desert English difficult to comprehend. They gunned the engine. We leaned back into the shadow of the sandstone.

Raven Cooper roared up on a shiny motorbike and halted under us. He hopped from his saddle and bent over a cholla cactus at the end of a bloom. A spiny, barbed mess of purple blossoms caught the last bursts of starlight. Raven was oblivious to everything else. His focus was compelling. Kehinde nodded. We resolved to know him better. A woman dashed through scraggly undergrowth, pumping her arms and flying with each step. That was Opal, running from the truck that snaked along the road toward us. Opal swerved to avoid a collision with Raven, and a cactus smacked her mouth. A barb ripped her lip, and blood flowed. Balance proved impossible; she tumbled onto the ground. Raven let her catch some oxygen then offered a hand. The pickup sped in, spraying dust at them as it came to a halt. Kehinde drew a blade, always wary of armed raiders in the night. Opal stood up slowly without Raven's help. Her spirit was compelling. We resolved to know her also.

"You fellas lost? Storm's coming." Raven waved at dark clouds. Two men grunted in harmony. No sign of a gun. "This ravine will be a raging river soon. You don't want to get caught messing 'round in that." Raven sounded reasonable, as if rape and murder weren't in the air. Opal studied him.

"Hey, Raven, how you doing?" The truck men knew him.

"Is it that bad?" The driver stuck his head out the window, sounding reasonable too. Wind snatched his big cowboy hat away. Rain splashed his eyes. The hat skipped down the road. "Oooh shit. Turn on the radio, Frank, see what they say."

"You're out fifty bucks." Frank glanced up at us sitting on the ledge. Kehinde's blade glinted. He slugged the driver's shoulder. "Nothing but static on the radio."

"Damn." The driver squinted at the sky. "Fuck this. The road could be underwater in a snap." He spun the steering wheel and yelled. "You all better take cover." He glanced at the truck bed. Nobody asked for a ride. "Be seeing you folks later." They sped off without retrieving the hat. The storm chased after them leaving clear sky over us.

Had I imagined the gun?

"You know them?" Opal quietly accused Raven of a crime.

He shrugged. "Were they after you?"

Opal shuddered.

"Skip lets Frank talk him into stupid shit. No excuse for either of them."

Opal spit blood, shook fear from her body, and stared at Raven's hair snapping in the storm's updraft. No dreads then, just a thick mane of black. He had smooth brown skin, large hazel eyes, and high cheekbones. He wore a Navajo squash blossom necklace, tight jeans, and cowboy boots.

"You goin' say anything more?" Raven asked.

Opal's heart pounded. Sweat dripped from every pore. She scanned the horizon then locked her eyes on him. He didn't flinch or blink. After several long minutes her muscles relaxed, and she licked at the blood on her lips. A pulse spiked across Raven's nerves. Opal almost smiled. Perhaps she read his magnetic field. He was forty-something and all muscle, sinew, and intensity.

"What are you staring at?" Raven growled.

"You," she said. "'Cause, damn, you are pretty." She grinned. "That ain't only concern in your eyes." She read him like an open book.

More menacing clouds rolled in from the west.

Raven huffed. "I'm not a tourist attraction or a goddamned museum exhibit."

"Flesh and blood, huh? Glad to hear it." Opal shook sand from an Afro. She must have been twenty-five. A flimsy T-shirt hugged her breasts and belly. Running shorts clutched buttocks and hips. She was a womanly spectacle, sparking Raven's nerves. He wasn't as bold as she and didn't speak passion. It was a tense situation. "Don't know what I'd do if you were an on-display-do-not-touch kinda experience." Opal grinned.

"What do you want, woman, talking at me like that?" Raven said.

"What you think?" Opal raised an eyebrow. "You aren't the type I usually go for."

"What type is that?"

"Who cares? It's time to change." She shook and flung sweat and sand at him. "Those crackers got my blood up. I want to kill somebody, get high, or make love."

Raven laughed. "That's quite a come-on."

"Oughta be a law or at least a city ordinance against someone fine as you riding around, causing traffic jams and accidents." Her leg muscles cramped. She bent over to stretch and grinned at him from between her thighs. Kehinde put away her blade and chuckled. Watching Opal work tension out, Raven took short breaths.

"What are you doing out here?" He kept reaching for reason. "Who are you?"

"Nobody yet." She stood up and stepped closer to him. Big lazy splats of rain got sucked up by hot sand and turned to mist. Kehinde held a Navajo blanket over our heads. "You smell like a painter," Opal said. "Catching the whirlwind, the lightning, and throwing it on a canvas, huh?"

Raven's back stiffened. "How do you know that?"

"I know things sometimes, out of nowhere. It's like I can read minds—if there's a good connection. My name is Opal Jones, pleased to meet you." She stuck out her hand, unafraid, trusting a good connection. "You're a storm child if ever I saw one." She gazed into his painterly eyes, totally in lust. "Your call, sugar."

Raven clasped Opal's rough hand with thin delicate fingers. "I stood in the lightning once, it knocked me down, stopped my heart, but I lived."

"A big heart like yours—" Opal put her hand on Raven's chest. "It'd take more than one bolt to stop that beat."

"Is that so?" Raven ran his hands through the beads of water in her Afro. He shook wetness at the cactus blossoms.

Kehinde gripped my arm. Melinga would have had elemental children and grandchildren, reaching into the spaces between things, pouring libation to the master of uncertainty. The signs would be easy to recognize.

"Romance after running for your life? You sure about that?" Raven said.

"You got wide eyes seeing clear into next week."

Raven lurched back from her, as if she'd punched him. "Don't tell me. You had a medicine woman dream," he said.

"What?" Opal said.

"You came out West to sweat with the people and have a vision, right?"

"Hell no. I'm just appreciating a fine hunk of manhood." Her hands on her hips, her chin a blade aimed at him, she was a fine doorful of a woman as Liam might say.

"Please don't tell me your great-grandma was a Cherokee princess."

"Cherokee didn't have princesses, no tipis neither." She walked a spiral in the dust getting closer to him again. "You Cherokee? Indian blood turning you brown?"

"Seminole." Raven eyed her, ready and not ready to risk love with a bold stranger.

Opal bounced on her springy calf muscles. "I ran hurdles in high school. Gotta quit smoking. It's ruining my game." She enjoyed defying gravity. "You get a lot of tourists who want to go back to nature with you?"

"Not runners." He folded his hands over his chest. "Other types."

Opal laughed. "White folk always getting in between everybody."

"Who says these types are only white?"

She wiggled her ankles. "Don't even know your name, and you're mad at me."

"Raven Cooper."

"Really?"

"That's what I use in the galleries. My real name's for friends."

"What if I call you Lightning?"

He grinned at her. "Seriously. Can you read minds?"

"I'd like to see your art, be your friend." She walked close again, feeling his pulse, testing his magnetic field. "I've been around the block. I've got a son and a few busted dreams. If you're married or don't like what you see, I'll keep on running. That ole motel gotta be somewhere. But if you're a free man, a man of adventure . . ."

"You'll what?"

"Ask you to buy me an ice cream."

He laughed and dabbed the blood off her lips. "Does that hurt?"

"Not too much."

The wind howled through the ravine. In a flash, buckets of water fell.

"Get on," Raven yelled. Opal hopped with him onto the long motorbike seat. He stomped the pedal several times. The engine didn't turn over. "Damn."

"Climb up here!" Kehinde yelled.

The clouds came down fast. Raven and Opal had no time to be mad at us for spying. As we hauled them up to our ledge, the desert turned to a water world. A river carried Raven's motorcycle away. In the huddle of our bodies, I illuminated Star's map with a flashlight. Eshu favored our meeting. Raven had rented the studio next to Star's and sometimes stayed overnight in the loft. He had a map of the desert in his body. He pointed up. Opal was uncertain about the slick steep surface. With a grunt, Kehinde scrambled up ahead of us. Raven and Opal followed. I came last.

Bolts of electricity crackled and thunder boomed. Below us water sluiced through the ravine, ripping and roaring like a happy child. When we reached level ground, the rain stopped. We were soaked, and the air was icy. Kehinde complained of achy joints. Opal took the pack from her back and tramped on, not looking to see if we followed. For hours, we borrowed her energy to slog through wet sand. The lock on Star's door was rusted shut, so Kehinde and I stayed in Raven's loft. He and Opal made a braid of their bodies on a drop cloth in his studio. Cyclones of trucks, billboards, airplanes, adobe houses, factories, and busted skyscrapers surrounded us in vivid surreal colors. Beyond exhaustion, even I feel asleep.

"Are you too good to be true?" Opal whispered. I was awake. It was morning.

"Maybe you're bringing out the best in me," Raven replied.

"I don't want to be nobody's muse."

"I like whatever I bring out of you."

Raven painted the future on her belly, breasts, and thighs. Opal thought it a shame to wash such beauty off in the shower. She showed us the image. I can't remember it, but we talked all day about the tomorrows we might make.

"Usually, I'm not like this," Opal told us.

"How are you?" Kehinde asked.

"Not optimistic, that's for damn sure." Opal smiled. "I'd like to be better. I need to be around the right people for that."

"Ashe," Kehinde murmured.

"She evokes the power to make things be," I translated.

"Can people change?" Opal shivered.

Raven hugged her. He poured hot tea for everyone and laid a table of biscuits, fruit, and fragrant beans. "*Gilidinehuyi*, Cherokee for lightning—Star Deer muttered that when I came to, after being struck." He showed the scar on his back where the bolt had hit. "I went walking in an electrical storm, the tallest thing for miles except Star, out there dancing. She says I pushed her out of the way. Is that possible? My heart stopped; I blacked out. I'm not a reliable witness. In the dark, I heard *Gilidinehuyi*. Star banged my chest and blew breath in my throat. I wanted to know what the word meant. *Gilidinehuyi* brought me back from the dead. It's my secret name."

Opal buttered a biscuit and stuffed it in Raven's mouth. "If you dared to come back from the dead, so can I."

Chewing, Raven put on a record—Marvin Gaye:

Talk to me, so you can see, what's going on

He and Opal shimmied around the studio. Kehinde pulled me up to slow dance.

Two of Melinga's children had found us. So had love.

Book VI

Pittsburgh, PA, 1987 & Pittsburgh, PA, 1982

There is another world, and it is in this one.

—Paul Éluard

Mallemaroking

Only one thing a BMW can do for me, and that's drive me to a Caddy.
Sekou's quip was as quiet as the mist drizzling down Cinnamon's cheeks. He'd been silent the last few weeks. Without her Squad it was hard to tell memory from ghost talk, especially with Uncle Clarence fussing. His fancy BMW had died, no warning. Wilson's Towing hauled the disabled car to the shop, and Kevin was driving Clarence to Opal's house with Cinnamon and Aunt Becca in the back seat. As they cruised through the Hill District, Clarence sulked. Riding shotgun in a beat-up Toyota offended his butt.

How could German engineers have failed him like that? Sekou was louder this time, but Clarence never tuned in to the spirit channel. *He's such a tightwad. How much you want to bet, Clarence still has the first nickel he earned?* Cinnamon chuckled.

"What's so damned funny?" Clarence said. "Are we trying to hit every pothole?"

"Just for you." Becca squeezed Kevin's hunky muscles.

Old and all, Kevin was a doorful of a man. Every day now, he was breaking records with Becca. You didn't have to be a fast-talking shark of a lawyer to make a woman happy. Kevin smiled into the rearview mirror. He enjoyed adventures with Becca's wild family. Getting him in on the mission had taken only one piece of Iris's chocolate cake.

As Clarence busted out of the car into cold April drizzle, Cinnamon popped the question. "We're doing a celebration for Daddy at the nursing home. Want to come?"

Becca exchanged glances with Kevin as he locked the car.

"A celebration seems premature," Clarence said.

"That's not what I'm asking." Cinnamon didn't want to invite her uncle: that was Iris. She and Star Deer wanted her to invite everybody.

"Way too soon to get slap happy."

Rain growled at Clarence.

"That attack dog don't like your tone." Becca took off her three-inch heels. "I'm not ruining my hair." She charged up slippery steps, faster than everybody.

"Why do people own killer dogs?" Clarence stepped back from the fence.

Rain looked to Cinnamon, ready to snap the chain and bite Clarence's head off.

"Hush, Rain. This is your weather. Sit." Rain dropped down. "Good girl." Cinnamon tossed a treat from lunch over the fence and headed up behind Becca.

"After you," Kevin said to Clarence.

"Raven just rolls his eyeballs around." Clarence raced up two steps at a time. "If he wakes up, he'll be disabled, maybe severely." He slammed the screen door for emphasis, barely missing Kevin's nose. "Sorry, man, didn't see you there."

"You're on a roll, counselor." Kevin stepped in behind him. "But—"

"Somebody has to be realistic. Raven's muscles won't work right. He might not walk or talk, and forget picking up a brush again." Clarence halted at the kitchen island. The Wanderer burst into this world from the spaces between things. Only a painting, but Clarence freaked, as if he'd turned the corner into a horror movie. He gaped at Raven's canvases hanging around the living room and kitchen. "Who put this surreal Sun Ra stuff up?"

"Aunt Iris helped me find Mom's stash." Cinnamon didn't mention Star Deer. Noble Indians and hoodoo Negroes got on Clarence's nerves.

"It was too gloomy," Becca said. Her iridescent hat and dress fit right in.

"Wait till I get the lights on a dimmer," Cinnamon said. "This corner wasn't up at the Rain Forest Lounge." She pointed at the former TV alcove. "They're untitled. Daddy wasn't done."

"No wonder Opal's staying with you, Rebecca." Clarence's voice was shaky. "Raven lived to throw paint. He always said, *Man, when I get too feeble to paint, take me out back and shoot me.*"

"Yeah," Cinnamon said, "whenever you harped on getting a *real* job. Daddy said it was paint or die."

"He won't be the Raven you lost."

"We don't care. He'll be who he is. We're ready."

Clarence wagged his finger. "He won't be the man who got shot, the man everybody loved. He'll be a stranger, and that'll be hard, maybe *impossible*." He paused, a real drama queen like everyone in the family. "That's *if* the man ever wakes all the way up. This isn't a grade-B soap opera where the dead come walking back into your life."

"He's not dead," Cinnamon said.

"You're right." Clarence stood stiff and tall, his courtroom persona in place. "Maybe dead would be better for him and for us."

Cinnamon had already done this stupid argument with herself, over and over without getting anywhere. Nowhere to get to.

"Don't give me those death-ray eyes, Rebecca," Clarence shouted. "I'm speaking the unvarnished truth. Stupid convictions are more dangerous foes of truths than lies."

He's quoting Nietzsche, Sekou hissed. *Don't let him get away with that!*

How could she argue with Nietzsche? Cinnamon grinned. "So drop your stupid convictions and try an open mind." Kevin whistled at her smart comeback.

"Are you going to the celebration or not?" Becca held up a folder of papers.

Clarence refused the folder and prowled the kitchen and living room. "Is Opal going to spend the rest of her life taking care of a cripple?"

"That's her choice, isn't it?" Becca said.

Clarence stumbled by two paintings of the Wanderer eating zigzags of electricity. "How are they going to get a wheelchair up and down twenty-three steps? And a second floor? *I* can't fit through that ancient bathroom door. How's he going to pee?"

"I know a good carpenter." Becca smiled at Kevin. He was an old-style handyman who did woodwork, plumbing, even electrical under the table. Clarence and everybody hired him on the cheap, instead of pricey union people. That's how he and Becca met.

Clarence snorted. "How will Opal pay for even budget renovations if she's taking care of Raven twenty-four seven and can't work? Driving her shift, she's already sick as a dog. She won't take a dime from anybody." He bumped into Kevin. "How many times did Raven run out on her?"

"Beats me," Kevin replied. "I didn't know them, *before*."

Clarence shuddered and kept moving. "Did Raven ever sell anything? If you're not making money, you're making excuses. He might as well have been shaking a tin cup."

"I'm an artist like Daddy," Cinnamon said, "painting the world with words and gestures. That's a hard road."

"It's a dead end. For you too."

"You don't get to write my future." Talking slow, Cinnamon barely controlled her rage. "No matter how reasonable you sound."

"You're smart as a whip, little girl, I'll give you that. But you're not movie star material. So put your megawatt brains to good use." Clarence made a sharp turn to avoid Kehinde whirling a cutlass in a desert storm, but ran into Star Deer dancing with spirit rocks. He was surrounded. "Why did I come across town for a party invite? You backward Negroes don't know how to use phones?"

"Don't get mean." Cinnamon spoke softly.

"Iris wanted you to see the paintings," Becca said. "You've hardly looked."

Clarence halted and stared at the floor. "The truth is mean, not me."

Cinnamon rolled her eyes. "Sekou used to say that shit when he got nasty."

"Shit? You're comparing me to your dead brother?"

The faggot, druggy, suicide! Sekou chuckled. *Don't give up, Sis. He's on the run.*

Iris said they needed Clarence's help, otherwise . . . "Maybe

Sekou used *your* line to weasel out of sticky situations. Look, we can't manage the impossible by ourselves."

"Cornball wisdom doesn't work on me." Clarence headed for the door.

"Your battery died or worse, remember?" Kevin said.

"So, call me a cab!" Nobody moved. "Cinnamon's too young to see what she's in for."

"Nothing wrong with being young and naïve and fresh," Kevin said. "How else you goin' change the world back 'round right?"

"It's never been right." Clarence groaned. "You're one of those throwback Negroes who thinks if we find our roots in Mother Africa we'll live happily ever after."

"Don't Negro me." Kevin stood his ground. "Any plan but yours must be dead in the water before it gets started good?"

"I didn't shoot Raven and leave him for dead." Clarence sat on the couch. It swallowed his behind; he scrambled up. "I just want what's best for everyone."

Becca slipped her arm through his. "You're always saying we don't let you help."

"You and Opal never listen to a word I say." Clarence eyed Cinnamon. "Raven and Opal quit each other, you know."

Becca waved the folder in his face. "I have something important for you to do."

"Right before he got shot," Clarence said. "He split."

"Hush." Becca patted him. "We got legal issues."

Clarence talked over his sister's head. "They were always breaking up."

"How many wives have you had?" Cinnamon blurted. "And other women too? Maybe even a few stray kids?"

Clarence gasped.

Kevin grabbed Cinnamon and tried to shake the mess out of her. "Don't get mean either, hear me?" He let Cinnamon go.

Clarence snorted. "Young people, talking in your face like that—"

"Serves you right." Becca pulled him toward the kitchen table.

"Quit acting the fool and listen to me. Raven and Opal were never married, that's the thing."

"Where's the phone? I'll call my own goddamned cab." Clarence crashed around the room, trying to avoid the paintings. He snatched up the receiver on the end table, almost knocking over a lamp. He banged the hook for a dial tone. He couldn't hoodoo it like Miz Redwood. "Is this just for show?" He wanted to smash the phone. His temper was worse than Opal's, a fire-breathing dragon burning up on the inside . . .

Yo, Sis, don't let your mouth write checks your ass can't cash! Keep your eyes on the prize.

"I didn't mean the stuff about the kids, Uncle Clarence." Cinnamon did spell #7, *talking love instead of screaming.* "You're serious about your responsibilities. I admire that." Almost true. "We're serious about Daddy. No matter if it's hard, harder, or impossible." Almost an apology.

"Opal won't throw him away without a fight," Becca said.

"What the hell is *Mallemaroking*?" Clarence said. A painting with this title in bold block letters hung over the elders' hoodoo altar.

"Sekou did the titles," Cinnamon explained. "A dictionary-boy thing."

Mallemaroking was a black, white, and purple rendering of *La Vérité* lost in fog. Heaving jugs to their lips, sailors danced on the deck; Kehinde sliced phantom enemies; Somso was a sensuous undulation by her side; Bob, his cap pulled low, cavorted in the shadows; Liam pranced beside him, tattoos shifting in candlelight; the Wanderer leapt from frothy waves, a mermaid/merman half as big as the boat, and Melinga clung to claws and seaweed hair. Everyone looked happy.

"So what's *Mallemaroking* mean?" Clarence asked. "I know you know."

"It's a synonym for carousing," Cinnamon replied. "Literally, the carousing of drunken sailors on icebound Greenland whaling ships."

"You don't say." He managed a weak smile.

Clarence is a sucker for juicy words he's never heard before. He used to enjoy ideas he'd never thought of too.

"Yeah," Cinnamon muttered. When they were younger, arguing with him was fun.

Clarence was grooming you to be the next lawyer in the family. I was going to be a fancy journalist.

Before Raven got shot . . . Cinnamon sighed. The bullet had pierced Clarence too. "The party's for everybody, even you." That came out wrong.

"Opal shouldn't waste herself on a lost cause." Clarence gripped Becca.

Becca flicked her fingers, a twentieth-century Amazon. "We need you to—"

"Raven is a mess. Opal's a cigarette puff away from a stroke."

"Mom has quit smoking," Cinnamon declared.

"Ha! Opal stays mad at me, but she might listen to reason coming from her baby sister." Clarence was actually pleading.

Becca chuckled. "Listen to me? No way!"

"Have you tried? Opal's been hurt so much." Clarence never sounded this vulnerable. "Do you want her hurt more?"

"Miz Redwood and Granddaddy want Mom to be Daddy's guardian," Cinnamon said.

"They figure you know how to do that," Kevin said. "They're too old."

"Opal lied about being his legal wife." Becca pressed the folder against Clarence's chest. "So we need you to sort that out."

Cinnamon hugged Clarence from behind and said what she thought was true. "Mom would ask you herself, but she can't stand to hear no."

"Here's your chance, man," Kevin said.

"Say yes," Cinnamon whispered. He had to say yes. He wouldn't be a lawyer if it wasn't for Opal.

You got him, Sekou said and faded.

Clarence clutched the folder.

Danger Fans

The Tempest ended its run with a matinee. Klaus, Marie, and Griot Joe had front row seats. Cinnamon quashed jealousy, a waste of good vitamins and minerals. She checked her watch: 6:30. By now, the Monongahela Playhouse was in the throes of strike and put-in for the next show. Union actors would split immediately, so snagging elusive Ariel might be impossible. Cinnamon put doubt and worry on the bus heading downtown and wrestled with Rain.

"Guests are coming." She fed Rain choice scraps from Iris's pot roast. "Don't snarl at them, OK?" Cinnamon climbed back over the fence and stomped around the porch. She was the logical choice to rig the lights and do front of house. It was her house. She was a techie, eating grit and grease and doing theatre magic. "I hate logic sometimes."

Cinnamon went inside, straightened the paintings, and checked the lights and dimmers she'd rigged for each one. The gobos made a dappled forest effect on the whole first floor. Nothing had changed up on her. She put on Sekou's T-shirt—WE'RE ALL MOSTLY SPACE AND THE FORCE TO HOLD IT TOGETHER—and threw a mud cloth robe on top: *Basiaba*, for young women at the crossroads, and *ce farin jala*, a brave man's belt. She stuck the eagle feather in her braids. Aidan's *mojo* hung from waist beads, seashells, and the Dahomey bead hung around her neck. In full armor but with shields down, she stomped back to the porch. 6:50 P.M.—Klaus and Marie should have been here already.

Commander Williams pulled up in her good German car at 7 P.M. with Mrs. Beckenbauer riding shotgun. They were bosom buddies since *Vati* went off on his "business trip" to a rehab facility. Slender, graceful Ariel got out of the back, dressed in mud cloth like Cinnamon. *Coincidental affinity*. Cinnamon's heart pounded.

She would have kissed Ariel anytime! Rain grumbled as Ariel surveyed the hilly street. One whistle from Cinnamon, and Rain muzzled it. 7:05 P.M. Marie, Klaus, and the other half of this chicken-head scenario were supposed to arrive before everybody else.

"I've biked around here." Ariel drifted past Opal's house. "There were Christmas lights."

"You biked these cliffs? In winter?" Commander Williams shuddered. "Why?"

"Are you the danger fan?" Mrs. B said, her *th* drifting toward *d*.

Ariel shrugged. "Two, three years ago, maybe five, I was doing a show. A contemporary tragedy." The photo hung in the Playhouse gallery of the stars. "We had tough rehearsals. I couldn't find my character. One evening I biked off into sleet. There's a hairpin turn down that way." Ariel's muscles tensed. "Dusk. I couldn't see a thing, thinking so hard. I almost wiped out." A story storm had Ariel: Cinnamon read the signs from twenty-three steps up. "Some wild creature jumped out of the weeds at me and saved me from smashing into the guardrail. I slipped by a vintage Cadillac, then ran a red light. I cruised all night, up and down these hills. Come morning, my muscles were jelly. I pushed the bike instead of pedaling. A very sad woman was out back there burning memories. The ink boiled to black smoke. Paper ash landed on my tongue. She turned the hose on me. It made no sense."

Cinnamon remembered a crazy biker on the drive home from Sekou's funeral. The next morning Opal had set fire to the past and sprayed icy water on Ariel, a scattered bit of the Wanderer.

"Why am I thinking of that?" Ariel asked.

"Why not?" Commander Williams locked the car. "It sounds—"

"Nothing made sense," Ariel said. "I went to a bar afterward or, no, maybe before. No, I'm confusing two different times. Four years ago. A man with a gun shot up that bar before I got there."

"Sounds traumatic." Commander Williams exchanged worried glances with Mrs. B.

"I came after the shooting. Too much blood, so I jumped on

a bike—it wasn't mine—pedaling like a demon, and there was a hairpin turn. I went downhill thirty miles per hour, but I survived."

Mrs. B looped her arm through Ariel's. "Good for you."

Ariel shook off the trance. "I never think about those nights."

Commander Williams hustled up the steps. "I don't blame you."

Cinnamon was dying for the whole story. It was 7:10. Rain wagged her tail at Klaus and Marie tumbling out of the cab of Lexy's truck, twenty minutes late! Griot Joe stood up by his cart in the flatbed. He wore a cape and a pointy hat fashioned from aluminum foil and Saran Wrap. Foil boots were splattered with mud. He must have been quite a front row sight at the Playhouse. The crow rode Joe's shoulder as he hobbled over uneven ground. Klaus and Marie unloaded the cart and shoved it to the back door path. Lexy took off to get the elders. Prancing up the front steps, Ariel didn't notice their arrival. Cinnamon still had the surprise factor.

Mrs. B ushered Ariel into the dim hallway.

"I'm so glad you came." Cinnamon bowed. "Welcome."

"We'll leave you to your fans," Commander Williams said, breathing hard.

Ariel startled. "You're going already?"

"The kids prepare good shock for you," Mrs. B said. "Everyone wonders how Klaus gets two girlfriends." She leaned close to Ariel. "I tell nosy ones, Klaus has two-for-one special. Two *bunte*—colored? Colorful girls." She laughed.

Ariel and Commander Williams looked embarrassed.

"Actually, we're—" breaking up as soon as the mission was over. Cinnamon couldn't say it. Falling out of love with Klaus and Marie was hard.

"They've got more than sex on the brain," Commander Williams declared.

"Yeah," Cinnamon said. The Squad never got around to more than kissing and touching. They did get *naked* together—not bare asses, bare souls.

Mrs. B ruffled Ariel's hair. "While you enjoy shock, Juanita and I go have dessert."

Ariel forced a smile. "Shock?"

Commander Williams squeezed Ariel's hands. "We must support our young people, when they think about more than themselves."

"Of course," Ariel said. "But—"

"I wanted to be an actress. Everybody stomped that dream. Today is a new world." Commander Williams nodded until Ariel did too. "We'll pick you up in an hour. Have fun." She marched off with Mrs. B.

Hoodoo Spell #7b

"What's going on?" Ariel squinted in the dim light and fingered opal beads that anchored several strands of green and yellow—*ide Ifa.*

"Nice bracelet," Cinnamon said.

Ariel held it up. "It's old, from Africa. I found it in a theatre or a gallery or somewhere. It's probably costume jewelry, but . . ."

"What?" Cinnamon's tongue tingled. "Tell me."

"I'm waiting for someone to know its secret, the owner maybe. Isn't that silly?"

"No." Cinnamon knew just the person for that.

Marie slammed through the back screen door into the kitchen. "No one will steal your cart," she assured Joe as he tiptoed in.

"It'll be fine. Rain is an attack guard dog." Klaus followed them.

Muscles in Ariel's jaw jumped. Fire flickered in both eyes.

The crow cawed and pecked Joe's cheek. "You sit in shadows long enough, you become one." Joe hobbled a few more steps, stopping an arm's length from Ariel. *The Chronicles* sat on the coffee table between them. Pages fluttered in the cross breeze.

"Are you stalking me?" Ariel took a step back.

"I saw the *Tempest* masquerade this afternoon." Joe smiled. The crow hopped onto his head. Joe took off the foil cape. Underneath was a patchwork of cloth, pinned and taped in patterns resembling Kente cloth, well-worn but clean. Joe smoothed fraying edges. "I'm a fan. I've seen many of your shows."

Ariel pulled the mud cloth robe tight. "You look—"

"Like a thousand miles of bad road," Joe said.

The crow spread its wings. Black silky feathers glistened as it glided to Ariel and perched on a bare shoulder.

"Familiar, I was going to say." Ariel was enchanted by the crow.

Joe grinned. "The bird of my head and yours."

The crow rubbed Ariel's cheeks. "How did you train this crow?"

"Not a pet," Joe replied. "Ariel, free as a bird, who do you mean to be now?"

"What? The next show? I'm not sure. My agent is working hard."

Cinnamon slid the master dimmer from zero to full on a ten count. Scenes from the Wanderer's and Kehinde's travels in Dahomey, Paris, and the US melted out of darkness into sharp relief. Steamships sailed down from the clouds. African villagers painted clay walls and dyed cloth. Trains skipped over mountain peaks. Kehinde and the Wanderer danced across lightning bolts to carnival stages and desert canyons rimmed by sculpted rock. Melinga opened a gate to a suspension bridge that hung from cables of light.

"What is this?" Ariel's voice was stony.

"Miz Redwood's hoodoo spell #7b," Klaus said. His cheeks burned.

"Go out and find stories nobody has heard or everybody almost forgot." Marie flipped a cascade of braids and beads.

"We're Guardians," Cinnamon said. "We want to bring you two back together."

"What lies has this person been telling you?" Ariel's eyes burned.

Joe pointed at Raven's paintings. "No lies."

Ariel clutched the bracelet.

"You wear *ide Ifa*." Joe offered a broken-tooth grin. "Father of mysteries."

Cinnamon hoisted *The Chronicles*. "Joe has the nineteenth century, you've got the twentieth."

"You forgot yourself, when you scattered," Marie said.

"Didn't you?" Klaus asked.

Ariel howled an Eshu laugh. "Is this a teenage prank?" The crow glided back to Joe. "What nonsense did you tell those nice ladies?"

Cinnamon set *The Chronicles* down. Doubt and worry had caught a ride back to her street and were morphing into panic. It had never occurred to her that Ariel might not see the same light at the end of the tunnel as Joe and her Squad. Ariel believed in poetry and art. Wouldn't anybody who believed see that Raven's paintings were memory conjured and restored?

Ariel circled the Squad. "Mrs. Williams said you wanted advice on alternative theatre. Not help with—" Ariel read the back of Joe's cape. "*Homeless Eshu. Will Do Magic for Small Change.* Are you kidding?"

"Say something." Cinnamon shook Joe's arm.

He was silent. The crow shat a dribble of white.

"I did a play about tricksters of the diaspora—Eshu and Papa Legba. I don't remember the title. I always get androgynous trickster roles. My breakout show was *The Tempest.* Everybody calls me Ariel now. The roles you play can take over your life. After a long run, how do you even remember yourself?"

"So what's your real name?" Klaus asked. "Or have you forgotten?"

"I'm usually on to the next play as soon as possible, so I don't have to—"

"Don't talk over or down to us," Marie said. "We hate it, and we're snarky."

Ariel sighed. "I don't know what figment of your imagination I'm supposed to be—tinker, dragon, soldier, spy."

"Careful," Joe muttered. "Even—"

"*Even a dragon brushing against thorns will tear its wings,*" they all said simultaneously.

"You can't know that." Ariel's face crumpled. "A friend of mine, an old actress from Africa, used to say that."

"Kehinde," the Squad said.

"She's dead now. I haven't thought about her in . . ." Ariel's eyes darted around the room. "You don't get to dredge up my worst nightmares, and—I have to go."

The dimmer board whined and spat sparks. The gobos pulsed on and off like a strobe. Ariel disappeared, a blur into the wall. The lights blazed bright and died. The Squad stood several moments in darkness. Curtains fluttered in an open window.

"Did Ariel vanish?" Klaus asked.

"Nobody can do that," Marie said.

Cinnamon wanted to scream. At least she wasn't crushed on Ariel anymore. "The fuse on the dimmer board blew." She fell into Klaus and Marie. They caught her, of course, and it turned into a group hug. Joe flicked on the overhead. Everyone squinted.

"I'm sorry our spell didn't work." Cinnamon hung her head.

Klaus shook Joe. "Say something."

"I try to find words." Joe spoke slowly. "For *aje* thoughts."

"No lame excuses." Marie's weird hand sparked. "These two are nice. I'm not. Is the Wanderer bit true?"

"Or are you crazy, like Ariel said?" Klaus asked.

"True and not true." Joe hobbled to the TV alcove and gazed at the paintings Raven never put on display—a bouquet of colored glass skyscrapers, ghostly amusement parks, a flock of jets trailing smoke—twentieth-century images. "A new world," Joe said. With the crow on his head, Joe leapt, stumbled, and shook his behind in the air—the dance he'd done at Sekou's funeral. The Squad joined him dancing around the coffee table.

"For eighteen seasons, visions and ghosts have haunted me. I've been running in snow drifts, over green sprouts, through the first breeze of summer, across fallen leaves. Running from myself, for four years, four months. No more running." Joe touched the brush-strokes on a rainbow-Wanderer bursting from the spaces between things. Sekou had titled this *Adumbration*. "Translation?"

"It means shadow," Marie said.

"Foreshadow," Klaus added.

"Images that talk to tomorrow," Cinnamon said.

"A good word." Joe chuckled.

"Piss on good words!" Marie was still mad.

"We thought we could make it right." Cinnamon hugged her from behind.

Joe pulled the foil cape on. The crow jumped to his shoulders. "Reversing entropy, putting broken pieces back together, a challenge, so much energy." The crow pecked Joe's head as they headed for the back door. "Scattering is mostly in my mind, how can you fix that?"

"We don't want you scattering into nothing." Marie's voice quivered.

Klaus took her hand. "Promise not to jump off any bridges going nowhere!"

"I am grateful to you." Joe stepped onto the porch.

"Wait." Cinnamon rushed him. "I hoped we could, not just fix your . . ."

Joe waited. The crow jumped from his shoulder and flew into the cart's purse perch. Joe stroked a shiny wing. "This bird healed a long time ago, but won't fly far."

Klaus and Marie leaned into Cinnamon. She closed her eyes. "I wished you and Kehinde dead, or in a coma, instead of my dad, and Kehinde turned out to *be* dead."

"Not from your wishing," Joe replied.

"I had a fantasy that if you were the whole Wanderer," Cinnamon said, "*aje,* Ariel, and whoever—you could help Daddy come back to himself, using weird science and the power of the spaces between things."

"Bring Raven back?" Joe glanced at Melinga, clapping her hands by an open gate on a light bridge. "I'd like to believe that story too, but, I'm tired. I must go. The bird of my head is famished. I can't wait for Lexy's truck."

Marie and Klaus poked Cinnamon. Her mouth was desert dry.

Klaus spoke up. "We're doing a celebration for Mr. Cooper at the nursing home tomorrow."

"Two o'clock, during visiting hours," Marie said. "It's his birthday."

They should cancel the party. It was a stupid optimist thing.

"Come if you can," Klaus and Marie said.

Joe refused help and wrestled the cart down the back way. Rain barked like a fiend as he coasted around the hairpin turn and zoomed out of sight.

Cinnamon clutched Klaus and Marie.

"You're not mad at us anymore . . ." Klaus said, a question and a statement.

"She's still mad," Marie said.

"Give me some time." Cinnamon darted inside. They followed.

"Joe will come." Klaus and Marie talking together gave her goose bumps.

Light leaked from *The Chronicles*. Marie opened to new words flooding onto the page. Klaus pointed at Cinnamon.

"Me?" After swallowing the bitter spit in her mouth, Cinnamon read softly.

Chronicles 26: Final Entry— Defying Gravity

Dear Guardians, thanks to your generosity, memory is conjured.

December 27, 1982, was bright and dazzling, a voluptuous day. Raven Cooper had finished his paintings for *The Chronicles of the Warrior Woman and the Great Wanderer.* The few he still fussed over were hidden somewhere. This night was the opening of an exhibition at Raven's favorite watering hole. The owners had agreed to hang his thirty-piece series during January. They offered a slow Monday, after the Jesus festivals, for a party. Dr. Bug-Man would deejay. Sekou lined up a world music band, and Star Deer rehearsed a contact dance. Poets prepared praise songs. Sekou asked us to dress up and tell tall tales. He planned to create a book to go with the paintings.

It was a warm day for December in Pittsburgh. I still shivered in layers of clothing. Kehinde loved winter—the challenge of cold and snow, the clarity in the sky. As the home star set, a cloud burst and turned to slush, coating the sidewalks and roads with glittery water crystal. We lived by one of three rivers. A bridge was right outside our window. It disappeared in a snow squall.

All thundered-up, a spectacle worthy of a Paris museum, we scrambled up and down treacherous Pittsburgh hills heading for the Rain Forest Lounge. Houses clung to the cliffs and grinned in the darkness at us, jack-o'-lanterns up to no good. Stripped of leaves, swaying in the wind, the trees were giant brooms sweeping sleet from the sky. Steep shortcuts from one cobblestone street to the next winded Kehinde. She didn't complain. Walking was her idea. She hated riding stinky, lumbering buses.

"The more you sit down, the harder it will be to stand up," she said.

A good pair of boots was her favorite winter transport. Sneaking through inky woods, Kehinde held on to me. *Aje* eyes worked well in twilight. Kehinde told stories, adventures from last week and last century, practicing for the celebration. It was slow-going; she stopped often to marvel at a memory. We'd given ourselves plenty of time.

You never have as much time as you think.

"That clerk looked like Melinga, grown into herself." Kehinde smiled. "All these children, they belong to us . . . Stretch your hands out as far as they reach."

"Here? Now?" I said. We teetered at the edge of a steep drop.

"You must be willing to die in order to live." When Kehinde was happy, she talked like this, full of old wisdom, still teaching me to be human. "Aren't I your *stillpoint*?"

We reached our hands into sheets of hard water, balancing with one another. It was thrilling.

"Are you going to do magic tricks tonight?" She kissed my cheek. "Everyone always went wild for that."

"I don't remember this."

"Disappearing. Breathing fire. Flying."

"I never flew."

"You called it defying gravity. Would I make this up?"

I laughed. "We both defied gravity."

"Don't swallow lightning. That's too dangerous."

"We need a thunderstorm for that." I shivered. "How do you remember all this?"

"We paid our passage through the Great Depression with your magic. Nobody believed their eyes. They begged me to divulge your secret. I wouldn't. Fellows calling themselves magickers offered to make me a rich woman for a hint."

"That greasy fellow chased us. You sliced his belt, and he tripped on his pants—in the desert. You left him his head."

"I'm a good keeper of secrets, yours and Brother-Taiwo's."

"You never told me what he said, the day we met."

"No." She sucked a cold breath. The wind whistled about us, a melody of hills, ravines, bridges, and rivers. "We must go down to come back up?"

"Yes," I said.

"In a minute. Hold me."

I gathered her close.

"Do we still have sand from the desert windstorm that tried to kill us?"

"It was a flash flood." I held up Bob's blue *mojo* bag. I had added eight things from New World adventures to the Jumbo hair. Kehinde gripped it.

"You haven't forgotten everything." She scattered a pinch of sand. "I dreamt that Opal and Raven were our grandchildren—Melinga's children who found us in the desert and saved us from choking in a dirt storm."

"It was a flash flood," I said. "I've had the same dream."

"Flood, sand storm, no matter." She flicked her fingers. "We share dreams. We're twins, sharing a destiny."

"I never got you or Somso to explain twins."

"I carry my brother's spirit." Kehinde returned the *mojo* and leaned against me. "What is lost or cannot be found can be conjured. Change is always possible."

"You believe that still?" I was amazed.

"Now more than ever." She traced my face with her palm. "The Igbo believe twins are abominations. The Yoruba revere them. One twin is mortal, material, one spiritual, but they share a soul." Kehinde squeezed me. "I'm careful and reflective, a *stillpoint*. You're bold and adventurous, a Wanderer. Together we are balance."

No one was nearby, only desperate squirrels and sleepy pigeons. I drew her into the circle of my being. I whispered, "My head belongs to you."

Crows chattered at us. We tasted tongues. The surge of blood, the rush of sweet electricity across skin and through muscles was the best carnival of sensations I could remember. It was too cold to make a braid of our bodies. We would do that later. To arrive on time, we had to keep moving. When we finally reached the Rain Forest Lounge, Kehinde was sweaty and wheezing. She paused under a streetlight to struggle for breath. She was frail, despite what the *aje* did to hold her to life.

"Coming from another century is a greater distance than traveling the ocean between continents," she said. "We're too old for the Rain Forest crowd."

"I'm here for the stories, for the people on fire for each other."

"Bob was on fire for you. He knew how to love." Kehinde held me close. "I have a story for you."

"Later."

"Now." She sounded urgent. "One I don't want to tell."

"OK." I could never resist her stories.

"Before he disappeared, Bob told me his plan in French." She paused as I absorbed this. "He begged Somso to let us take Melinga and disappear. She refused."

"No good solution."

"Bob offered to run away with Somso and Melinga and never search for us. Somso was moved by this sacrifice. She didn't need our blood. Taking what we loved, as I had taken Brother-Taiwo, would suffice. Bob begged me to search for him and Melinga, but insisted I not tell you until—"

"Until what? He didn't trust me?"

"I agreed too quickly. Perhaps I wanted you for myself."

"You were delirious."

"Bob wanted to save you from murder, to offer Melinga a good life. He wanted us to know love. He gave up one self to become another. If the road ends, fly."

My heart ached. Bob left us for love. "Such is life on Earth." I danced with Kehinde into the middle of the street.

"You're not sad?"

"I've already mourned losing Melinga and Bob. Now I find his love again and yours. Why be sad?"

She shook her head. "I never feel worthy of your love."

"I hold all of you. You hold all of me."

"Yes." Kehinde pushed the door open. "Let's go in. Today we celebrate with Melinga's children."

Incense, rum, oil paint, cigarette smoke, and sweaty humans welcomed us. Musicians pounded drums, plucked hunter's harps, and several played balaphon—West African marimba. Lighting was dim except for glowing alcoves where the magic moments of our lives burst out of darkness. From Dahomey to the capitals of the Old World and across the land of the free, Raven had made sense of this world on his canvases. He said his mother could snatch a hurricane from the sky; his father could carve the wind. He was keeping company with them.

"All we need is the poetry," Sekou said. He had an arm around Lexy, the DJ who had captured his heart. They grinned at us. "Party time!" Sekou shouted.

Raven wore a colorful patchwork coat and a knot of silver around his neck. He greeted us with his bear hug.

"Where is Opal?" Kehinde looked around. The place was jammed.

"We had an argument," Raven said quickly. "Woman tried to break up with me tonight. Can you believe that? We'll get it straightened out tomorrow."

"It's a shame she couldn't be here." Kehinde sighed.

"We're not enough fun for you?" Sekou teased.

"We wanted to see her and your little sister," I said.

"Moms would never bring Cinnamon to this den of iniquity," Sekou muttered.

"Opal's trying to wrap her mind around a lot of hard things right now," Raven said. "Don't forget that when you're mad at her."

"You choose to love her," Sekou said. "I'm stuck with her."

"You don't have to love anybody," Raven said. "It doesn't work that way."

Sekou sulked a second. "It doesn't work any way with Mom."

"She'll come around," Dr. Lexy said.

"Give us a tour?" Kehinde squeezed Sekou's arm, distracting him.

In the first painting, Kehinde and I balanced on a log in a white-water stream.

"What is *Bascule*?" Kehinde asked.

The titles were Eshu words. Sekou had to crack open their secrets. "A device like a drawbridge, where one end counterbalances the other," he said.

Kehinde laughed. "Taiwo always loved bridges."

"The Brooklyn Bridge is my favorite," I said. "A woman built that, did you know?"

We circled the bar and exclaimed at what was more vivid on canvas than in our memories. A crowd trailed us. We ended on the dance floor. Star Deer swooped down from the balcony. Other dancers jumped out of nowhere. Musicians plucked melancholy strings. The dancers ended flat on the ground, looking up.

I followed Star's gaze to the ceiling. "What is this?"

"You don't remember?" Kehinde laughed.

A water creature leapt from the waves. Electric bolts of hair glowed. A fat tail poked a hole in the sky and hooked a spiral galaxy. Eyes reflected an infinity of other eyes.

"I painted the feeling I got from those wild stories." Raven sounded uncertain.

"Your *aje* masquerade," Kehinde whispered in Yoruba. "Raven paints your secrets without knowing it."

Enchanted, we tasted tongues. Kehinde bent me back for a moving-picture kiss. The crowd applauded and cheered us. A man yelled, "God hates you all." He waved a gun. Under a hooded jacket, he had no eyes.

Raven and Kehinde gave themselves away, and—my mind reeled with Igbo words—*If you are running out of the way, whom do you want the bull to hit?*—and Akan words—*Don't let me die at all, but let me die.* Part of me ran away, part of me gave up, part of me held on. Too much space and not enough force to hold it together. I scattered.

My crow companion finally lifts its wings and soars into a cloud of black feathers.

Is this Earth journey a Good Mission?

What Do We Do?

Cinnamon was dazed and cold. Klaus put his hot cheek on her shoulder, and Marie curled in Cinnamon's lap, her hair a warm blanket. When Lexy returned with the elders, they were disappointed to hear that Joe and Ariel had already left. Iris made tea and hot chocolate. Aidan took out his banjo, and the strings vibrated with edgy energy.

Lexy strolled around the room, gazing at the paintings. Miz Redwood walked with him. The hot drinks cooled; the whipped cream sagged. On their fifth round Sekou recited, *Mallemaroking, Adumbration, Douroucouli, Magniloquent, Xenophilia . . .*

Cinnamon grinned at Lexy. "Remember you and Sekou behind the washing machine, like the best roller-coaster ride at Kennywood, or crawling after ants on Fifth Avenue, or rapping together? Wow . . . Sekou loved you more than words."

"More than words?" Embarrassed, Lexy downed his cold tea. "That's a lot of love."

"Maybe you could tell us about that night at the bar," Redwood said.

"I don't, I haven't, I can't . . ." Lexy bit his cracked lip. It bled.

Aidan played tender licks on the banjo and soothed everybody's jagged nerves.

"Back in Georgia, when I was a girl, I had big plans, don't you know?" Redwood danced backcountry steps. "A singing and dancing sensation, I was goin' take the whole world by storm. I had me a banjo-playing secret sweetheart." Redwood halted. "A man caught me in the fog on a country road and took me against my will. I snatched the life right out of him." She balled her storm hand. "Snatched the life right out of my own self too. For the longest time, I wasn't sure I could have a child." This was the past that Opal hoped they could all forget. Redwood opened her storm hand and patted Lexy's arm. "It took me a long time to pick myself up off that road."

"Hmm-hmm." Iris could have been sitting in the Amen corner of church.

"Aidan and I had a good life, a sensation on stage and screen. I turned forty-two, surprise! I had Raven. Crows squawking outside the window kept me company when he was born." She was close to tears. "So, Dr. Lexy, if you can stand telling it, we could stand hearing what happened when my only son got shot in the head."

Aidan played softly, gently. Redwood sang a wordless harmony. The Squad joined in. Rustling and crackling, Sekou flickered in the gobos and hit the ghost backbeats. Lexy caught that rhythm and perked up. "The art show at the Rain Forest Lounge was Sekou's big idea. He convinced the owners. He was always doing that. Nobody could outtalk Sekou. Nobody could keep up, except his baby sister. That's what *he* said, always bragging on you." Lexy scratched the rash on his neck.

"Do you mind if I take notes?" Cinnamon tapped her magic words journal. Lexy nodded. "Wait." She grabbed *The Chronicles* and one of Raven's calligraphy pens from her orca knapsack. "I should write in here for the Wanderer." She opened to a blank page, and, writing as fast as thought, dashed off what Lexy had already said. "Ready."

Lexy stood up straight and turned his cap to the side. Dr. Bug-Man was in the house. "Star brought her contact crew over for the opening. Sekou had a poetry-jam lined up. Everybody wanted to bust a few rhymes for the old folks. Raven Cooper was an art hero, old-school. He'd die poor before he'd sell out. Stare at his paintings long enough, you start talking in tongues, so rhyming fierce words was easy. I was surprised Mr. Cooper was doing his show in a gay bar. People claimed he was AC-DC. I don't know about that.

"The fool with the gun was yelling heinous crap, *faggots and dykes are abominations* and *God hates you all*. Sekou told him to take his mess outside. A young guy, close to our age. The way he moved, talked—hard rock or hip-hop, not R&B. Nobody wants to admit that. Who knew he was packing heat? We thought he'd just come to talk some shit. A rumor went around that he was a jilted lover, mad at Mr. Cooper for turning him queer, like how a vampire makes another vampire out of an innocent soul minding his own business. Can you beat that? So I shut that rumor down. Why does the shooter have to be a gay man who doesn't want to be a gay man? Anyway, he got away . . . with murder. The case went cold in a minute. I don't know how hard those detectives looked. They never found a clue, a trail, a hair to trace. He had a hood over his face and leather gloves. Didn't leave a fingerprint or a nasty note. We don't know what the shooter was besides a sick bastard. He shot up a few pictures, but he wasn't aiming at the art. He was just mad shooting.

"Mr. Cooper knocked Sekou and one of the old warrior Africans out of the way, and then the other one twisted around in front of him, so fast. I couldn't move like that. Star Deer couldn't move like that. Nobody could. That warrior lady was flying. Bullet went through her back and slowed down a bit before hitting Mr. Cooper's head, or he would have been dead too. Her organs bled out. Everybody cowering in the corners, under the table, me too, and the heroes were out on the dance floor dying. Sekou had jumped behind the bar. I saw him from where I was hiding under a table. He couldn't move. Star Deer was holed up in the ladies' room. She didn't come out till the cops arrived. We thought this maniac with the gun was going to go around shooting everybody. Nobody was packing heat except for him. It wasn't that kind of joint. As the old warrior lady, Kehinde, was dying, I remember every word.

Abla was wrong. That was Kehinde talking. *I ate the bullet this time, for love.*

Foolish woman. The other warrior was crying.

Save him and let me go. What do we do? Kehinde gasped. *Let it be the last words I hear.*

We search for Melinga. We tell her the story. She is the Guardian at the gate to tomorrow.

They stole my world, Kehinde said. *I should have died in the water or at the end of a bayonet. I killed my twin brother, but I swore an oath and I loved you. No good solution, only love. What do we do?*

We search. We . . . The other warrior's voice ran down.

Promise me, on the oath you swore. Save him.

"That was it. I don't know, waiting to get whacked, time got funny, then Sekou was waving at me. My man shrugged, like what the hell were we waiting to die like dogs for. He took a quick peek and crawled out. Nobody shot him, so I crawled out too.

"There was this raggedy homeless guy, safety-pinned together, smelling like burnt air before a storm. He was holding onto Mr. Cooper, mumbling, *Don't leave me, I can't bear it,* and crying. His hand was on Mr. Cooper's wound, stopping the blood. Somebody I didn't recognize dashed out the wide-open door, chasing the gunman, maybe. My mind was a mess. Kehinde was dead, her eyes wide open, not seeing anything. The homeless guy howled at Sekou or anybody trying to close her eyes. So much blood everywhere and shit too, I mean the warrior woman shit herself dying. Sekou left her eyes open and sat down in the blood. The other warrior was gone, nobody knew where.

"The ambulance took forever to get there. Nasty weather, or maybe they didn't give a crap. I don't want to think like that, but I've seen it. Anyhow the EMTs said the homeless guy was a magic man, said it was a miracle. Mr. Cooper should have been dead, with blood and stuff swelling up his brain, blowing his mind out. But he wasn't dead. He was breathing, stable. I don't know if it felt like a miracle to Sekou. He was sitting there, rocking in the blood, moaning stupid talk, like the shooting was his fault. 'Cause it was his big idea, 'cause Mr. Cooper knocked him to safety and took the bullet himself. Who can think straight while something foul like that is going down? And Mr. Cooper, you know he would have told Sekou. He loved him, the way a man loves a son. He would have told him. He would have set Sekou straight."

Lexy paused again, scratching a long time. Redwood eased her storm hand under his fingernails. He stopped digging.

"You don't ever want to bury your son. That's hell, for sure."

Lexy choked up. Redwood nodded, and he continued. "Mr. Cooper wanted Sekou to have a life. He was trying to give him that. So he wasn't thinking: *I'll die or be in a coma for the rest of my life because of your trifling, faggot ass.* But some people tried to make Sekou feel low. I can't forgive them for that. Him doing the needles—OK that was Sekou's choice, not anybody else's fault, but maybe it could have gone another way." He hung his head. "Actually Sekou started blaming himself before anybody else did."

"Nothing you could have done about that," Cinnamon said. Her hand ached from writing so quickly. "Who ever won an argument with Dictionary Boy?"

"That warrior lady, eyes open and all, she looked, I don't want to say peaceful, but Kehinde knew what she was doing, like Mr. Cooper, they were, uhm, at the end, you know, I feel they loved us. That's what it was about."

Black Bird Take My Spirit High

Rehearsing inside taped-down dimensions had not provided the full claustrophobic effect of Raven's nursing home room. Cinnamon hugged *The Chronicles* under the folds of a long robe, trying to squelch preshow jitters. She set the heavy tome down on Raven's lap. Klaus and Marie scooped her up into a group hug. They were ragged and jagged too. The bold colorful designs of their African bohemian costumes clashed with puke peach cement-block walls. The funky air laced with disinfectants made them cough. Even pushing the other beds to the wall and stuffing busted chairs in the closet, there was hardly room to move or breathe. They held on to each other in a Mod Squad secret-society huddle. Hooded robes shrouded their heads; fat pants hugged ankles and covered jitters. Grown-ups could not see what was going on.

Her Squad had performed the *Black Bird* piece for a talent show at Cinnamon's school last week. They would never have to play a harder crowd. Everybody knew Cinnamon had pipes, but nobody was expecting Marie. A big rapper kid shouted, *Damn, the Asian girl can blow!* and the audience was laughing and cracking on each other rather than the act onstage. Not a peep about white boys. Klaus and Cinnamon had talked down *Flugzeuge* flitting around their tummies in German before going on. Despite consonant clusters, some idiot assumed they were talking Spanish and spread the tale that Klaus was a blond Puerto Rican. Cherrie Carswell and Patty Banks said he was cute.

Klaus tugged Cinnamon's crown of braids. "You look good enough to eat."

"Like a tropical fruit chocolate delight?" Cinnamon said.

"No!" Marie blew her lips at Cinnamon. "A *surprise!*" She kissed Cinnamon and then Klaus. Marie was the best kisser, no contest, sneaking her tongue in on a gasp. "What do we have to say for ourselves? Huh?" Marie shook them. "Don't think. Don't giggle. Talk to me."

"When you're onstage, give Doubt a comfortable seat in the wings." Klaus spoke Redwood's lines. "Let Doubt watch you soar." He leaned his full weight onto Cinnamon and Marie. They entwined arms and tangled up their legs, becoming a single creature toying with gravity on the scuffed linoleum. Klaus put a finger to Marie's and Cinnamon's foreheads, noses, and lips, then his own.

"Go with our hearts. We got this." Cinnamon spoke Ariel's prompt. Still tasting Marie's kiss and shivering with Klaus's hot contact, she traced her fingers across their cheeks and sent warm breath down their necks. Sex would be a good offering to Eshu. Together, they chanted their version of an Eshu praise poem from the Wanderer:

We are all blessed with contradiction
Eshu is a shapeshifter
Pour libation
to the master of masquerade
to the master of improvisation
Everything at once, yet not any one thing

"What does that mean, for each of us?" Klaus asked.

"I don't know yet," Cinnamon admitted.

"Me neither," Marie said.

"We'll find out when we do this," Klaus said.

"Right." Cinnamon and Marie hit an upbeat reply together.

"What are we risking? What are we giving up?" Marie said.

"I wanted revenge," Cinnamon confessed.

"Me too," Klaus and Marie said.

"Like folks from the old country say, forgiveness is the best revenge."

"Verzeihen ist die beste Rache," Klaus and Marie repeated in German.

"We've been waiting for love to come on back in style," Marie whispered.

Cinnamon tingled. "Maybe we don't have to break up."

The Squad swung a long moment through upbeat silence, doing the small dance, falling toward the center of the Earth, catching each other and falling again. Contact improv readiness, waiting. Iris would give the cue for the beginning.

Raven's bed had been cranked up as far as it would go. If his eyes and visual cortex were hooked up and turned on, he would have the best seat in the house. Dr. Elliott had admitted a birthday party would probably do no harm. "Consciousness is an elusive mystery," he said. "Raven is responding to stimulation. A twelve or almost thirteen. Who knows how far he'll go? Just don't get your hopes up too high."

Clarence, looking corporate and important with a snazzy briefcase, hulked in the corner and grumbled to Lexy and Kevin about false hope. Star Deer screwed up her face and slipped away from bad vibes. At least Clarence had shown up. He didn't say a word about Georgia crackers, hillbilly music, or *noble savages and hoodoo Negroes*. It wasn't like Sekou's funeral. Clarence was outnumbered.

Everybody on Daddy's team had come to the nursing home, almost everybody. Opal and Aunt Becca were caught in a traffic jam but on their way, according to Kevin. No sign of Ariel/Griot Joe yet. Cinnamon refused to worry about that. Thirteen on a scale of three to fourteen was cause for celebration, not pointless negative speculation.

With a twist of the pegs, Aidan got the banjo tuned to a sweet spot. He wore a Seminole patchwork coat and a turban tied around his loose white hair. Redwood sported a crown of river silk, chains of silver bangles at the waist of harem pants, and seashells and seed pods around graceful ankles. She kept time with the machines beeping and whirring. Iris wore a *gele*—Yoruba head wrap—and a red and black sheath to honor Eshu, master of uncertainty, weaver of the cosmic interface. Over the sheath she'd draped a Seminole mantle. She and Kevin, who styled a blue velvet cowboy shirt and boots with two-inch heels, arranged a feast table of delicious food.

Iris jerked as if a jolt of energy had hit her. "Excuse me." She patted Kevin's shoulder and headed for the door. While Kevin fussed with his famous barbecue and whiskey brownies, Yoruba words tumbled from Iris's lips. The show was about to begin. Cinnamon spoke the English translation.

Eshu, do not undo me
Do not falsify the words of my mouth
Do not misguide the movements of my feet
You who translate yesterday's words into novel utterances
Do not undo me
I bear your sacrifice

Clarence rolled his eyes.

Shaking her powwow jingle dress, Star Deer lit a bunch of sage in front of him. "Chippewa elders teach us always to purify a place and the people who have gathered—before any ceremony. I'm not Chippewa. I am Cherokee. I honor their wisdom. Sage smoke drives out bad spirits and bad feelings." Star moved slowly around the room. When she reached Clarence again, she pulled out a braid of sweetgrass. "Sweetgrass calls in the good spirits. Gather the smoke to you. Rub it against your body." She whispered, "If you can't go with the spirit thing or the theatre thing, think of yourself as activating the placebo effect."

Clarence snorted, but drew the smoke toward him. Iris opened the door to reveal a shadowy figure filling the frame. A page from *The Chronicles* come to life, the Wanderer was here and not here, fuzzy as a weak broadcast, then sharp as a spotlight. Breath on fire, skin turning to crystals, eyes flickering between rainbows, the Wanderer stepped over the threshold, through the spaces between things and onto the scuffed gray linoleum floor. The Wanderer might have been naked except for the *ide Ifa* on one wrist and a lightning bolt headdress. Nobody quite knew what they were seeing.

True and not true.

"You theatre folks sure know how to make an entrance." Kevin applauded the special effects.

"Hot dog, one of Raven's pictures coming to life," Aidan said.

"We've been walking around in his landscapes for a while, sugar," Redwood said.

"Thank you for the end of the story, for giving me back to myself." The Wanderer pointed at *The Chronicles* and faded a little. "What destiny will Raven Cooper choose?"

Cinnamon shrugged. "Not knowing is torture!" She danced the Wanderer right up to the bed and headed back to Klaus and Marie. Outside in the hall, Opal hid under a busted light, wiping away tears. "We're all here, Daddy," Cinnamon said.

Raven opened his eyes at that. He looked disoriented, confused. His gaze drifted through the room, not settling on anything.

"Good to see you, Son." Aidan wrapped Raven's right hand around the walking stick he'd carved—wind-storming into a Georgia swamp. Leather strands of beads cascaded down the side.

"Sorry I stayed away so long." Redwood put Raven's favorite brush into his painting hand and then handed Iris a *mojo* bag.

The smell of rum stung Cinnamon's nose. The Squad helped the elders collect nine ornery things: a busted banjo string, an elephant hair, a splinter from Ariel's broken wand, goober dust from Sekou's grave, a poison mushroom, truncated definitions on half a dictionary page, a rock from the badlands, Opal's last cigarette butt, and a broken crow feather. Iris placed this *mojo* around the Wanderer's neck.

Star finished smudging the room. Marie smoothed Sekou's thunderbird shirt under her billowy robes. Her hair was held back from her face by a grandmother's jade comb and the Oshun comb she shared with Cinnamon. Klaus sneezed as Star danced sweetgrass smoke by him. He waved Sekou's bear claw in the air. Cinnamon felt shy in her Yoruba and Fon finery, but didn't let on. They whirled their robes into a tangle and let them float to the ground. Aidan played furious licks on the banjo.

"Sacrifice means to give up one self for another." Cinnamon launched her center of gravity at Marie and pivoted across her muscular back. Klaus dropped to the floor and snagged Cinnamon as she flew over Marie's shoulders. Rolling with their momentum, Cinnamon shifted to the ground and lifted Klaus who caught Marie with the edge of his shoulder. After that it was hard to say what happened: fast Newtonian physics processed below consciousness into thrilling art. They landed too out of breath for singing. Aidan and Redwood had to go one time through the song as a duet.

> *Can't help loving somebody*
> *Who can soar, who can fly*
> *Who can take your spirit up in the sky*
> *A black bird with a broken wing*
> *Hopping down there on the ground*
> *Why's that ole black bird sticking 'round*
> *Ain't got nothing good to sing*
> *Can't help loving somebody*
> *Who can soar, who can fly*
> *Who can take your spirit up in the sky*
> *Black bird sing a worm in my ear*
> *Can't get the tune to leave me alone*
> *Black bird sing a worm in my ear*
> *Hear it all day and all night*
> *Black bird flap that ole broken wing*
> *The pain sure get him to sing*
> *Black bird, black bird*
> *Can't work the wind to take flight*
> *It's the song black bird get to soar*
> *It's the song black bird get to fly*
> *Black bird take my spirit up in the sky*

Even Clarence was dazzled. He clapped his hands and looked from Lexy over to Raven, who jiggled the wind staff, his eyes tracking everybody. His facial muscles twitched, forming a grin or a grimace. Opal stepped over the doorframe, wheezing burbly short breaths. She clutched one of Raven's paintings to her gurgling chest.

Iris pressed Lexy toward her. "Go on now."

"We've been missing you around here." Lexy beamed at Opal. "We're celebrating. Mr. Cooper is a thirteen on a scale of three to fourteen, on his birthday." He pulled Opal close to Cinnamon, Klaus, and Marie. "Dr. Elliott said he might show up, all of him, anytime now. A shame for you to miss out on any of that."

"You were a friend of my son's," Opal said.

"I, uh." Lexy teetered around a maze of emotions. "We were more than friends."

"Yes. That too." Opal squinted at Lexy. "You've gained a few pounds. Didn't recognize you at first."

"We never met before, officially. Only here."

"Sekou had a picture of you two." She handed the photo to him.

"What else you got there?" Redwood said.

"You started too soon." Opal turned to Cinnamon. "Becca's still looking for a parking space."

"No, ma'am, she's right here." Aidan nodded at Becca striding in.

"I been at this nursing home plenty, you know," Opal said.

"We are grateful," Iris said. "And so glad you are here now."

Raven gurgled and everyone got still, holding one breath together.

"Show us what you brought, Mom," Cinnamon said. "Please."

"Raven is someone who sees things beautiful." Opal turned the painting around: a spiral galaxy of colors, shadows, and ghosts morphing into creatures, musical instruments, flying machines. "He was working on this before . . ." Opal halted. "He sees things beautiful. When he looks, the beauty is there, vivid, clear, and he paints that."

That's number thirty. Sekou was here! Marie and Klaus heard him too. They held up the title: *Kitab al-jabr wa'l-muqabalah—The Book of Restoring and Balancing.*

"Raven painted my memory back." The Wanderer spoke softly, flickering across the dimensions.

The wind staff spilled out of Raven's grip. Clarence picked it up and curled Raven's fingers around it again. "This is going to be very hard." Clarence had tears in his eyes. Iris put an arm around his shoulder.

"So we're counting on your help, Brother," Opal said. Star Deer nodded.

Opal pushed past Clarence and sat down in the chair waiting for her by Raven's bed. She lifted his painting hand and kissed it. Redwood, Aidan, and Iris crowded around the bed too, holding onto each other. Cinnamon was light-headed and wobbly. Klaus and Marie wobbled next to her. Nobody was going to fall on their faces. Raven shook the staff at Redwood and Aidan. They dipped and twirled in his gentle beat.

"*Gilidinehuyi*," Opal whispered Raven's secret name. Star and everyone echoed her. "*Gilidinehuyi*." Opal leaned her ears to his lips as soft sounds spilled out. Words? Opal's poker face gave nothing away.

"Children of thunder, *Gilidinehuyi*," the Wanderer murmured then faded out as if a hoodoo light-board operator was sliding the dimmer from full down to zero on a ten count.

"Easy is overrated." Cinnamon, Klaus, and Marie came together on an upbeat.

"Who you mean to be is always hard." Cinnamon poured libation to the master of uncertainty. "But we will do magic for small change."

Acknowledgments

Thanks to my agent, Kris O'Higgins, who believes in the stories I write, and also to L. Timmel Duchamp and Kathryn Wilham, who gave this novel a chance when I first wrote it in 2014. Thanks to Lee Harris and the amazing Tordotcom team for bringing my work to a wide audience.

Every novel is a challenge, a journey through dangerous and marvelous territory. Writing *Will Do Magic for Small Change* was an epic, around-the-world voyage. Thanks to the good folks who danced in the dark and sang to the moon with me: Rowland Abiodun, Sally Bellerose, Pearl Cleage, Grace L. Dillon, Jonathan Gosnell, Eileen Gunn, Daniel José Older, Kathleen Mosley, Susan Stinson; Wolfgang and Beate Schmidhuber and the whole Schmidhuber clan; Bill Oram and Micala Sidore; Joel Tansey and Kiki Gounaridou; Bobby, Mary, and Theo Welland.

Special thanks to Lucille Booker, Holly Derr, Erika Ewing, Kara Morin, Bill Peterson, Kevin Quashie, and Joy Voeth for generously offering me their impressions of growing up in the 1980s, to John Hellweg for his inspiring, unforgettable production of *The Tempest*, and to Nic Uluru for conjuring an image for the story.

Blessings on the Beyond 'Dusa Wild Sapelonians: Liz Roberts, Ama Patterson, Sheree R. Thomas, and Pan Morigan, who sent power to my writing hand.

Pan Morigan and James Emery make the writing possible.

Appendix

Adinkra—visual symbols on cloth created by the Akan to embody ideas or proverbs

ahosi—Fon, member of the king's household, wife of the king, warrior woman

ajaho—Fon, head of the Dahomean king's secret agents

aje—Yoruba, the power Olodumare gave to Oshun; a being with such power

ajo mmuo—Igbo, evil spirits, *alu* (abomination) against *Ani*—the Earth Deity

Akan—ethnic group in what is now Ghana and Côte d'Ivoire

akewi—Yoruba, storyteller, griot

Allahu akbar—God is great in Farsi

alu—Igbo, abominations

Ani—Igbo, the Earth Deity

ashe—English transliteration of Yoruba term, the power to make things be

ASM—Assistant Stage Manager

ausgezeichnet—German, outstanding, wonderful

Babalawo—Yoruba, father of mysteries, an *Ifa* diviner

Bambara or Bamana—an African people in Mali

basiaba—Bambara or Bamana, mud cloth pattern for young women

Béhanzin—king of Dahomey

bògò—Bambara or Bamana for earth or mud

bògòlan—Bambara or Bamana for mud cloth

bògòlanfini—Bambara or Bamana for mud cloth

ce farin jala—Bambara or Bamana, a brave man's belt

chi—the Igbo personal life force

Eshu—English transliteration of Yoruba term, an orisha, master of crossroads, life and death, master of uncertainty, weaver of the cosmic interface

fini—Bambara or Bamana for cloth

Flugzeuge im Bauch—German, airplanes in the stomach, butterflies, nerves

Fon—ruling ethnic group in Dahomey

gawlo—griot in Fula

gbeto—Fon, elephant huntress, sharpshooter

gilidinehuyi—Cherokee for lightning

Hau ab, Arschloch—German for beat it, asshole

ide Ifa—Yoruba, beaded bracelet worn by *Babalawo*

Ifa—divination wisdom of the Yoruba

Igbo—ethnic group in what is now Nigeria

Iyalawo—Yoruba, a priestess of Ifa, a mother of secrets

Kannst du Deutsch?—German, Do you speak German?

Kannst du eine Fremdsprache?—German, Can you speak a foreign language?

kpojito—Fon, reign-mate of the king in Dahomey

kposi—Fon, literally leopard's wives—sovereign's highest ranking spouses

lan—Bambara or Bamana for with or by means of

logisch—German, logical

maamajomboo—Mandinka, a masquerade

Maskókî—Seminole for Creek language

Mère d'eau—Mami Wata in French, mother of waters

minkisi—plural of *nkisi*

mino—Fon, our mothers—the warrior wives of the king

Mist—German, crap, dung

mojo—prayer in a bag

natürlich—German, of course, naturally

nkisi—Kikongo, spirit or vessel of spiritual forces from the land of the dead

Nne mmiri—Igbo, water goddess

nzumbe—Mbunde word for animated corpse, zombie

odu Ifa—Yoruba, the bag of wisdom that Olodumare gave to the orisha

Ohrwurm—German, a tune, a saying that is stuck in your mind

Olodumare—Yoruba, the supreme being, the creator

Omotaiyelolu—Yoruba, the twin who excels

orisha—English transliteration of Yoruba term, Yoruba deities, ancestors, forces of nature, cosmic deities

Osanyin—Yoruba deity of herbalistic medicine

Oshoosi—Yoruba deity of hunters, the archer

Oshun—Yoruba water deity, akin to Mami Wata

Ouidah—capital, royal city of Dahomey

oun—Yoruba, he or she

sehr gut—German, very good

Sie kann ein bißchen. Hörst du das nicht?—German, She speaks a little. Can't you tell?

Verdammt—German, Damn it!

vodun—Fon religion related to Yoruba Orisha worship (*Voodoo*)

Yemoja—Yoruba water deity, akin to Mami Wata